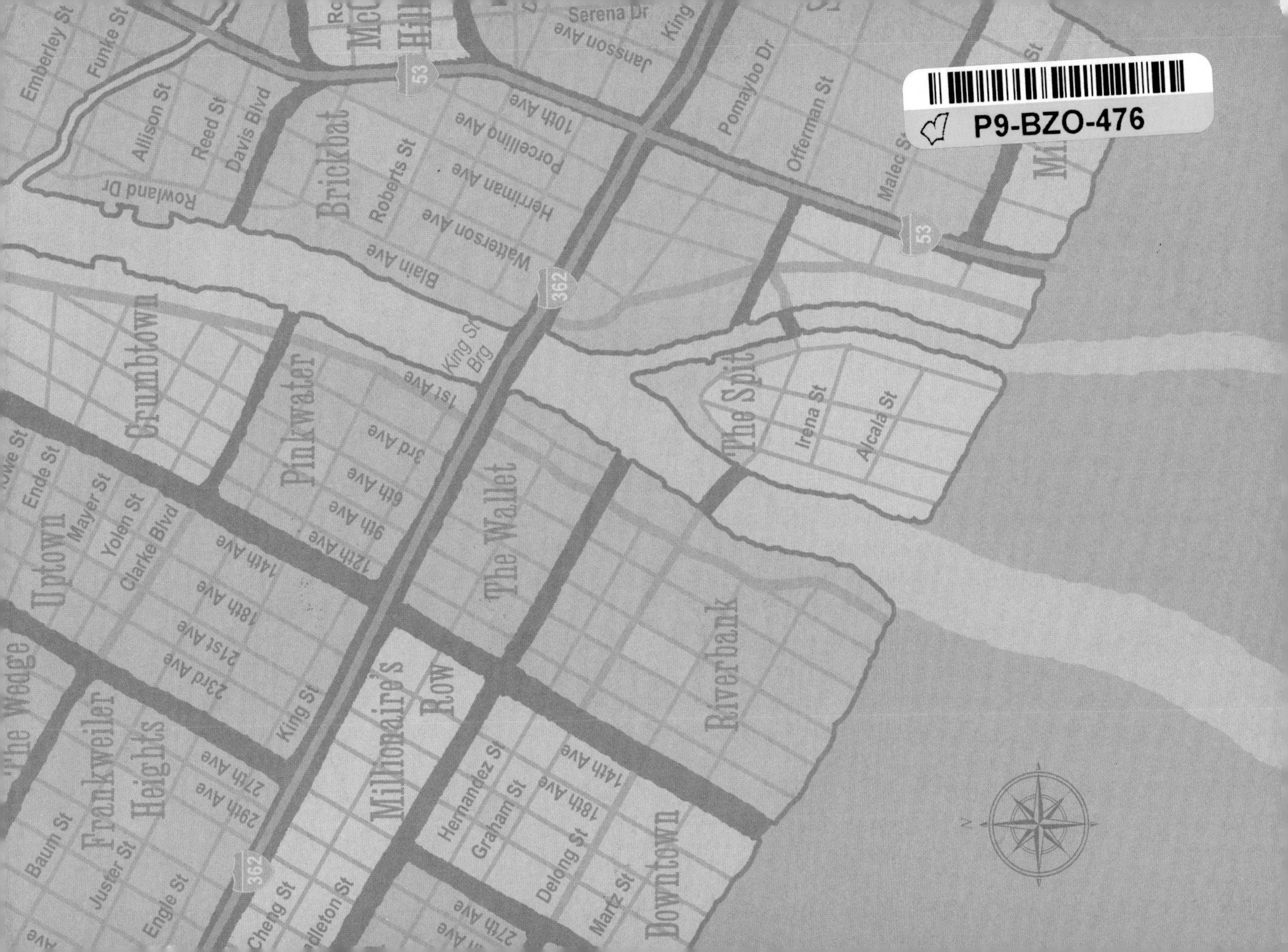
Emberley St
Funke St
Allison St
Reed St
Davis Blvd
Rowland Dr
Brickbat
Roberts St
Serena Dr
Jansson Ave
King
10th Ave
Porcellino Ave
Herriman Ave
Waterson Ave
Blain Ave
Pomaybo Dr
Offerman St
Malec St
53
53
362
Crumbtown
Pinkwater
King St Brg
1st Ave
3rd Ave
6th Ave
9th Ave
12th Ave
The Wallet
The Spit
Irena St
Alcala St
Ende St
Mayer St
Yolen St
Clarke Blvd
Uptown
14th Ave
18th Ave
21st Ave
23rd Ave
King St
The Wedge
Frankweiler Heights
27th Ave
29th Ave
Baum St
Juster St
Engle St
362
Cheng St
Millionaire's Row
Riverbank
Hernandez St
Graham St
14th Ave
18th Ave
Delong St
Martz St
Downtown
27th Ave
N

THE CREEPY CASE FILES OF

MARGO MALOO

DREW WEING

:01

First Second
NEW YORK

:01

First Second

Published by First Second

First Second is an imprint of Roaring Brook Press, a division of Holtzbrinck Publishing Holdings Limited Partnership

175 Fifth Avenue, New York, New York 10010

All rights reserved

Library of Congress Control Number: 2015951852

ISBN: 978-1-62672-339-9

Our books may be purchased in bulk for promotional, educational, or business use. Please contact your local bookseller or the Macmillan Corporate and Premium Sales Department at (800) 221-7945 ext. 5442 or by e-mail at MacmillanSpecialMarkets@macmillan.com.

First Edition 2016

Book design by Danielle Ceccolini

Printed in China by Toppan Leefung Printing Ltd., Dongguan City, Guangdong Province

10 9 8 7 6 5 4 3 2 1

Drawn with a Zebra .05mm mechanical pencil. Inked with a Platinum Carbon fountain pen, Platinum Carbon Ink Cartridges, PH Martin Bombay Ink, any old cheap brush for areas of black, and Daler Rowney Pro White for corrections. Drawn on Strathmore 400 Series smooth bristol. Colored with Photoshop, with a Monoprice Graphic Tablet and a lot of scribbling.

FOR ELEANOR, WHO WAS DOWN FROM THE START.
AND TO ALL THE KIDS WHO WANT TO KNOW THE **TRUTH.**

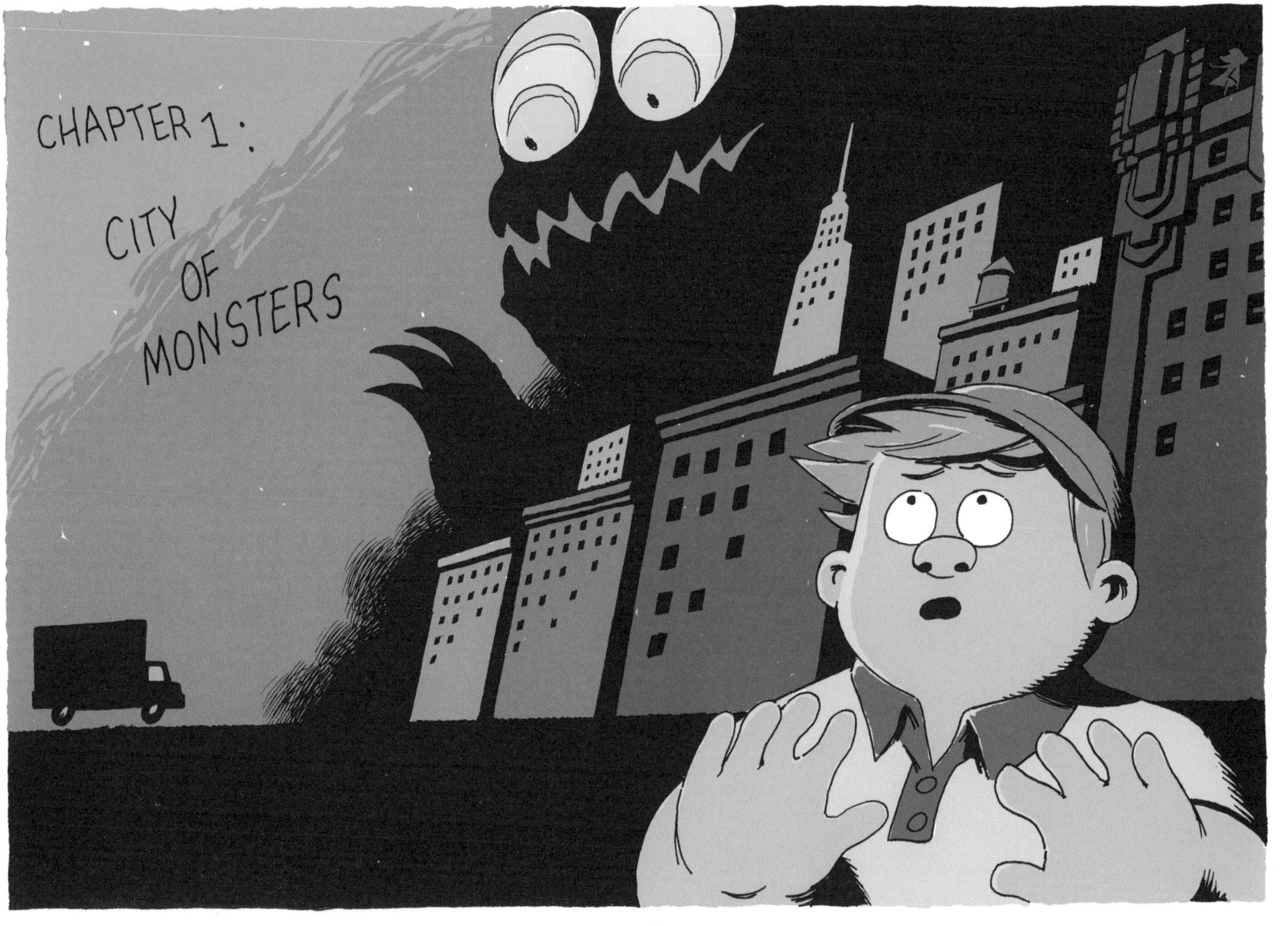
CHAPTER 1:
CITY
OF
MONSTERS

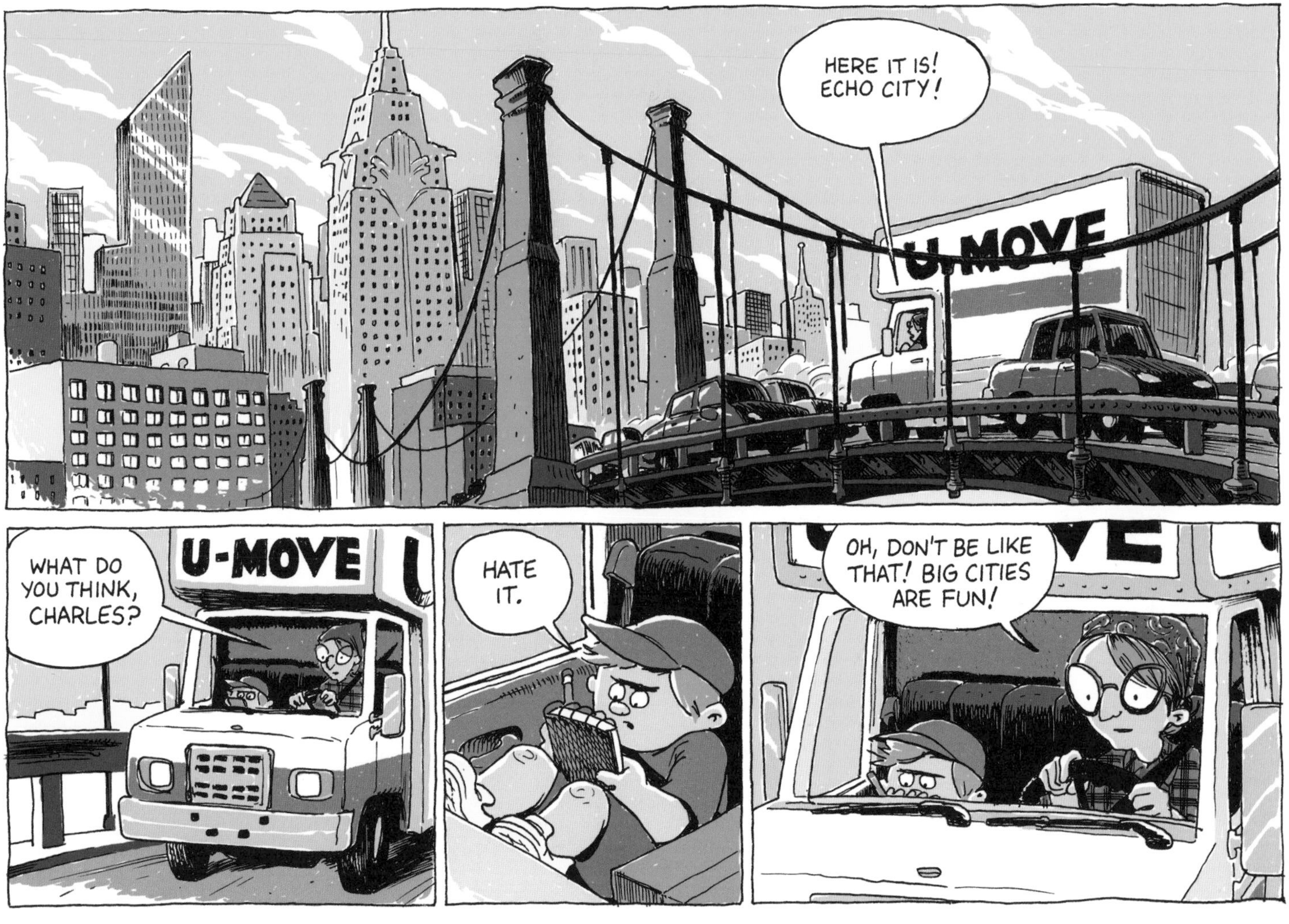
HERE IT IS! ECHO CITY!
U-MOVE
U-MOVE
WHAT DO YOU THINK, CHARLES?
HATE IT.
OH, DON'T BE LIKE THAT! BIG CITIES ARE FUN!

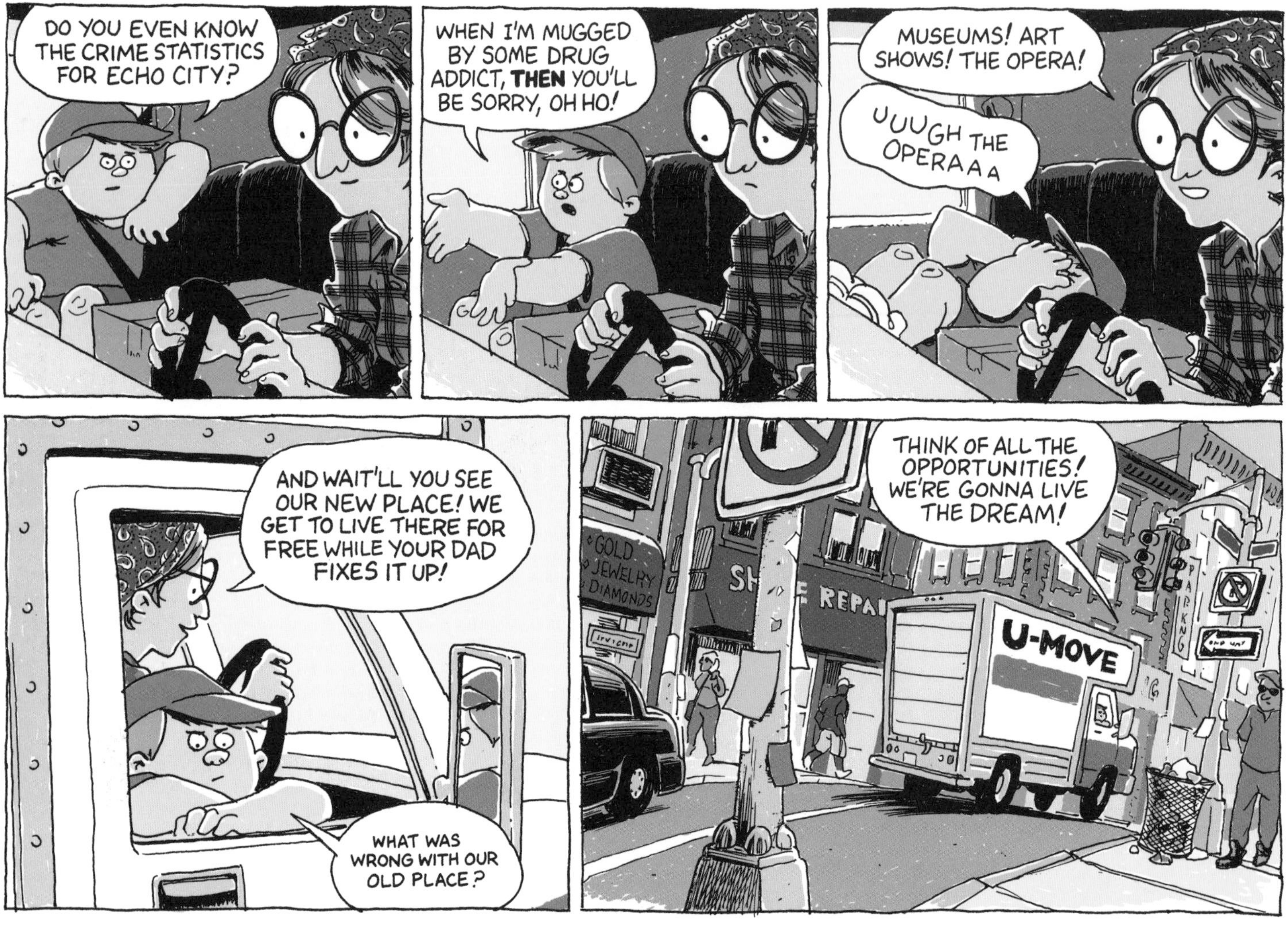
DO YOU EVEN KNOW THE CRIME STATISTICS FOR ECHO CITY?
WHEN I'M MUGGED BY SOME DRUG ADDICT, **THEN** YOU'LL BE SORRY, OH HO!
MUSEUMS! ART SHOWS! THE OPERA!
UUUGH THE OPERAAAA
AND WAIT'LL YOU SEE OUR NEW PLACE! WE GET TO LIVE THERE FOR FREE WHILE YOUR DAD FIXES IT UP!
WHAT WAS WRONG WITH OUR OLD PLACE?
THINK OF ALL THE OPPORTUNITIES! WE'RE GONNA LIVE THE DREAM!
GOLD JEWELRY DIAMONDS
U-MOVE
PARKING

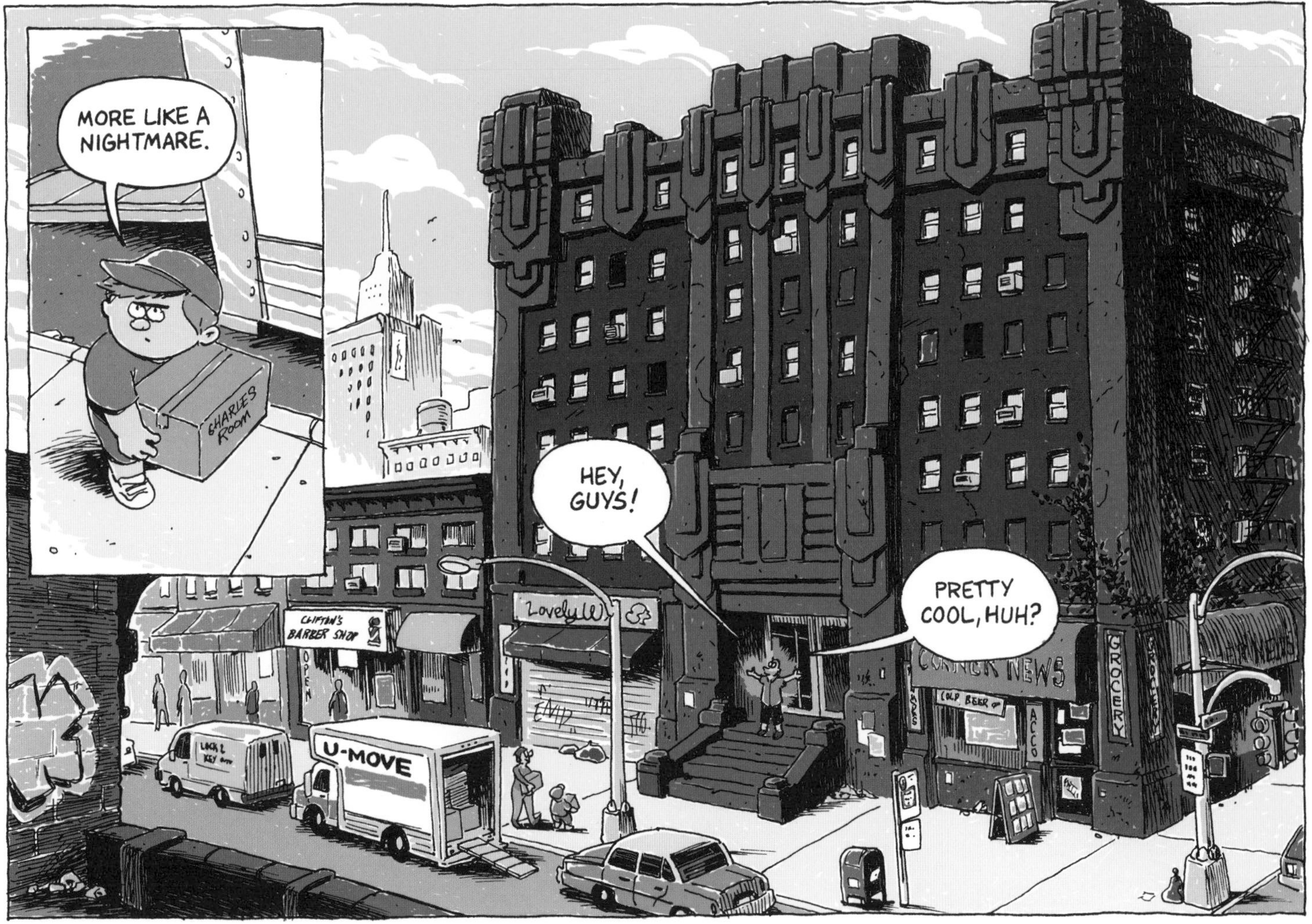
MORE LIKE A NIGHTMARE.
HEY, GUYS!
PRETTY COOL, HUH?
CHARLES ROOM
CLIFTON'S BARBER SHOP
U-MOVE
CORNER NEWS
GROCERY

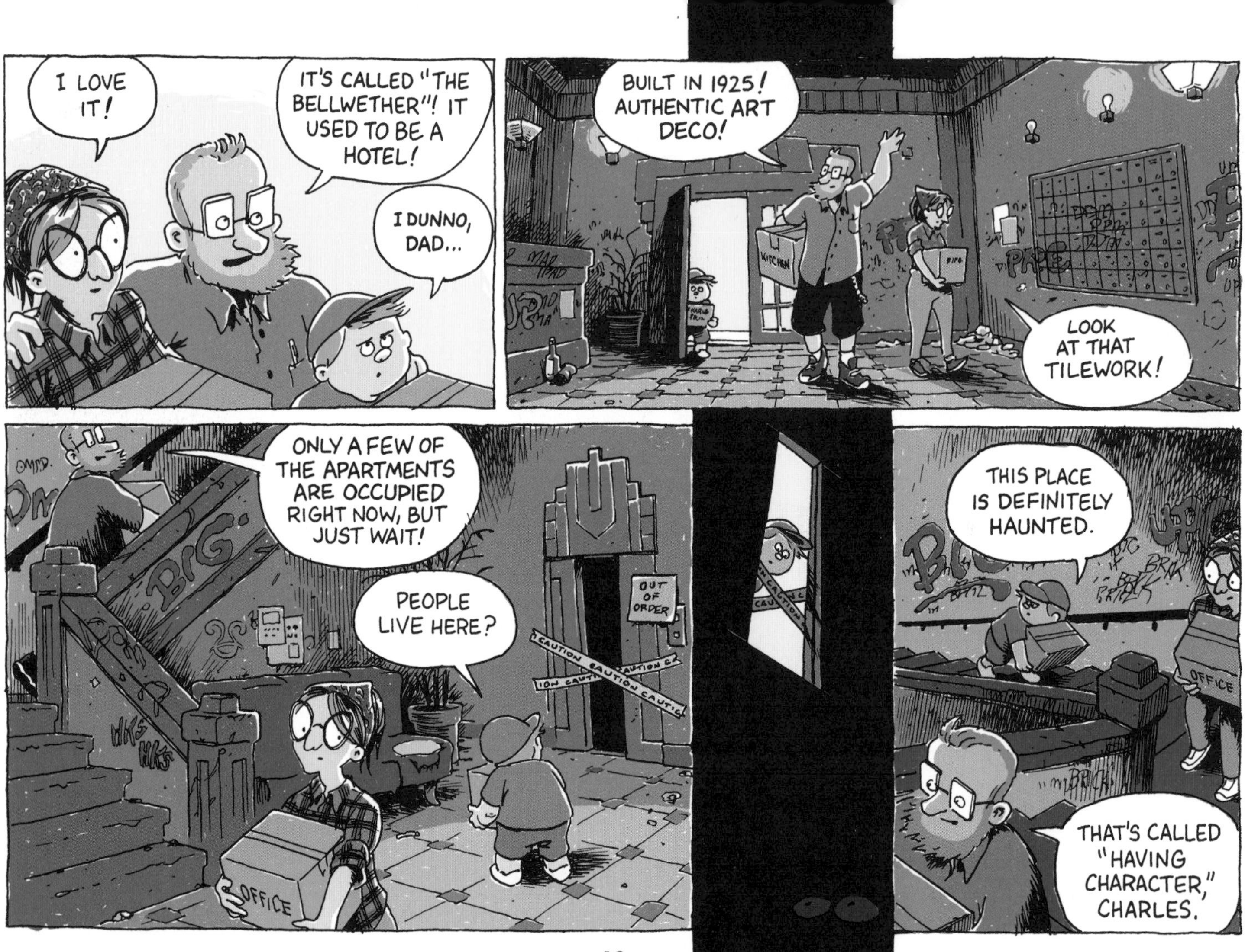
I LOVE IT!
IT'S CALLED "THE BELLWETHER"! IT USED TO BE A HOTEL!
I DUNNO, DAD...
BUILT IN 1925! AUTHENTIC ART DECO!
LOOK AT THAT TILEWORK!
ONLY A FEW OF THE APARTMENTS ARE OCCUPIED RIGHT NOW, BUT JUST WAIT!
PEOPLE LIVE HERE?
THIS PLACE IS DEFINITELY HAUNTED.
THAT'S CALLED "HAVING CHARACTER," CHARLES.

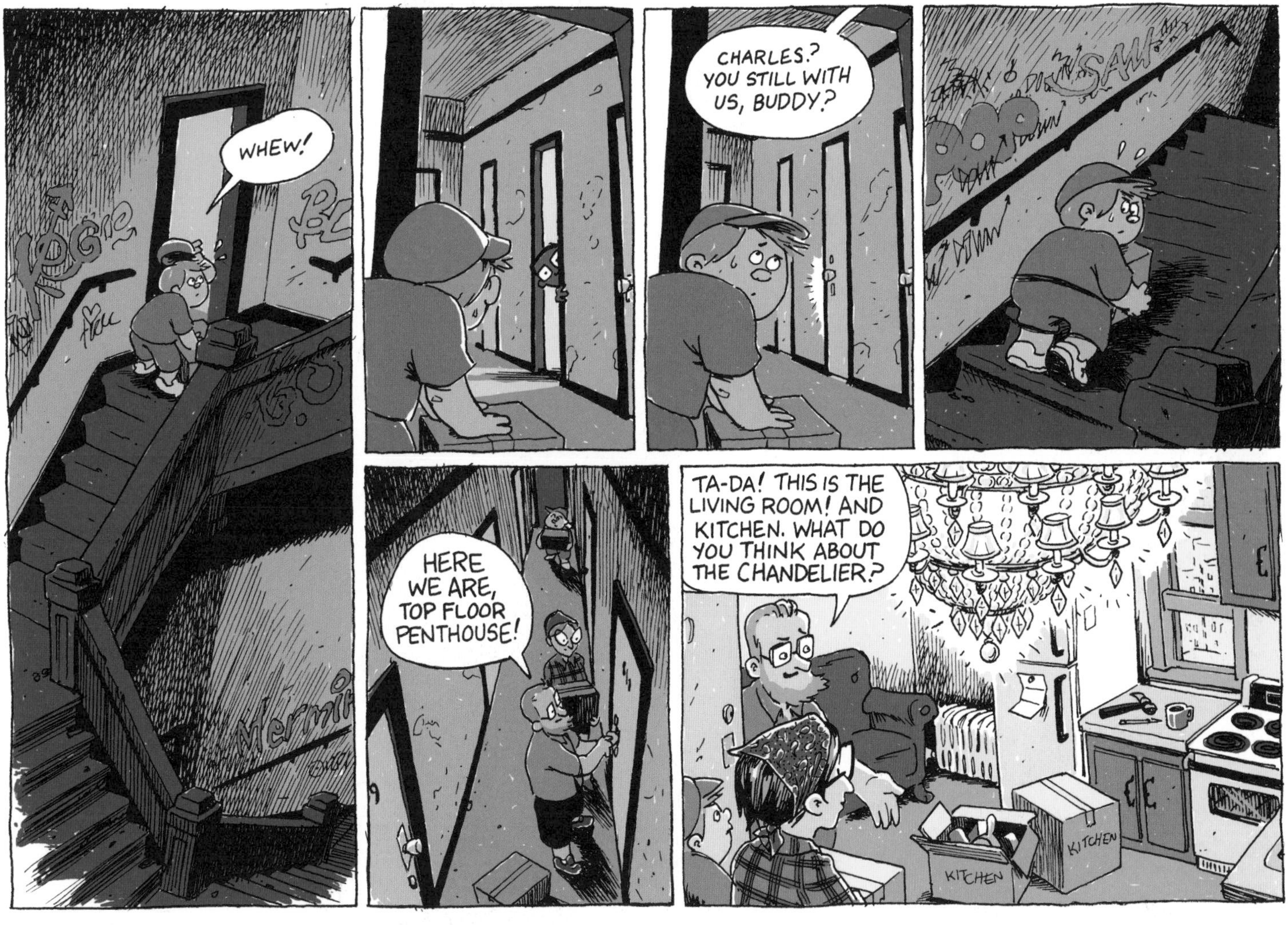
WHEW!
CHARLES? YOU STILL WITH US, BUDDY?
HERE WE ARE, TOP FLOOR PENTHOUSE!
TA-DA! THIS IS THE LIVING ROOM! AND KITCHEN. WHAT DO YOU THINK ABOUT THE CHANDELIER?
KITCHEN
KITCHEN

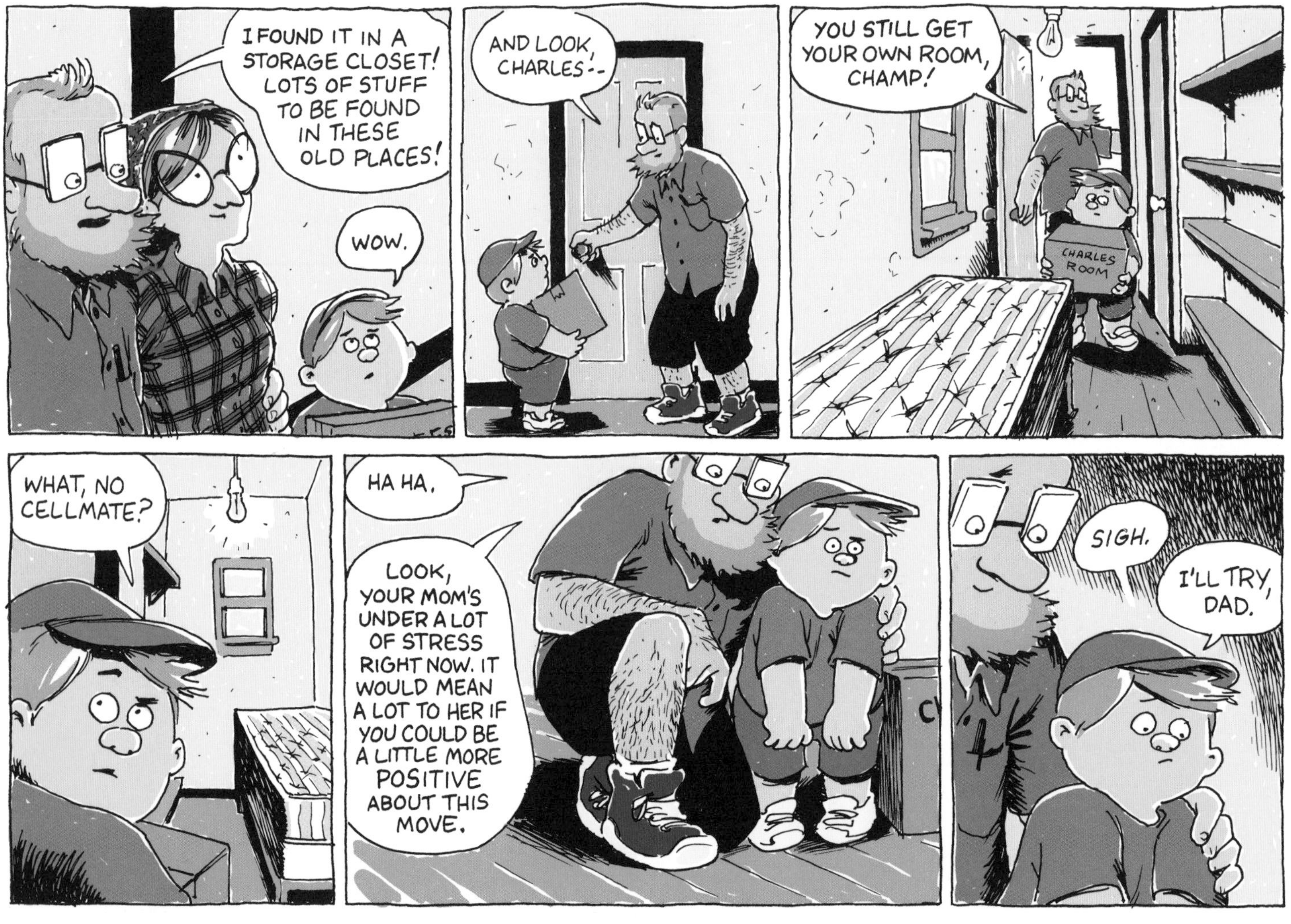
I FOUND IT IN A STORAGE CLOSET! LOTS OF STUFF TO BE FOUND IN THESE OLD PLACES!
WOW.
AND LOOK, CHARLES--
YOU STILL GET YOUR OWN ROOM, CHAMP!
CHARLES ROOM
WHAT, NO CELLMATE?
HA HA.
LOOK, YOUR MOM'S UNDER A LOT OF STRESS RIGHT NOW. IT WOULD MEAN A LOT TO HER IF YOU COULD BE A LITTLE MORE POSITIVE ABOUT THIS MOVE.
SIGH.
I'LL TRY, DAD.

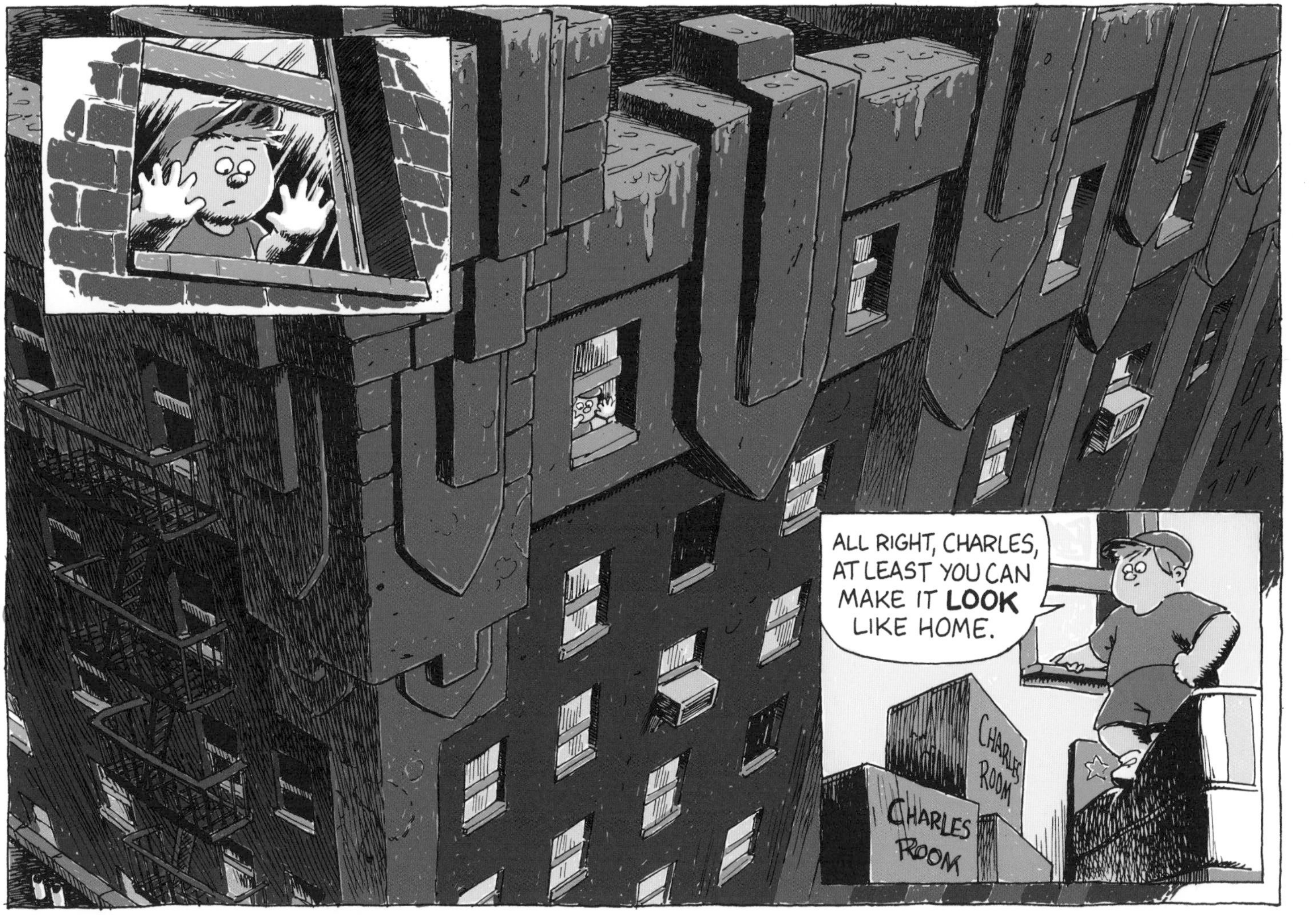
ALL RIGHT, CHARLES, AT LEAST YOU CAN MAKE IT **LOOK** LIKE HOME.
CHARLES ROOM
CHARLES ROOM

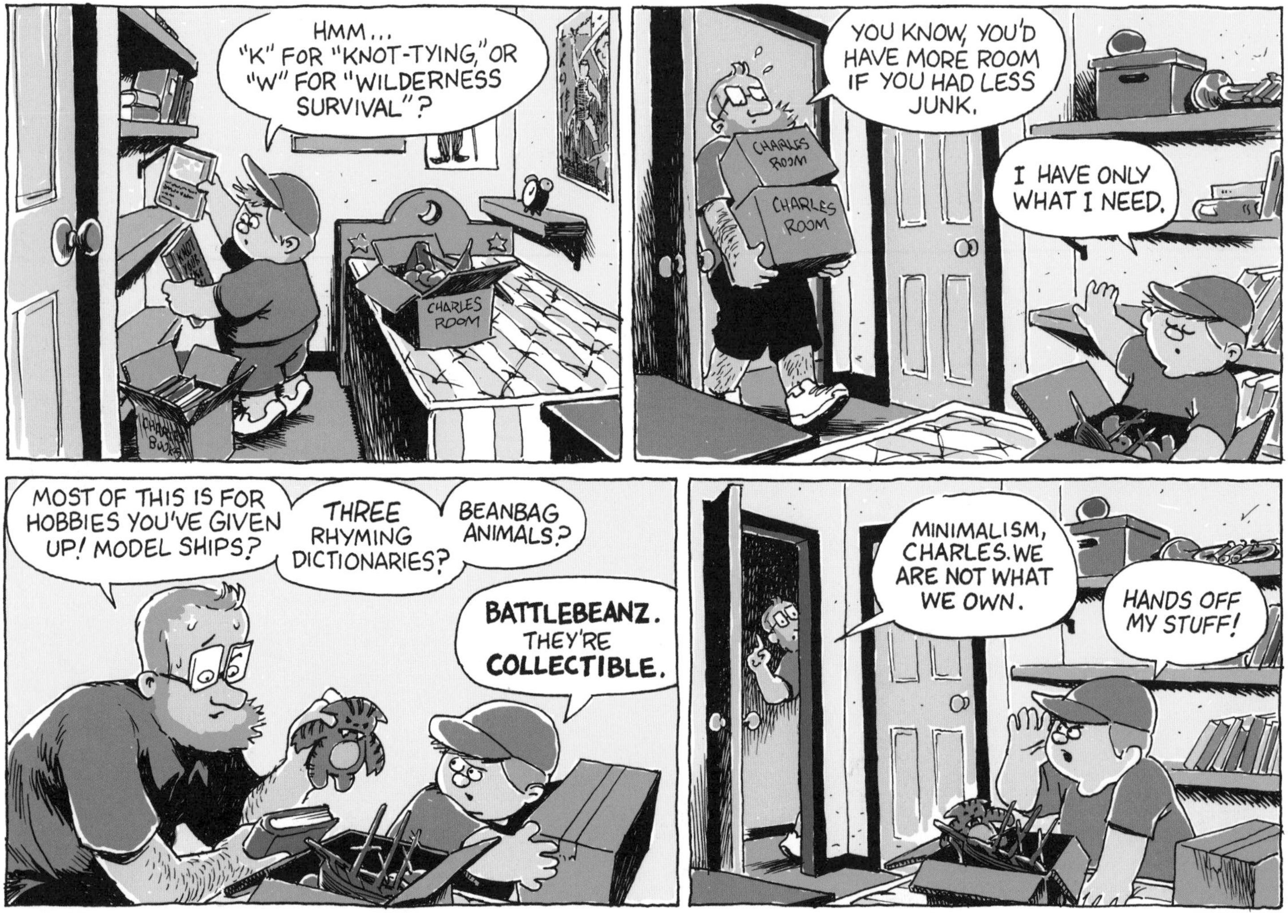

HMM... "K" FOR "KNOT-TYING," OR "W" FOR "WILDERNESS SURVIVAL"?
CHARLES ROOM
YOU KNOW, YOU'D HAVE MORE ROOM IF YOU HAD LESS JUNK.
CHARLES ROOM
CHARLES ROOM
I HAVE ONLY WHAT I NEED.
MOST OF THIS IS FOR HOBBIES YOU'VE GIVEN UP! MODEL SHIPS?
THREE RHYMING DICTIONARIES?
BEANBAG ANIMALS?
BATTLEBEANZ. THEY'RE **COLLECTIBLE.**
MINIMALISM, CHARLES. WE ARE NOT WHAT WE OWN.
HANDS OFF MY STUFF!

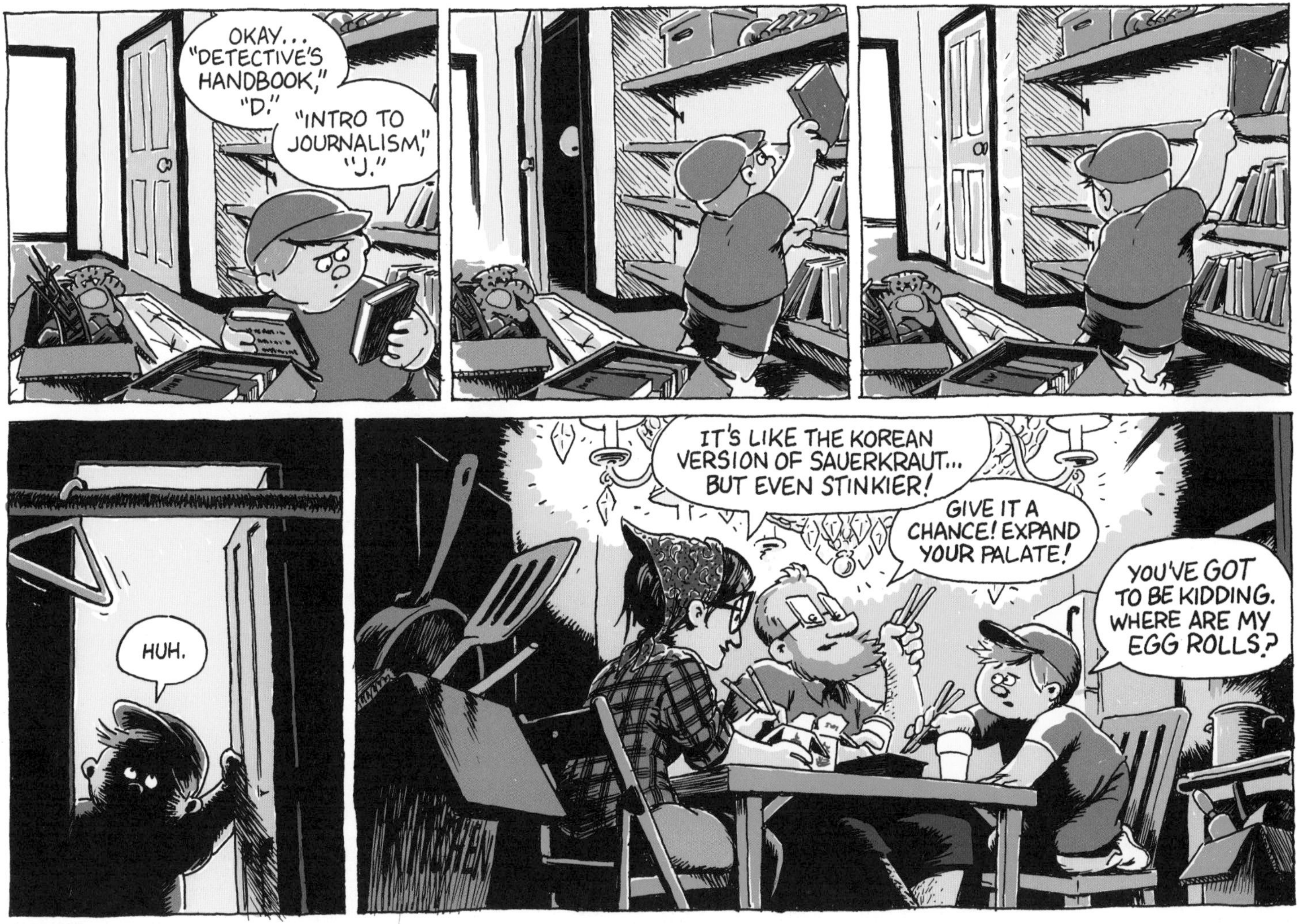
OKAY... "DETECTIVE'S HANDBOOK," "D."
"INTRO TO JOURNALISM," "J."
HUH.
IT'S LIKE THE KOREAN VERSION OF SAUERKRAUT... BUT EVEN STINKIER!
GIVE IT A CHANCE! EXPAND YOUR PALATE!
YOU'VE GOT TO BE KIDDING. WHERE ARE MY EGG ROLLS?

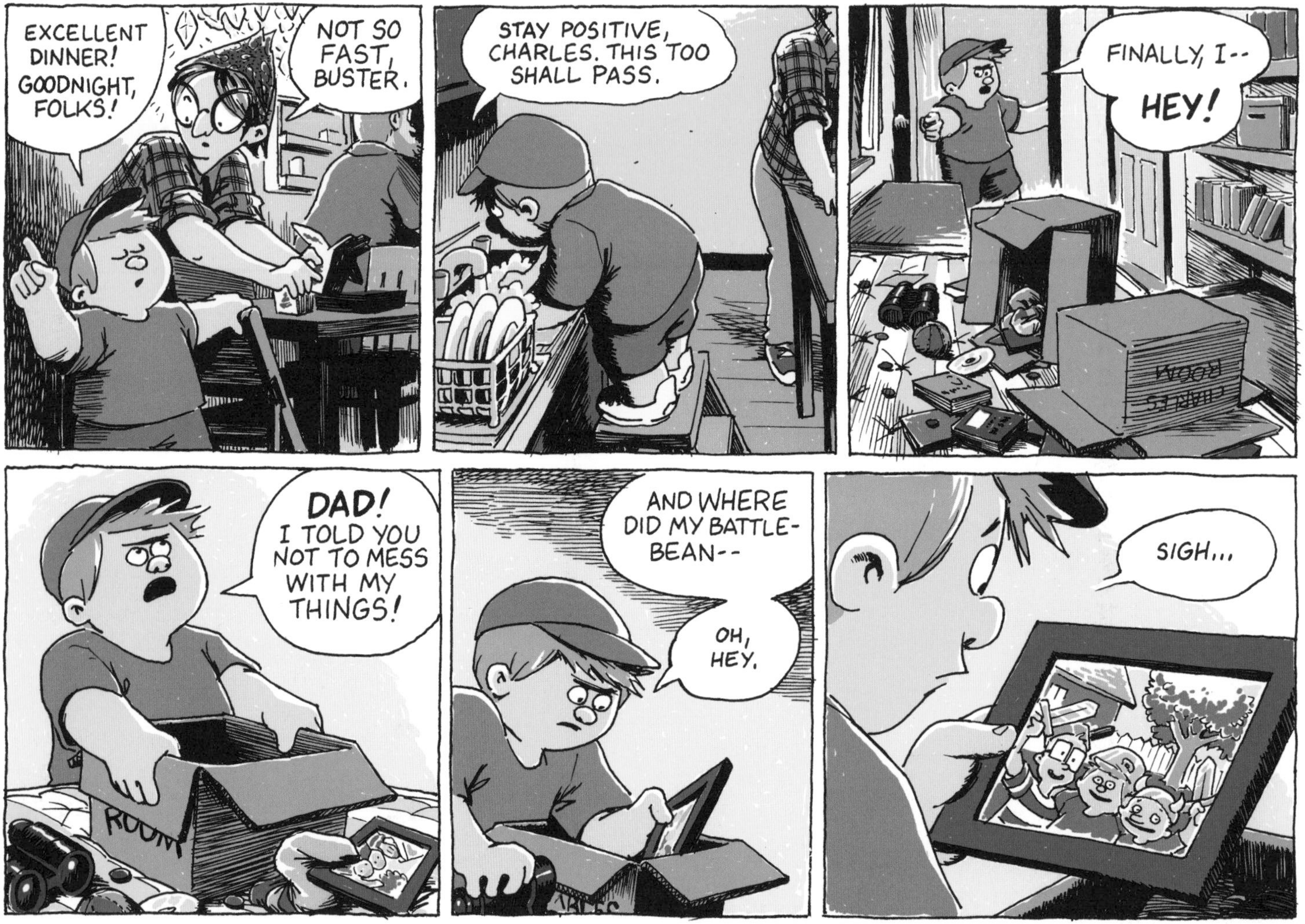
EXCELLENT DINNER! GOODNIGHT, FOLKS!
NOT SO FAST, BUSTER.
STAY POSITIVE, CHARLES. THIS TOO SHALL PASS.
FINALLY, I--
HEY!
CHARLES ROOM
DAD! I TOLD YOU NOT TO MESS WITH MY THINGS!
ROOM
AND WHERE DID MY BATTLE-BEAN--
OH, HEY.
SIGH...

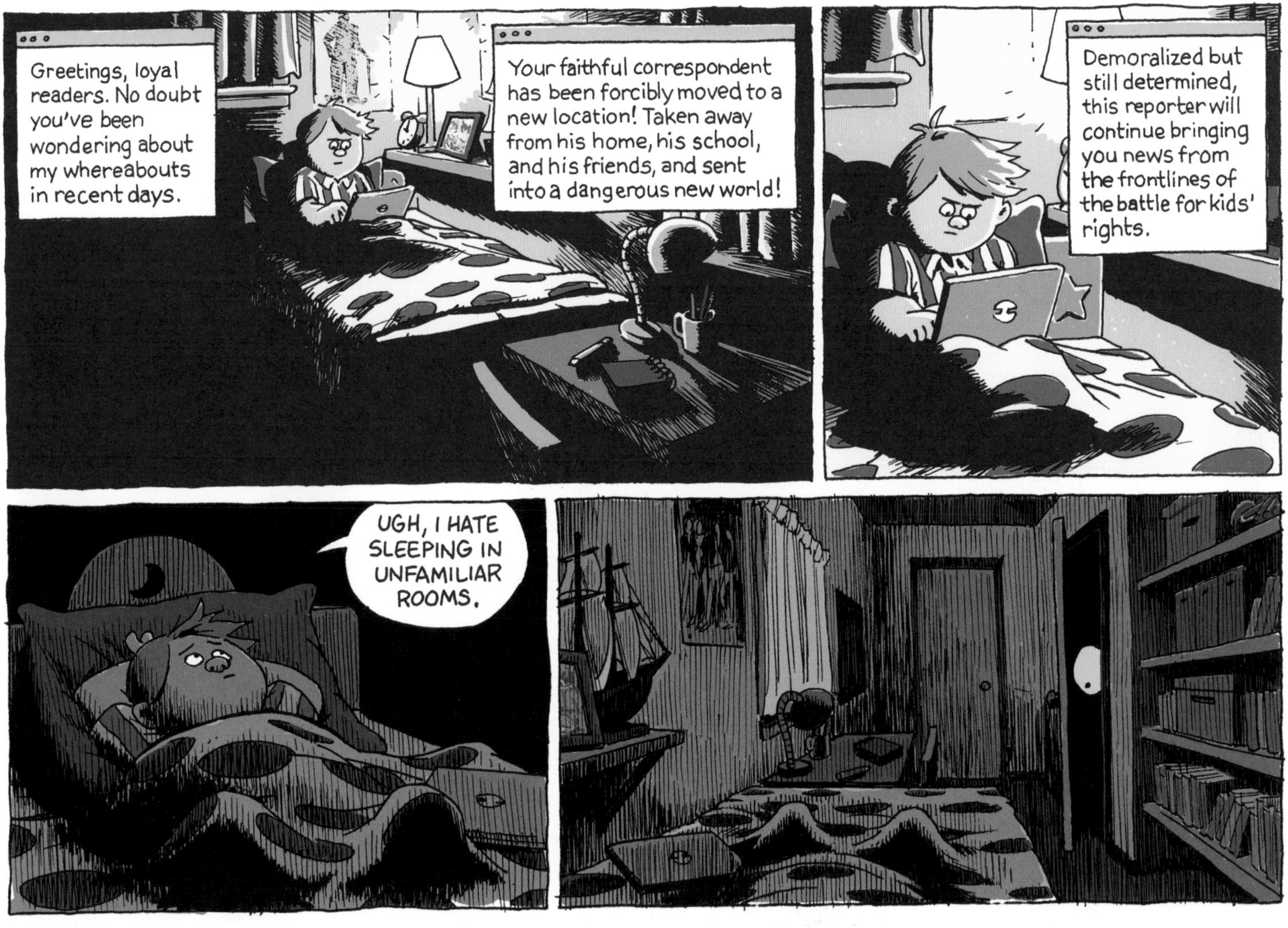

Greetings, loyal readers. No doubt you've been wondering about my whereabouts in recent days.
Your faithful correspondent has been forcibly moved to a new location! Taken away from his home, his school, and his friends, and sent into a dangerous new world!
Demoralized but still determined, this reporter will continue bringing you news from the frontlines of the battle for kids' rights.
UGH, I HATE SLEEPING IN UNFAMILIAR ROOMS.

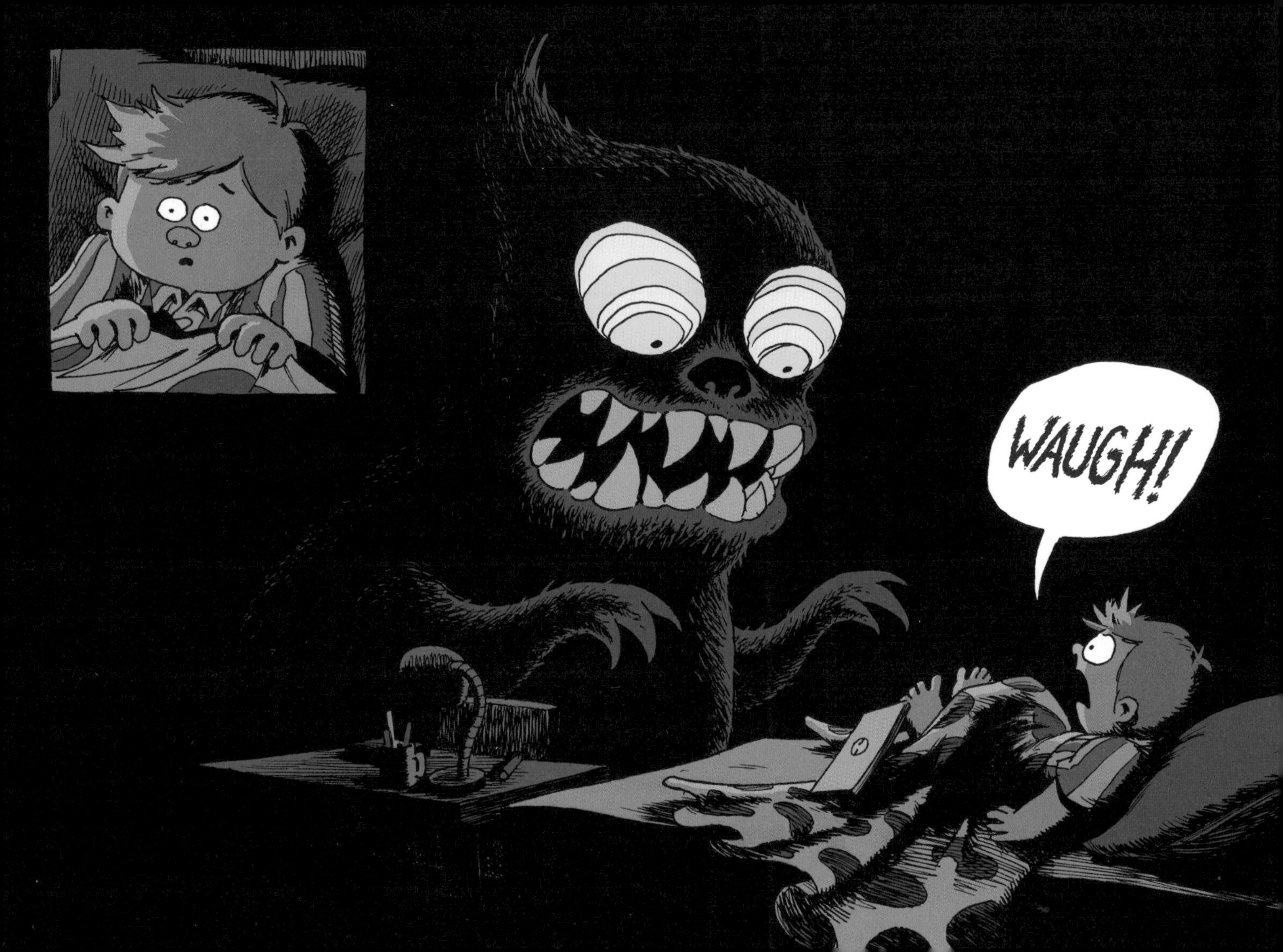
WAUGH!

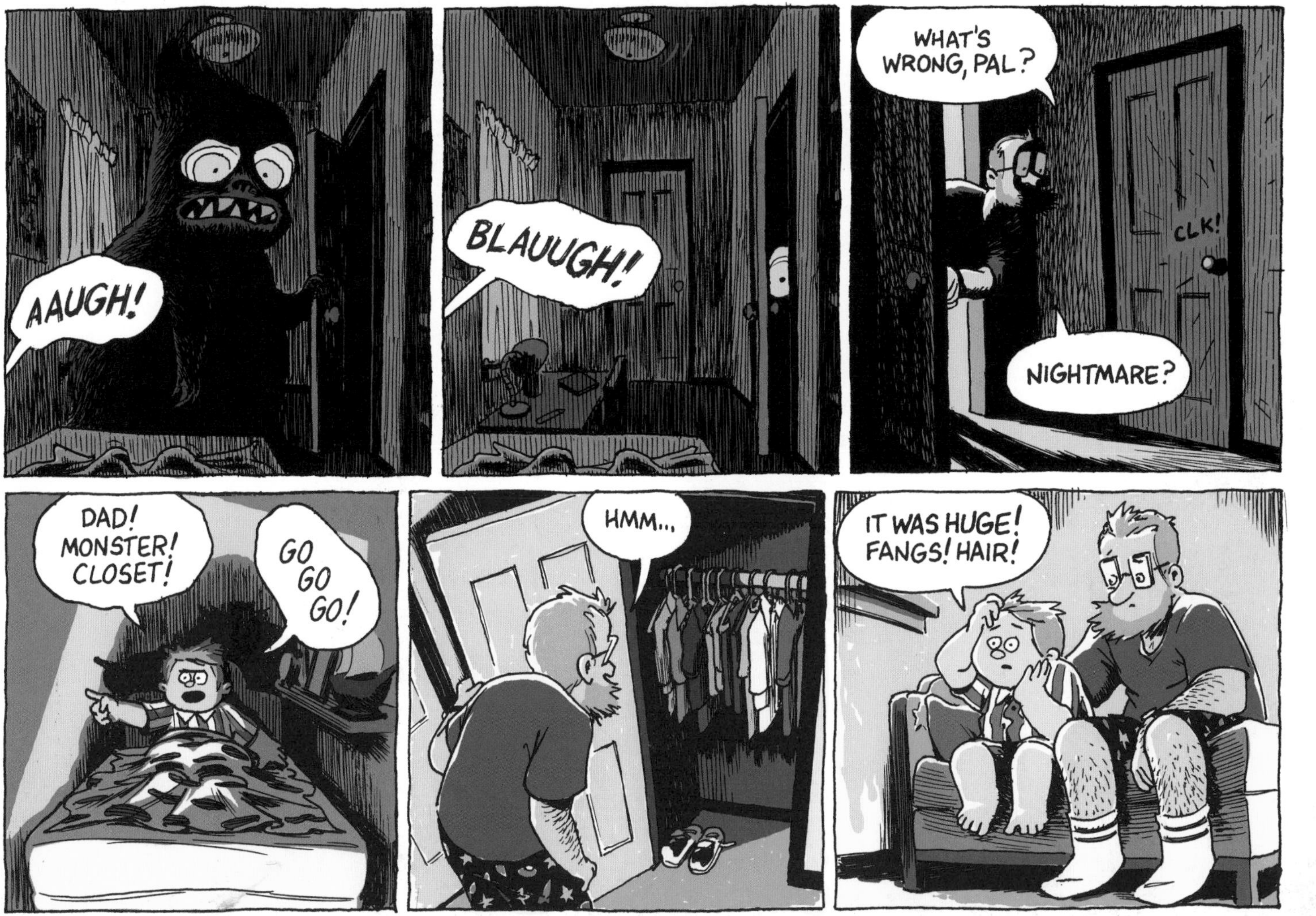
AAUGH!
BLAUUGH!
WHAT'S WRONG, PAL?
CLK!
NIGHTMARE?
DAD! MONSTER! CLOSET!
GO GO GO!
HMM...
IT WAS HUGE! FANGS! HAIR!

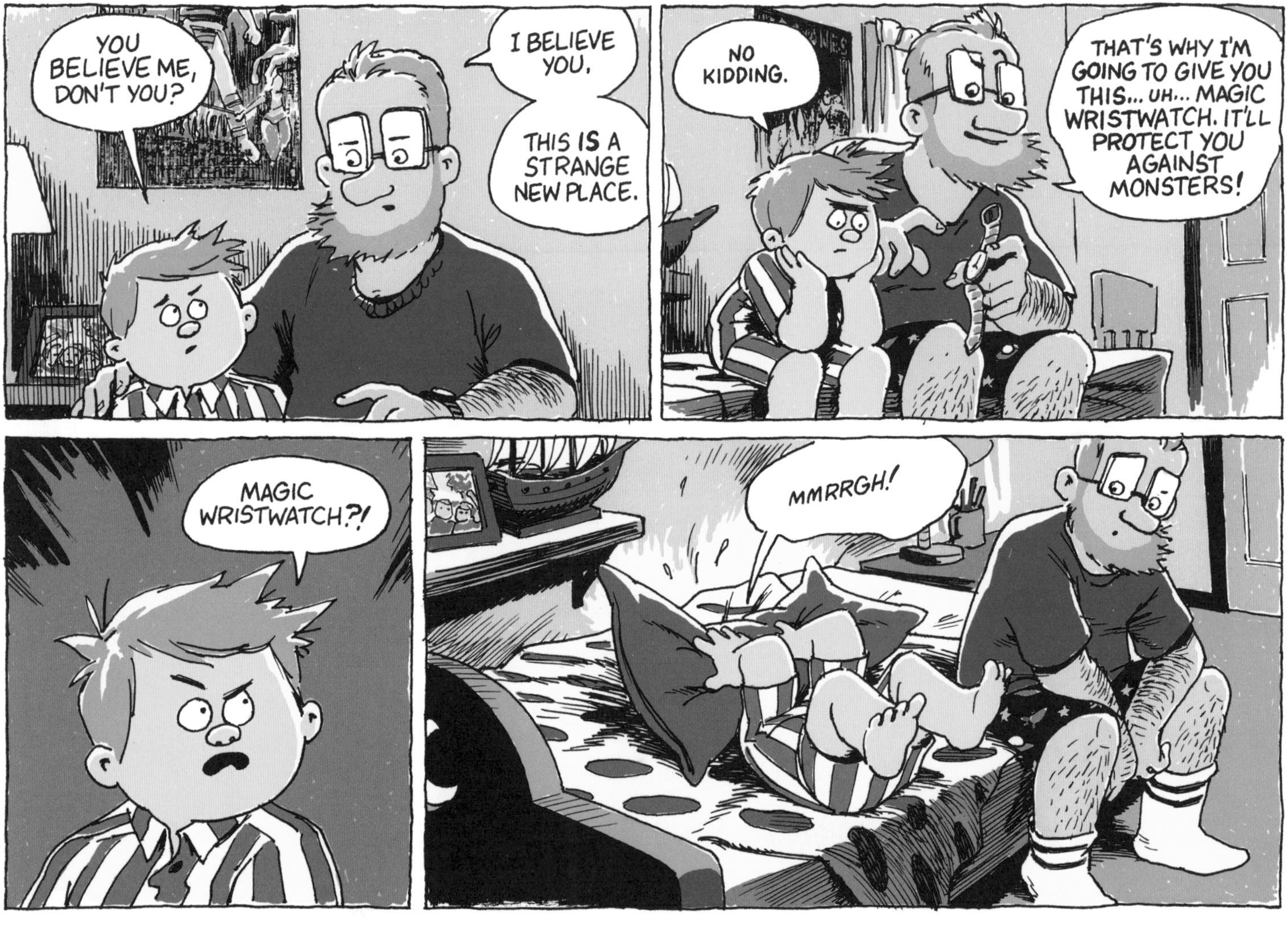
YOU BELIEVE ME, DON'T YOU?
I BELIEVE YOU.
THIS **IS** A STRANGE NEW PLACE.
NO KIDDING.
THAT'S WHY I'M GOING TO GIVE YOU THIS... UH... MAGIC WRISTWATCH. IT'LL PROTECT YOU AGAINST MONSTERS!
MAGIC WRISTWATCH?!
MMRRGH!

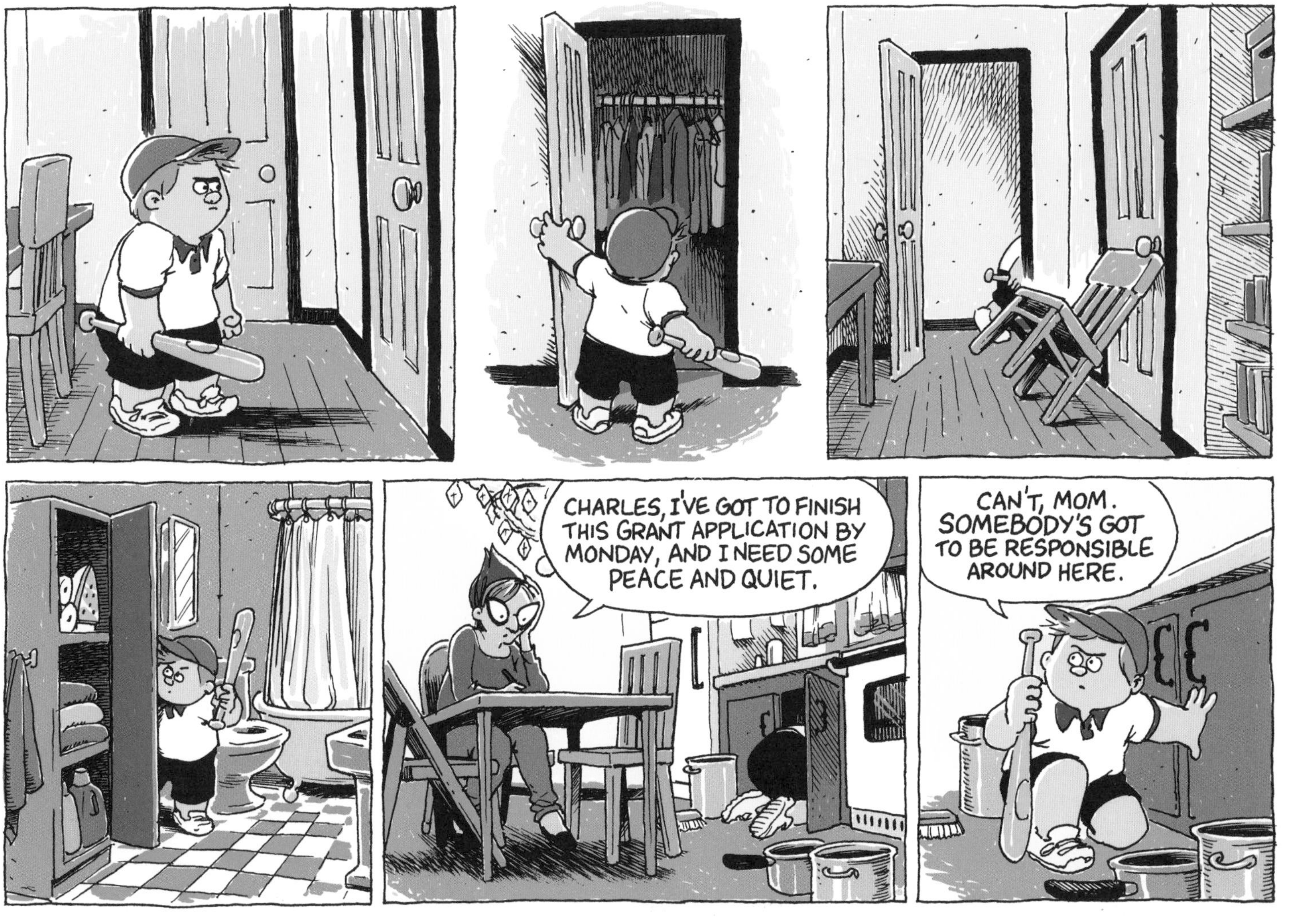
CHARLES, I'VE GOT TO FINISH THIS GRANT APPLICATION BY MONDAY, AND I NEED SOME PEACE AND QUIET.
CAN'T, MOM. SOMEBODY'S GOT TO BE RESPONSIBLE AROUND HERE.

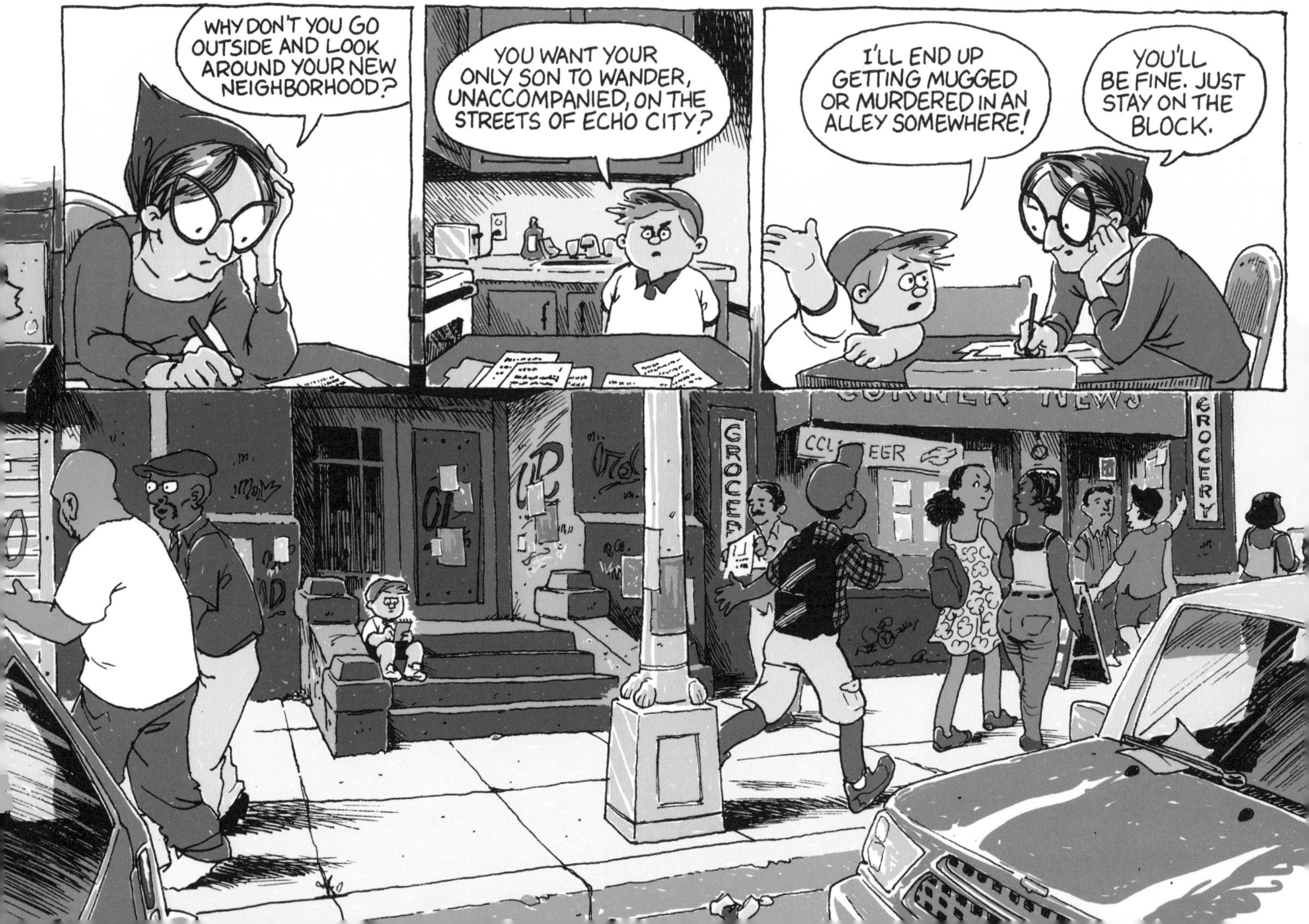
WHY DON'T YOU GO OUTSIDE AND LOOK AROUND YOUR NEW NEIGHBORHOOD?
YOU WANT YOUR ONLY SON TO WANDER, UNACCOMPANIED, ON THE STREETS OF ECHO CITY?
I'LL END UP GETTING MUGGED OR MURDERED IN AN ALLEY SOMEWHERE!
YOU'LL BE FINE. JUST STAY ON THE BLOCK.
GROCERY

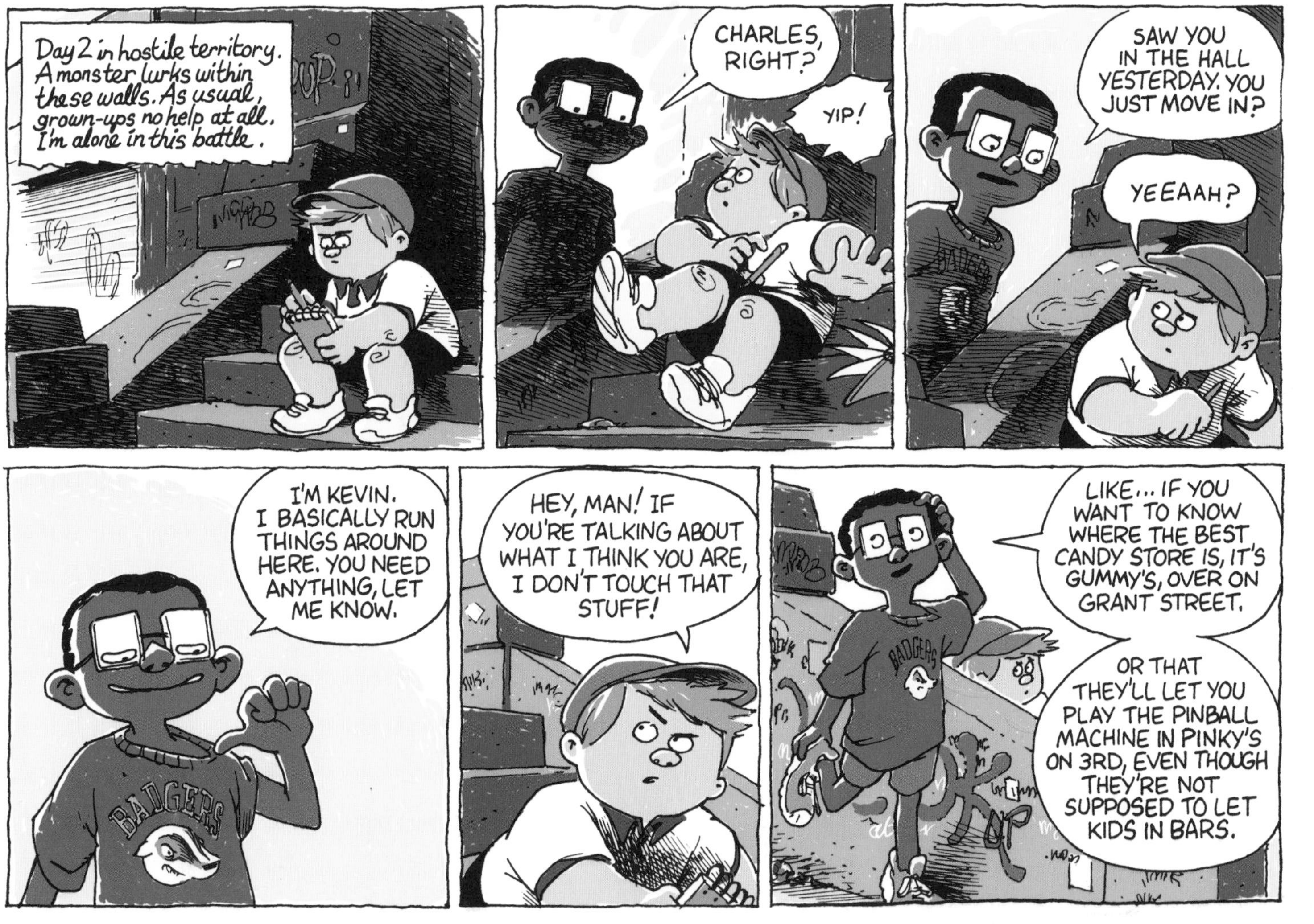
Day 2 in hostile territory. A monster lurks within these walls. As usual, grown-ups no help at all. I'm alone in this battle.
CHARLES, RIGHT?
YIP!
SAW YOU IN THE HALL YESTERDAY. YOU JUST MOVE IN?
YEEAAH?
I'M KEVIN. I BASICALLY RUN THINGS AROUND HERE. YOU NEED ANYTHING, LET ME KNOW.
HEY, MAN! IF YOU'RE TALKING ABOUT WHAT I THINK YOU ARE, I DON'T TOUCH THAT STUFF!
LIKE... IF YOU WANT TO KNOW WHERE THE BEST CANDY STORE IS, IT'S GUMMY'S, OVER ON GRANT STREET.
OR THAT THEY'LL LET YOU PLAY THE PINBALL MACHINE IN PINKY'S ON 3RD, EVEN THOUGH THEY'RE NOT SUPPOSED TO LET KIDS IN BARS.
BADGERS

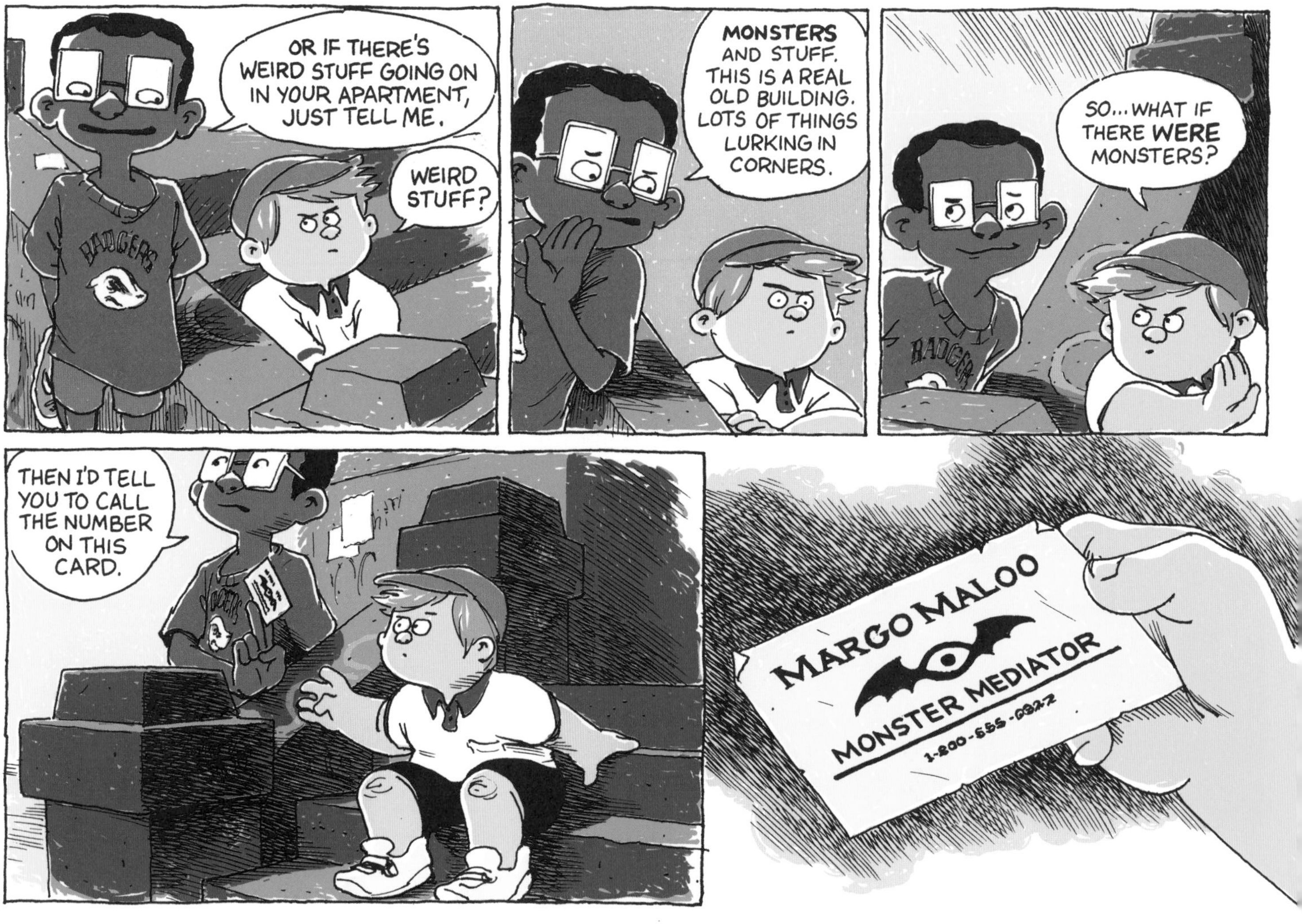
OR IF THERE'S WEIRD STUFF GOING ON IN YOUR APARTMENT, JUST TELL ME.
WEIRD STUFF?
MONSTERS AND STUFF. THIS IS A REAL OLD BUILDING. LOTS OF THINGS LURKING IN CORNERS.
SO... WHAT IF THERE **WERE** MONSTERS?
THEN I'D TELL YOU TO CALL THE NUMBER ON THIS CARD.
MARGO MALOO
MONSTER MEDIATOR
1-800-555-0272

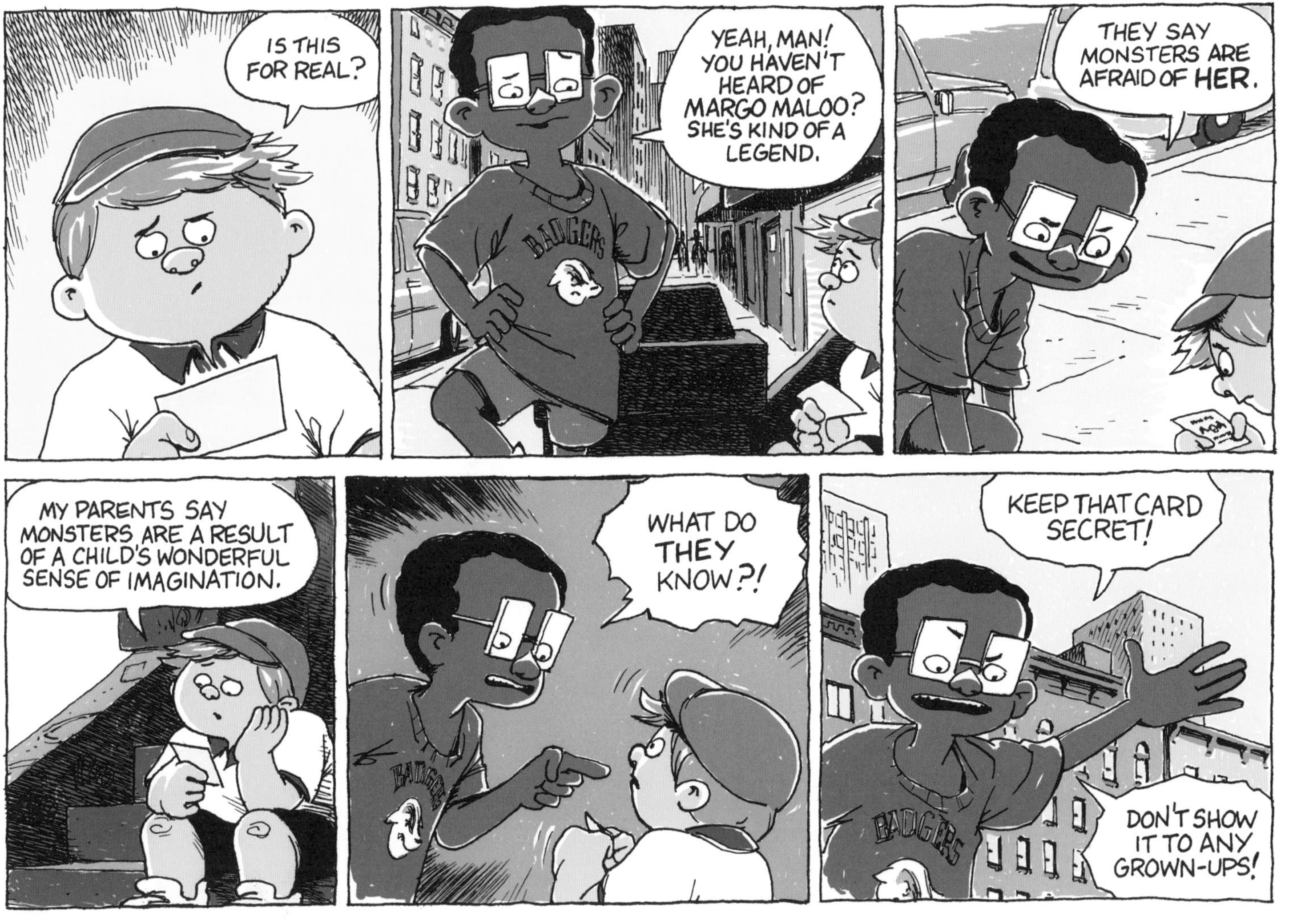
IS THIS FOR REAL?
YEAH, MAN! YOU HAVEN'T HEARD OF MARGO MALOO? SHE'S KIND OF A LEGEND.
THEY SAY MONSTERS ARE AFRAID OF HER.
MY PARENTS SAY MONSTERS ARE A RESULT OF A CHILD'S WONDERFUL SENSE OF IMAGINATION.
WHAT DO THEY KNOW?!
KEEP THAT CARD SECRET!
DON'T SHOW IT TO ANY GROWN-UPS!

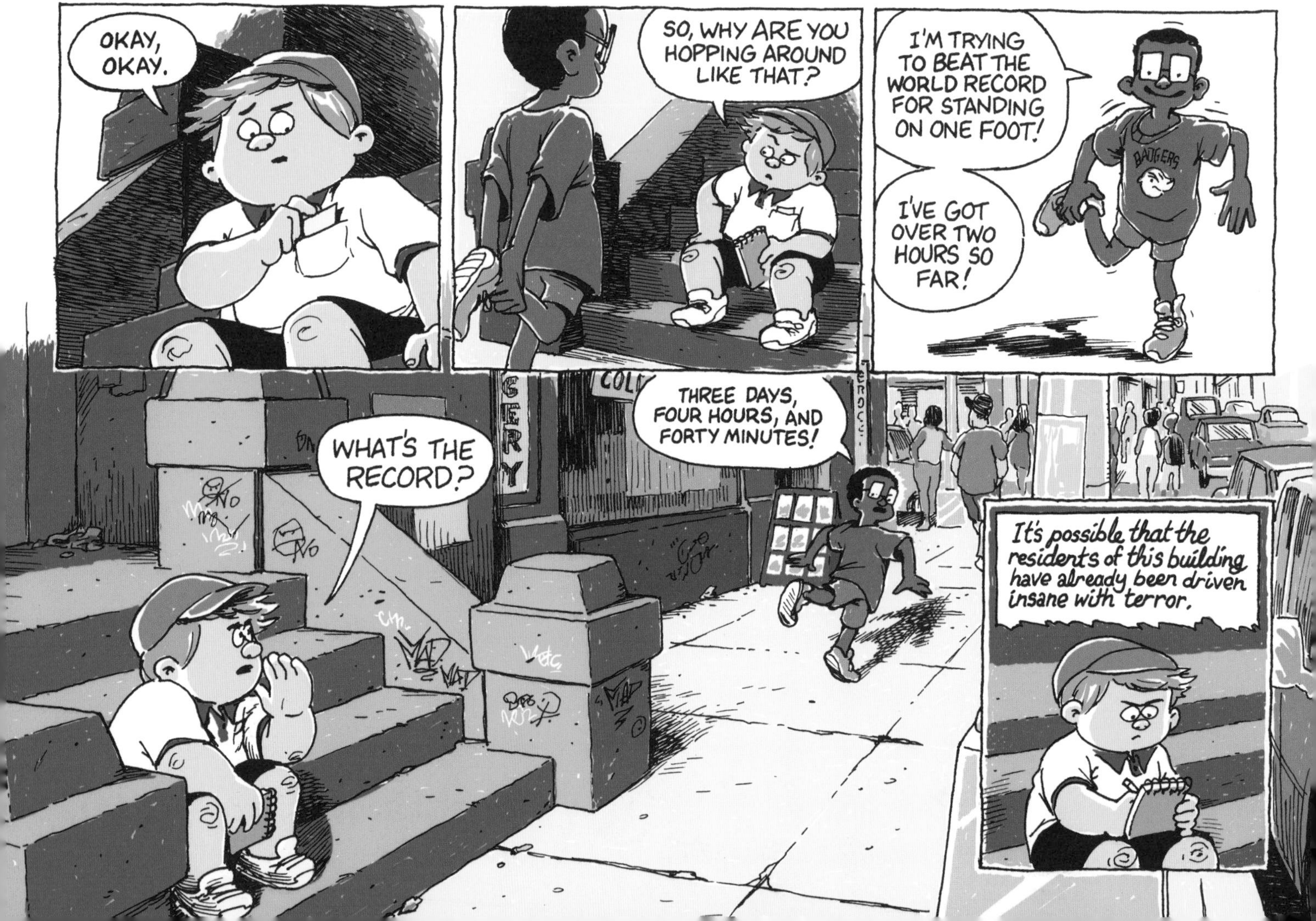
OKAY, OKAY.
SO, WHY ARE YOU HOPPING AROUND LIKE THAT?
I'M TRYING TO BEAT THE WORLD RECORD FOR STANDING ON ONE FOOT!
I'VE GOT OVER TWO HOURS SO FAR!
BADGERS
WHAT'S THE RECORD?
THREE DAYS, FOUR HOURS, AND FORTY MINUTES!
It's possible that the residents of this building have already been driven insane with terror.

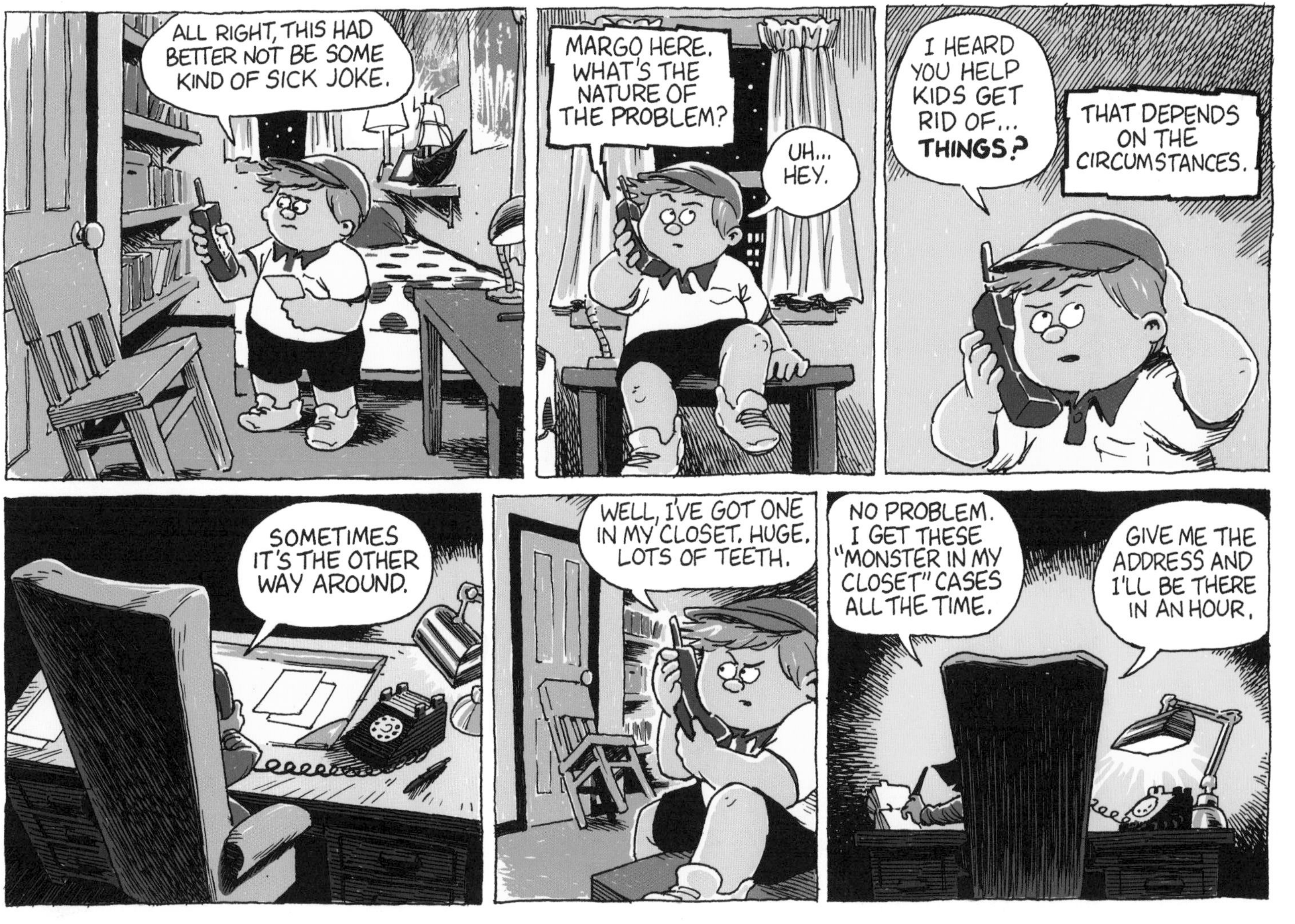
ALL RIGHT, THIS HAD BETTER NOT BE SOME KIND OF SICK JOKE.
MARGO HERE. WHAT'S THE NATURE OF THE PROBLEM?
UH... HEY.
I HEARD YOU HELP KIDS GET RID OF... **THINGS?**
THAT DEPENDS ON THE CIRCUMSTANCES.
SOMETIMES IT'S THE OTHER WAY AROUND.
WELL, I'VE GOT ONE IN MY CLOSET. HUGE. LOTS OF TEETH.
NO PROBLEM. I GET THESE "MONSTER IN MY CLOSET" CASES ALL THE TIME.
GIVE ME THE ADDRESS AND I'LL BE THERE IN AN HOUR.

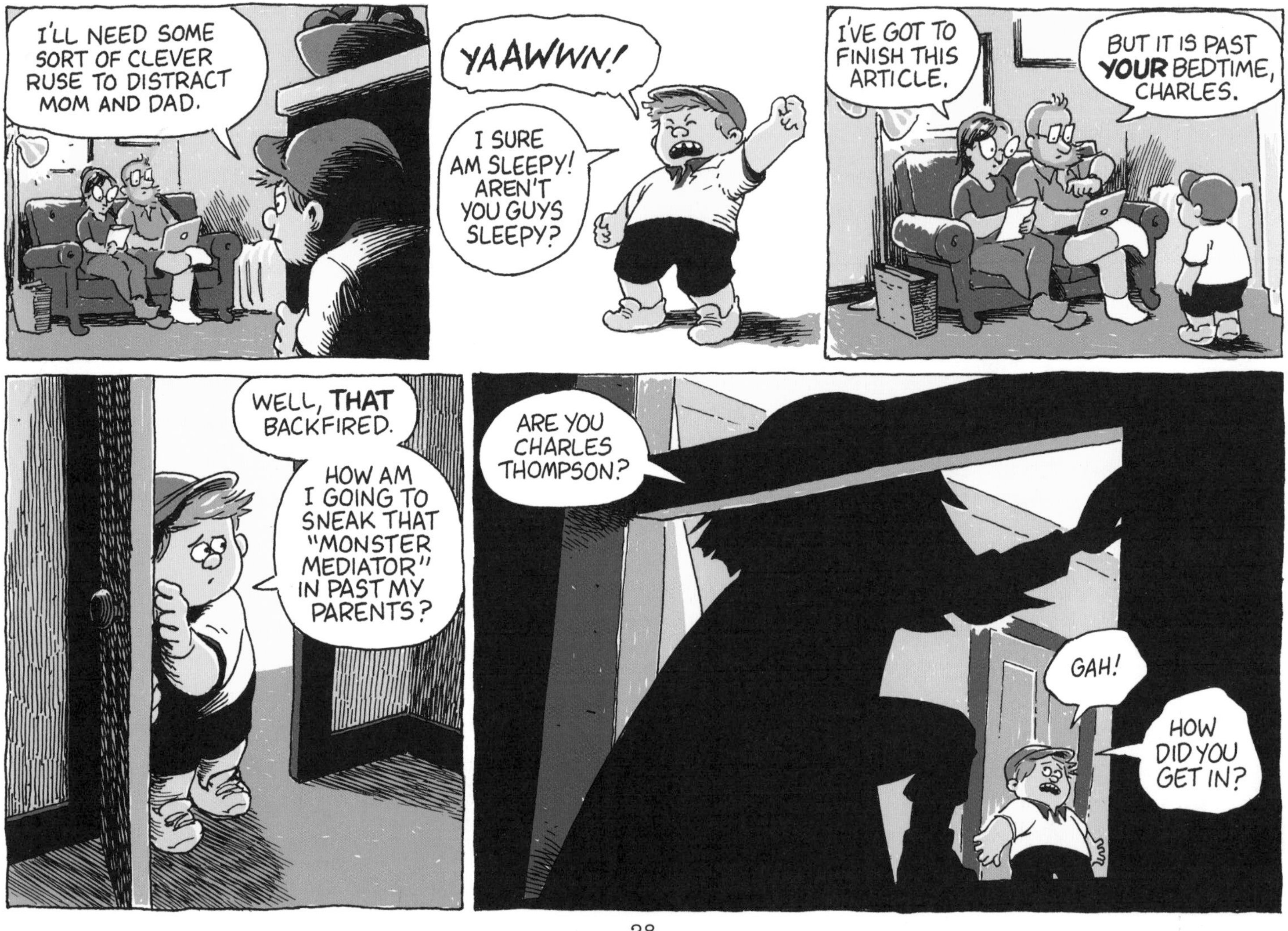
I'LL NEED SOME SORT OF CLEVER RUSE TO DISTRACT MOM AND DAD.
YAAWWN!
I SURE AM SLEEPY! AREN'T YOU GUYS SLEEPY?
I'VE GOT TO FINISH THIS ARTICLE.
BUT IT IS PAST **YOUR** BEDTIME, CHARLES.
WELL, **THAT** BACKFIRED.
HOW AM I GOING TO SNEAK THAT "MONSTER MEDIATOR" IN PAST MY PARENTS?
ARE YOU CHARLES THOMPSON?
GAH!
HOW DID YOU GET IN?

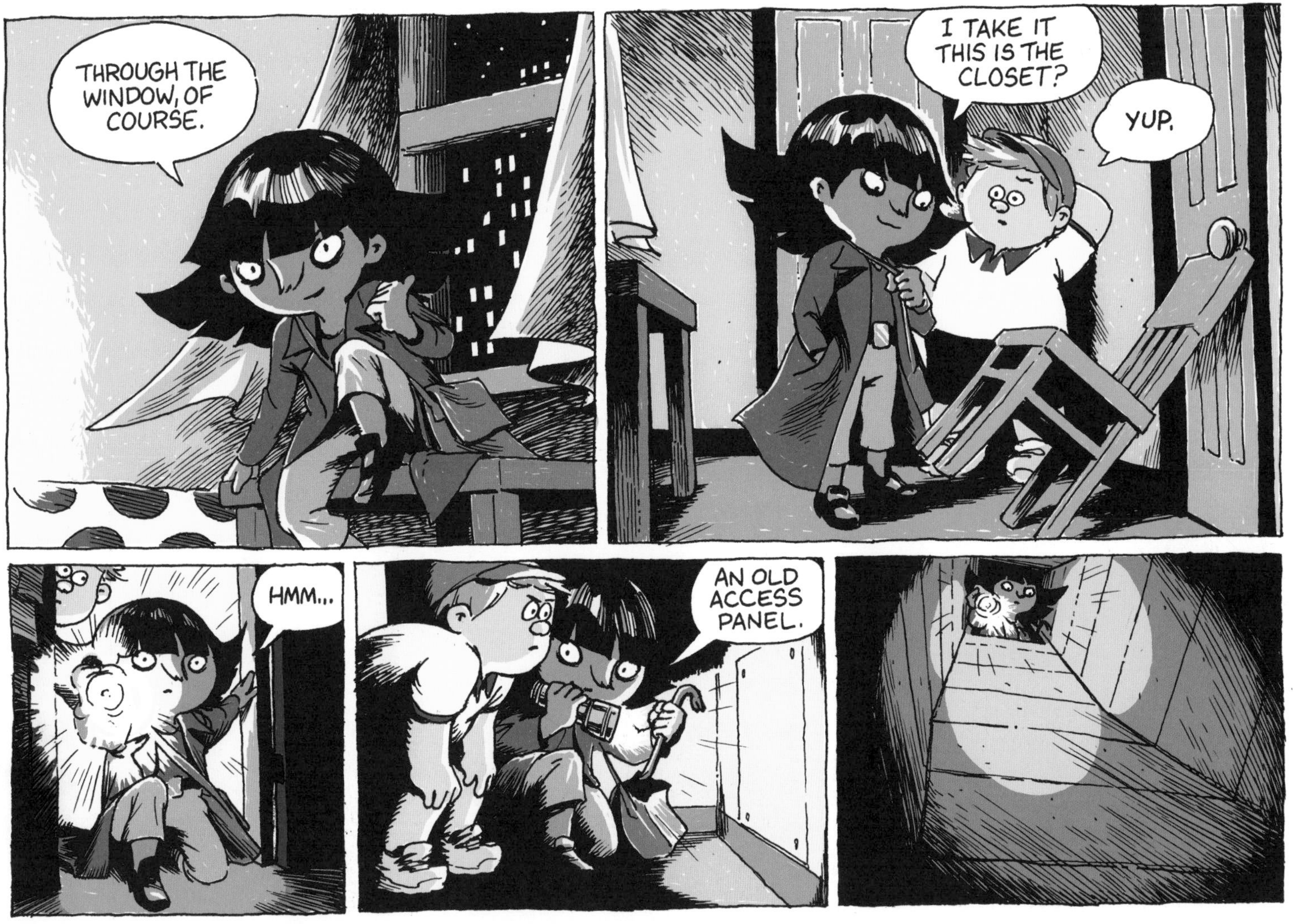
THROUGH THE WINDOW, OF COURSE.
I TAKE IT THIS IS THE CLOSET?
YUP.
HMM...
AN OLD ACCESS PANEL.

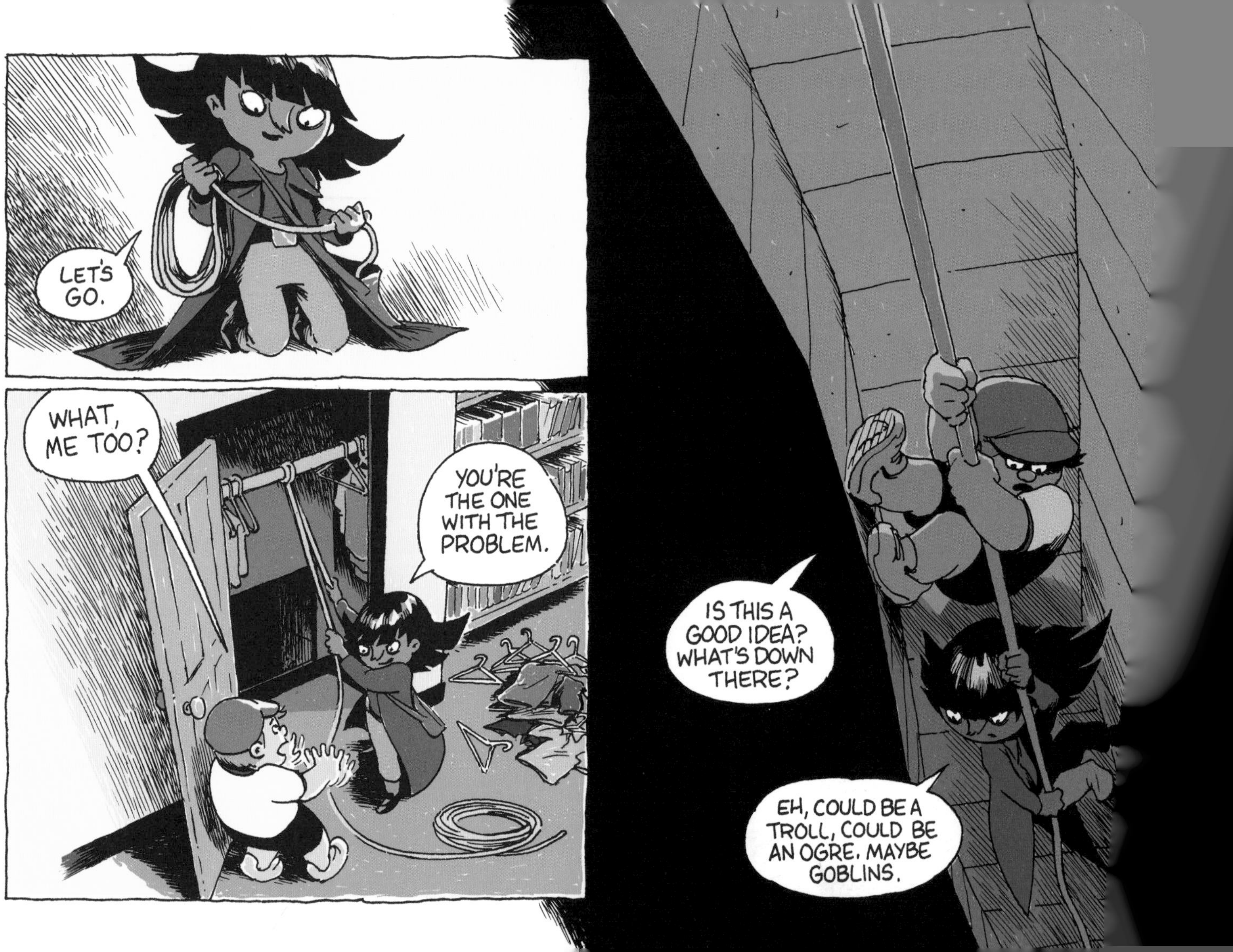
LET'S GO.
WHAT, ME TOO?
YOU'RE THE ONE WITH THE PROBLEM.
IS THIS A GOOD IDEA? WHAT'S DOWN THERE?
EH, COULD BE A TROLL, COULD BE AN OGRE. MAYBE GOBLINS.

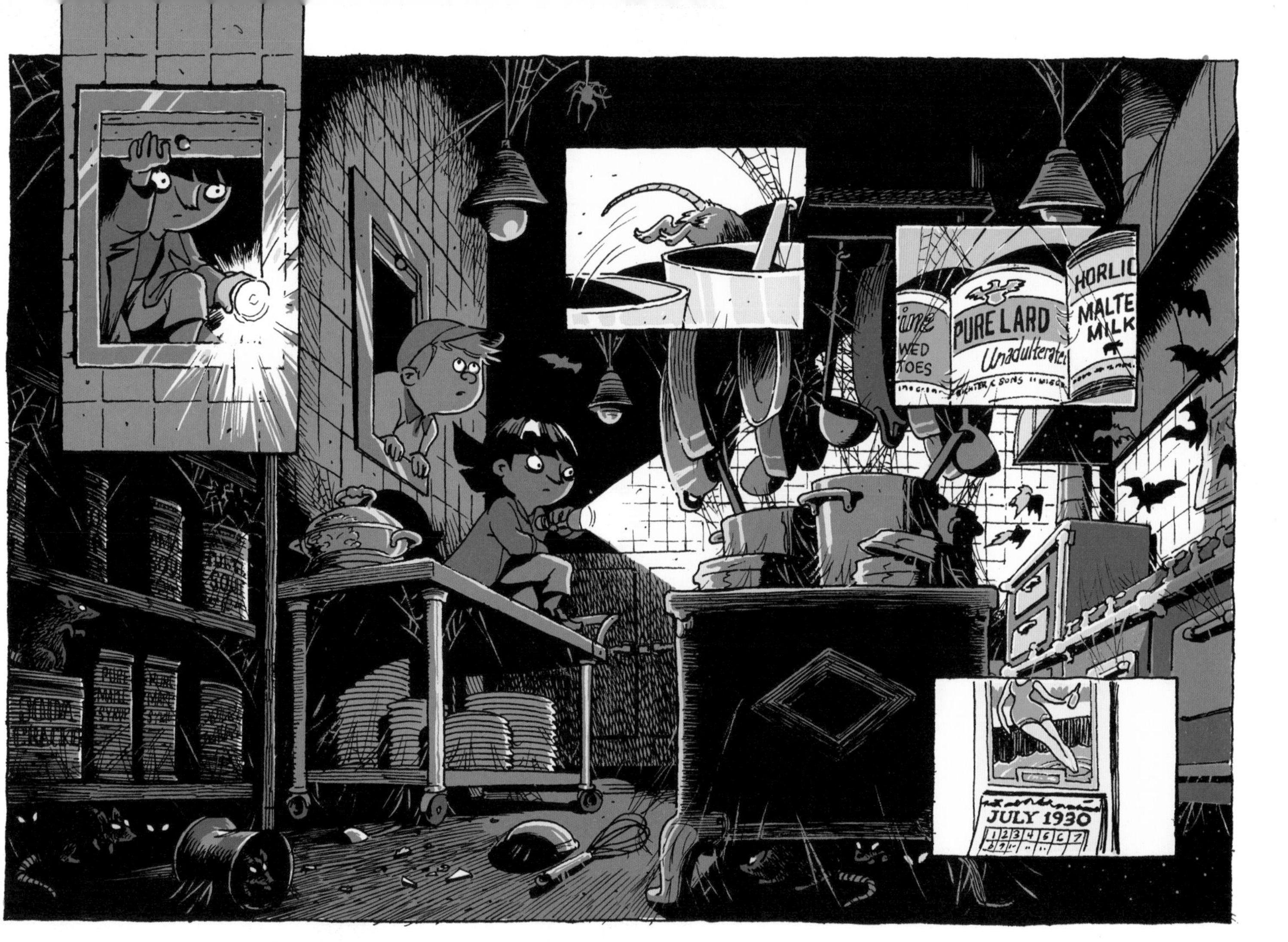
PURE LARD
Unadulterate
HORLIC
MALTE
MILK
JULY 1930

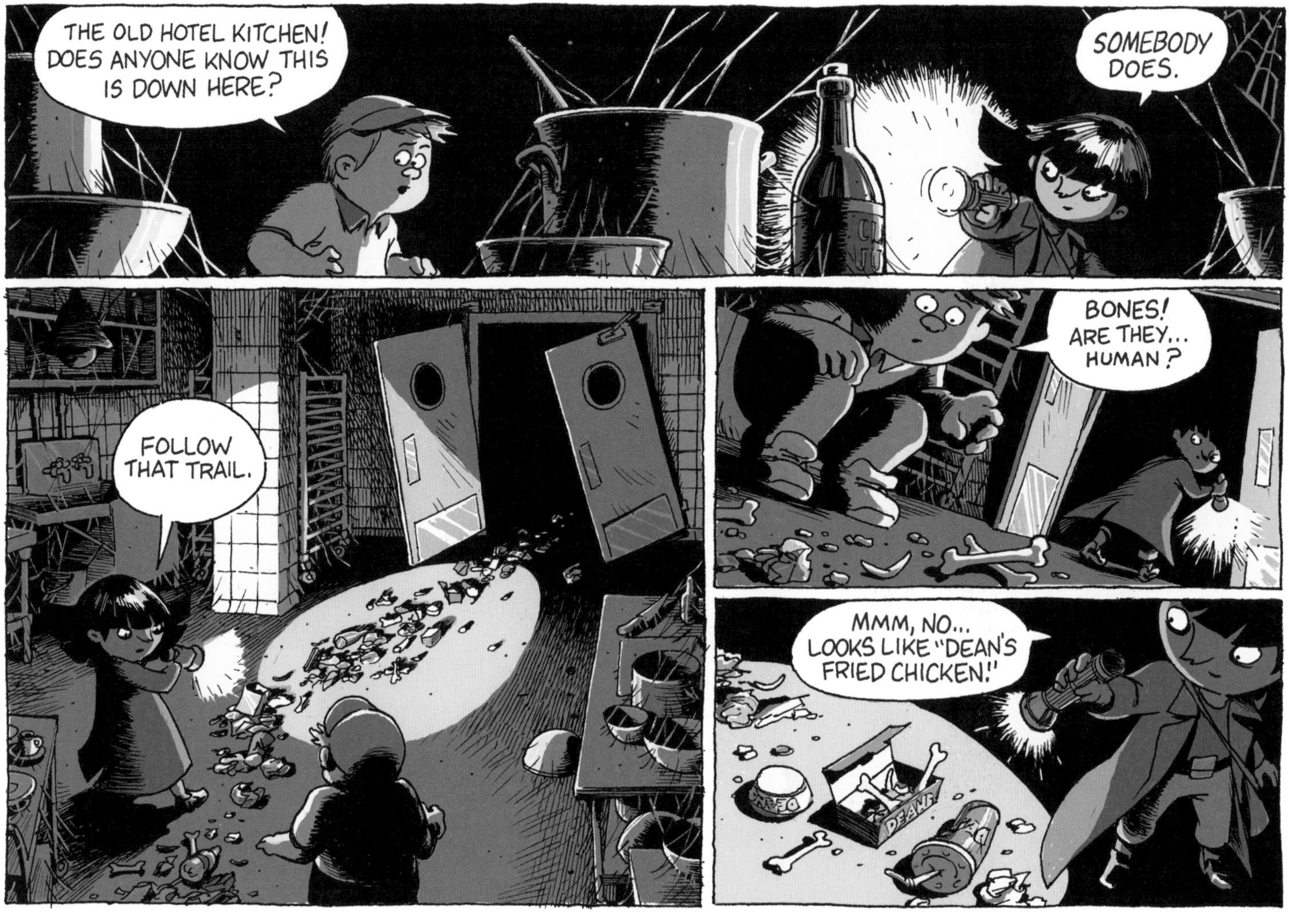
THE OLD HOTEL KITCHEN! DOES ANYONE KNOW THIS IS DOWN HERE?
SOMEBODY DOES.
FOLLOW THAT TRAIL.
BONES! ARE THEY... HUMAN?
MMM, NO... LOOKS LIKE "DEAN'S FRIED CHICKEN."

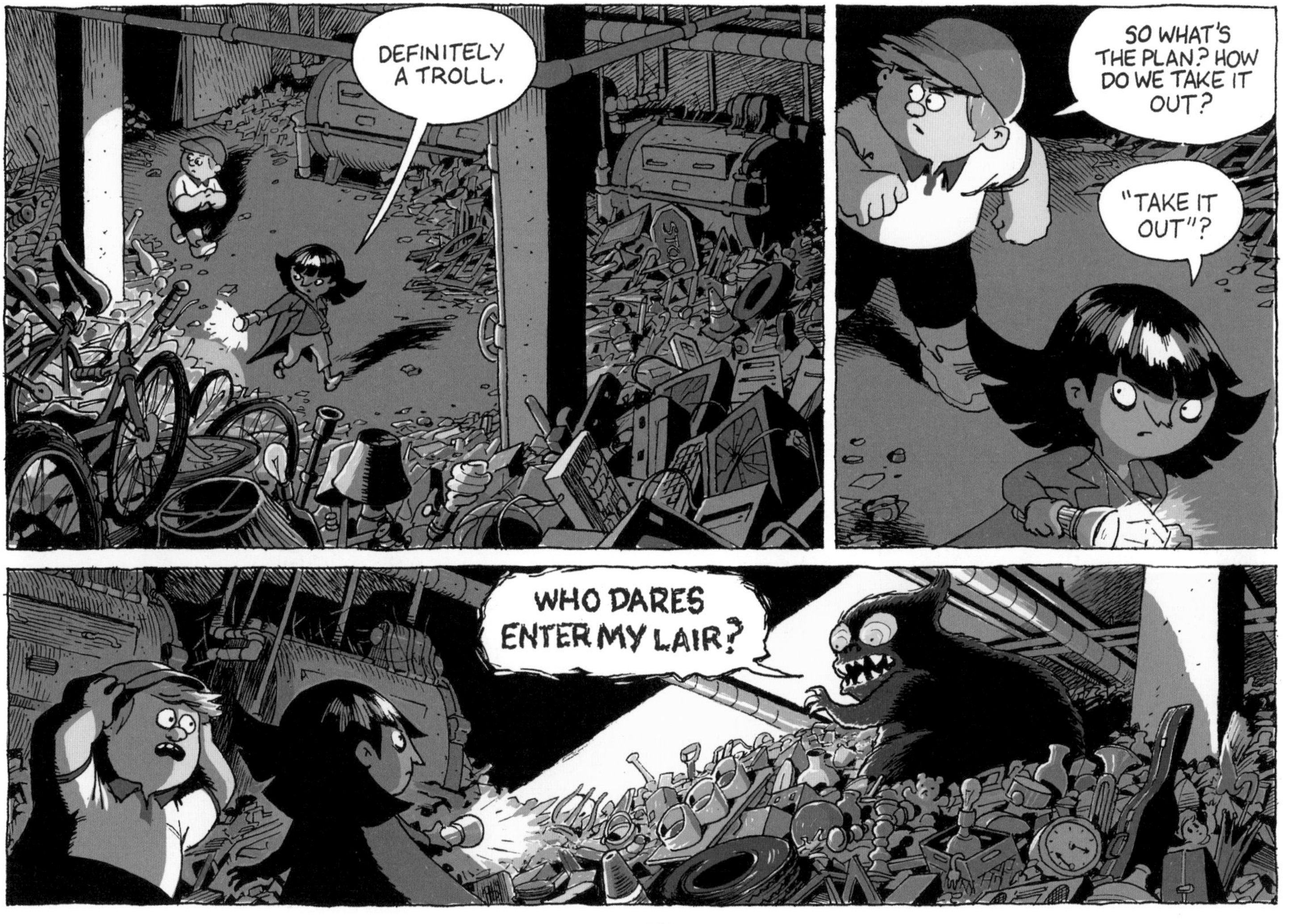
DEFINITELY A TROLL.
SO WHAT'S THE PLAN? HOW DO WE TAKE IT OUT?
"TAKE IT OUT"?
WHO DARES ENTER MY LAIR?

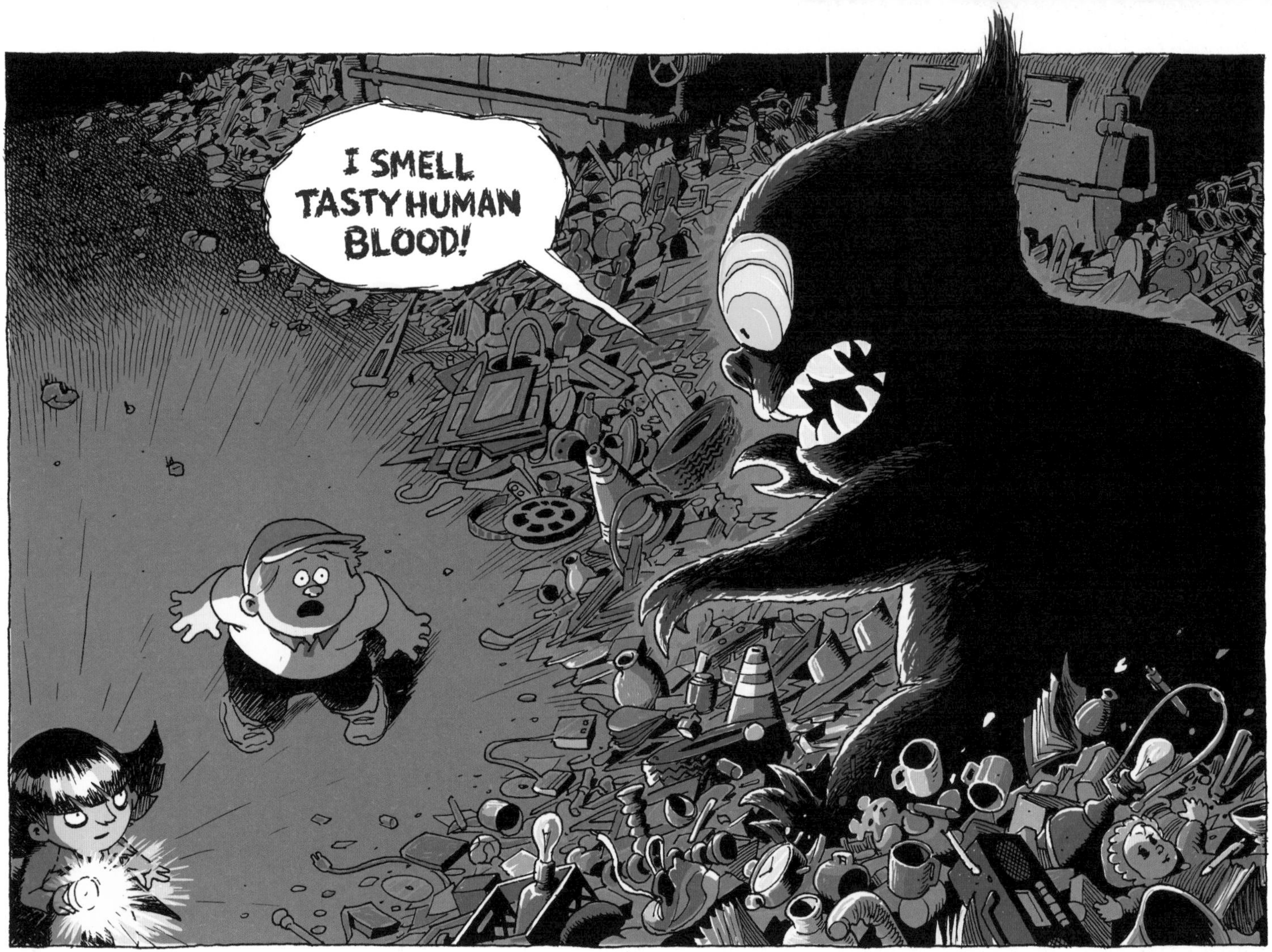
I SMELL TASTY HUMAN BLOOD!

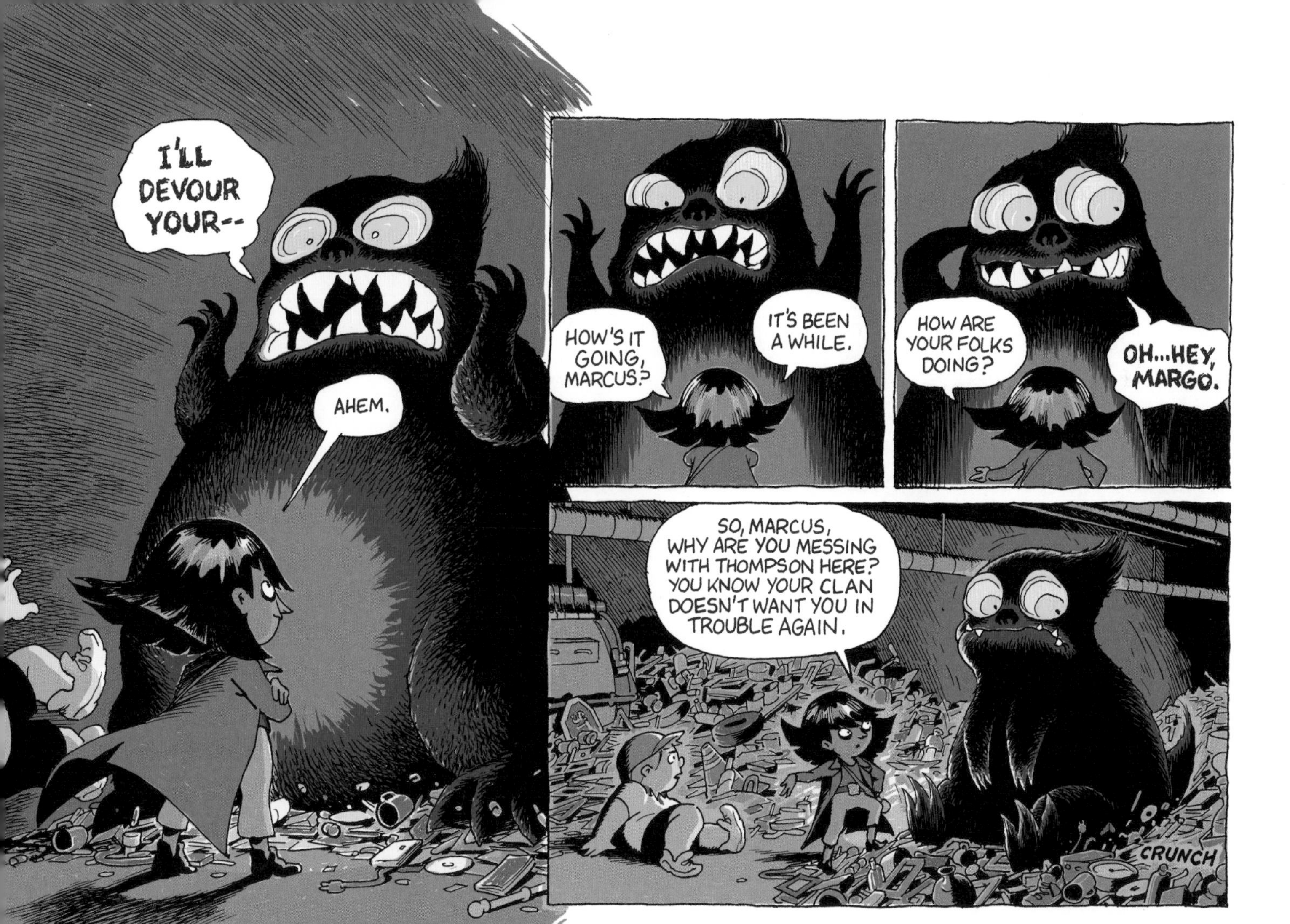
I'LL DEVOUR YOUR--
AHEM.
HOW'S IT GOING, MARCUS?
IT'S BEEN A WHILE.
HOW ARE YOUR FOLKS DOING?
OH...HEY, MARGO.
SO, MARCUS, WHY ARE YOU MESSING WITH THOMPSON HERE? YOU KNOW YOUR CLAN DOESN'T WANT YOU IN TROUBLE AGAIN.
CRUNCH

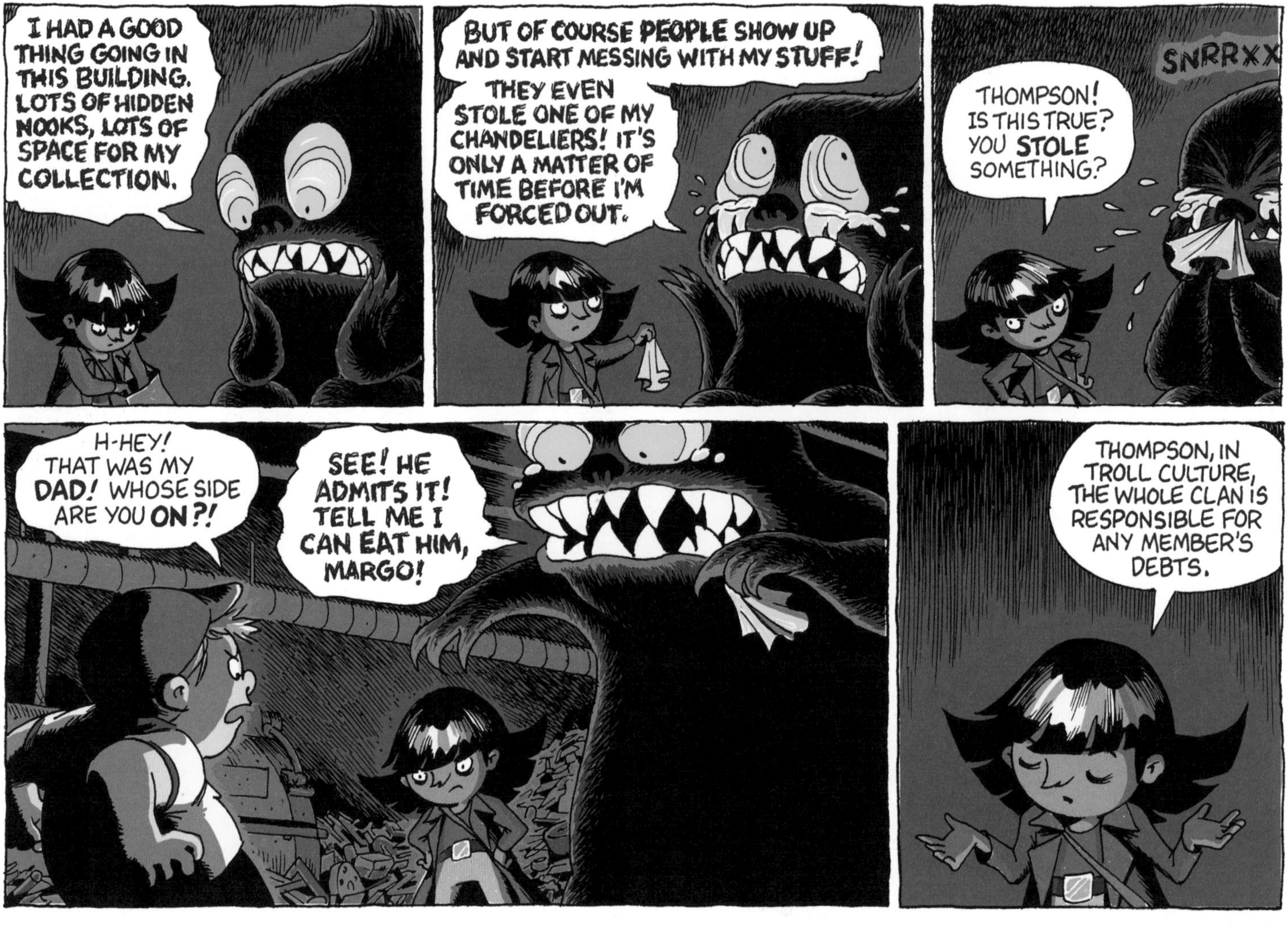
I HAD A GOOD THING GOING IN THIS BUILDING. LOTS OF HIDDEN NOOKS, LOTS OF SPACE FOR MY COLLECTION.
BUT OF COURSE PEOPLE SHOW UP AND START MESSING WITH MY STUFF!
THEY EVEN STOLE ONE OF MY CHANDELIERS! IT'S ONLY A MATTER OF TIME BEFORE I'M FORCED OUT.
SNRRXX
THOMPSON! IS THIS TRUE? YOU STOLE SOMETHING?
H-HEY! THAT WAS MY DAD! WHOSE SIDE ARE YOU ON?!
SEE! HE ADMITS IT! TELL ME I CAN EAT HIM, MARGO!
THOMPSON, IN TROLL CULTURE, THE WHOLE CLAN IS RESPONSIBLE FOR ANY MEMBER'S DEBTS.

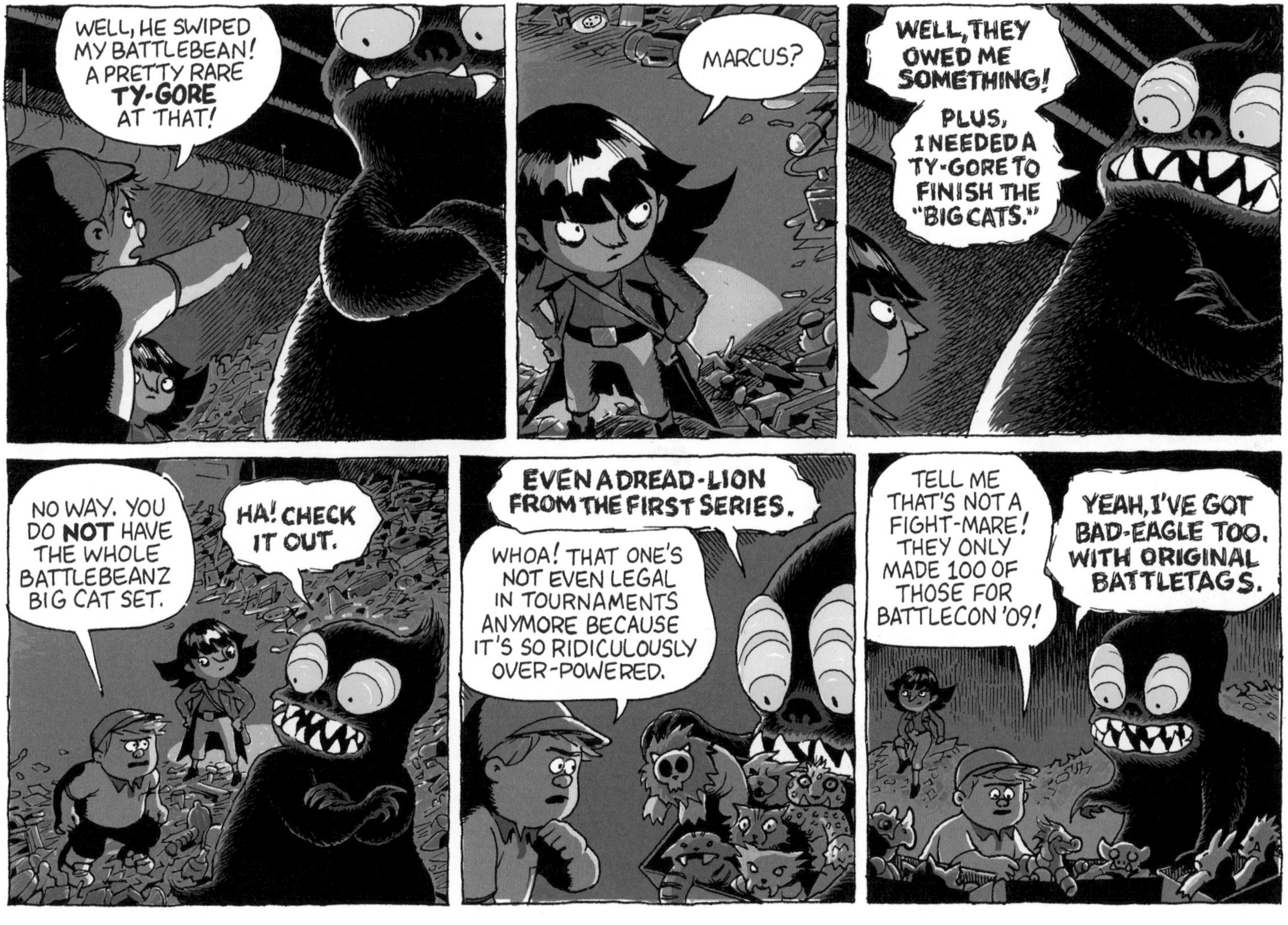
WELL, HE SWIPED MY BATTLEBEAN! A PRETTY RARE **TY-GORE** AT THAT!
MARCUS?
WELL, THEY OWED ME SOMETHING!
PLUS, I NEEDED A TY-GORE TO FINISH THE "BIG CATS."
NO WAY. YOU DO **NOT** HAVE THE WHOLE BATTLEBEANZ BIG CAT SET.
HA! CHECK IT OUT.
EVEN A DREAD-LION FROM THE FIRST SERIES.
WHOA! THAT ONE'S NOT EVEN LEGAL IN TOURNAMENTS ANYMORE BECAUSE IT'S SO RIDICULOUSLY OVER-POWERED.
TELL ME THAT'S NOT A FIGHT-MARE! THEY ONLY MADE 100 OF THOSE FOR BATTLECON '09!
YEAH, I'VE GOT BAD-EAGLE TOO. WITH ORIGINAL BATTLETAGS.

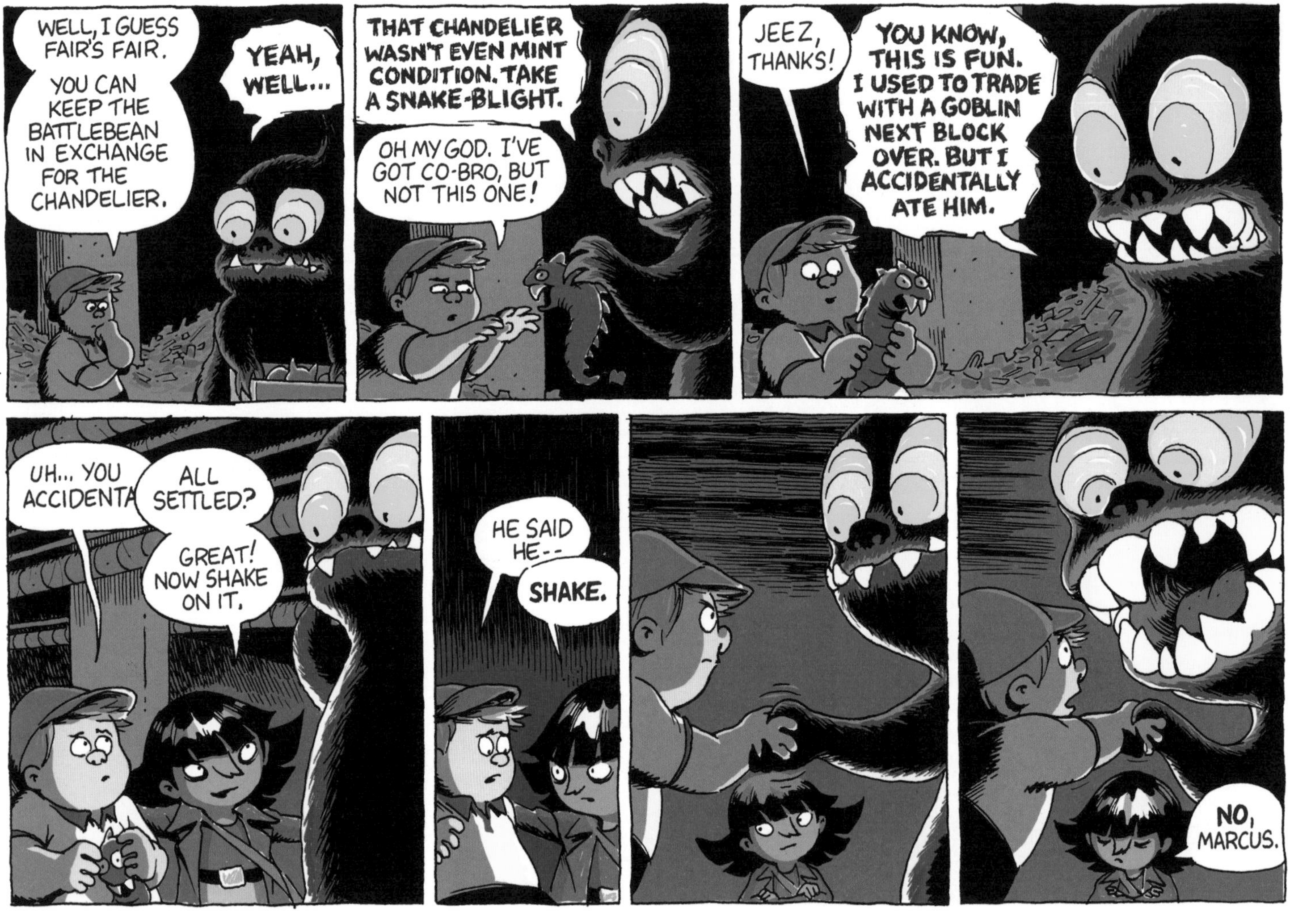
WELL, I GUESS FAIR'S FAIR.
YOU CAN KEEP THE BATTLEBEAN IN EXCHANGE FOR THE CHANDELIER.
YEAH, WELL...
THAT CHANDELIER WASN'T EVEN MINT CONDITION. TAKE A SNAKE-BLIGHT.
OH MY GOD. I'VE GOT CO-BRO, BUT NOT THIS ONE!
JEEZ, THANKS!
YOU KNOW, THIS IS FUN. I USED TO TRADE WITH A GOBLIN NEXT BLOCK OVER. BUT I ACCIDENTALLY ATE HIM.
UH... YOU ACCIDENTA
ALL SETTLED?
GREAT! NOW SHAKE ON IT.
HE SAID HE--
SHAKE.
NO, MARCUS.

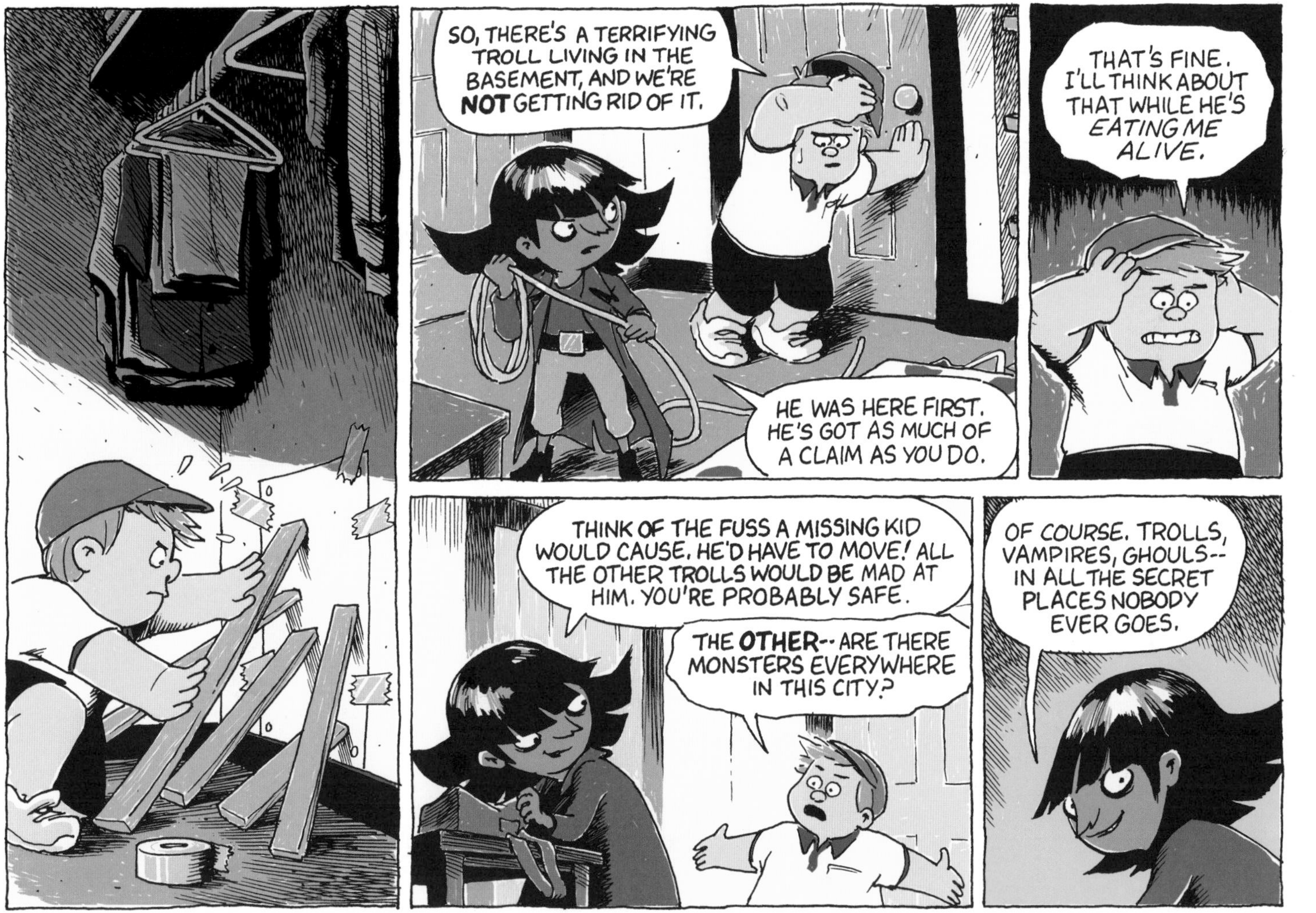
SO, THERE'S A TERRIFYING TROLL LIVING IN THE BASEMENT, AND WE'RE **NOT** GETTING RID OF IT.
HE WAS HERE FIRST. HE'S GOT AS MUCH OF A CLAIM AS YOU DO.
THAT'S FINE. I'LL THINK ABOUT THAT WHILE HE'S *EATING ME ALIVE.*
THINK OF THE FUSS A MISSING KID WOULD CAUSE. HE'D HAVE TO MOVE! ALL THE OTHER TROLLS WOULD BE MAD AT HIM. YOU'RE PROBABLY SAFE.
THE **OTHER**-- ARE THERE MONSTERS EVERYWHERE IN THIS CITY?
OF COURSE. TROLLS, VAMPIRES, GHOULS-- IN ALL THE SECRET PLACES NOBODY EVER GOES.

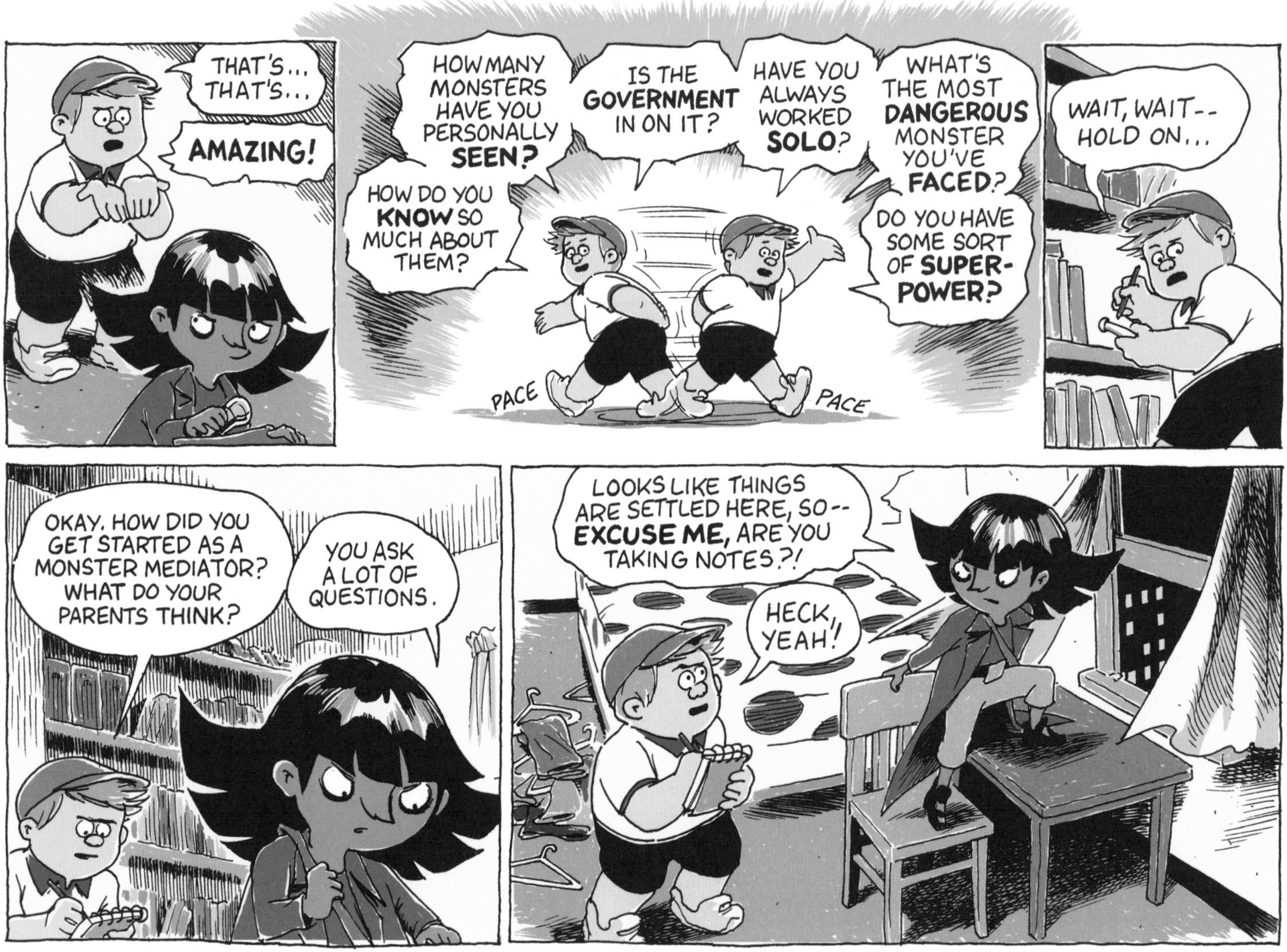

THAT'S... THAT'S...
AMAZING!
HOW MANY MONSTERS HAVE YOU PERSONALLY SEEN?
HOW DO YOU KNOW SO MUCH ABOUT THEM?
IS THE GOVERNMENT IN ON IT?
HAVE YOU ALWAYS WORKED SOLO?
WHAT'S THE MOST DANGEROUS MONSTER YOU'VE FACED?
DO YOU HAVE SOME SORT OF SUPER-POWER?
PACE
PACE
WAIT, WAIT-- HOLD ON...
OKAY. HOW DID YOU GET STARTED AS A MONSTER MEDIATOR? WHAT DO YOUR PARENTS THINK?
YOU ASK A LOT OF QUESTIONS.
LOOKS LIKE THINGS ARE SETTLED HERE, SO-- EXCUSE ME, ARE YOU TAKING NOTES?!
HECK, YEAH!!

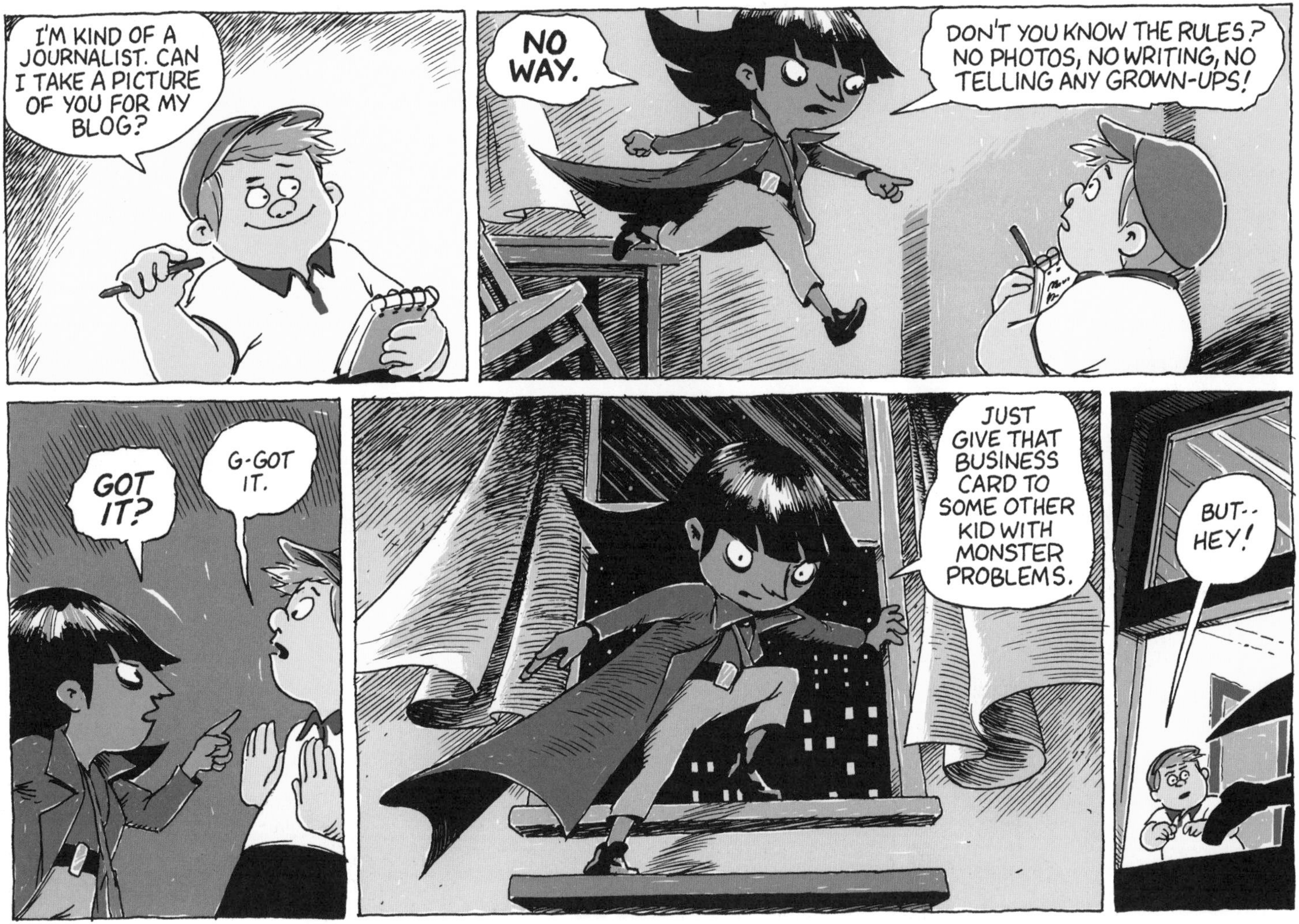
I'M KIND OF A JOURNALIST. CAN I TAKE A PICTURE OF YOU FOR MY BLOG?
NO WAY.
DON'T YOU KNOW THE RULES? NO PHOTOS, NO WRITING, NO TELLING ANY GROWN-UPS!
GOT IT?
G-GOT IT.
JUST GIVE THAT BUSINESS CARD TO SOME OTHER KID WITH MONSTER PROBLEMS.
BUT-- HEY!

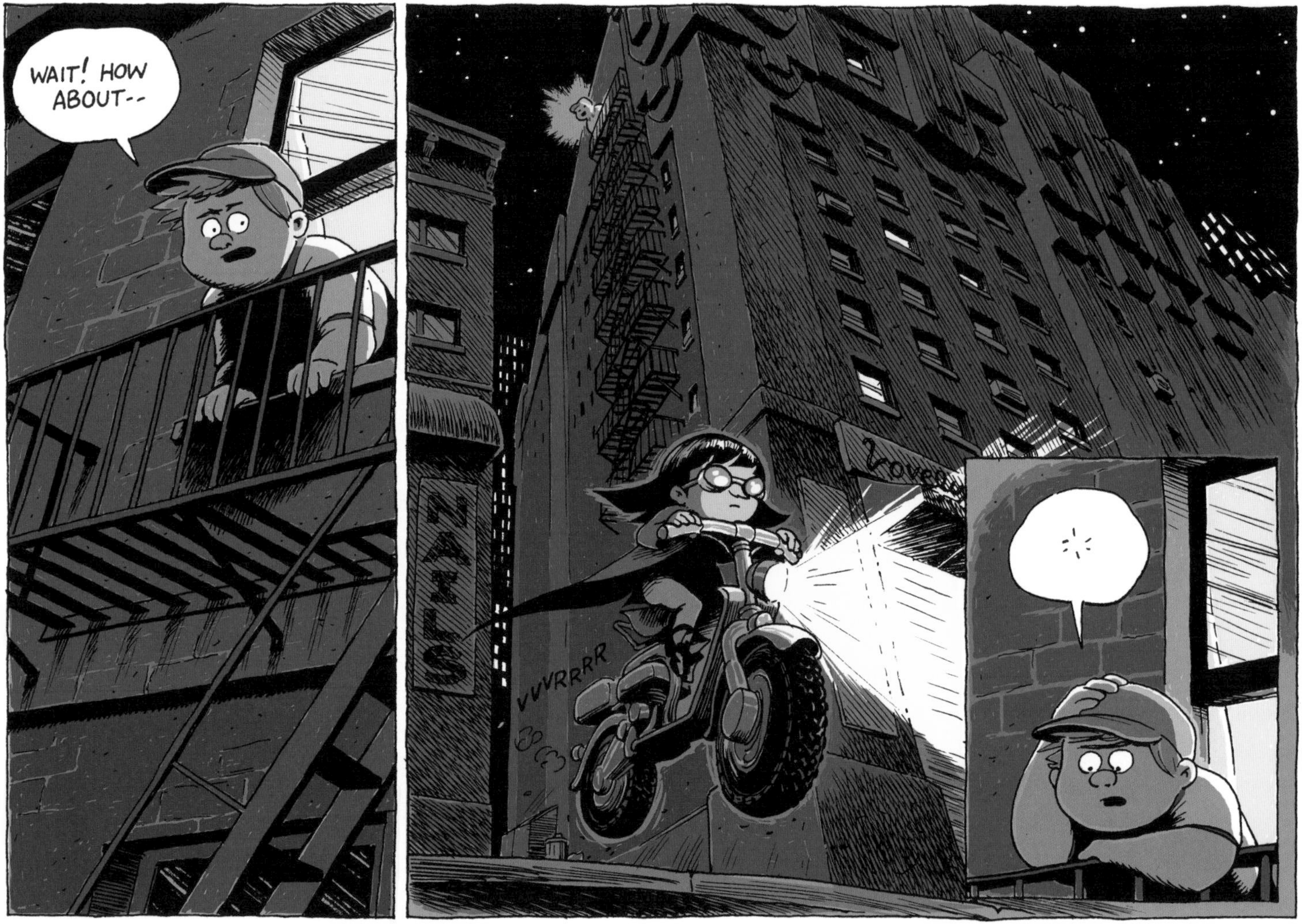
WAIT! HOW ABOUT--
NAILS
VVVRRRR

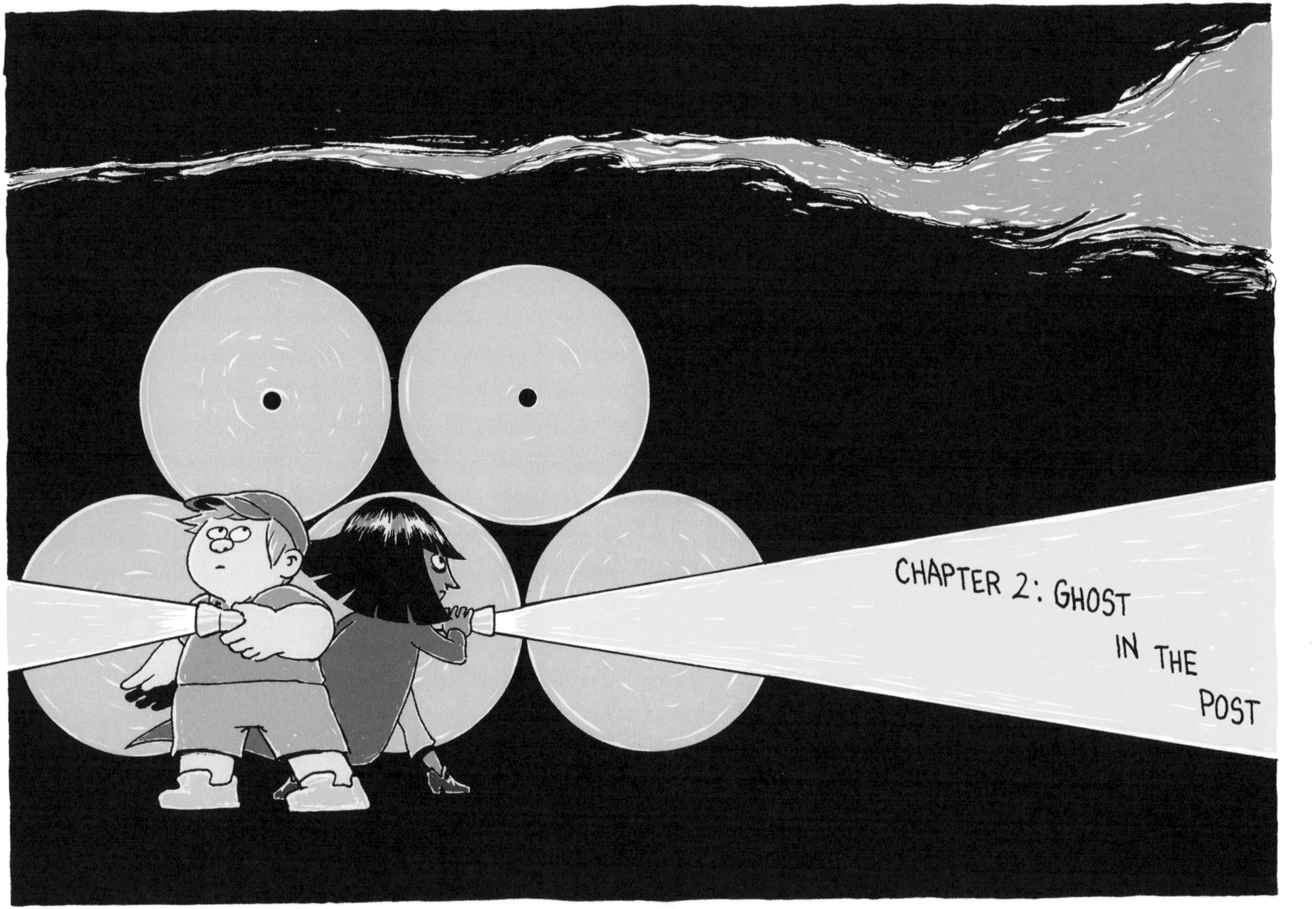
CHAPTER 2: GHOST IN THE POST

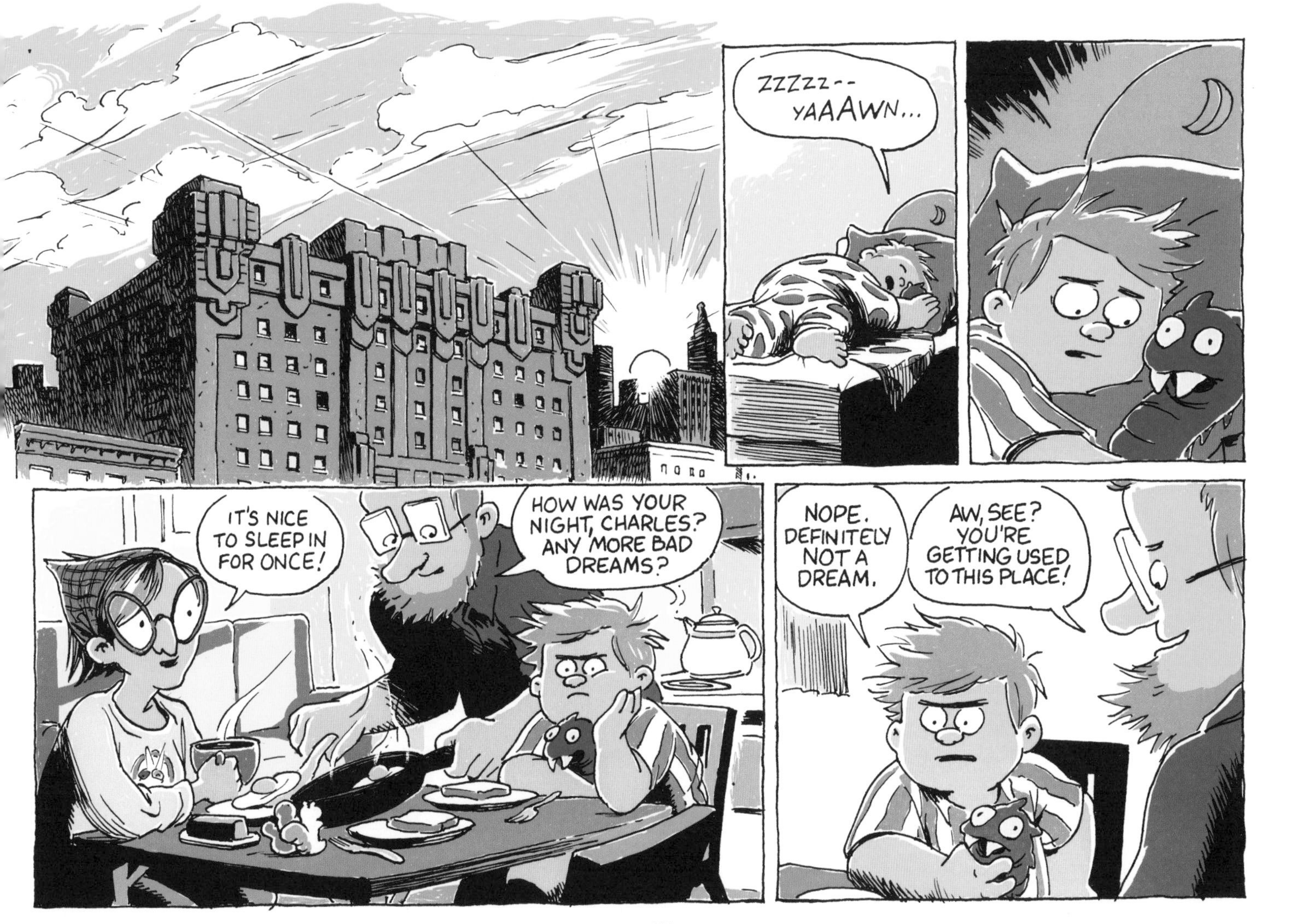
ZZZzz--
YAAAWN...
IT'S NICE TO SLEEP IN FOR ONCE!
HOW WAS YOUR NIGHT, CHARLES? ANY MORE BAD DREAMS?
NOPE. DEFINITELY NOT A DREAM.
AW, SEE? YOU'RE GETTING USED TO THIS PLACE!

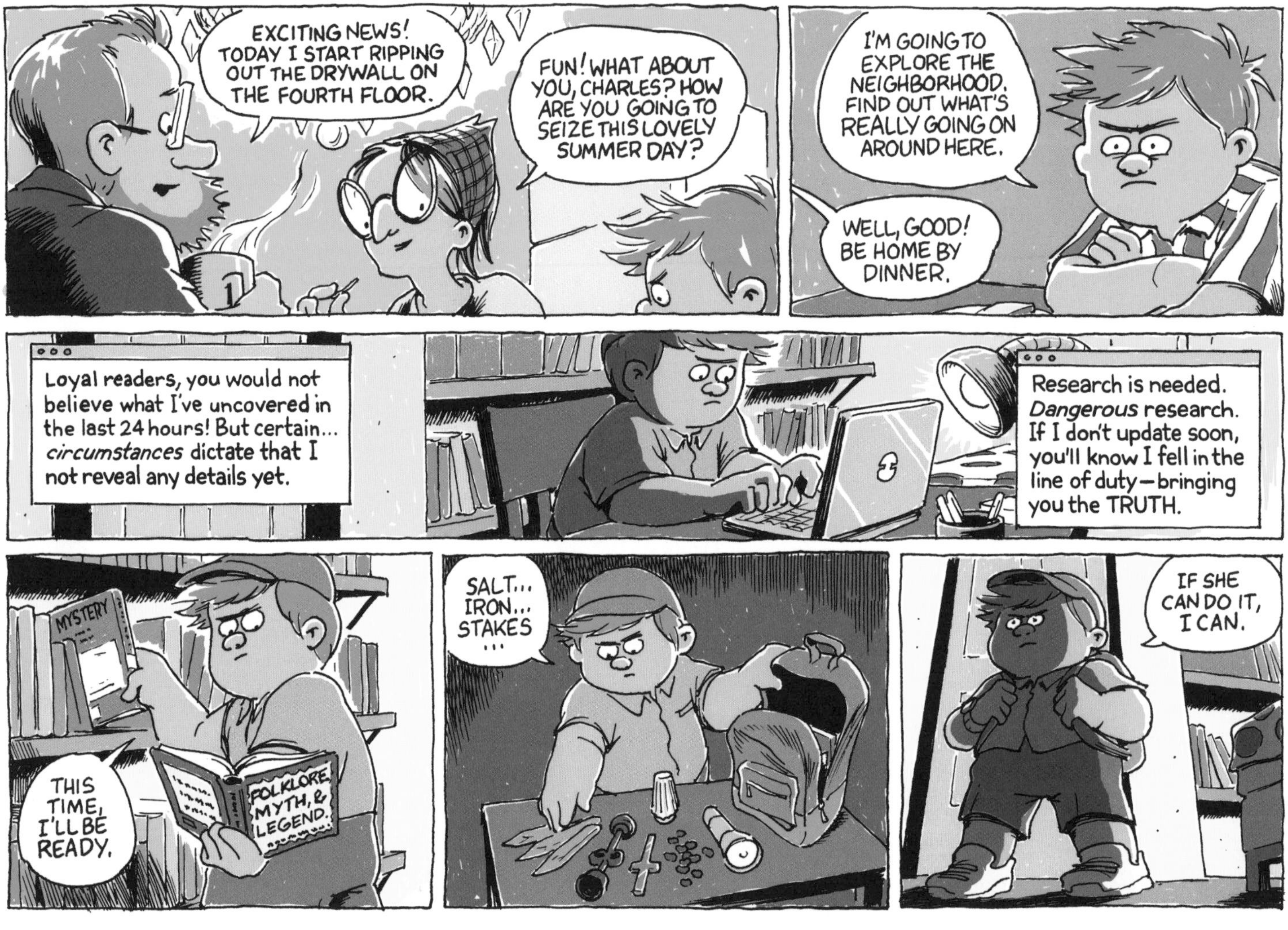
EXCITING NEWS! TODAY I START RIPPING OUT THE DRYWALL ON THE FOURTH FLOOR.
FUN! WHAT ABOUT YOU, CHARLES? HOW ARE YOU GOING TO SEIZE THIS LOVELY SUMMER DAY?
I'M GOING TO EXPLORE THE NEIGHBORHOOD. FIND OUT WHAT'S REALLY GOING ON AROUND HERE.
WELL, GOOD! BE HOME BY DINNER.
Loyal readers, you would not believe what I've uncovered in the last 24 hours! But certain... *circumstances* dictate that I not reveal any details yet.
Research is needed. *Dangerous* research. If I don't update soon, you'll know I fell in the line of duty—bringing you the TRUTH.
MYSTERY
THIS TIME, I'LL BE READY.
FOLKLORE, MYTH, & LEGEND.
SALT... IRON... STAKES ...
IF SHE CAN DO IT, I CAN.

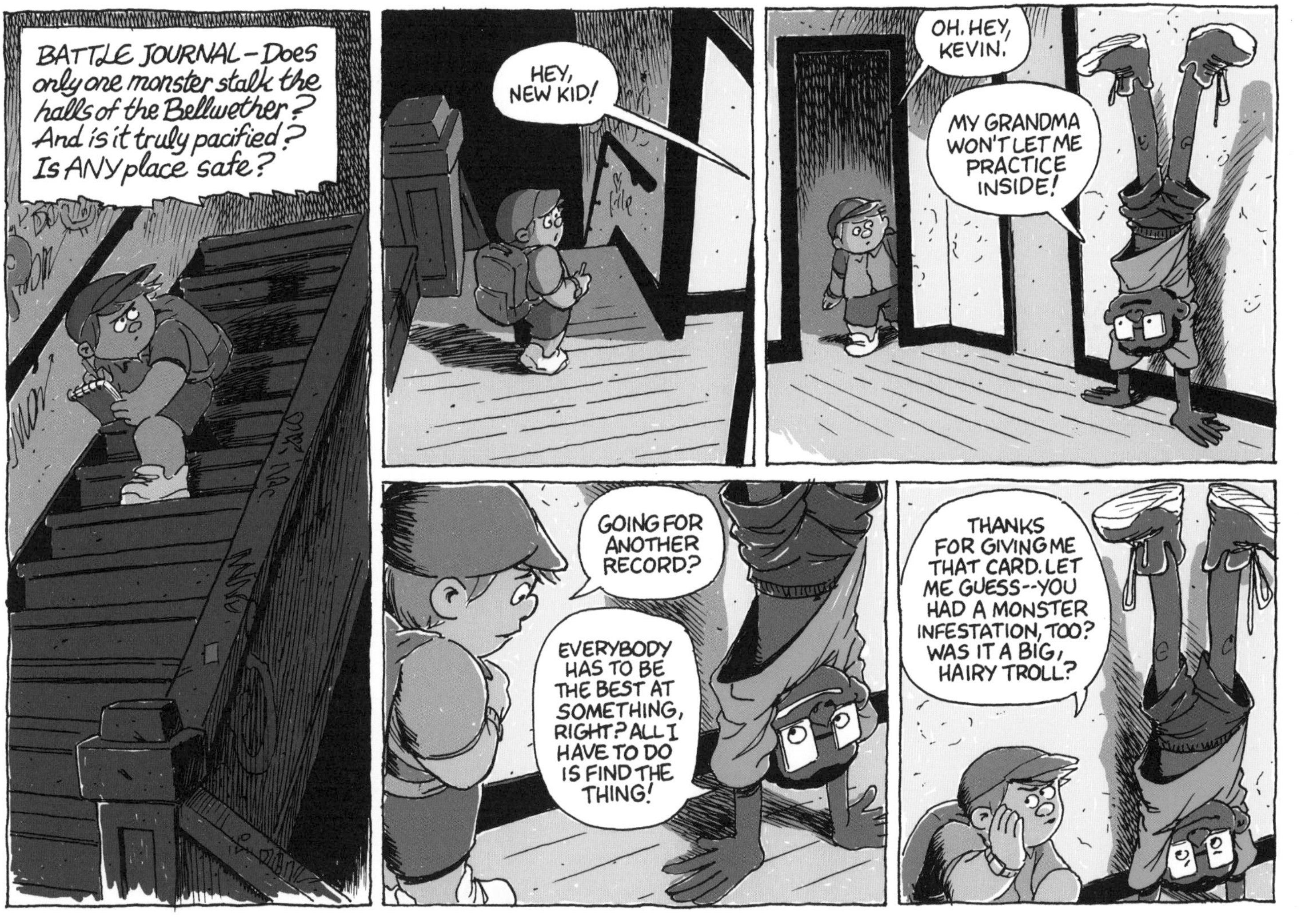
BATTLE JOURNAL - Does only one monster stalk the halls of the Bellwether? And is it truly pacified? Is ANY place safe?
HEY, NEW KID!
OH. HEY, KEVIN.
MY GRANDMA WON'T LET ME PRACTICE INSIDE!
GOING FOR ANOTHER RECORD?
EVERYBODY HAS TO BE THE BEST AT SOMETHING, RIGHT? ALL I HAVE TO DO IS FIND THE THING!
THANKS FOR GIVING ME THAT CARD. LET ME GUESS--YOU HAD A MONSTER INFESTATION, TOO? WAS IT A BIG, HAIRY TROLL?

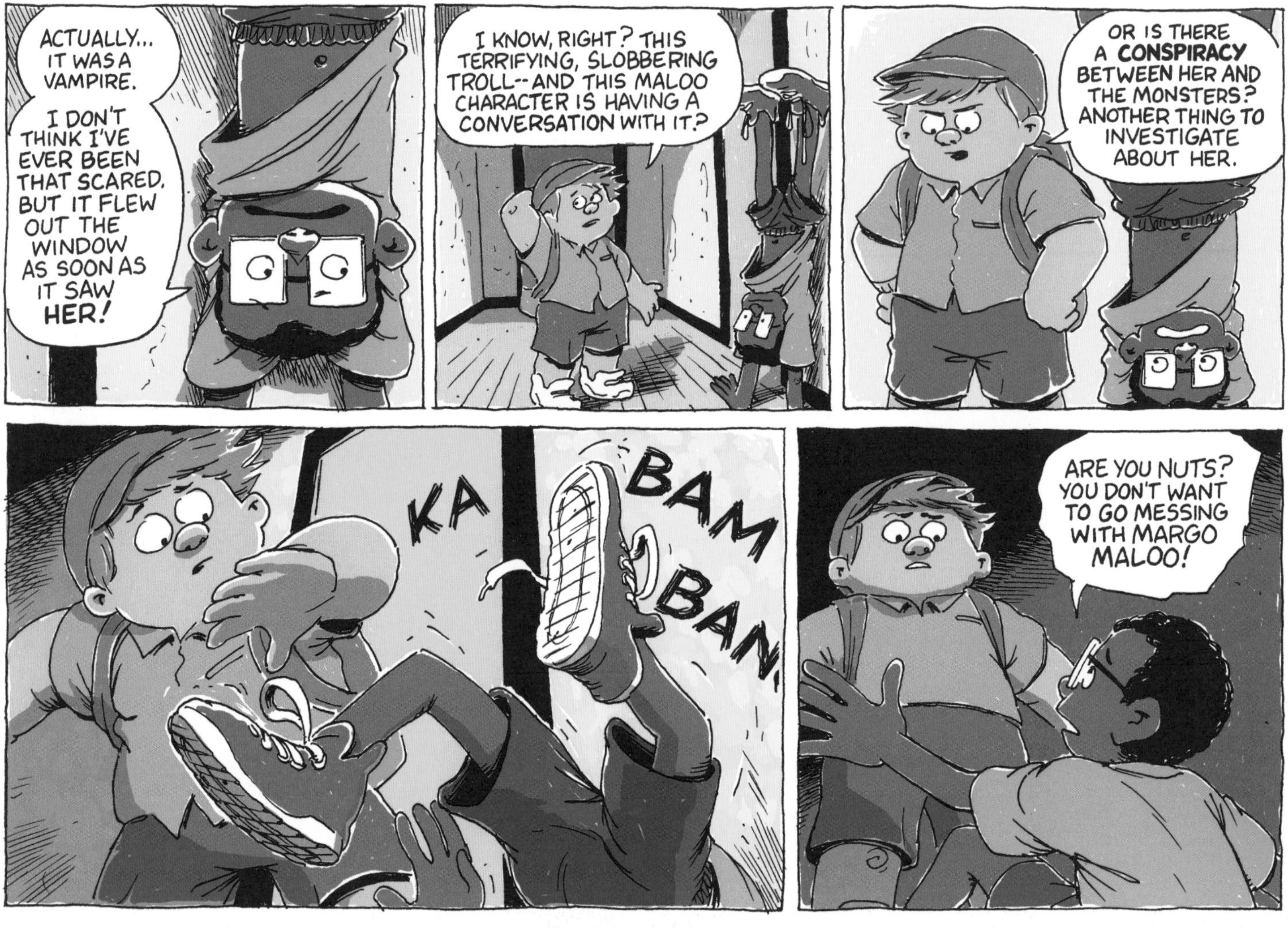
ACTUALLY... IT WAS A VAMPIRE.
I DON'T THINK I'VE EVER BEEN THAT SCARED, BUT IT FLEW OUT THE WINDOW AS SOON AS IT SAW **HER**!
I KNOW, RIGHT? THIS TERRIFYING, SLOBBERING TROLL--AND THIS MALOO CHARACTER IS HAVING A CONVERSATION WITH IT?
OR IS THERE A **CONSPIRACY** BETWEEN HER AND THE MONSTERS? ANOTHER THING TO INVESTIGATE ABOUT HER.
KA
BAM
BAN
ARE YOU NUTS? YOU DON'T WANT TO GO MESSING WITH MARGO MALOO!

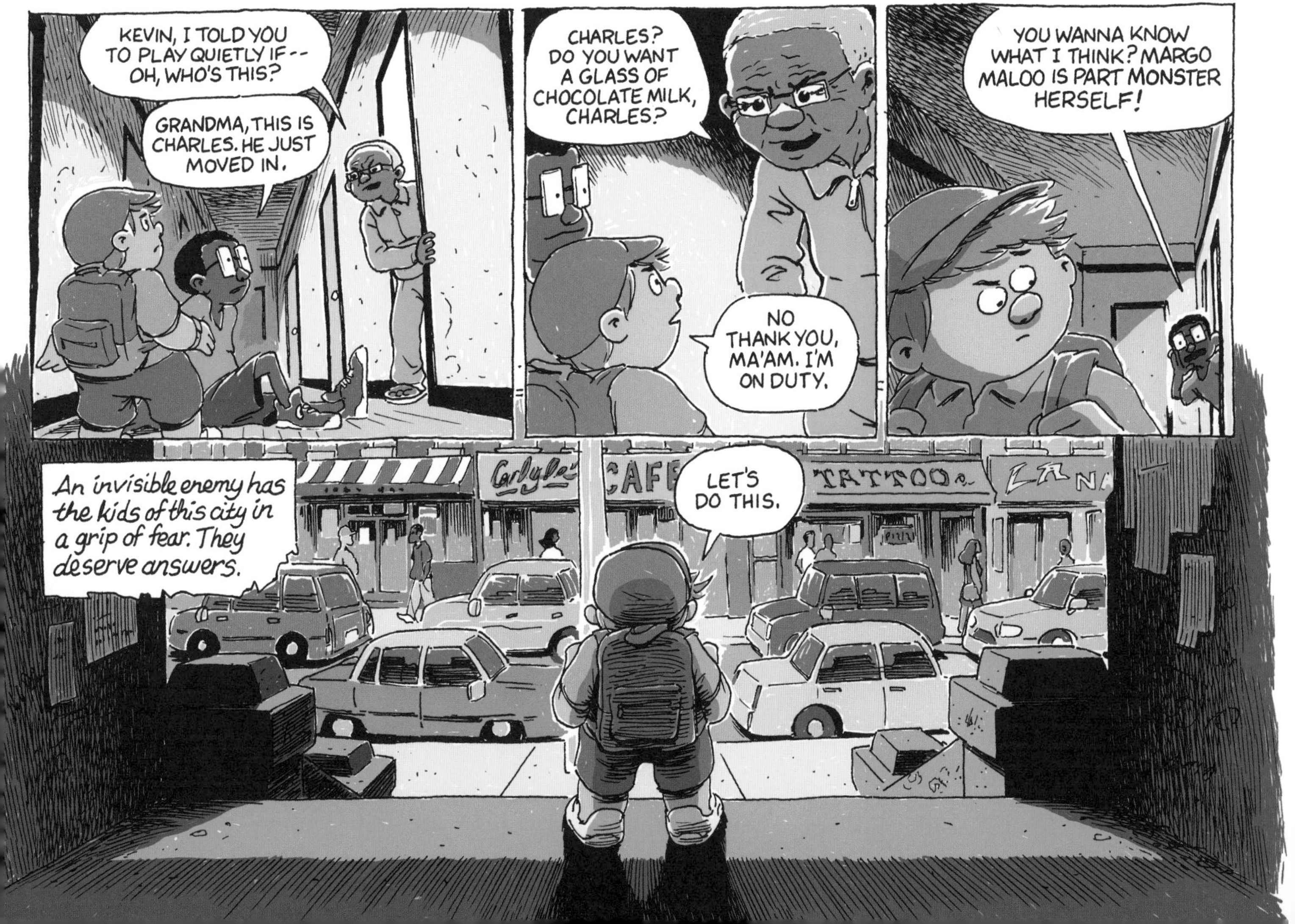
KEVIN, I TOLD YOU TO PLAY QUIETLY IF -- OH, WHO'S THIS?
GRANDMA, THIS IS CHARLES. HE JUST MOVED IN.
CHARLES? DO YOU WANT A GLASS OF CHOCOLATE MILK, CHARLES?
NO THANK YOU, MA'AM. I'M ON DUTY.
YOU WANNA KNOW WHAT I THINK? MARGO MALOO IS PART MONSTER HERSELF!
An invisible enemy has the kids of this city in a grip of fear. They deserve answers.
LET'S DO THIS.
CAFE
TATTOO

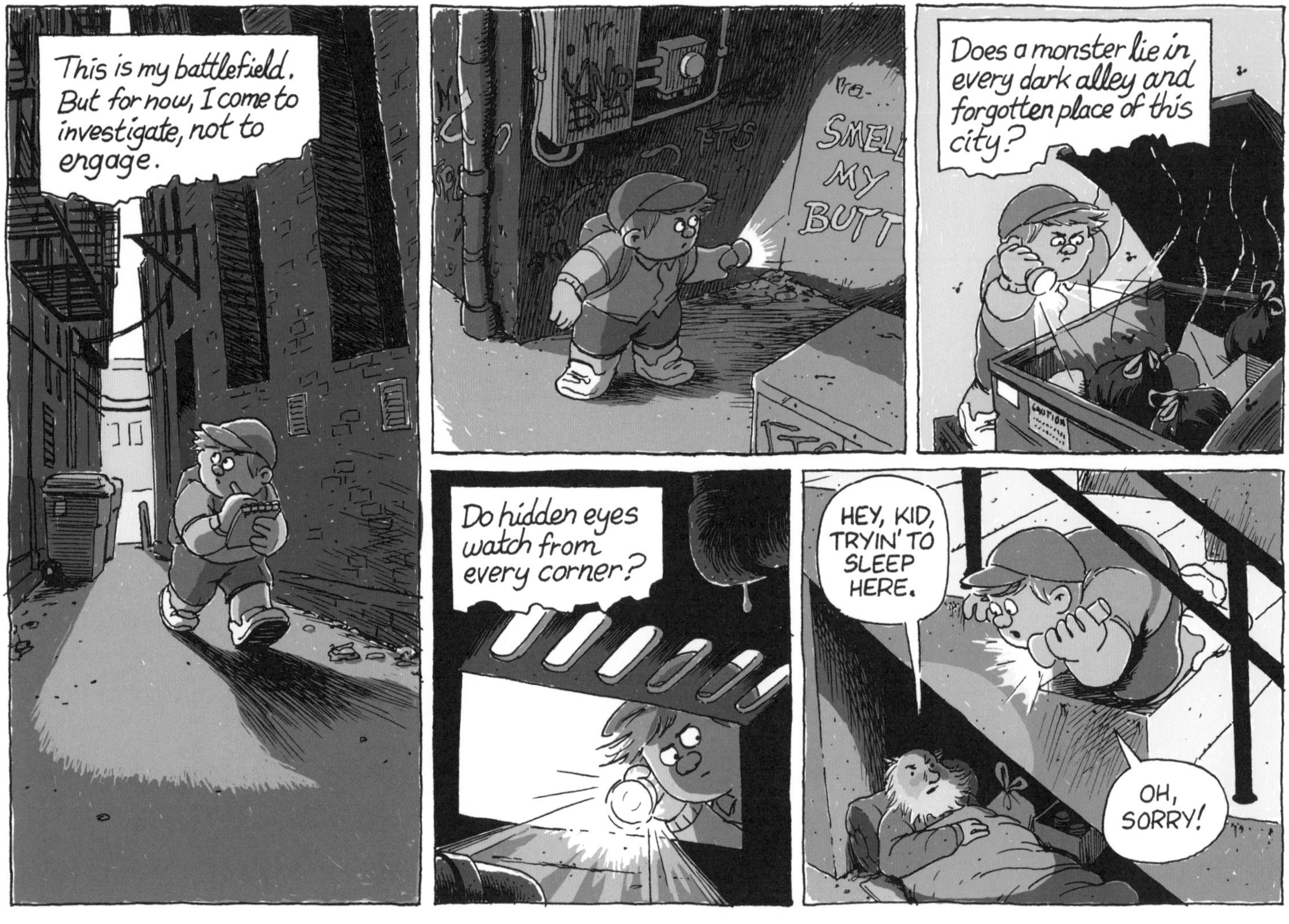
This is my battlefield. But for now, I come to investigate, not to engage.
Does a monster lie in every dark alley and forgotten place of this city?
Do hidden eyes watch from every corner?
HEY, KID, TRYIN' TO SLEEP HERE.
OH, SORRY!

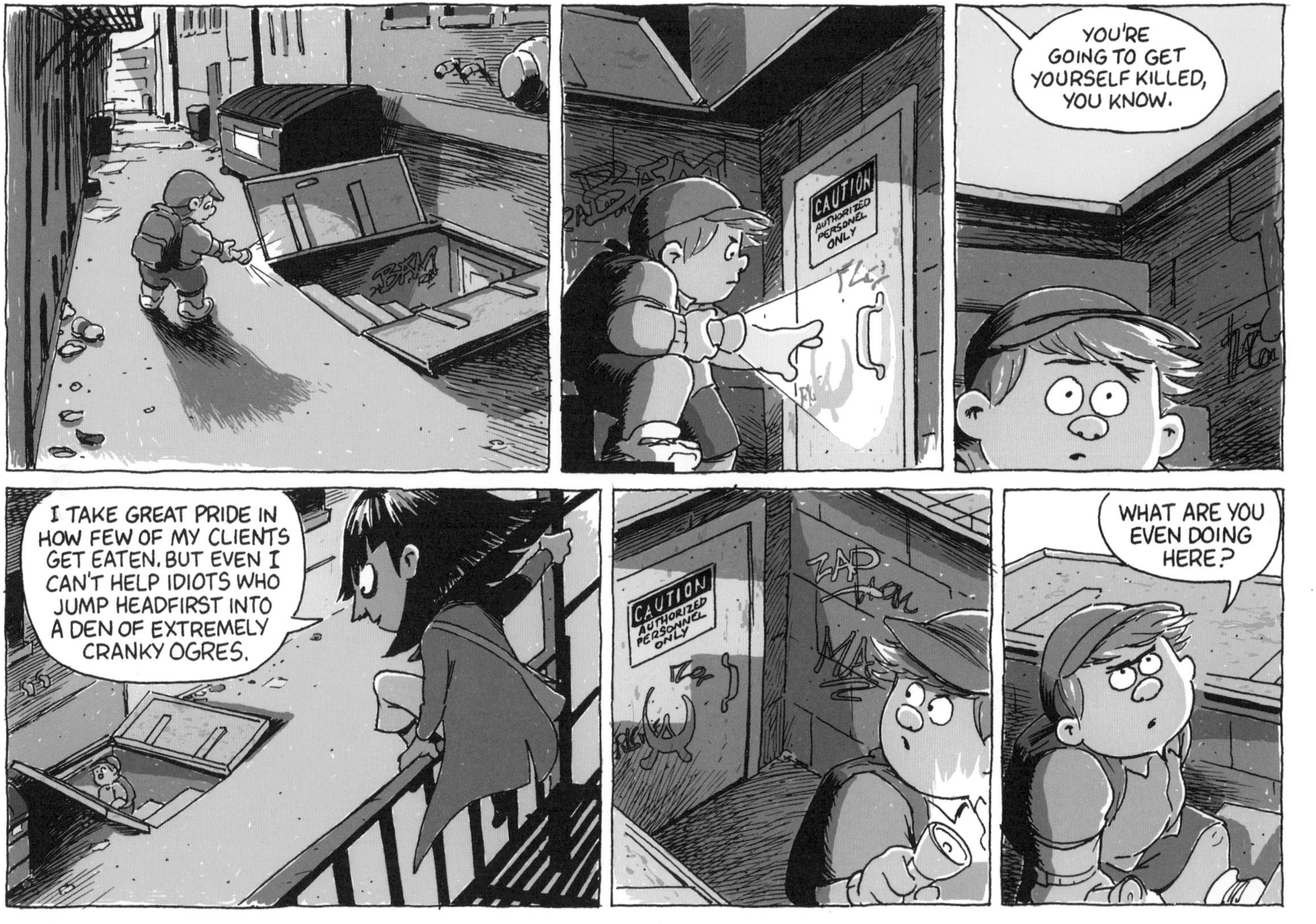
BAM
CAUTION AUTHORIZED PERSONEL ONLY
YOU'RE GOING TO GET YOURSELF KILLED, YOU KNOW.
I TAKE GREAT PRIDE IN HOW FEW OF MY CLIENTS GET EATEN. BUT EVEN I CAN'T HELP IDIOTS WHO JUMP HEADFIRST INTO A DEN OF EXTREMELY CRANKY OGRES.
CAUTION AUTHORIZED PERSONNEL ONLY
ZAP
WHAT ARE YOU EVEN DOING HERE?

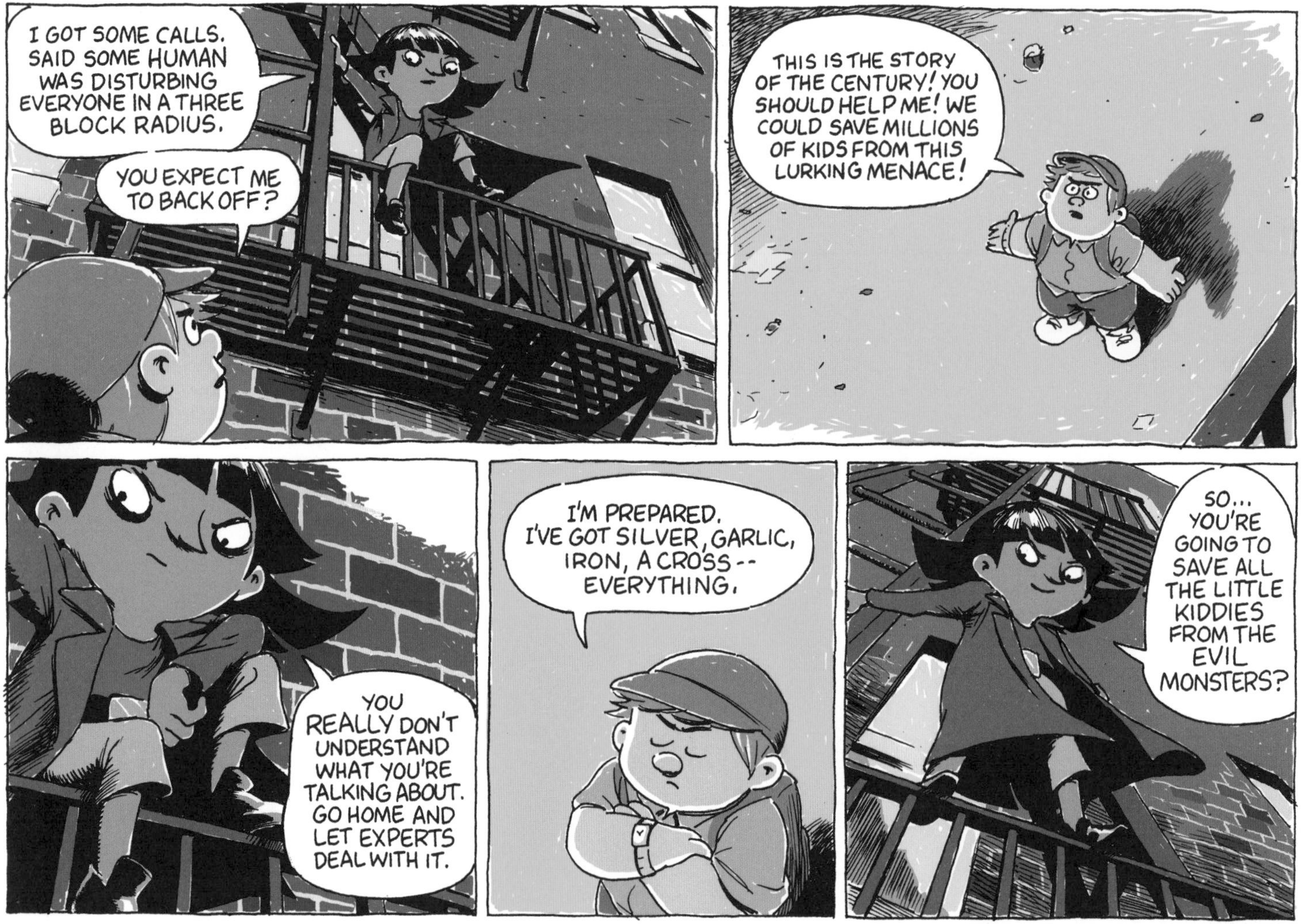

I GOT SOME CALLS. SAID SOME HUMAN WAS DISTURBING EVERYONE IN A THREE BLOCK RADIUS.
YOU EXPECT ME TO BACK OFF?
THIS IS THE STORY OF THE CENTURY! YOU SHOULD HELP ME! WE COULD SAVE MILLIONS OF KIDS FROM THIS LURKING MENACE!
YOU REALLY DON'T UNDERSTAND WHAT YOU'RE TALKING ABOUT. GO HOME AND LET EXPERTS DEAL WITH IT.
I'M PREPARED. I'VE GOT SILVER, GARLIC, IRON, A CROSS -- EVERYTHING.
SO... YOU'RE GOING TO SAVE ALL THE LITTLE KIDDIES FROM THE EVIL MONSTERS?

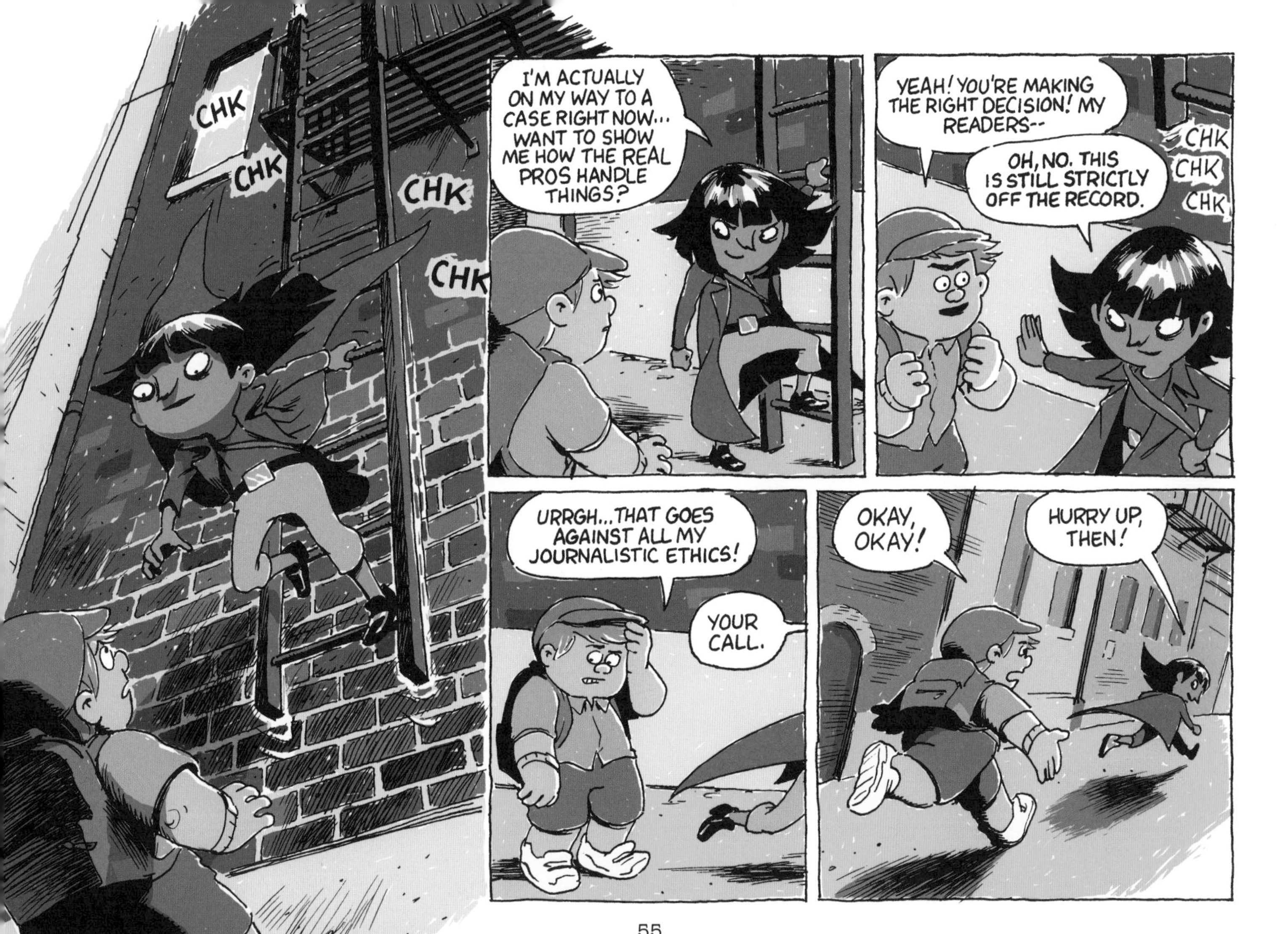
CHK
CHK
CHK
CHK
I'M ACTUALLY ON MY WAY TO A CASE RIGHT NOW... WANT TO SHOW ME HOW THE REAL PROS HANDLE THINGS?
YEAH! YOU'RE MAKING THE RIGHT DECISION! MY READERS--
OH, NO. THIS IS STILL STRICTLY OFF THE RECORD.
CHK
CHK
CHK
URRGH...THAT GOES AGAINST ALL MY JOURNALISTIC ETHICS!
YOUR CALL.
OKAY, OKAY!
HURRY UP, THEN!

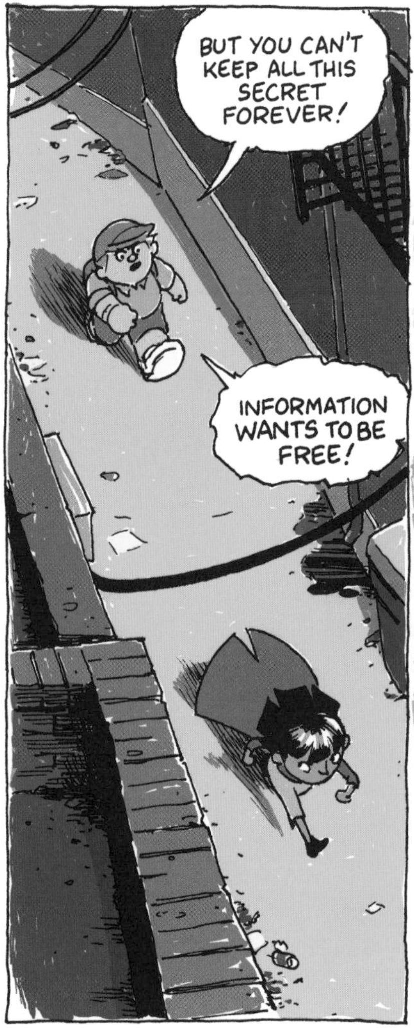
BUT YOU CAN'T KEEP ALL THIS SECRET FOREVER!
INFORMATION WANTS TO BE FREE!

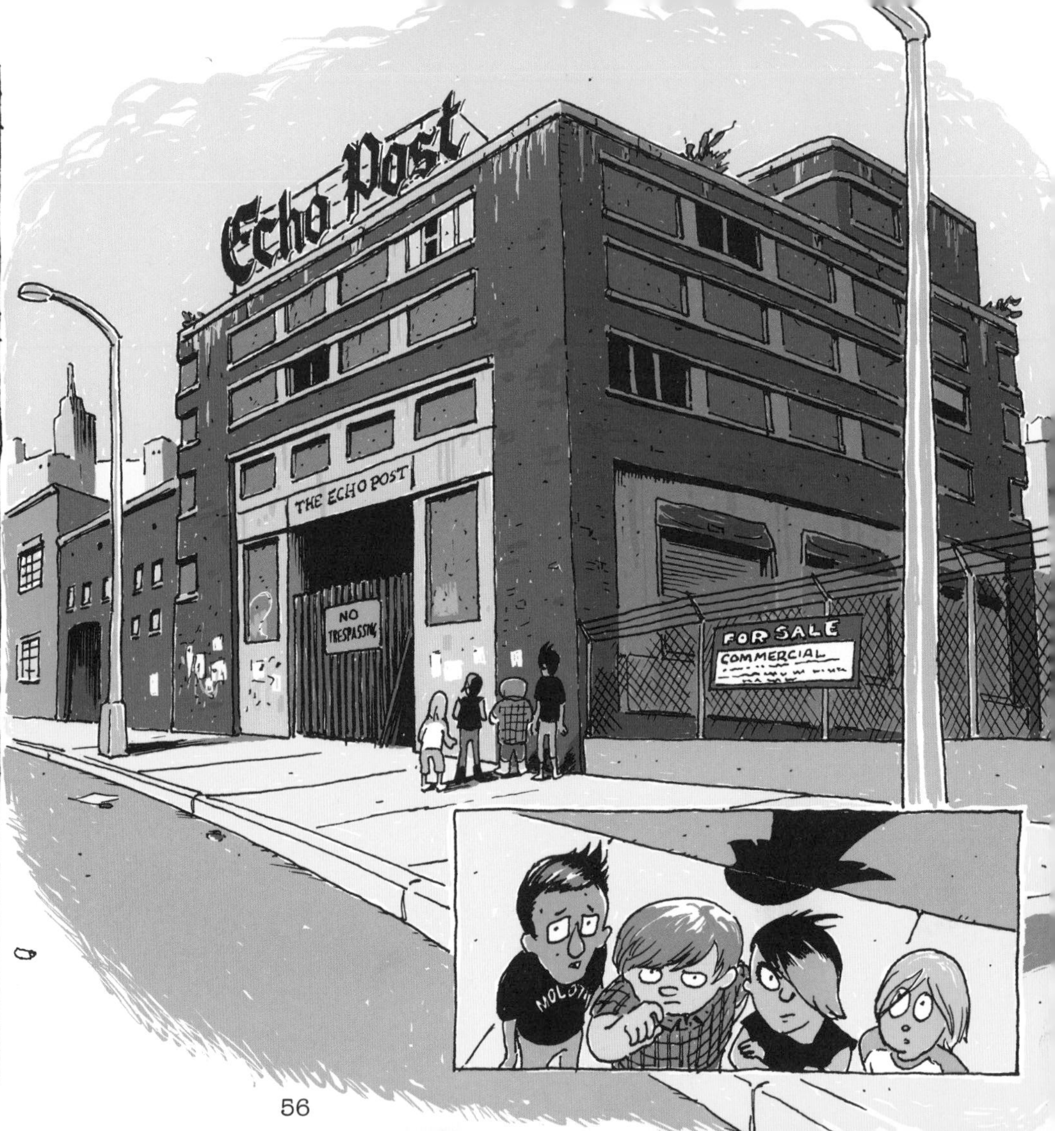
Echo Post
THE ECHO POST
NO TRESPASSING
FOR SALE
COMMERCIAL

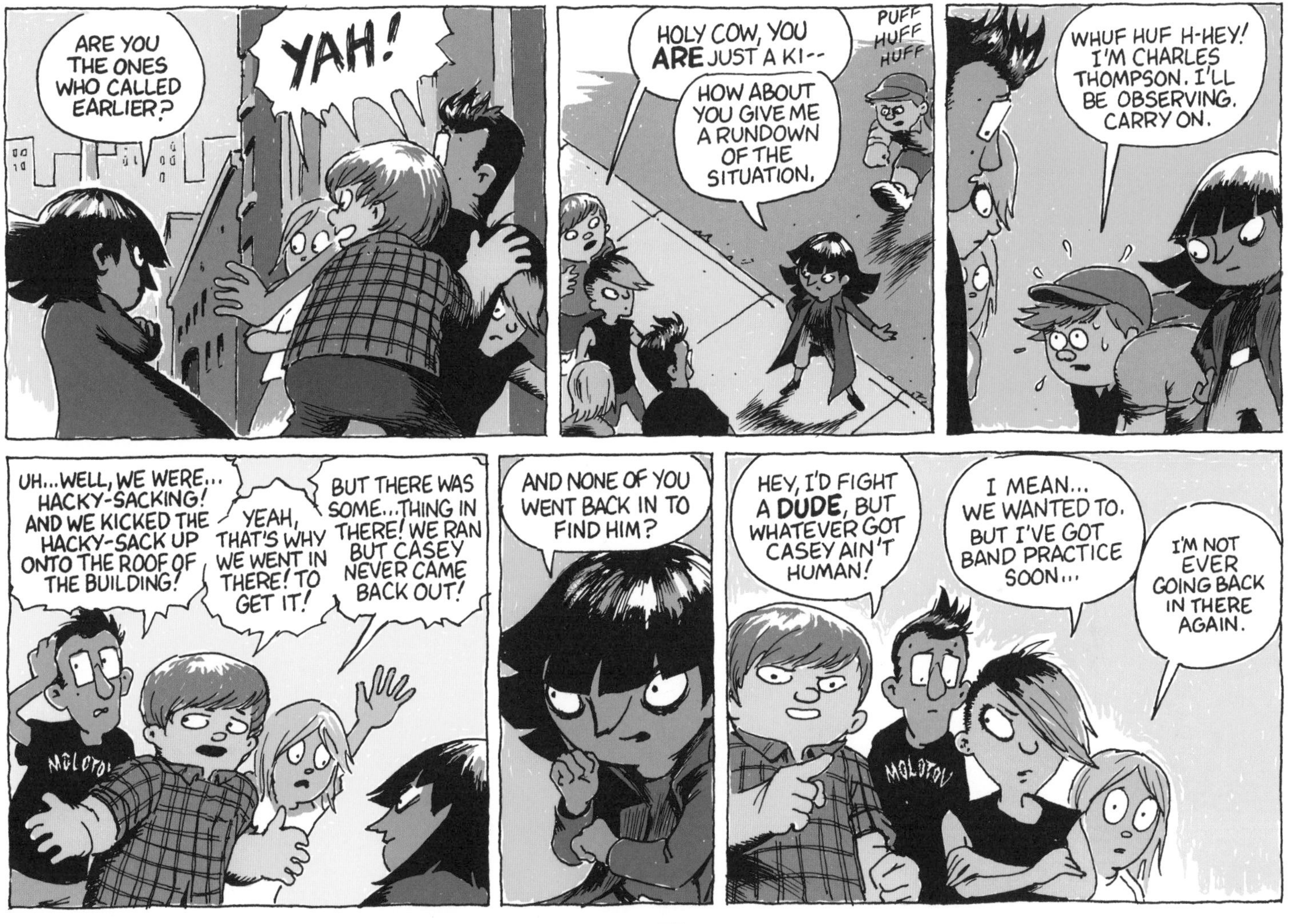
ARE YOU THE ONES WHO CALLED EARLIER?
YAH!
HOLY COW, YOU ARE JUST A KI--
PUFF HUFF HUFF
HOW ABOUT YOU GIVE ME A RUNDOWN OF THE SITUATION.
WHUF HUF H-HEY! I'M CHARLES THOMPSON. I'LL BE OBSERVING. CARRY ON.
UH...WELL, WE WERE... HACKY-SACKING! AND WE KICKED THE HACKY-SACK UP ONTO THE ROOF OF THE BUILDING!
YEAH, THAT'S WHY WE WENT IN THERE! TO GET IT!
BUT THERE WAS SOME...THING IN THERE! WE RAN BUT CASEY NEVER CAME BACK OUT!
MOLOTOV
AND NONE OF YOU WENT BACK IN TO FIND HIM?
HEY, I'D FIGHT A DUDE, BUT WHATEVER GOT CASEY AIN'T HUMAN!
I MEAN... WE WANTED TO. BUT I'VE GOT BAND PRACTICE SOON...
I'M NOT EVER GOING BACK IN THERE AGAIN.
MOLOTOV

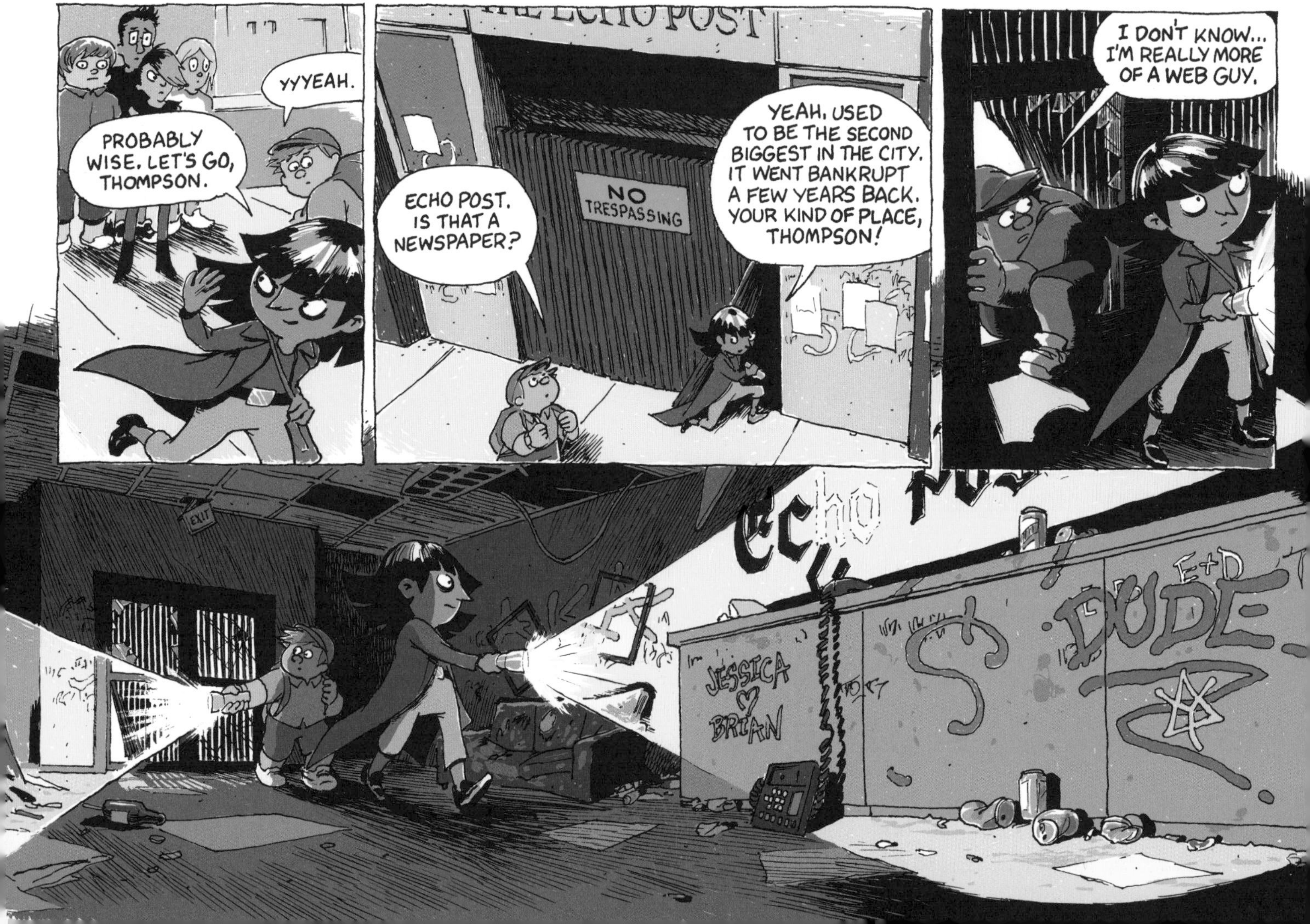
YYYEAH.
PROBABLY WISE. LET'S GO, THOMPSON.
THE ECHO POST
NO TRESPASSING
ECHO POST. IS THAT A NEWSPAPER?
YEAH, USED TO BE THE SECOND BIGGEST IN THE CITY. IT WENT BANKRUPT A FEW YEARS BACK. YOUR KIND OF PLACE, THOMPSON!
I DON'T KNOW... I'M REALLY MORE OF A WEB GUY.
EXIT
JESSICA ♡ BRIAN
DUDE
E+D

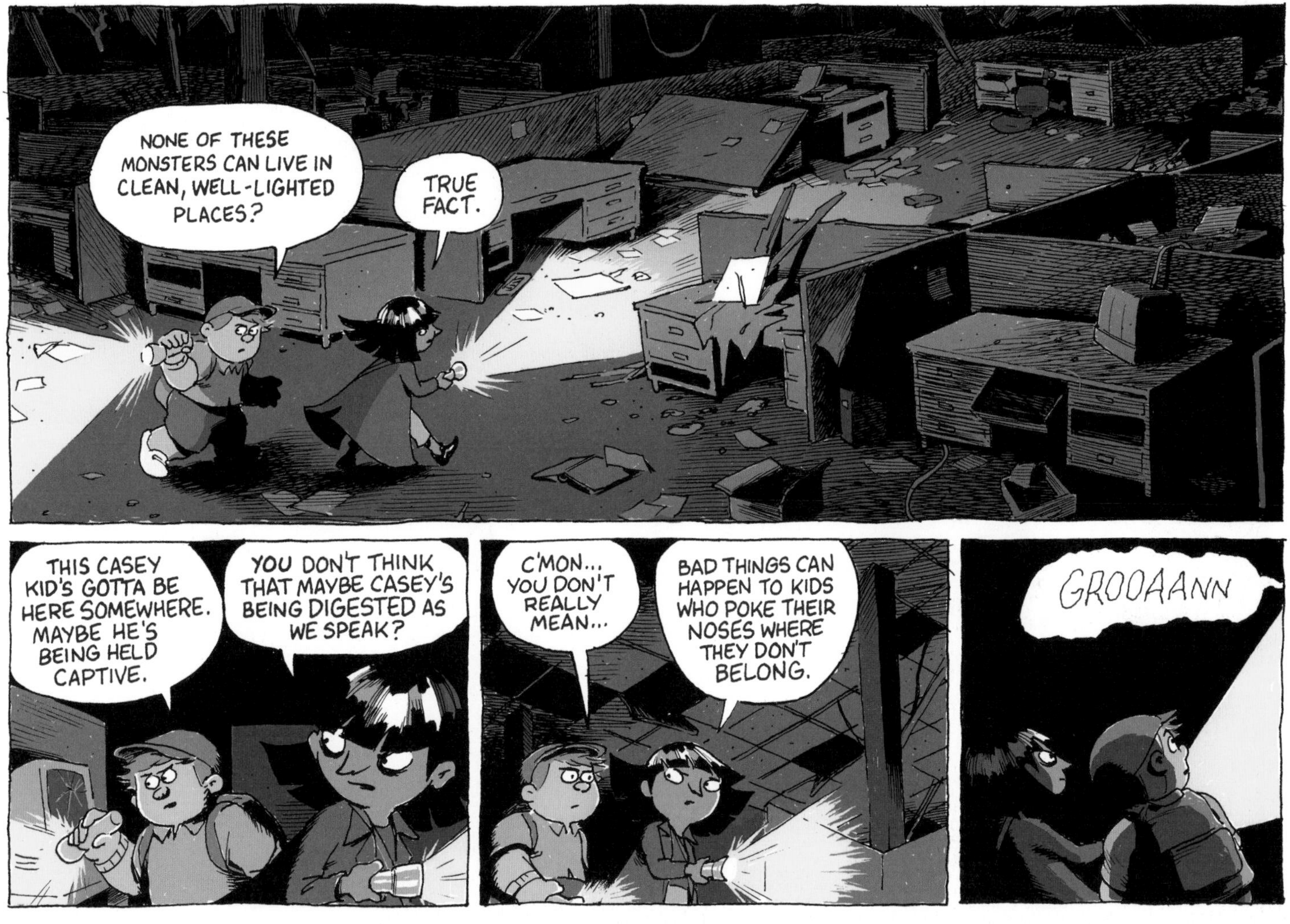
NONE OF THESE MONSTERS CAN LIVE IN CLEAN, WELL-LIGHTED PLACES?
TRUE FACT.
THIS CASEY KID'S GOTTA BE HERE SOMEWHERE. MAYBE HE'S BEING HELD CAPTIVE.
YOU DON'T THINK THAT MAYBE CASEY'S BEING DIGESTED AS WE SPEAK?
C'MON... YOU DON'T REALLY MEAN...
BAD THINGS CAN HAPPEN TO KIDS WHO POKE THEIR NOSES WHERE THEY DON'T BELONG.
GROOAANN

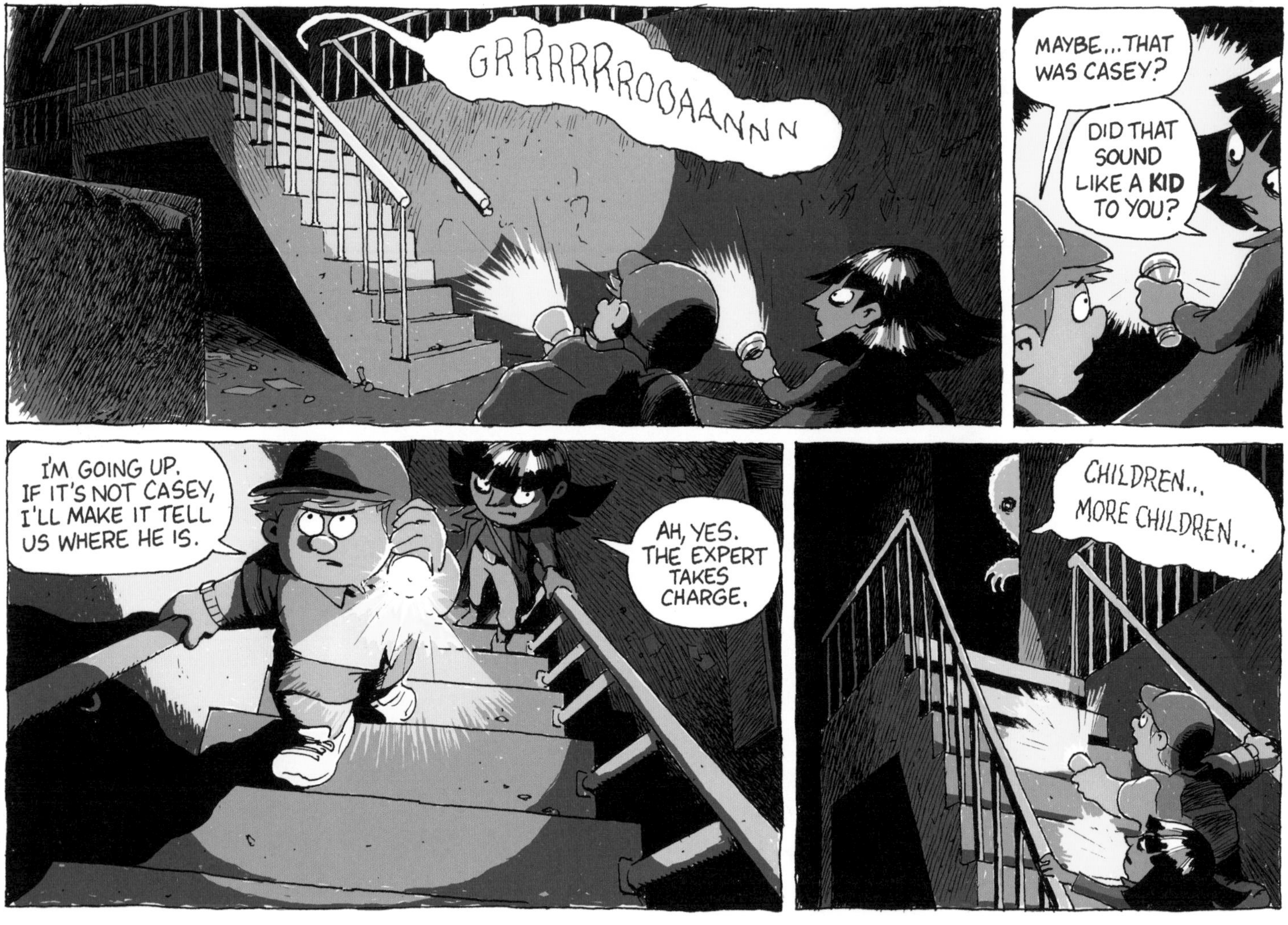
GRRRRRROOAANNN
MAYBE... THAT WAS CASEY?
DID THAT SOUND LIKE A **KID** TO YOU?
I'M GOING UP. IF IT'S NOT CASEY, I'LL MAKE IT TELL US WHERE HE IS.
AH, YES. THE EXPERT TAKES CHARGE.
CHILDREN... MORE CHILDREN...

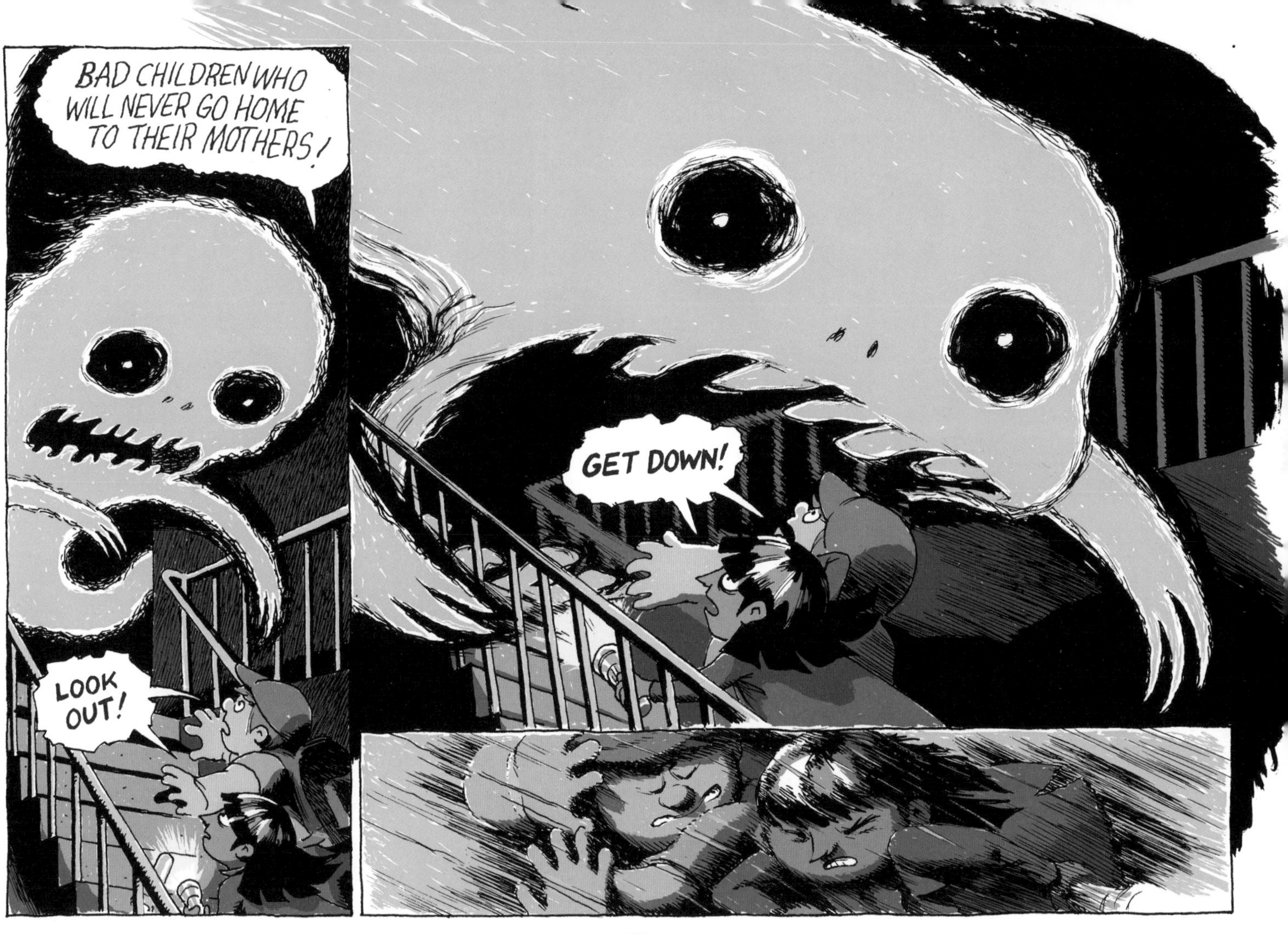
BAD CHILDREN WHO WILL NEVER GO HOME TO THEIR MOTHERS!
LOOK OUT!
GET DOWN!

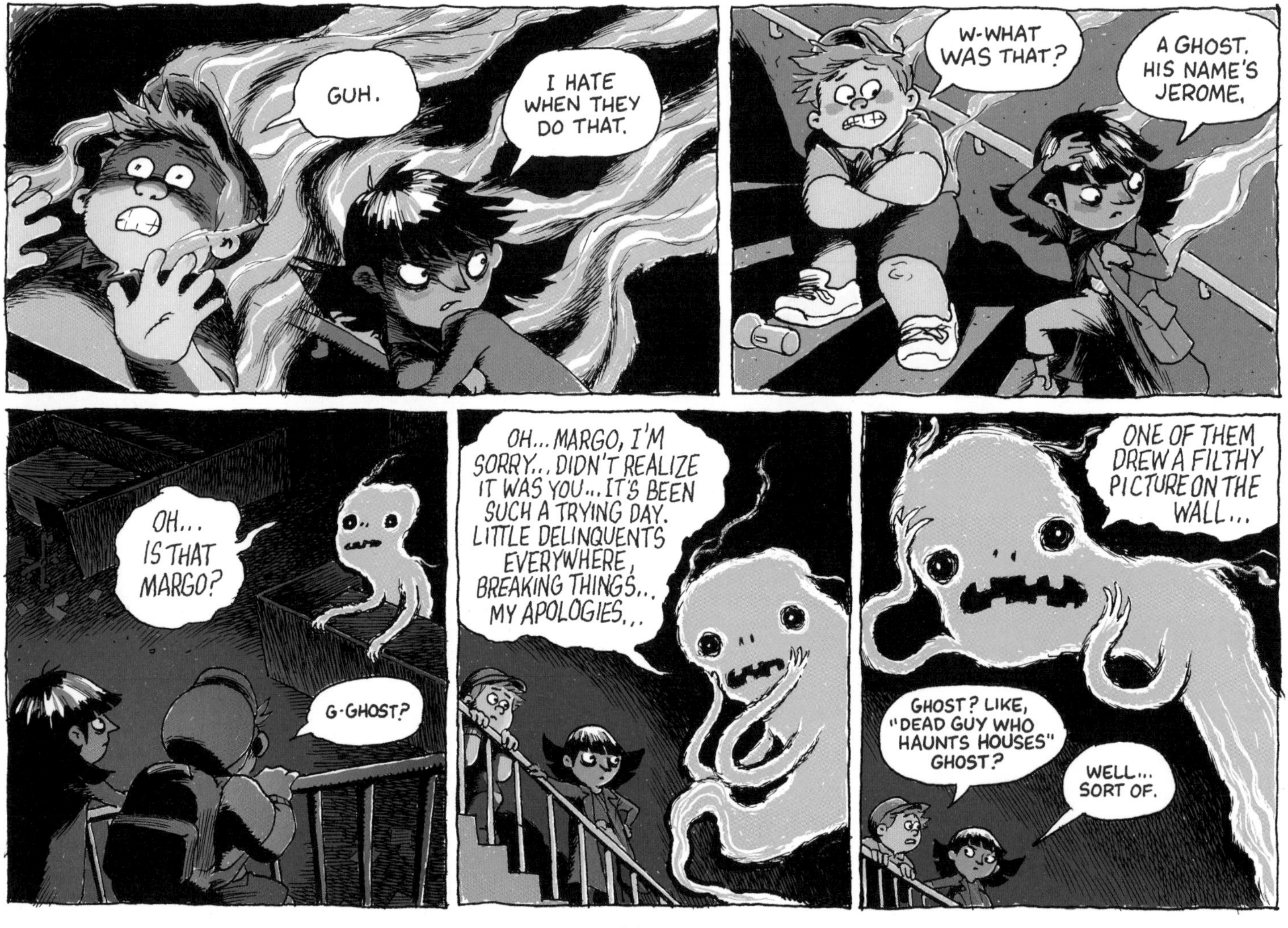
GUH.
I HATE WHEN THEY DO THAT.
W-WHAT WAS THAT?
A GHOST. HIS NAME'S JEROME.
OH... IS THAT MARGO?
G-GHOST?
OH... MARGO, I'M SORRY... DIDN'T REALIZE IT WAS YOU... IT'S BEEN SUCH A TRYING DAY. LITTLE DELINQUENTS EVERYWHERE, BREAKING THINGS... MY APOLOGIES...
ONE OF THEM DREW A FILTHY PICTURE ON THE WALL...
GHOST? LIKE, "DEAD GUY WHO HAUNTS HOUSES" GHOST?
WELL... SORT OF.

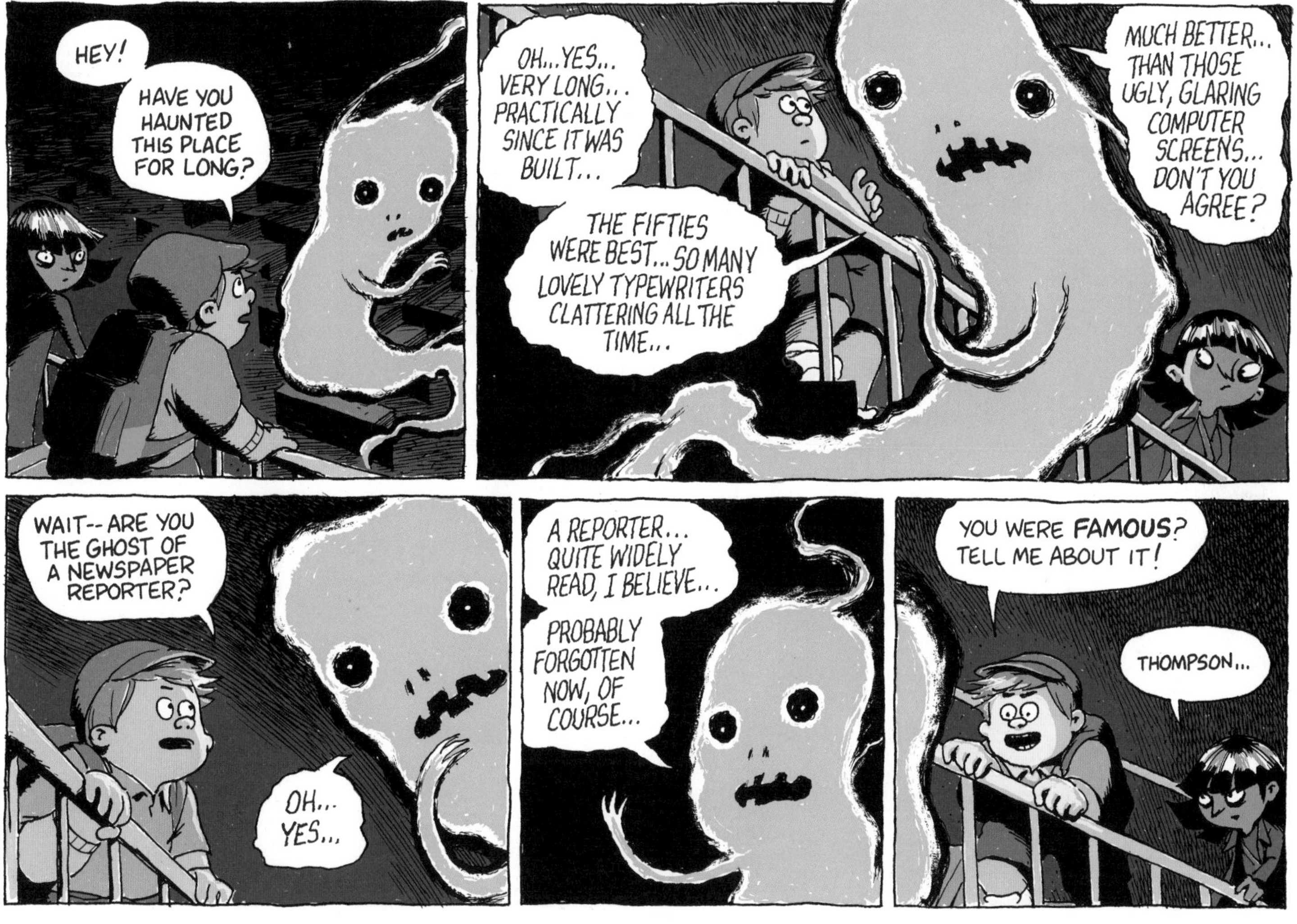
HEY!
HAVE YOU HAUNTED THIS PLACE FOR LONG?
OH... YES... VERY LONG... PRACTICALLY SINCE IT WAS BUILT...
THE FIFTIES WERE BEST... SO MANY LOVELY TYPEWRITERS CLATTERING ALL THE TIME...
MUCH BETTER... THAN THOSE UGLY, GLARING COMPUTER SCREENS... DON'T YOU AGREE?
WAIT-- ARE YOU THE GHOST OF A NEWSPAPER REPORTER?
OH... YES...
A REPORTER... QUITE WIDELY READ, I BELIEVE...
PROBABLY FORGOTTEN NOW, OF COURSE...
YOU WERE **FAMOUS**? TELL ME ABOUT IT!
THOMPSON...

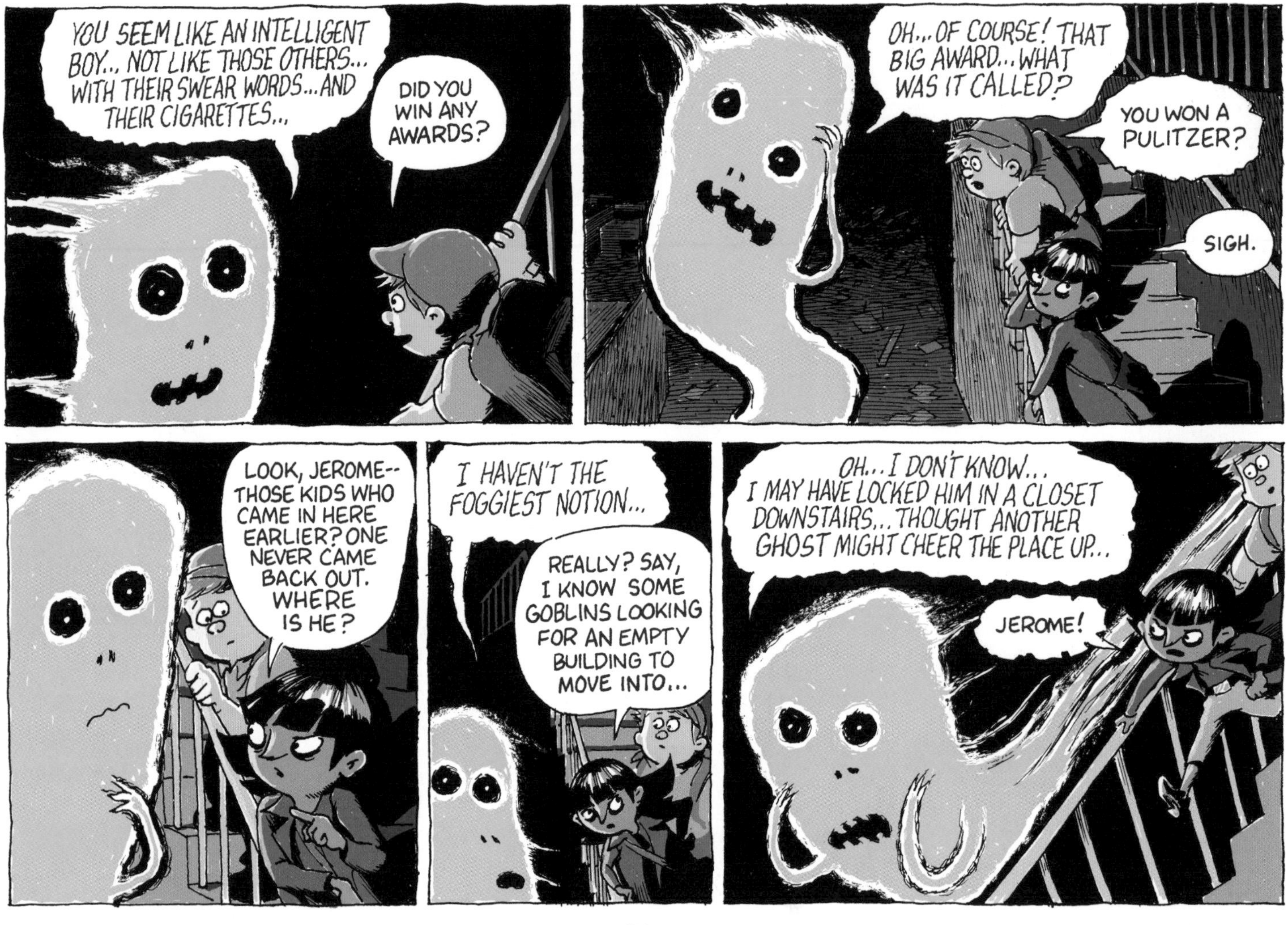
YOU SEEM LIKE AN INTELLIGENT BOY... NOT LIKE THOSE OTHERS... WITH THEIR SWEAR WORDS...AND THEIR CIGARETTES...
DID YOU WIN ANY AWARDS?
OH...OF COURSE! THAT BIG AWARD...WHAT WAS IT CALLED?
YOU WON A PULITZER?
SIGH.
LOOK, JEROME-- THOSE KIDS WHO CAME IN HERE EARLIER? ONE NEVER CAME BACK OUT. WHERE IS HE?
I HAVEN'T THE FOGGIEST NOTION...
REALLY? SAY, I KNOW SOME GOBLINS LOOKING FOR AN EMPTY BUILDING TO MOVE INTO...
OH... I DON'T KNOW... I MAY HAVE LOCKED HIM IN A CLOSET DOWNSTAIRS... THOUGHT ANOTHER GHOST MIGHT CHEER THE PLACE UP...
JEROME!

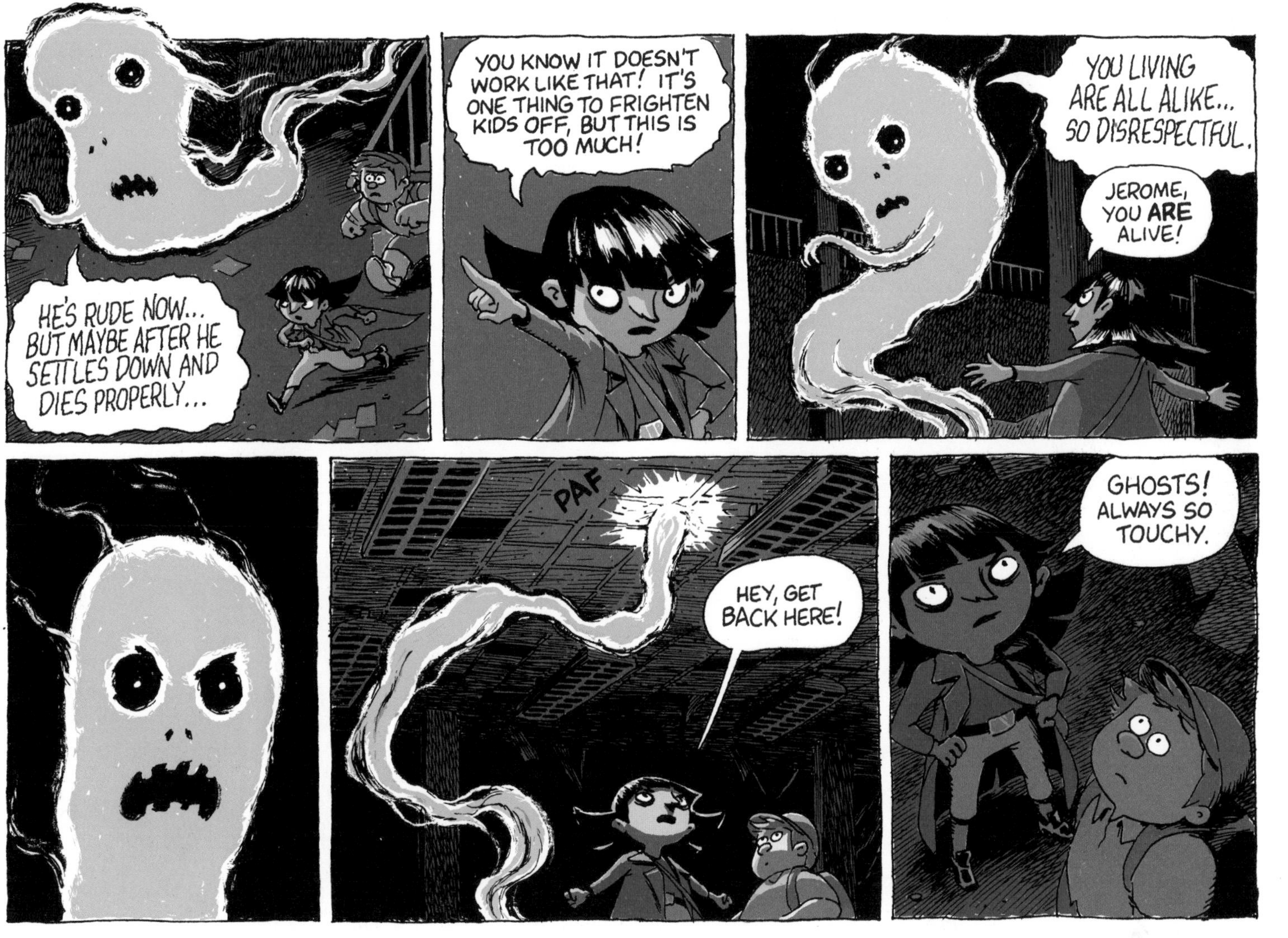
HE'S RUDE NOW... BUT MAYBE AFTER HE SETTLES DOWN AND DIES PROPERLY...
YOU KNOW IT DOESN'T WORK LIKE THAT! IT'S ONE THING TO FRIGHTEN KIDS OFF, BUT THIS IS TOO MUCH!
YOU LIVING ARE ALL ALIKE... SO DISRESPECTFUL.
JEROME, YOU **ARE** ALIVE!
PAF
HEY, GET BACK HERE!
GHOSTS! ALWAYS SO TOUCHY.

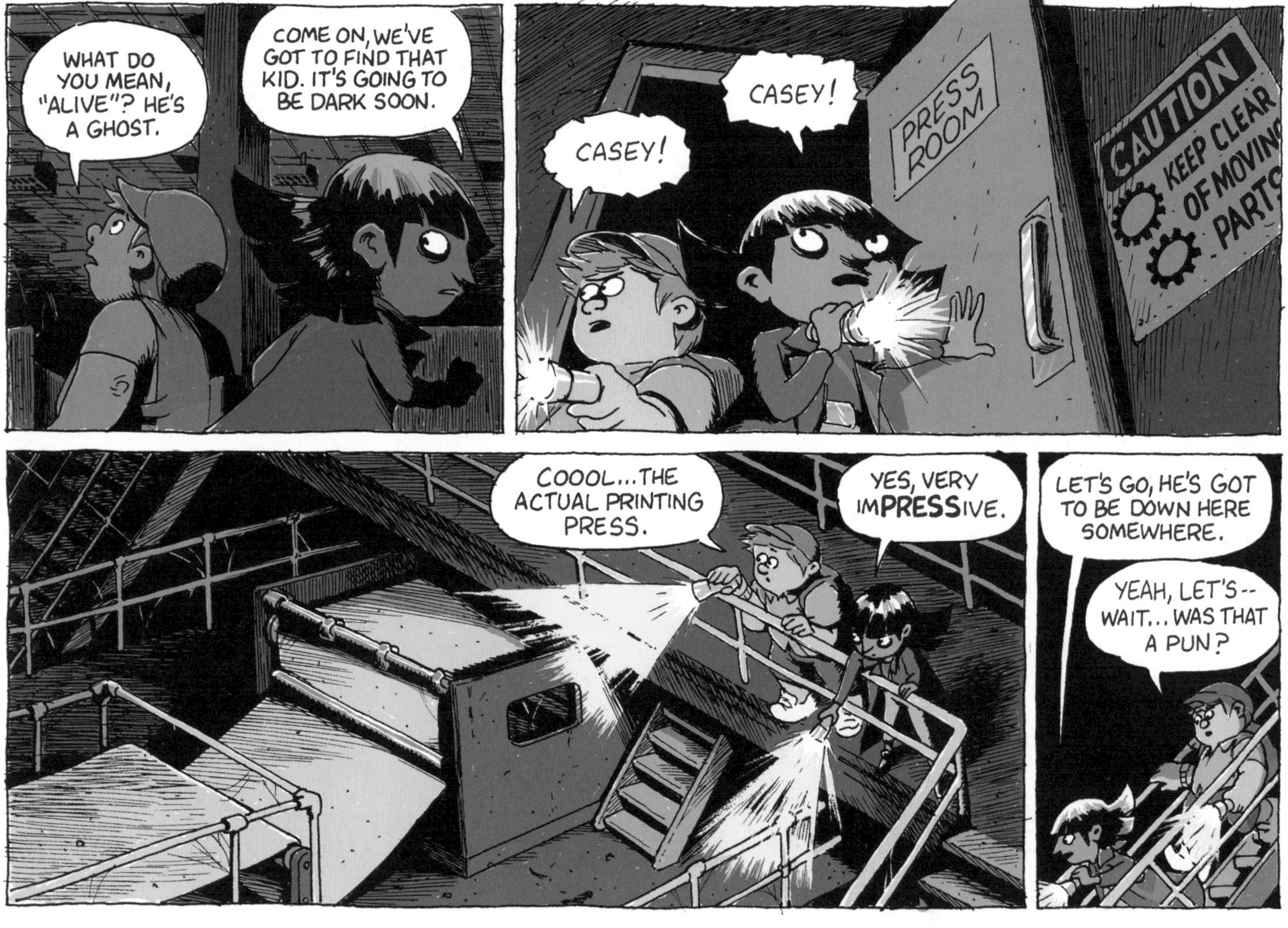
WHAT DO YOU MEAN, "ALIVE"? HE'S A GHOST.
COME ON, WE'VE GOT TO FIND THAT KID. IT'S GOING TO BE DARK SOON.
CASEY!
CASEY!
PRESS ROOM
CAUTION
KEEP CLEAR
COOOL...THE ACTUAL PRINTING PRESS.
YES, VERY IMPRESSIVE.
LET'S GO, HE'S GOT TO BE DOWN HERE SOMEWHERE.
YEAH, LET'S-- WAIT... WAS THAT A PUN?

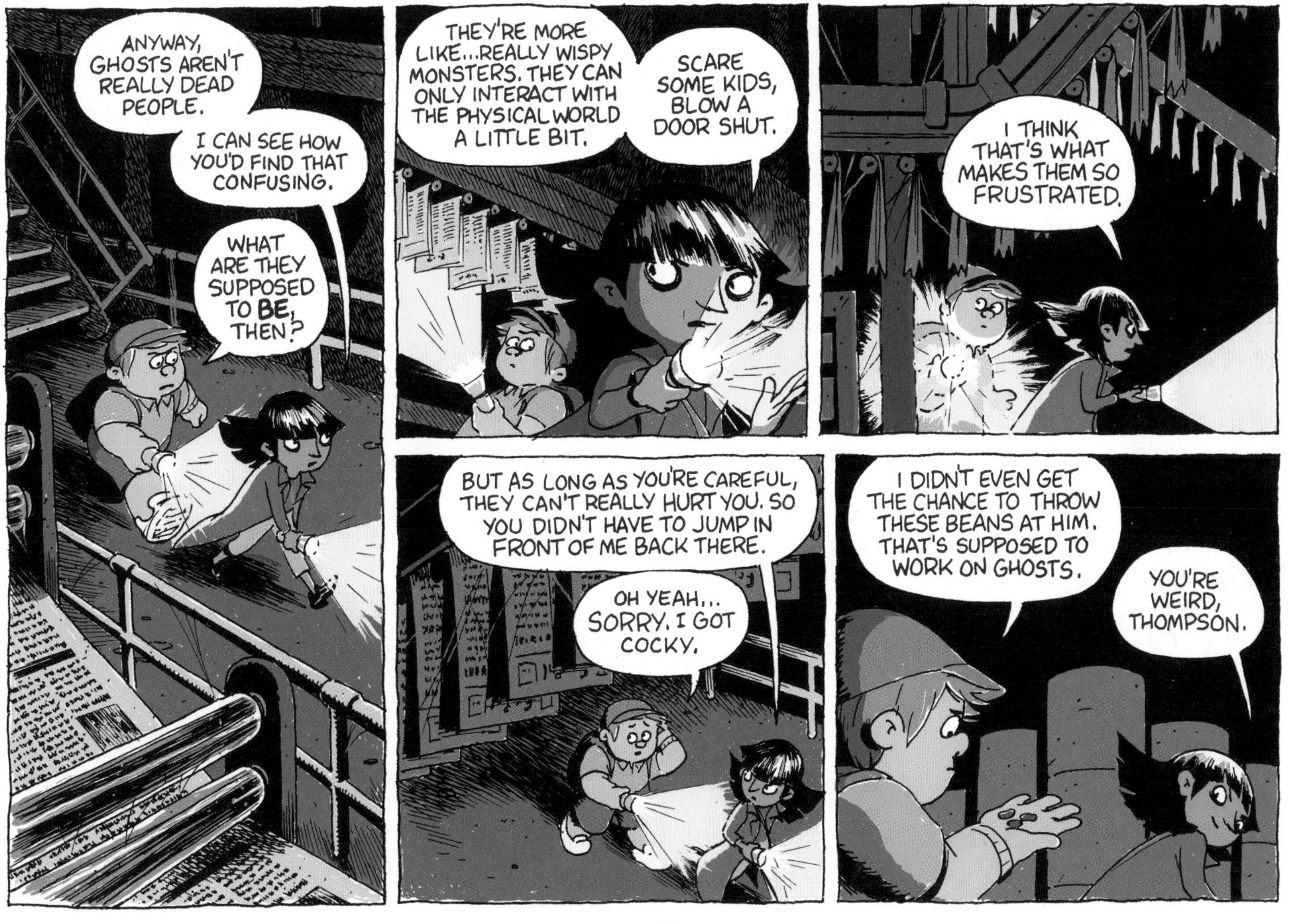

ANYWAY, GHOSTS AREN'T REALLY DEAD PEOPLE.
I CAN SEE HOW YOU'D FIND THAT CONFUSING.
WHAT ARE THEY SUPPOSED TO **BE**, THEN?
THEY'RE MORE LIKE...REALLY WISPY MONSTERS. THEY CAN ONLY INTERACT WITH THE PHYSICAL WORLD A LITTLE BIT.
SCARE SOME KIDS, BLOW A DOOR SHUT.
I THINK THAT'S WHAT MAKES THEM SO FRUSTRATED.
BUT AS LONG AS YOU'RE CAREFUL, THEY CAN'T REALLY HURT YOU. SO YOU DIDN'T HAVE TO JUMP IN FRONT OF ME BACK THERE.
OH YEAH... SORRY. I GOT COCKY.
I DIDN'T EVEN GET THE CHANCE TO THROW THESE BEANS AT HIM. THAT'S SUPPOSED TO WORK ON GHOSTS.
YOU'RE WEIRD, THOMPSON.

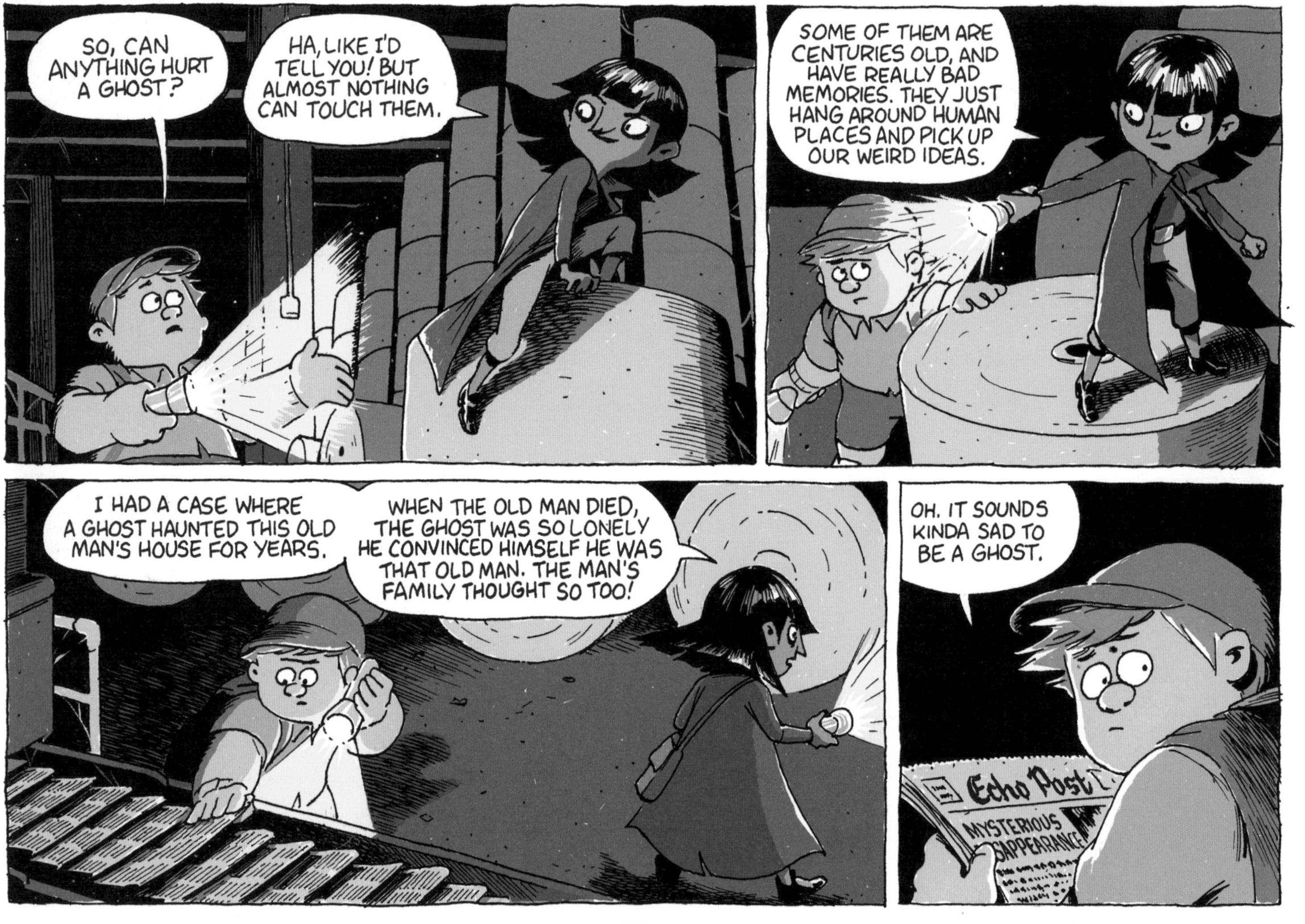
SO, CAN ANYTHING HURT A GHOST?
HA, LIKE I'D TELL YOU! BUT ALMOST NOTHING CAN TOUCH THEM.
SOME OF THEM ARE CENTURIES OLD, AND HAVE REALLY BAD MEMORIES. THEY JUST HANG AROUND HUMAN PLACES AND PICK UP OUR WEIRD IDEAS.
I HAD A CASE WHERE A GHOST HAUNTED THIS OLD MAN'S HOUSE FOR YEARS.
WHEN THE OLD MAN DIED, THE GHOST WAS SO LONELY HE CONVINCED HIMSELF HE WAS THAT OLD MAN. THE MAN'S FAMILY THOUGHT SO TOO!
OH. IT SOUNDS KINDA SAD TO BE A GHOST.
Echo Post
MYSTERIOUS DISAPPEARANCE

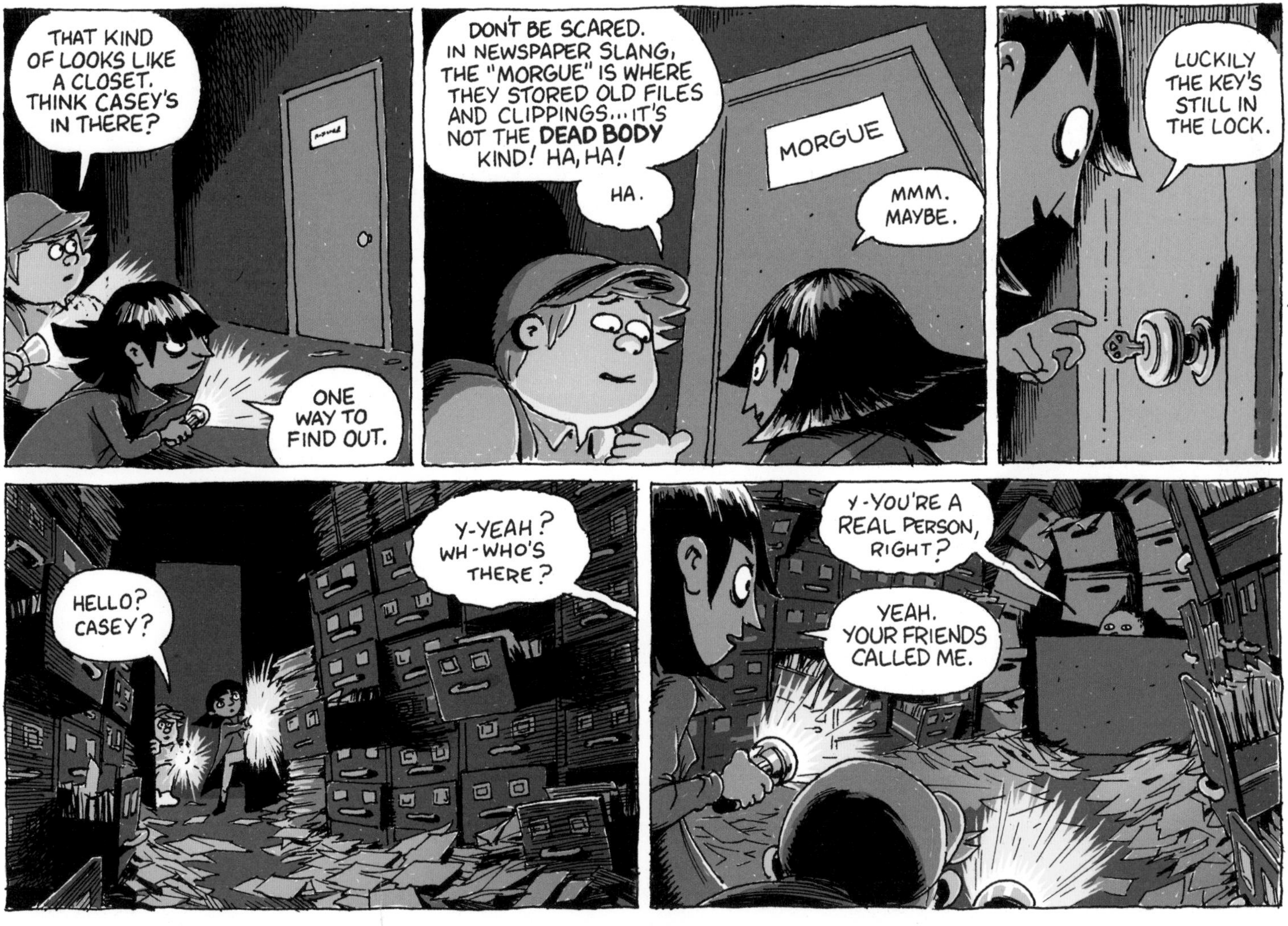
THAT KIND OF LOOKS LIKE A CLOSET. THINK CASEY'S IN THERE?
ONE WAY TO FIND OUT.
DON'T BE SCARED. IN NEWSPAPER SLANG, THE "MORGUE" IS WHERE THEY STORED OLD FILES AND CLIPPINGS... IT'S NOT THE **DEAD BODY** KIND! HA, HA!
HA.
MORGUE
MMM. MAYBE.
LUCKILY THE KEY'S STILL IN THE LOCK.
HELLO? CASEY?
Y-YEAH? WH-WHO'S THERE?
Y-YOU'RE A REAL PERSON, RIGHT?
YEAH. YOUR FRIENDS CALLED ME.

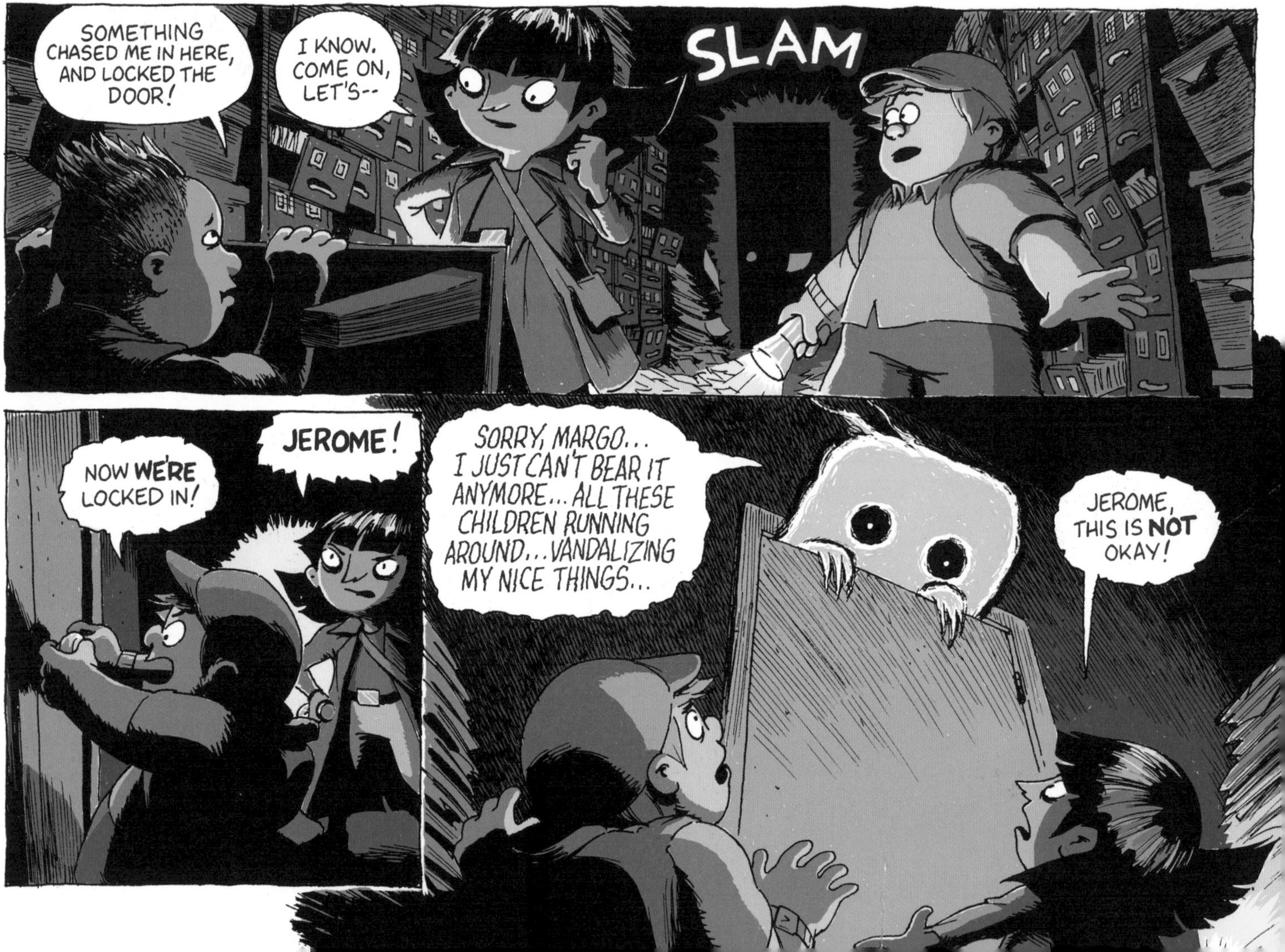
SOMETHING CHASED ME IN HERE, AND LOCKED THE DOOR!
I KNOW. COME ON, LET'S--
SLAM
NOW **WE'RE** LOCKED IN!
JEROME!
SORRY, MARGO... I JUST CAN'T BEAR IT ANYMORE... ALL THESE CHILDREN RUNNING AROUND... VANDALIZING MY NICE THINGS...
JEROME, THIS IS **NOT** OKAY!

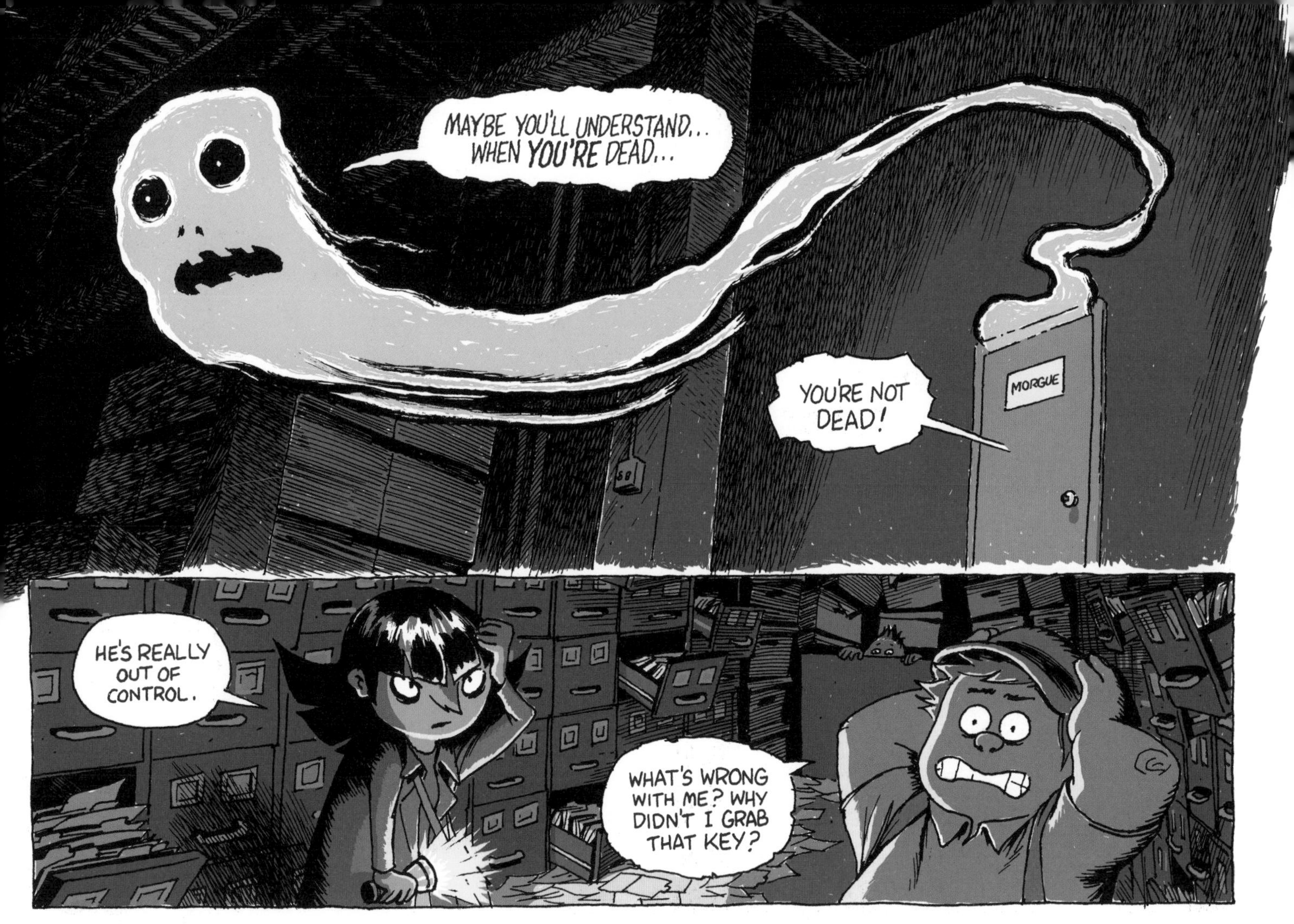
MAYBE YOU'LL UNDERSTAND... WHEN YOU'RE DEAD...
MORGUE
YOU'RE NOT DEAD!
HE'S REALLY OUT OF CONTROL.
WHAT'S WRONG WITH ME? WHY DIDN'T I GRAB THAT KEY?

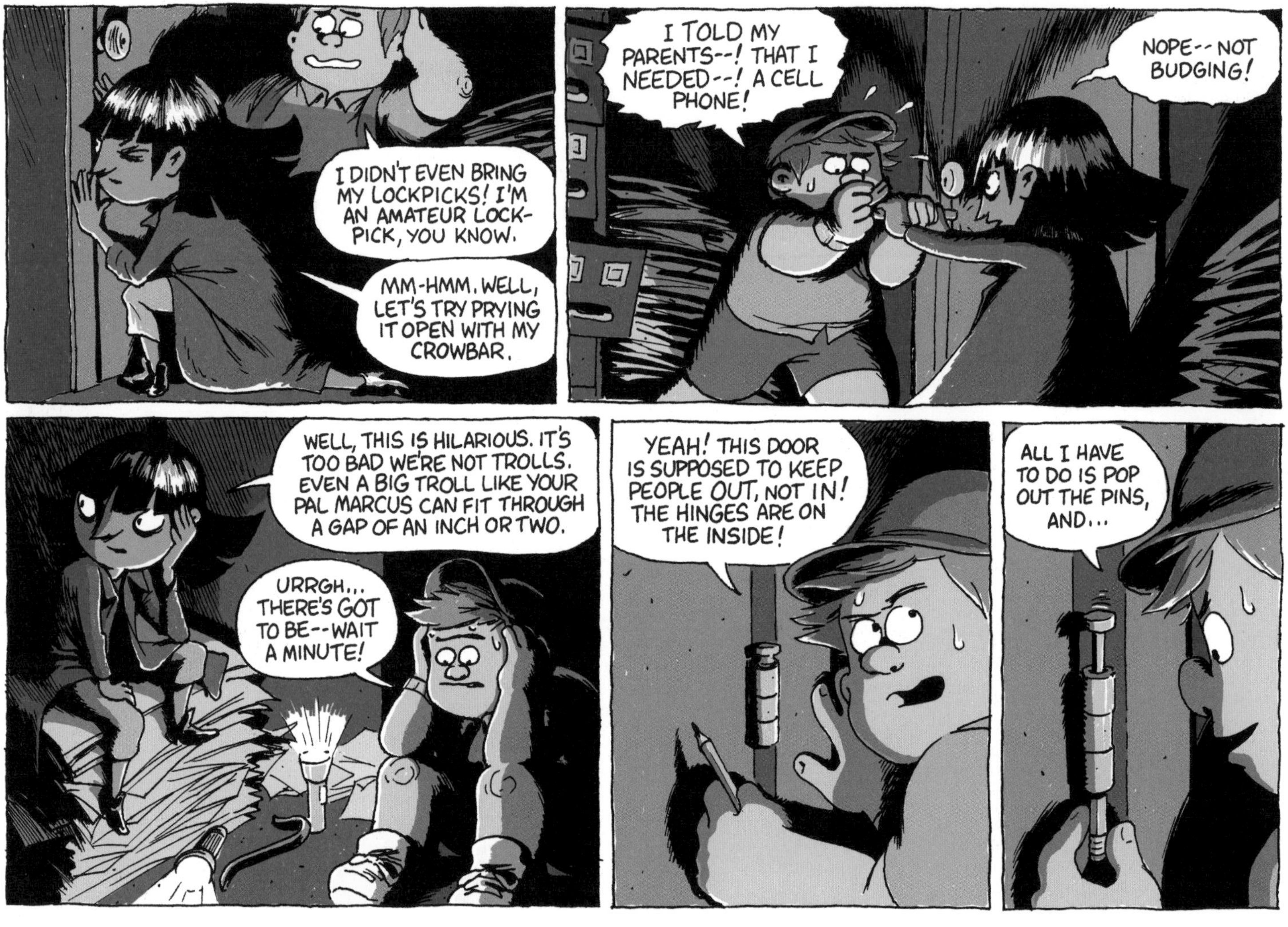
I DIDN'T EVEN BRING MY LOCKPICKS! I'M AN AMATEUR LOCK-PICK, YOU KNOW.
MM-HMM. WELL, LET'S TRY PRYING IT OPEN WITH MY CROWBAR.
I TOLD MY PARENTS--! THAT I NEEDED--! A CELL PHONE!
NOPE--NOT BUDGING!
WELL, THIS IS HILARIOUS. IT'S TOO BAD WE'RE NOT TROLLS. EVEN A BIG TROLL LIKE YOUR PAL MARCUS CAN FIT THROUGH A GAP OF AN INCH OR TWO.
URRGH... THERE'S GOT TO BE--WAIT A MINUTE!
YEAH! THIS DOOR IS SUPPOSED TO KEEP PEOPLE OUT, NOT IN! THE HINGES ARE ON THE INSIDE!
ALL I HAVE TO DO IS POP OUT THE PINS, AND...

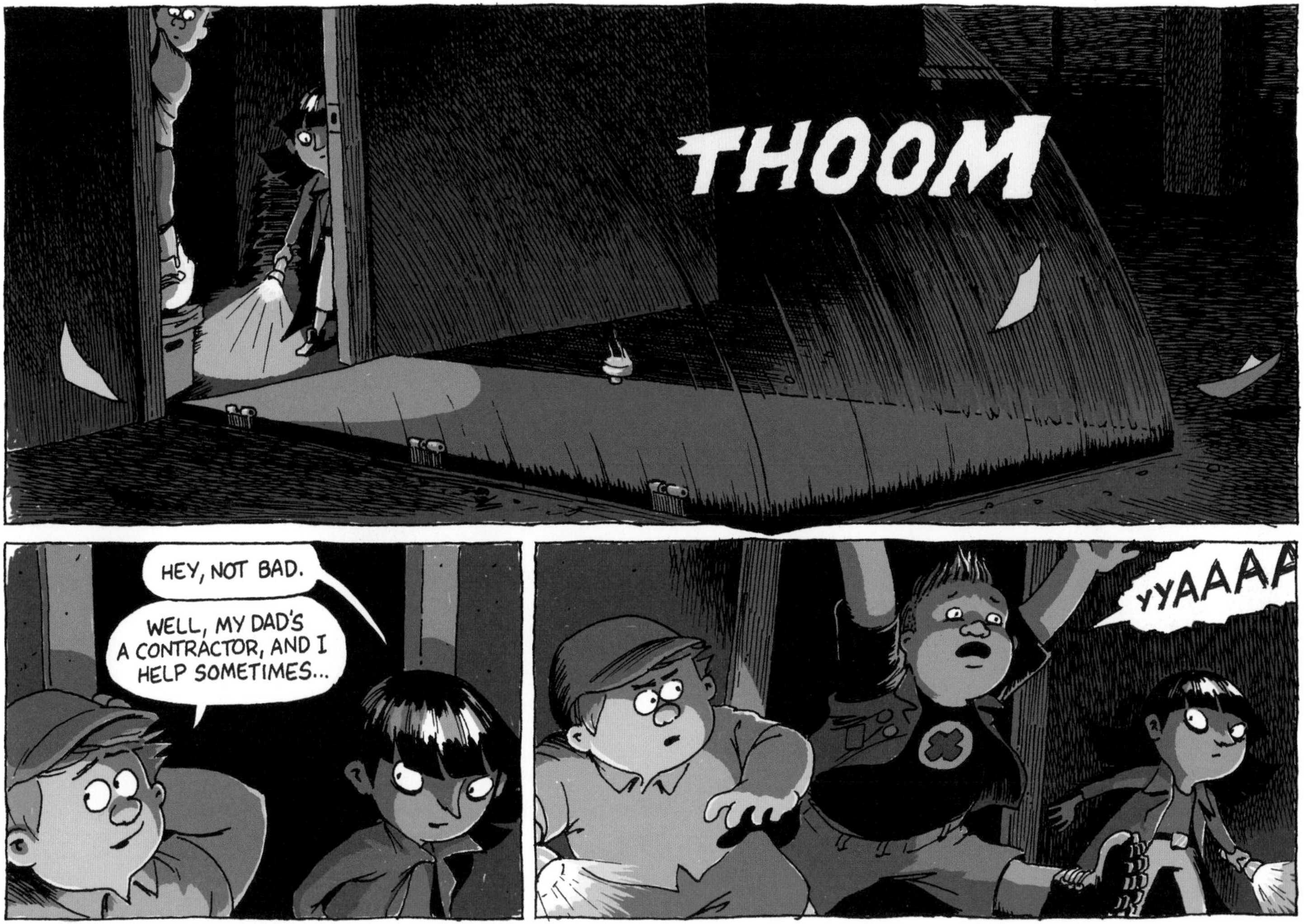
THOOM
HEY, NOT BAD.
WELL, MY DAD'S A CONTRACTOR, AND I HELP SOMETIMES...
YYAAAA

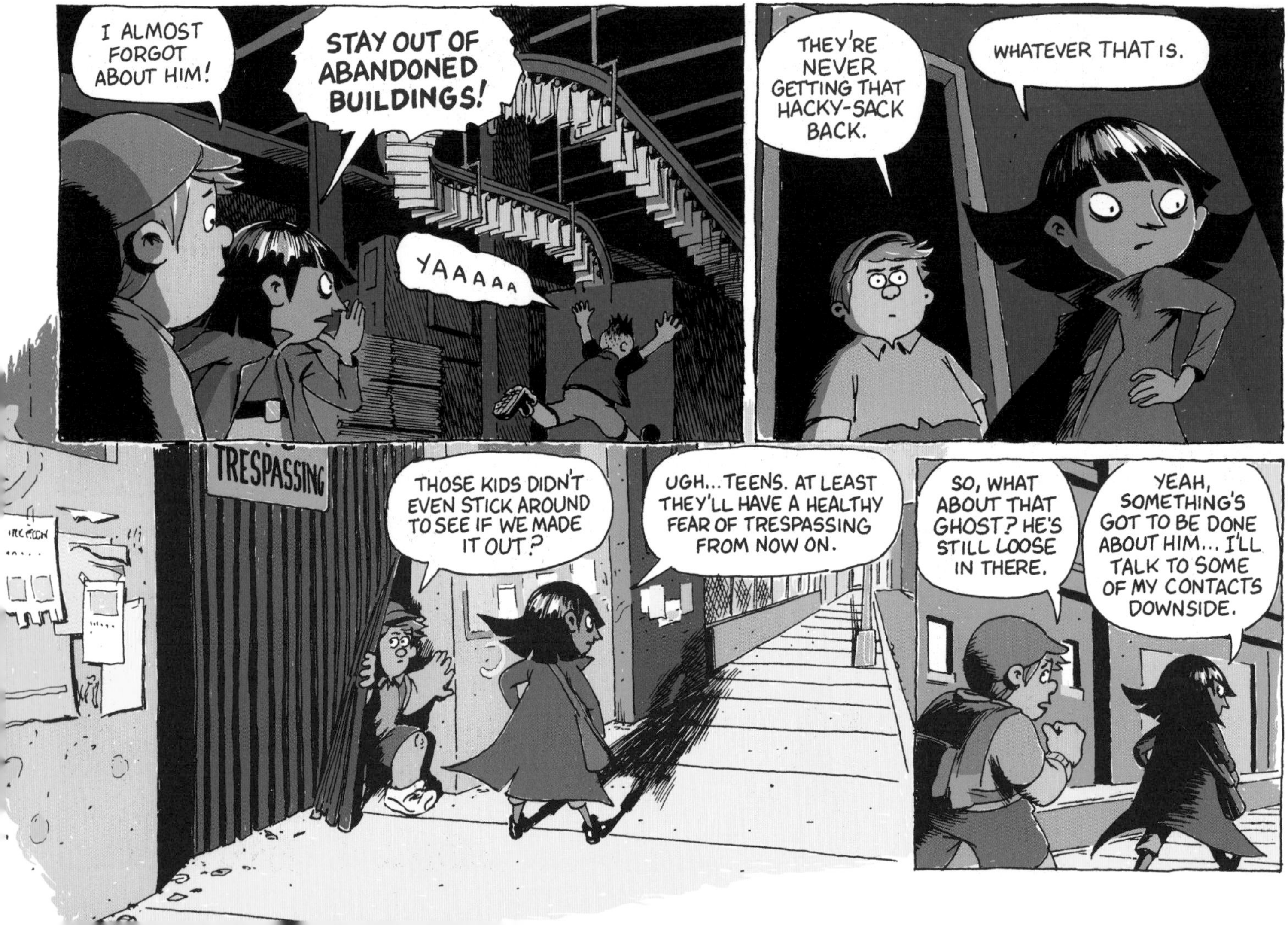
I ALMOST FORGOT ABOUT HIM!
STAY OUT OF ABANDONED BUILDINGS!
YAAAAA
THEY'RE NEVER GETTING THAT HACKY-SACK BACK.
WHATEVER THAT IS.
TRESPASSING
THOSE KIDS DIDN'T EVEN STICK AROUND TO SEE IF WE MADE IT OUT?
UGH... TEENS. AT LEAST THEY'LL HAVE A HEALTHY FEAR OF TRESPASSING FROM NOW ON.
SO, WHAT ABOUT THAT GHOST? HE'S STILL LOOSE IN THERE.
YEAH, SOMETHING'S GOT TO BE DONE ABOUT HIM... I'LL TALK TO SOME OF MY CONTACTS DOWNSIDE.

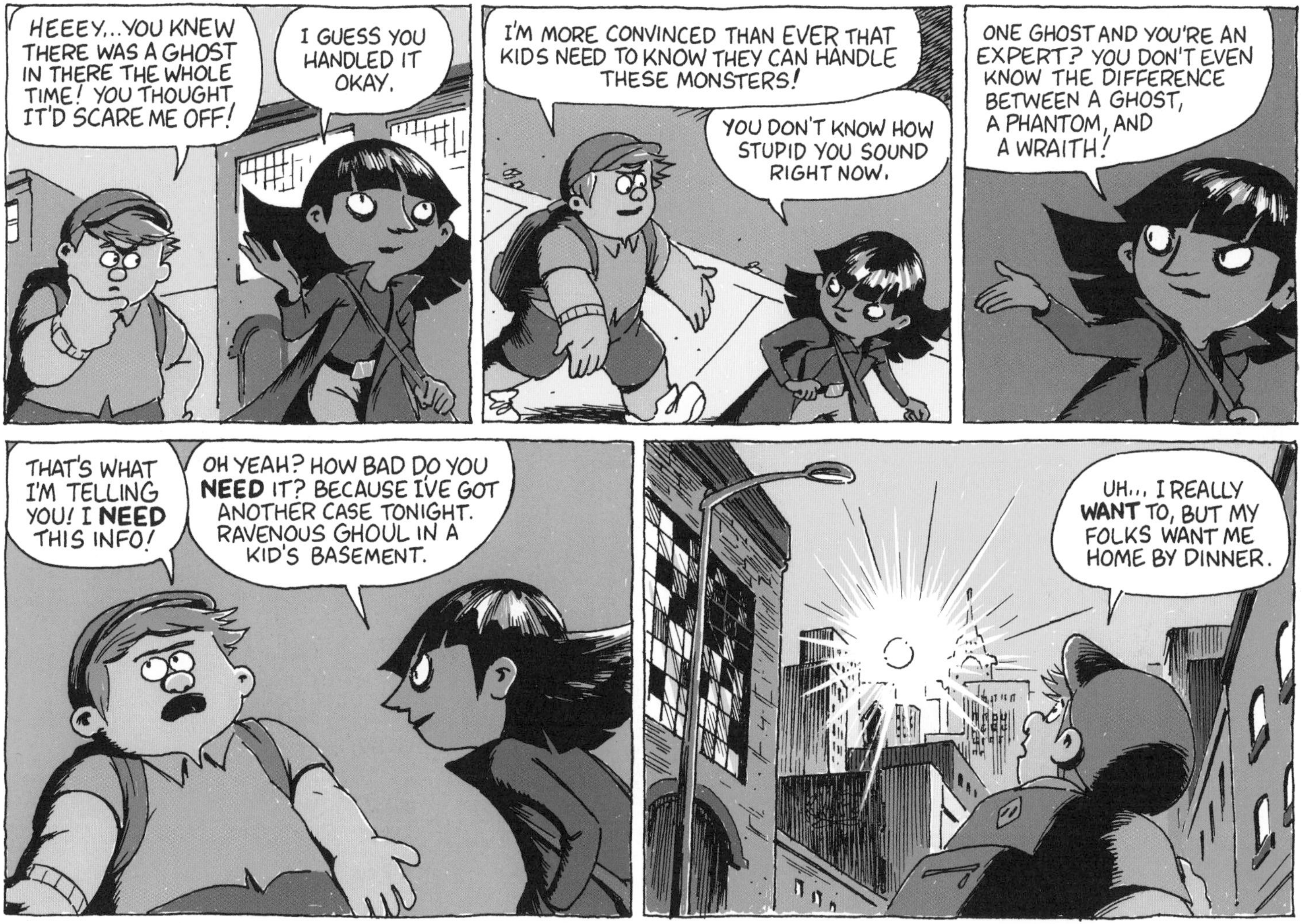
HEEEY...YOU KNEW THERE WAS A GHOST IN THERE THE WHOLE TIME! YOU THOUGHT IT'D SCARE ME OFF!
I GUESS YOU HANDLED IT OKAY.
I'M MORE CONVINCED THAN EVER THAT KIDS NEED TO KNOW THEY CAN HANDLE THESE MONSTERS!
YOU DON'T KNOW HOW STUPID YOU SOUND RIGHT NOW.
ONE GHOST AND YOU'RE AN EXPERT? YOU DON'T EVEN KNOW THE DIFFERENCE BETWEEN A GHOST, A PHANTOM, AND A WRAITH!
THAT'S WHAT I'M TELLING YOU! I **NEED** THIS INFO!
OH YEAH? HOW BAD DO YOU **NEED** IT? BECAUSE I'VE GOT ANOTHER CASE TONIGHT. RAVENOUS GHOUL IN A KID'S BASEMENT.
UH... I REALLY **WANT** TO, BUT MY FOLKS WANT ME HOME BY DINNER.

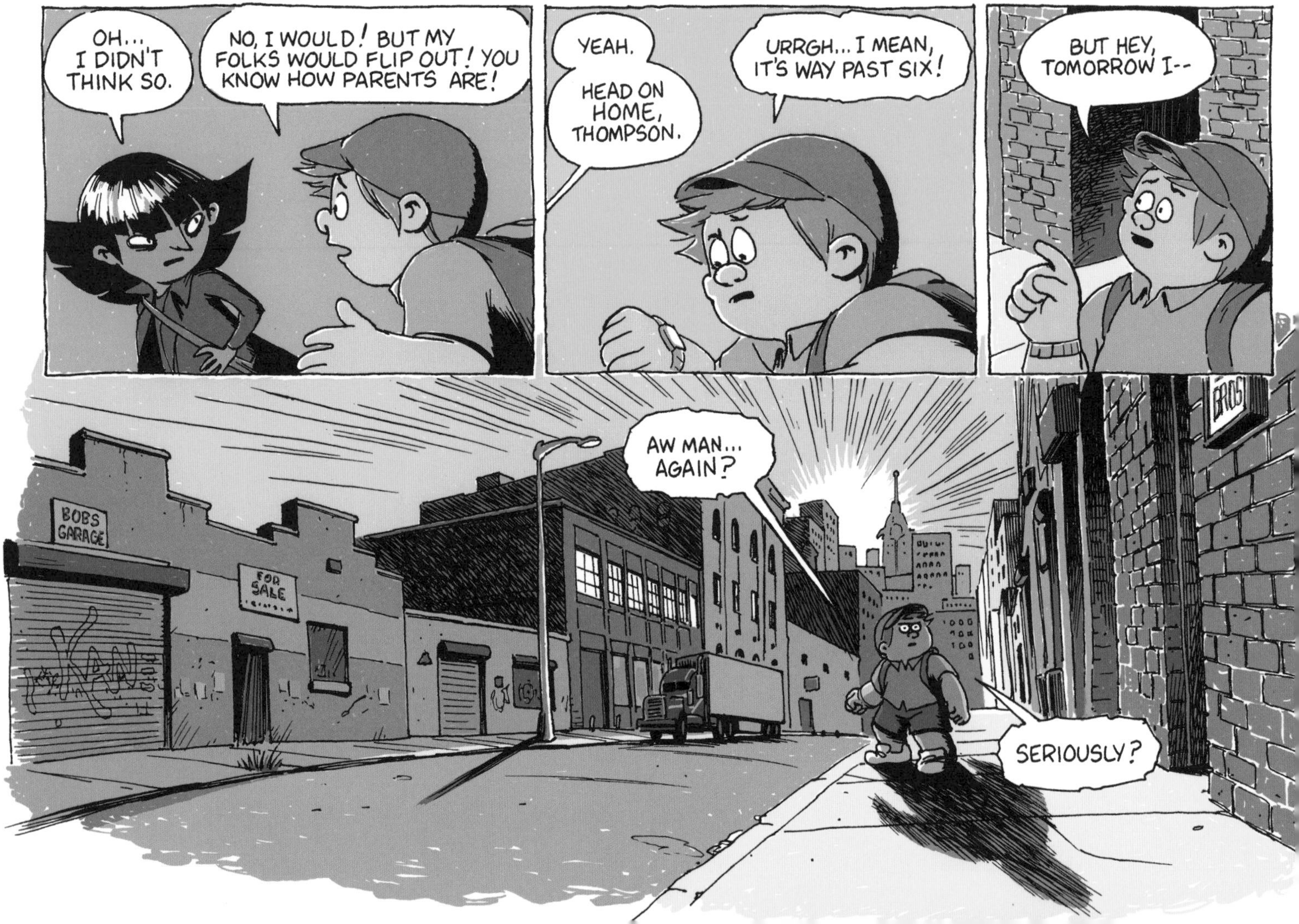
OH... I DIDN'T THINK SO.
NO, I WOULD! BUT MY FOLKS WOULD FLIP OUT! YOU KNOW HOW PARENTS ARE!
YEAH.
HEAD ON HOME, THOMPSON.
URRGH... I MEAN, IT'S WAY PAST SIX!
BUT HEY, TOMORROW I--
BOBS GARAGE
FOR SALE
BROS
AW MAN... AGAIN?
SERIOUSLY?

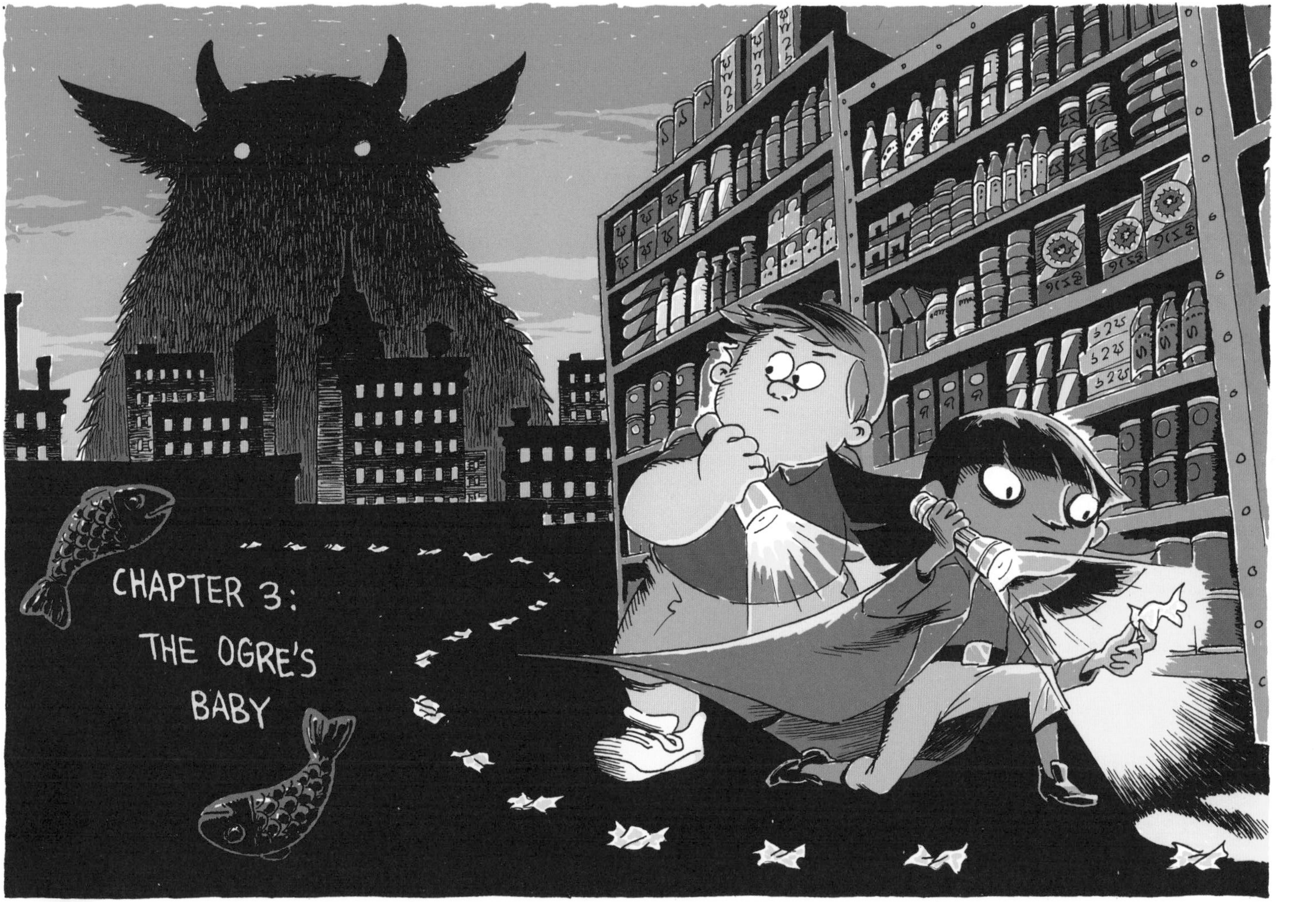
CHAPTER 3:
THE OGRE'S
BABY

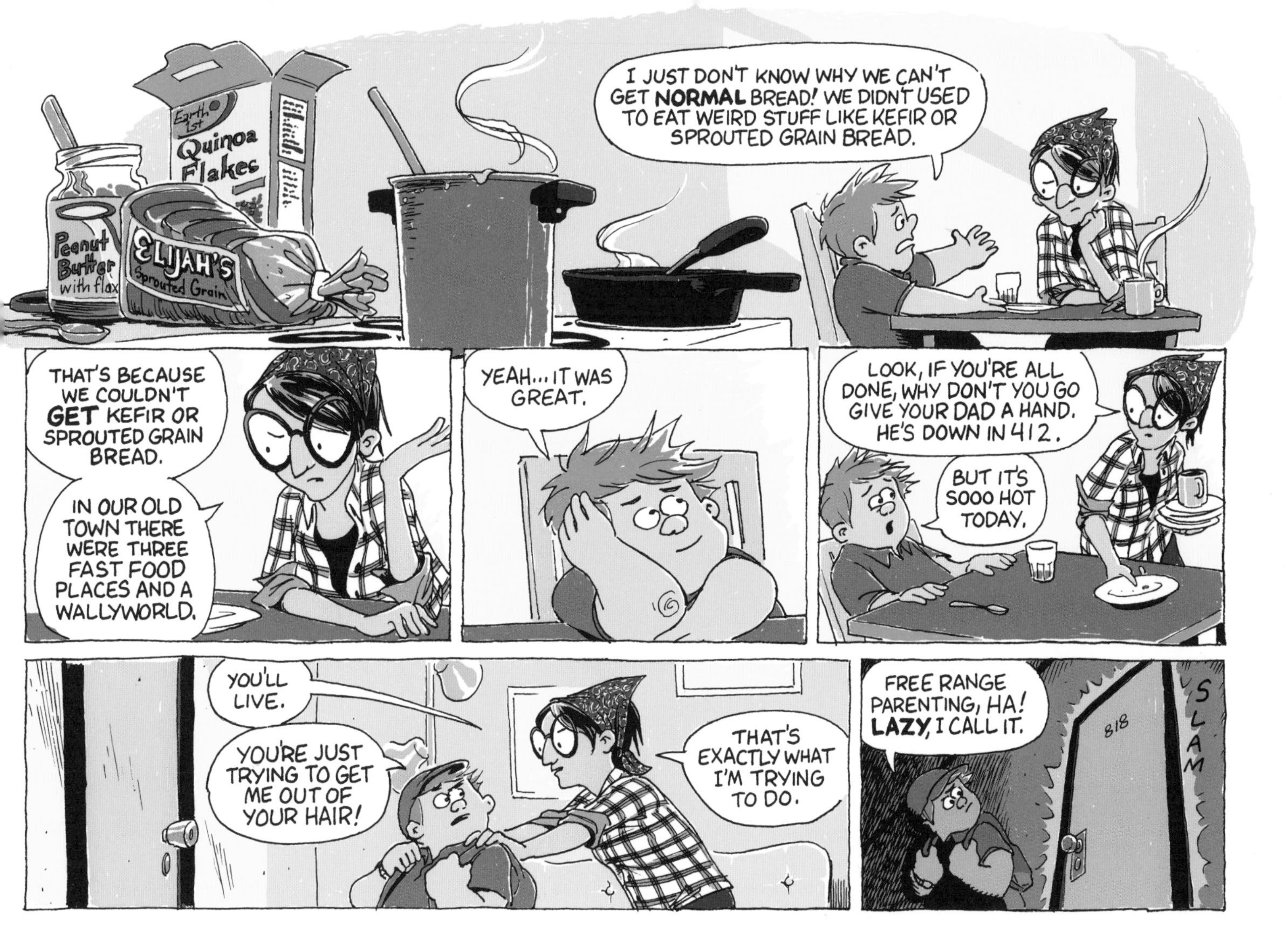
Earth 1st Quinoa Flakes
Peanut Butter with flax
ELIJAH'S Sprouted Grain
I JUST DON'T KNOW WHY WE CAN'T GET NORMAL BREAD! WE DIDN'T USED TO EAT WEIRD STUFF LIKE KEFIR OR SPROUTED GRAIN BREAD.
THAT'S BECAUSE WE COULDN'T GET KEFIR OR SPROUTED GRAIN BREAD.
IN OUR OLD TOWN THERE WERE THREE FAST FOOD PLACES AND A WALLYWORLD.
YEAH... IT WAS GREAT.
LOOK, IF YOU'RE ALL DONE, WHY DON'T YOU GO GIVE YOUR DAD A HAND. HE'S DOWN IN 412.
BUT IT'S SOOO HOT TODAY.
YOU'LL LIVE.
YOU'RE JUST TRYING TO GET ME OUT OF YOUR HAIR!
THAT'S EXACTLY WHAT I'M TRYING TO DO.
FREE RANGE PARENTING, HA! LAZY, I CALL IT.
818
SLAM

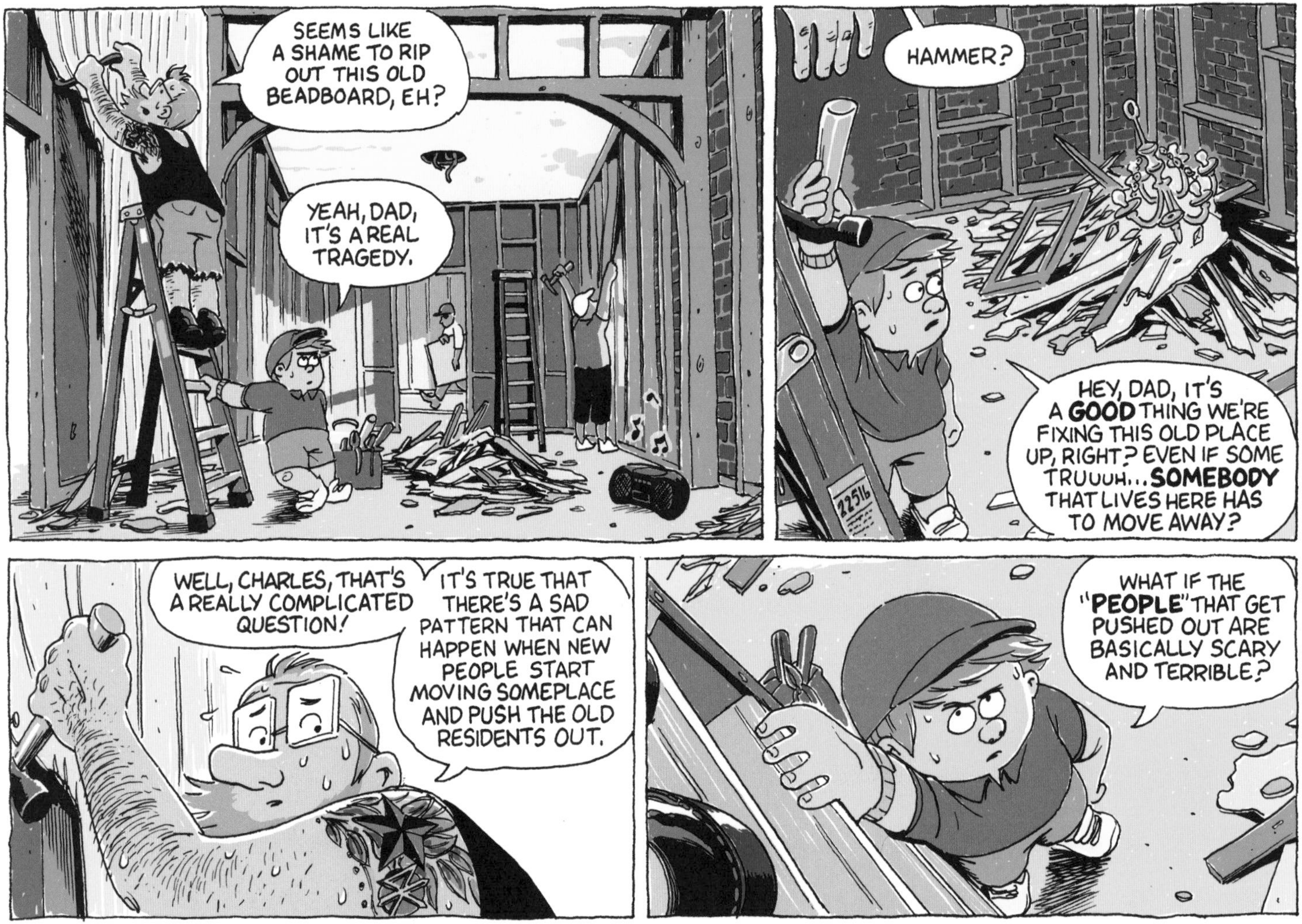
SEEMS LIKE A SHAME TO RIP OUT THIS OLD BEADBOARD, EH?
YEAH, DAD, IT'S A REAL TRAGEDY.
HAMMER?
HEY, DAD, IT'S A **GOOD** THING WE'RE FIXING THIS OLD PLACE UP, RIGHT? EVEN IF SOME TRUUUH... **SOMEBODY** THAT LIVES HERE HAS TO MOVE AWAY?
WELL, CHARLES, THAT'S A REALLY COMPLICATED QUESTION!
IT'S TRUE THAT THERE'S A SAD PATTERN THAT CAN HAPPEN WHEN NEW PEOPLE START MOVING SOMEPLACE AND PUSH THE OLD RESIDENTS OUT.
WHAT IF THE "**PEOPLE**" THAT GET PUSHED OUT ARE BASICALLY SCARY AND TERRIBLE?

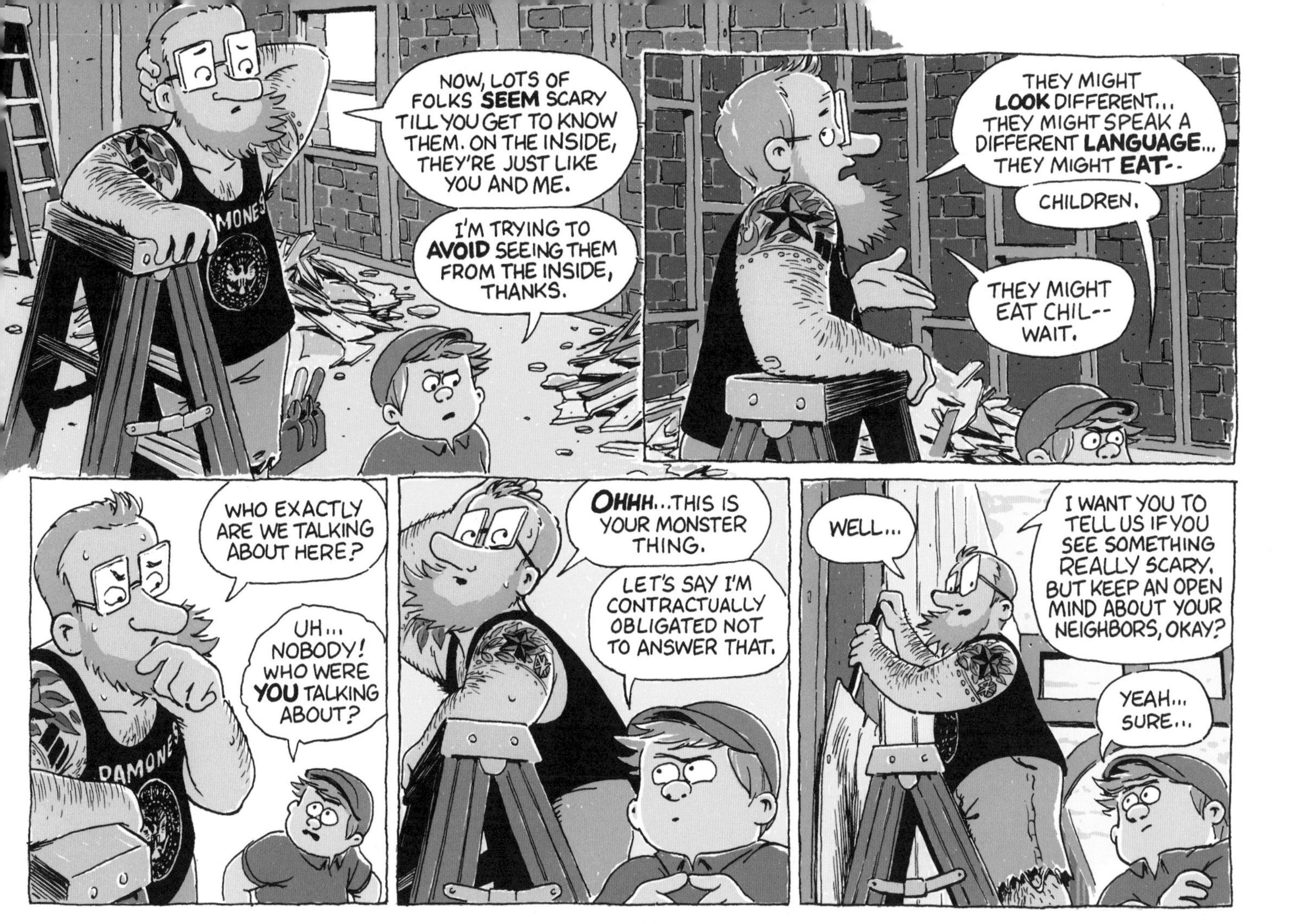
NOW, LOTS OF FOLKS SEEM SCARY TILL YOU GET TO KNOW THEM. ON THE INSIDE, THEY'RE JUST LIKE YOU AND ME.
I'M TRYING TO AVOID SEEING THEM FROM THE INSIDE, THANKS.
THEY MIGHT LOOK DIFFERENT... THEY MIGHT SPEAK A DIFFERENT LANGUAGE... THEY MIGHT EAT--
CHILDREN.
THEY MIGHT EAT CHIL-- WAIT.
WHO EXACTLY ARE WE TALKING ABOUT HERE?
UH... NOBODY! WHO WERE YOU TALKING ABOUT?
OHHH...THIS IS YOUR MONSTER THING.
LET'S SAY I'M CONTRACTUALLY OBLIGATED NOT TO ANSWER THAT.
WELL...
I WANT YOU TO TELL US IF YOU SEE SOMETHING REALLY SCARY, BUT KEEP AN OPEN MIND ABOUT YOUR NEIGHBORS, OKAY?
YEAH... SURE...

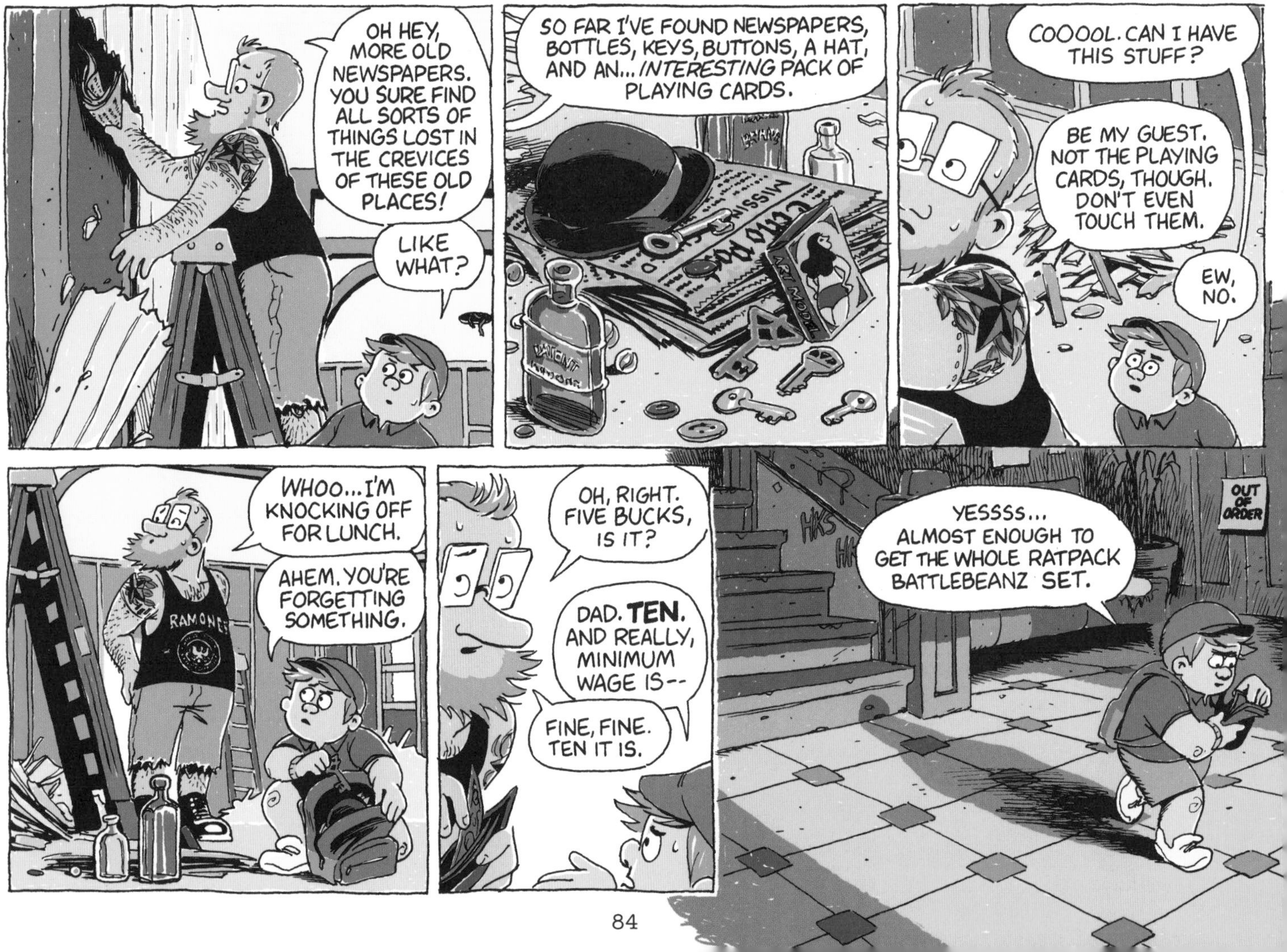
OH HEY, MORE OLD NEWSPAPERS. YOU SURE FIND ALL SORTS OF THINGS LOST IN THE CREVICES OF THESE OLD PLACES!
LIKE WHAT?
SO FAR I'VE FOUND NEWSPAPERS, BOTTLES, KEYS, BUTTONS, A HAT, AND AN... INTERESTING PACK OF PLAYING CARDS.
ART MODEL
PATENT
COOOOL. CAN I HAVE THIS STUFF?
BE MY GUEST. NOT THE PLAYING CARDS, THOUGH. DON'T EVEN TOUCH THEM.
EW, NO.
WHOO... I'M KNOCKING OFF FOR LUNCH.
AHEM. YOU'RE FORGETTING SOMETHING.
RAMONES
OH, RIGHT. FIVE BUCKS, IS IT?
DAD. TEN. AND REALLY, MINIMUM WAGE IS--
FINE, FINE. TEN IT IS.
OUT OF ORDER
HKS
YESSSS... ALMOST ENOUGH TO GET THE WHOLE RATPACK BATTLEBEANZ SET.

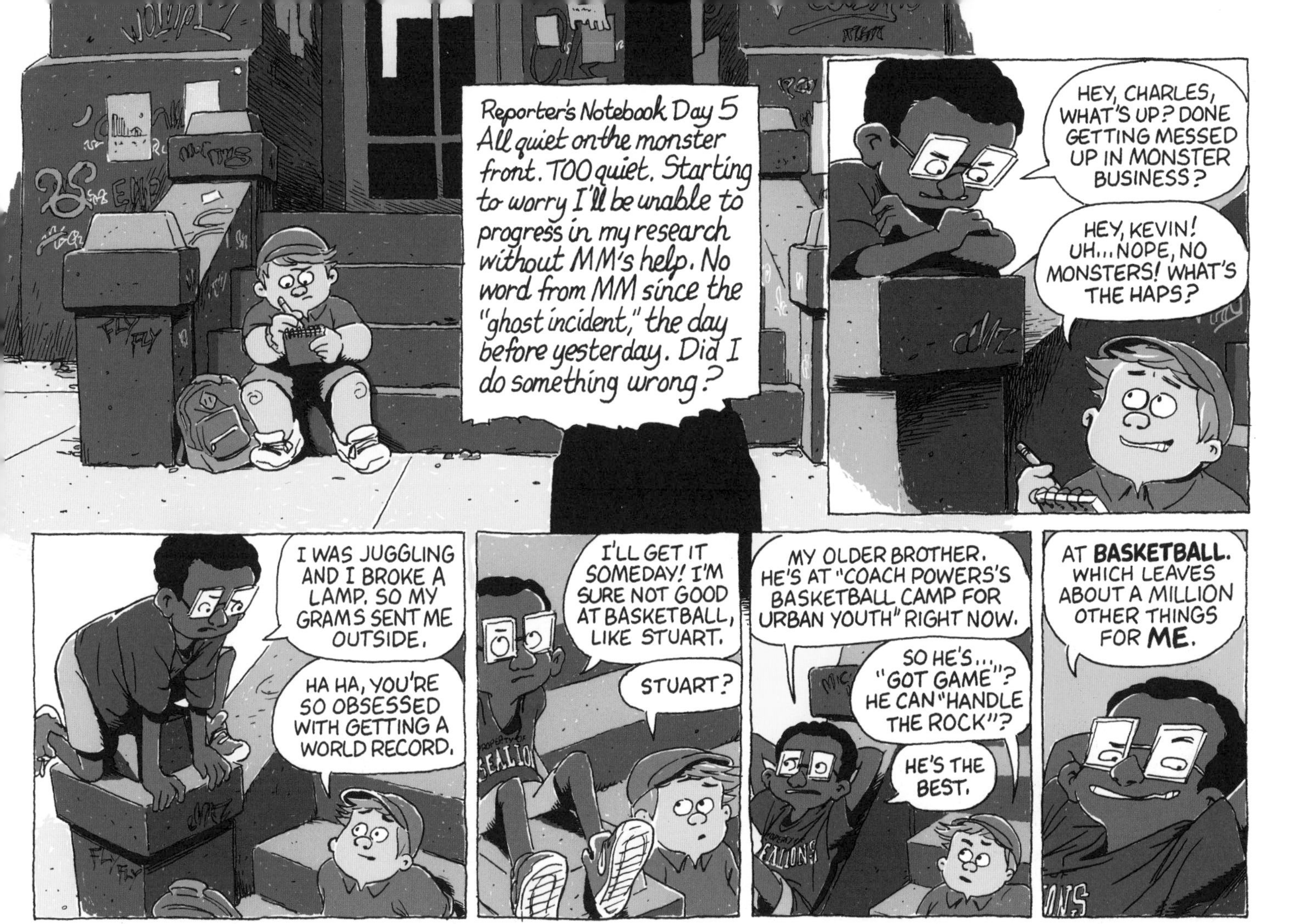
Reporter's Notebook Day 5 All quiet on the monster front. TOO quiet. Starting to worry I'll be unable to progress in my research without MM's help. No word from MM since the "ghost incident," the day before yesterday. Did I do something wrong?
HEY, CHARLES, WHAT'S UP? DONE GETTING MESSED UP IN MONSTER BUSINESS?
HEY, KEVIN! UH...NOPE, NO MONSTERS! WHAT'S THE HAPS?
I WAS JUGGLING AND I BROKE A LAMP. SO MY GRAMS SENT ME OUTSIDE.
HA HA, YOU'RE SO OBSESSED WITH GETTING A WORLD RECORD.
I'LL GET IT SOMEDAY! I'M SURE NOT GOOD AT BASKETBALL, LIKE STUART.
STUART?
MY OLDER BROTHER. HE'S AT "COACH POWERS'S BASKETBALL CAMP FOR URBAN YOUTH" RIGHT NOW.
SO HE'S... "GOT GAME"? HE CAN "HANDLE THE ROCK"?
HE'S THE BEST.
AT BASKETBALL. WHICH LEAVES ABOUT A MILLION OTHER THINGS FOR ME.

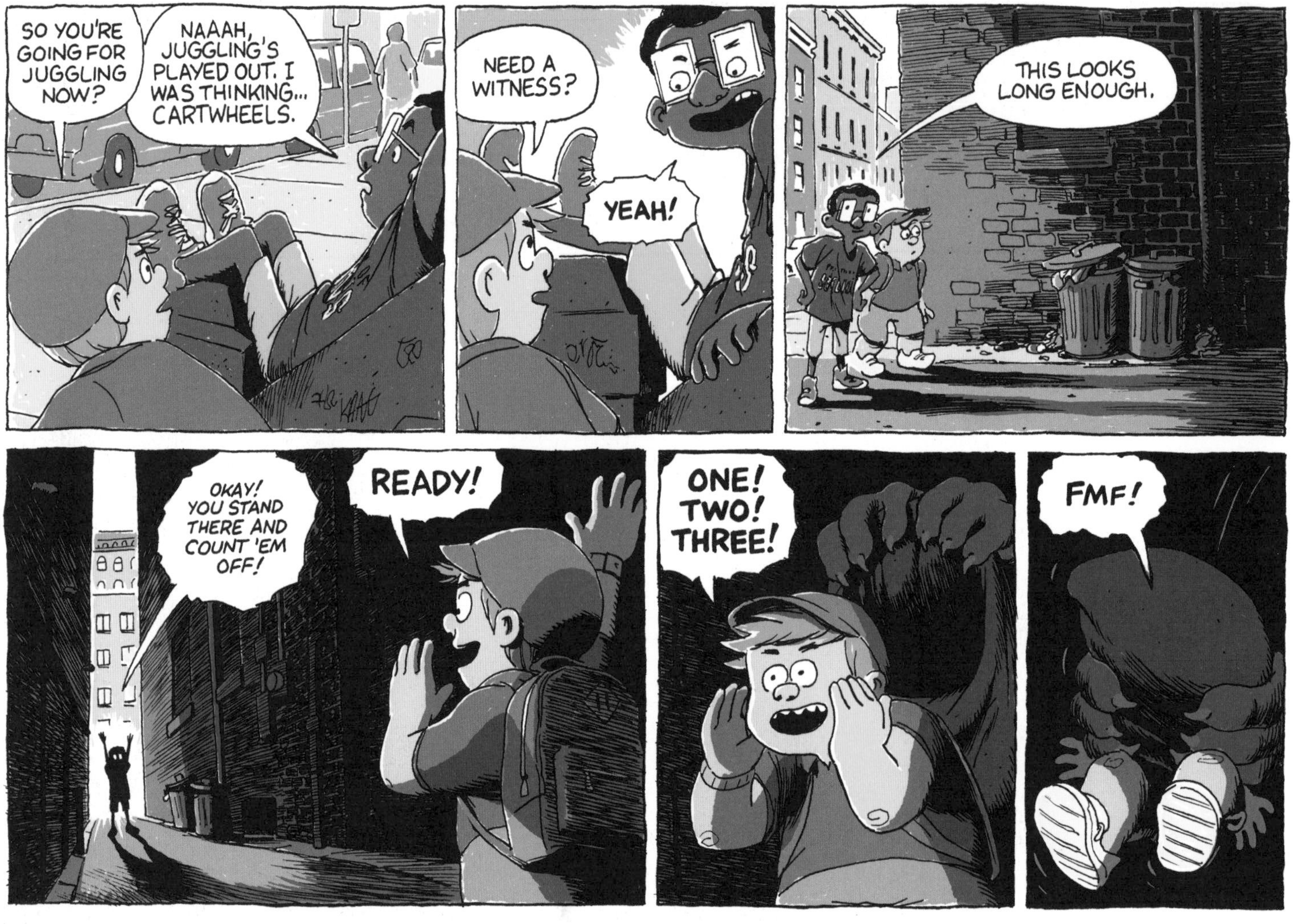
SO YOU'RE GOING FOR JUGGLING NOW?
NAAAH, JUGGLING'S PLAYED OUT. I WAS THINKING... CARTWHEELS.
NEED A WITNESS?
YEAH!
THIS LOOKS LONG ENOUGH.
OKAY! YOU STAND THERE AND COUNT 'EM OFF!
READY!
ONE! TWO! THREE!
FMF!

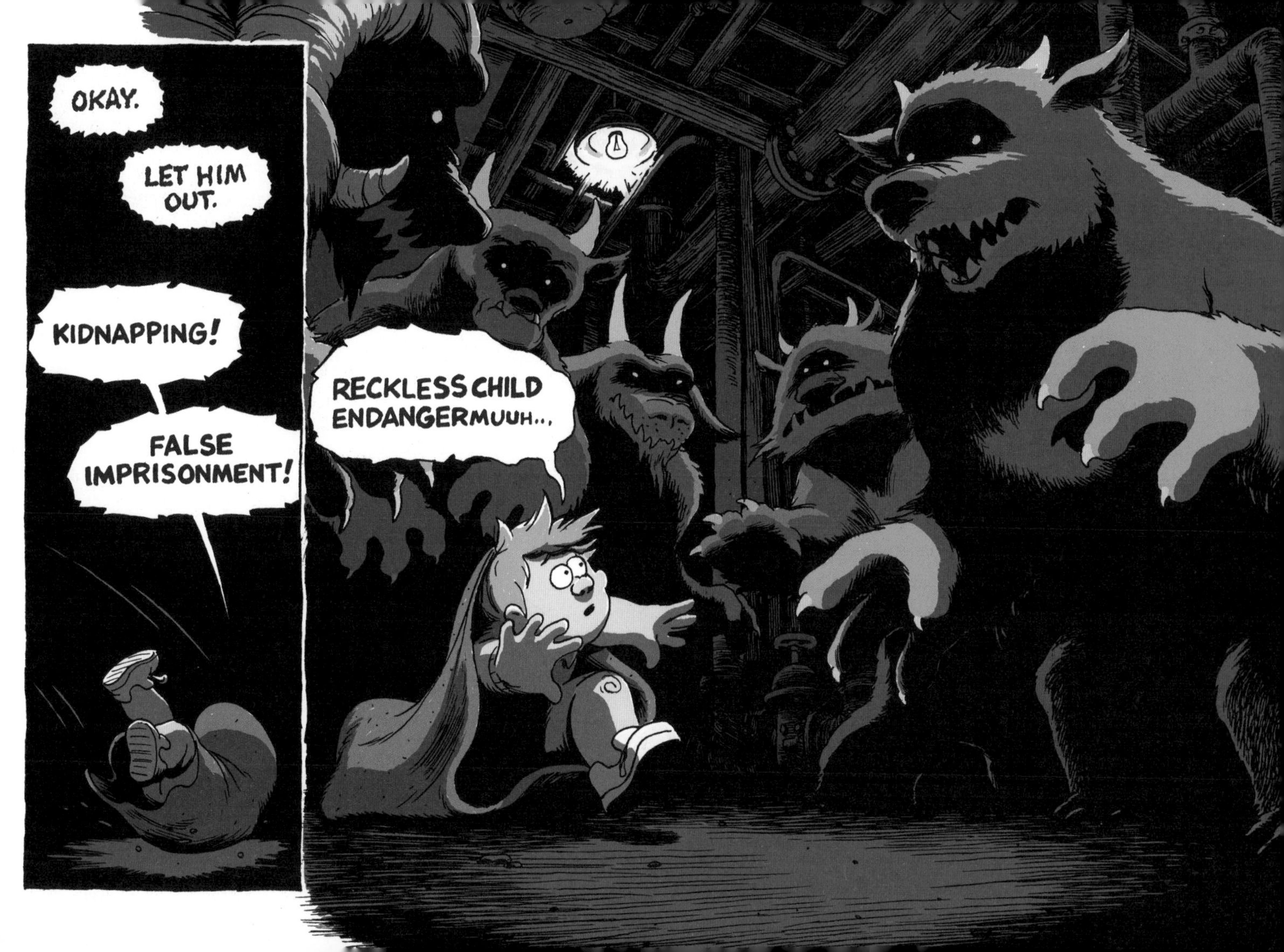
OKAY.
LET HIM OUT.
KIDNAPPING!
FALSE IMPRISONMENT!
RECKLESS CHILD ENDANGERMUUH...

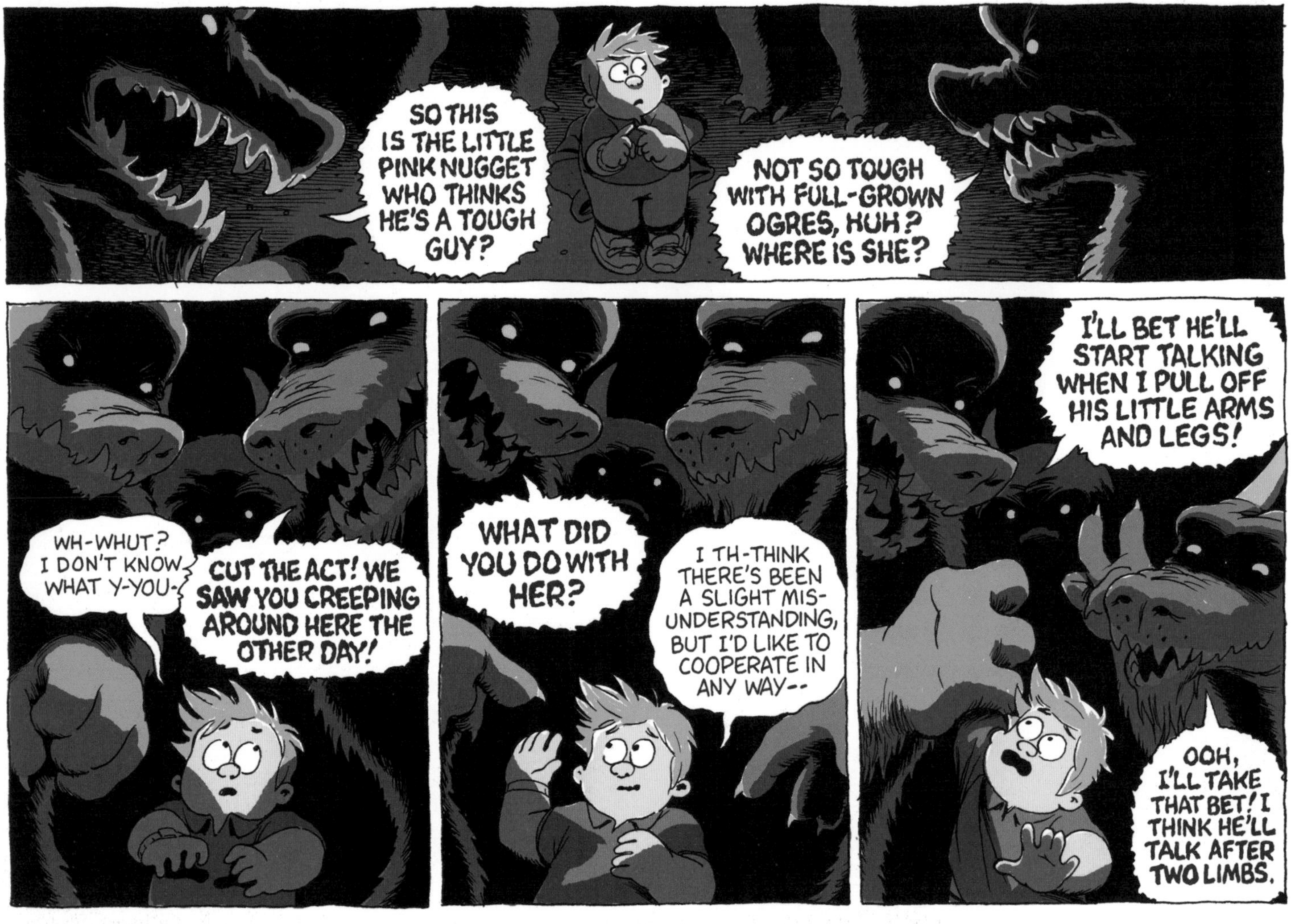
SO THIS IS THE LITTLE PINK NUGGET WHO THINKS HE'S A TOUGH GUY?
NOT SO TOUGH WITH FULL-GROWN OGRES, HUH? WHERE IS SHE?
WH-WHUT? I DON'T KNOW WHAT Y-YOU-
CUT THE ACT! WE SAW YOU CREEPING AROUND HERE THE OTHER DAY!
WHAT DID YOU DO WITH HER?
I TH-THINK THERE'S BEEN A SLIGHT MIS-UNDERSTANDING, BUT I'D LIKE TO COOPERATE IN ANY WAY--
I'LL BET HE'LL START TALKING WHEN I PULL OFF HIS LITTLE ARMS AND LEGS!
OOH, I'LL TAKE THAT BET! I THINK HE'LL TALK AFTER TWO LIMBS.

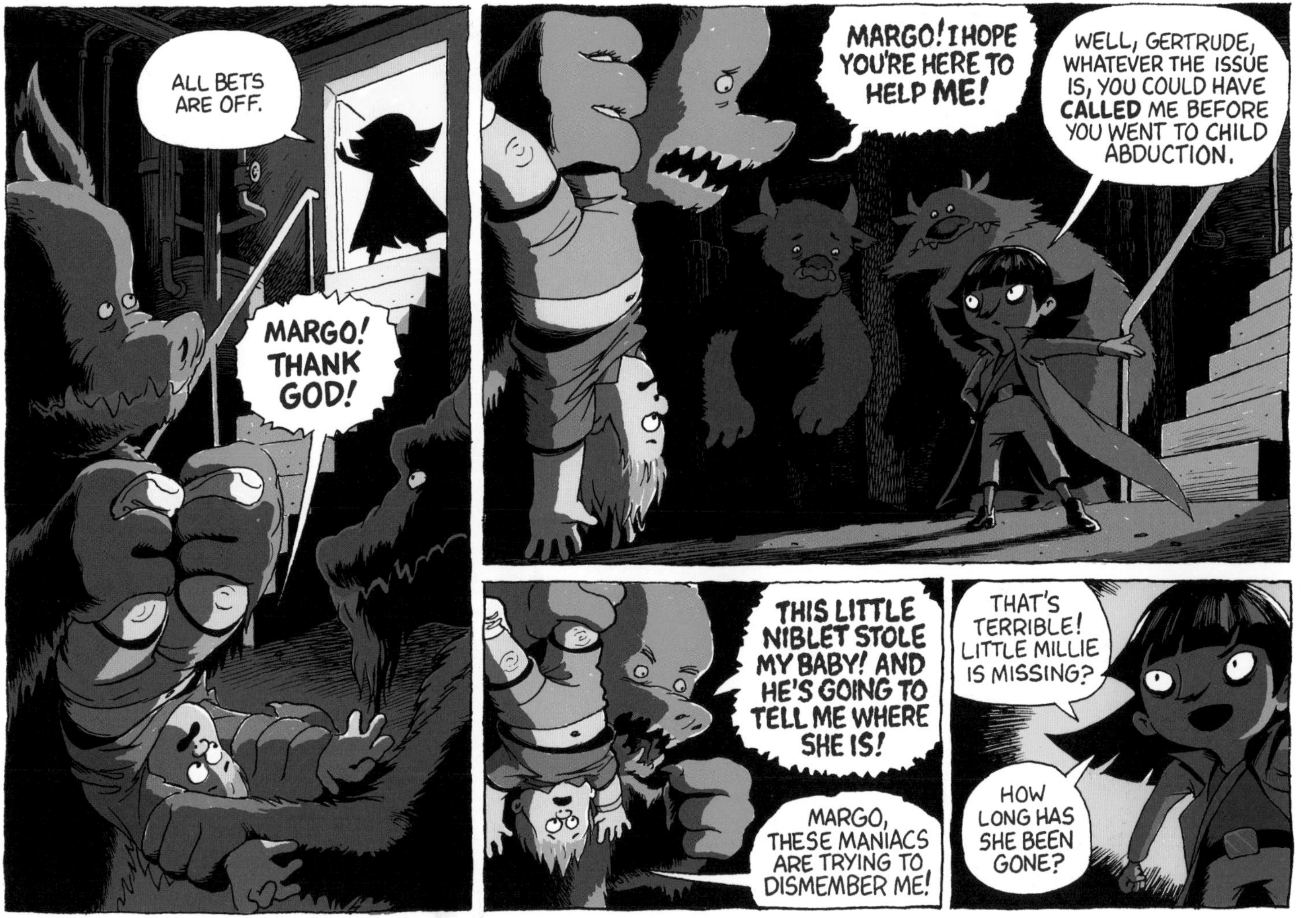
ALL BETS ARE OFF.
MARGO! THANK GOD!
MARGO! I HOPE YOU'RE HERE TO HELP ME!
WELL, GERTRUDE, WHATEVER THE ISSUE IS, YOU COULD HAVE CALLED ME BEFORE YOU WENT TO CHILD ABDUCTION.
THIS LITTLE NIBLET STOLE MY BABY! AND HE'S GOING TO TELL ME WHERE SHE IS!
MARGO, THESE MANIACS ARE TRYING TO DISMEMBER ME!
THAT'S TERRIBLE! LITTLE MILLIE IS MISSING?
HOW LONG HAS SHE BEEN GONE?

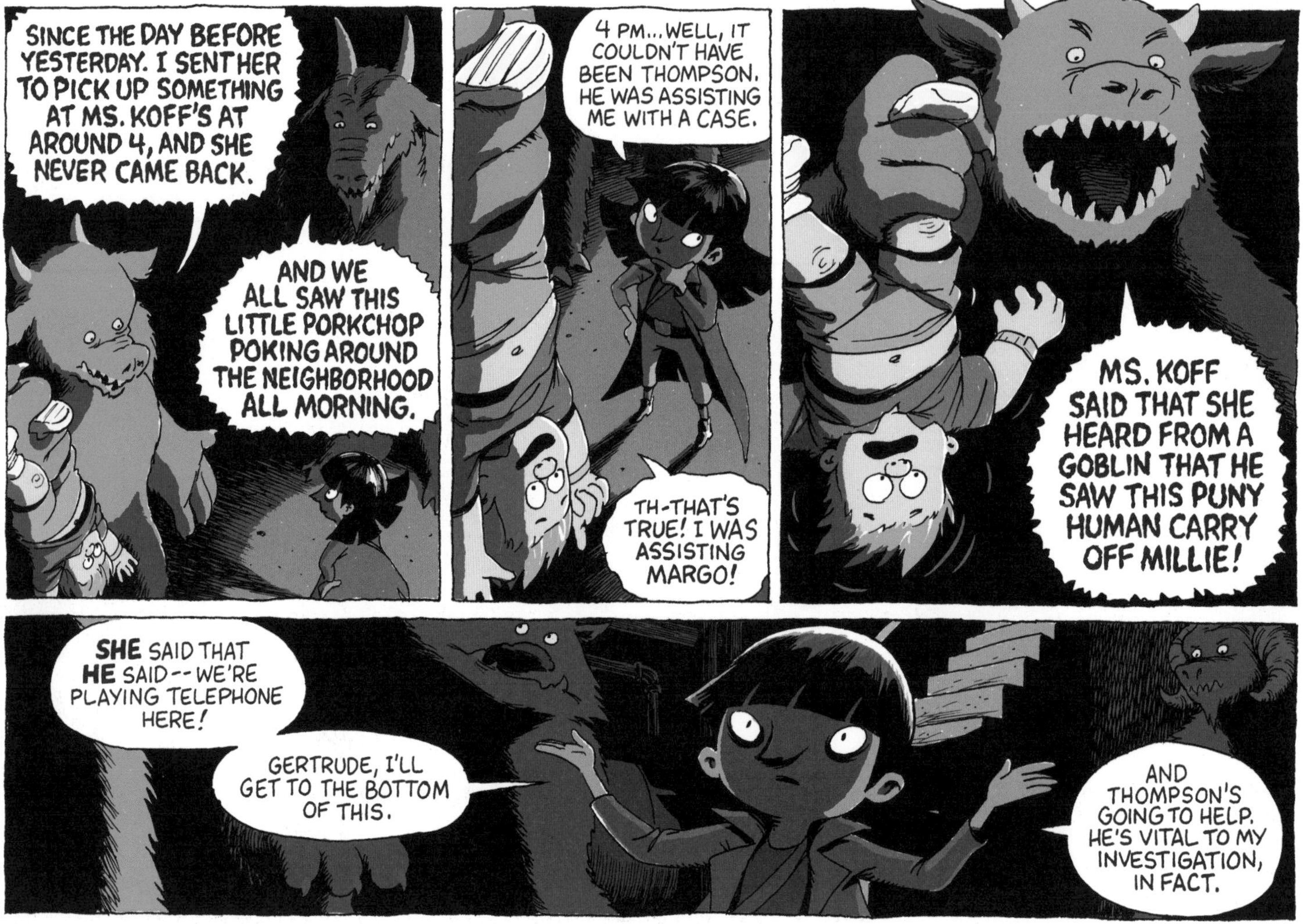
SINCE THE DAY BEFORE YESTERDAY. I SENT HER TO PICK UP SOMETHING AT MS. KOFF'S AT AROUND 4, AND SHE NEVER CAME BACK.
AND WE ALL SAW THIS LITTLE PORKCHOP POKING AROUND THE NEIGHBORHOOD ALL MORNING.
4 PM... WELL, IT COULDN'T HAVE BEEN THOMPSON. HE WAS ASSISTING ME WITH A CASE.
TH-THAT'S TRUE! I WAS ASSISTING MARGO!
MS. KOFF SAID THAT SHE HEARD FROM A GOBLIN THAT HE SAW THIS PUNY HUMAN CARRY OFF MILLIE!
SHE SAID THAT **HE** SAID-- WE'RE PLAYING TELEPHONE HERE!
GERTRUDE, I'LL GET TO THE BOTTOM OF THIS.
AND THOMPSON'S GOING TO HELP. HE'S VITAL TO MY INVESTIGATION, IN FACT.

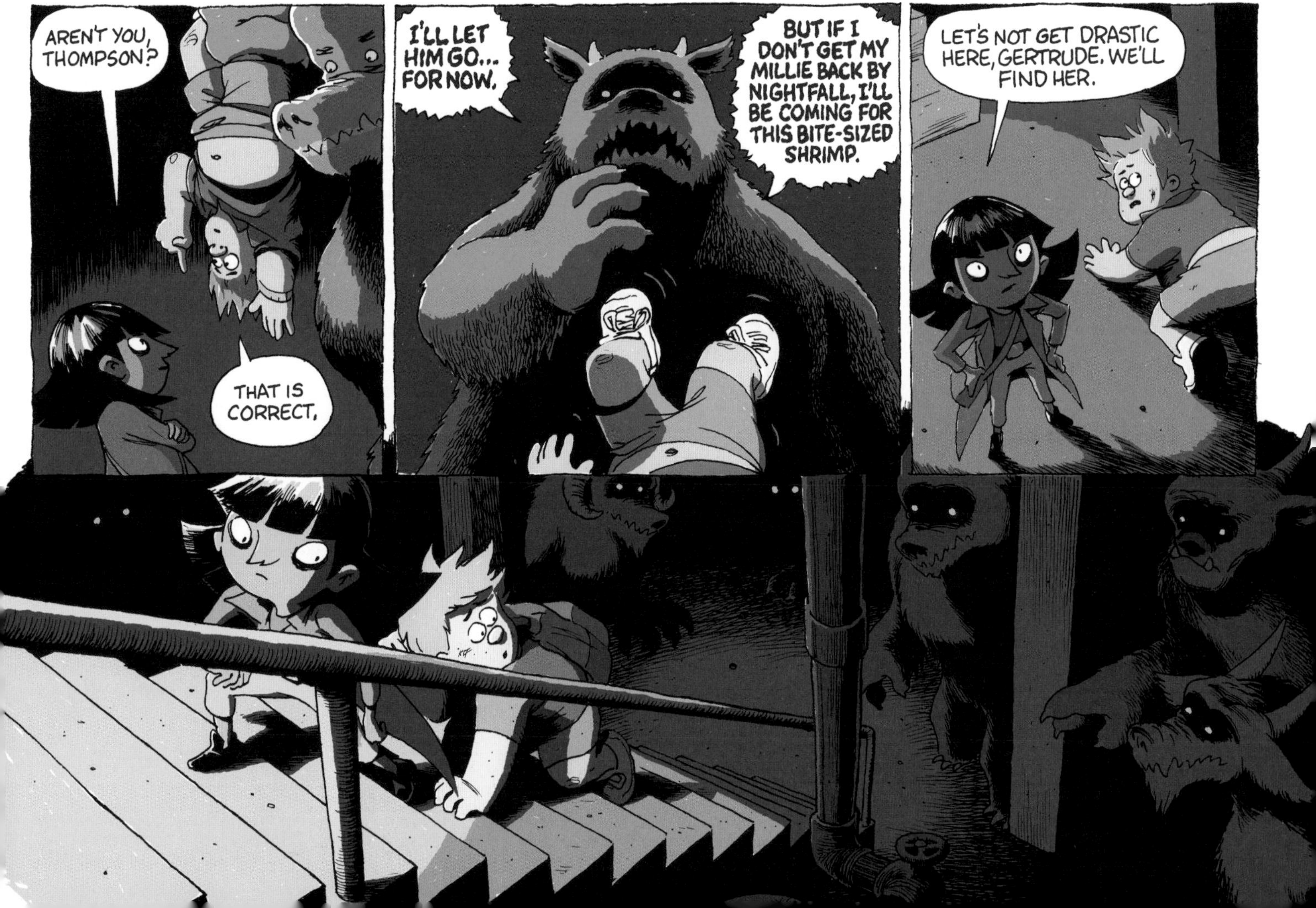
AREN'T YOU, THOMPSON?
THAT IS CORRECT.
I'LL LET HIM GO... FOR NOW.
BUT IF I DON'T GET MY MILLIE BACK BY NIGHTFALL, I'LL BE COMING FOR THIS BITE-SIZED SHRIMP.
LET'S NOT GET DRASTIC HERE, GERTRUDE. WE'LL FIND HER.

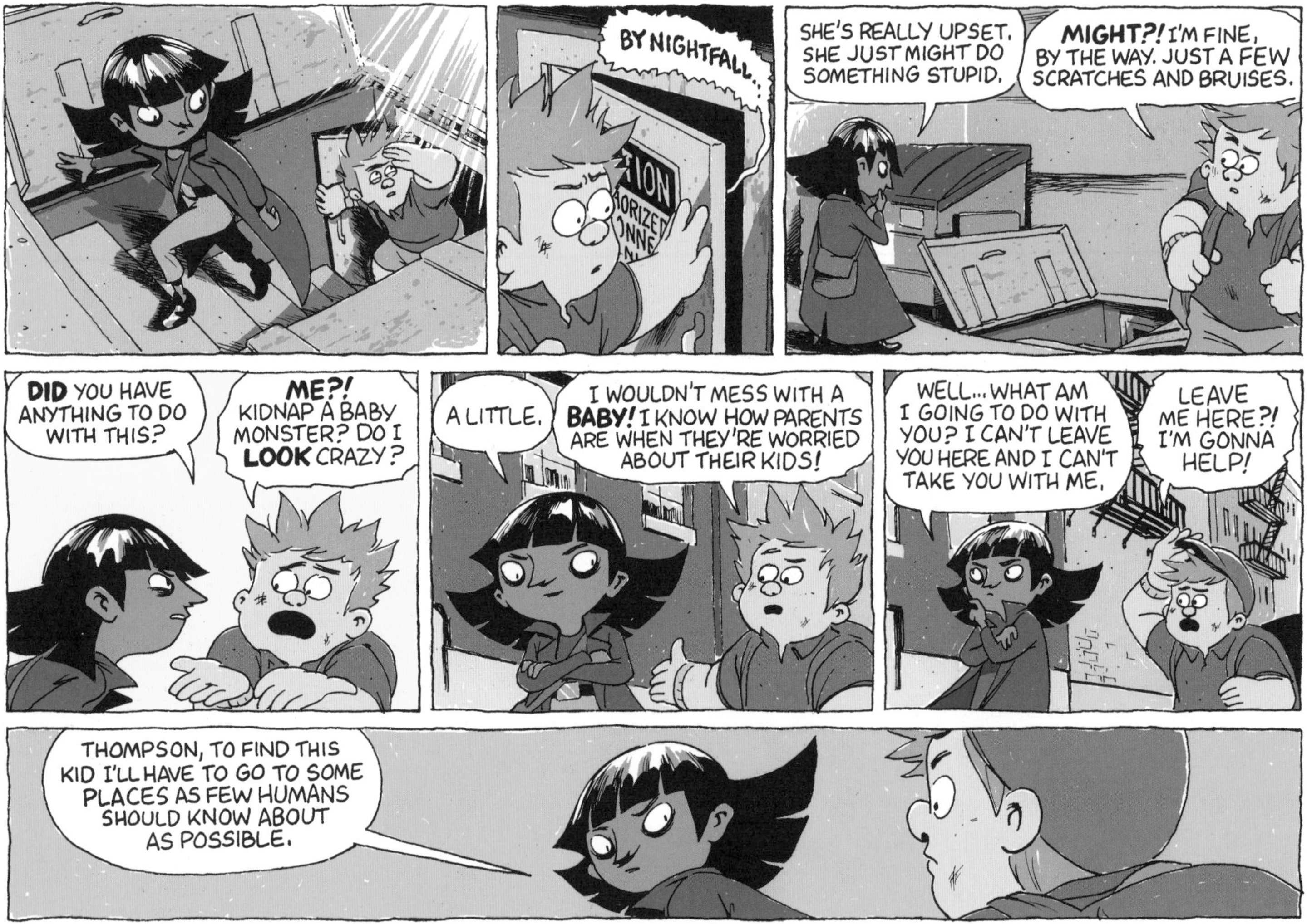
BY NIGHTFALL...
SHE'S REALLY UPSET. SHE JUST MIGHT DO SOMETHING STUPID.
MIGHT?! I'M FINE, BY THE WAY. JUST A FEW SCRATCHES AND BRUISES.
DID YOU HAVE ANYTHING TO DO WITH THIS?
ME?! KIDNAP A BABY MONSTER? DO I LOOK CRAZY?
A LITTLE.
I WOULDN'T MESS WITH A BABY! I KNOW HOW PARENTS ARE WHEN THEY'RE WORRIED ABOUT THEIR KIDS!
WELL... WHAT AM I GOING TO DO WITH YOU? I CAN'T LEAVE YOU HERE AND I CAN'T TAKE YOU WITH ME.
LEAVE ME HERE?! I'M GONNA HELP!
THOMPSON, TO FIND THIS KID I'LL HAVE TO GO TO SOME PLACES AS FEW HUMANS SHOULD KNOW ABOUT AS POSSIBLE.

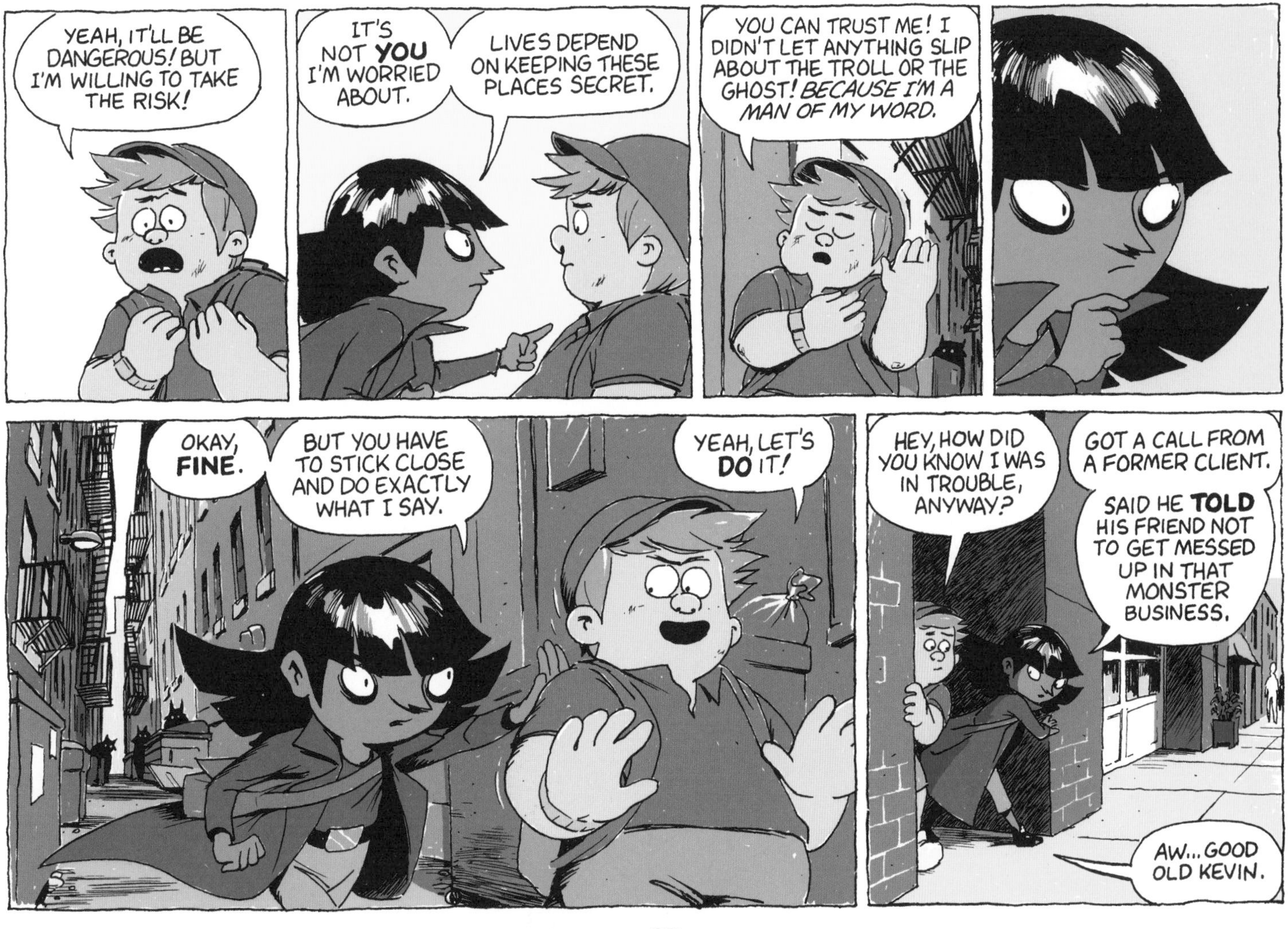

YEAH, IT'LL BE DANGEROUS! BUT I'M WILLING TO TAKE THE RISK!
IT'S NOT **YOU** I'M WORRIED ABOUT.
LIVES DEPEND ON KEEPING THESE PLACES SECRET.
YOU CAN TRUST ME! I DIDN'T LET ANYTHING SLIP ABOUT THE TROLL OR THE GHOST! *BECAUSE I'M A MAN OF MY WORD.*
OKAY, **FINE**.
BUT YOU HAVE TO STICK CLOSE AND DO EXACTLY WHAT I SAY.
YEAH, LET'S **DO** IT!
HEY, HOW DID YOU KNOW I WAS IN TROUBLE, ANYWAY?
GOT A CALL FROM A FORMER CLIENT.
SAID HE **TOLD** HIS FRIEND NOT TO GET MESSED UP IN THAT MONSTER BUSINESS.
AW... GOOD OLD KEVIN.

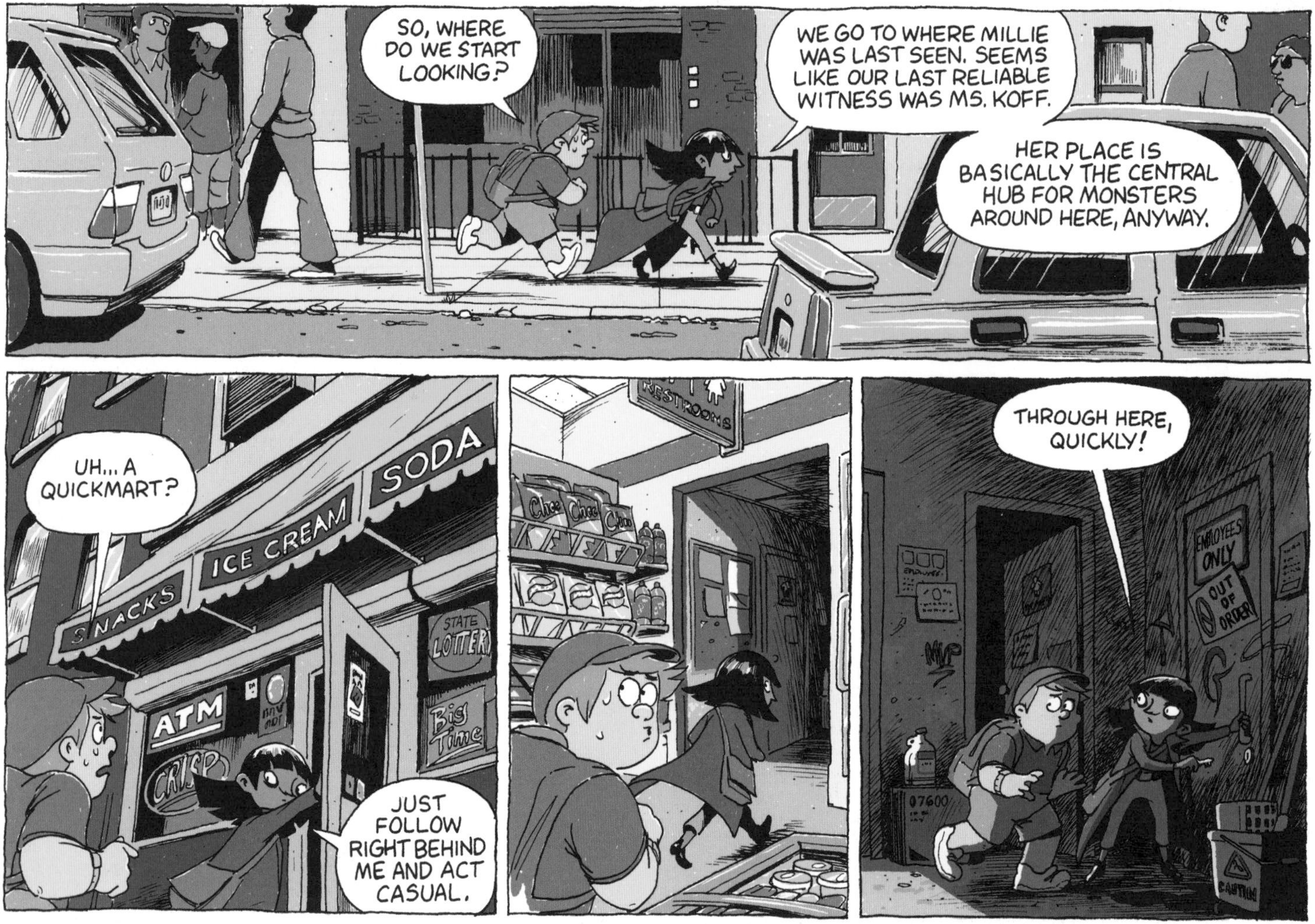
SO, WHERE DO WE START LOOKING?
WE GO TO WHERE MILLIE WAS LAST SEEN. SEEMS LIKE OUR LAST RELIABLE WITNESS WAS MS. KOFF.
HER PLACE IS BASICALLY THE CENTRAL HUB FOR MONSTERS AROUND HERE, ANYWAY.
SNACKS
ICE CREAM
SODA
UH... A QUICKMART?
STATE LOTTERY
ATM
Big Time
JUST FOLLOW RIGHT BEHIND ME AND ACT CASUAL.
RESTROOMS
THROUGH HERE, QUICKLY!
EMPLOYEES ONLY
OUT OF ORDER
CAUTION

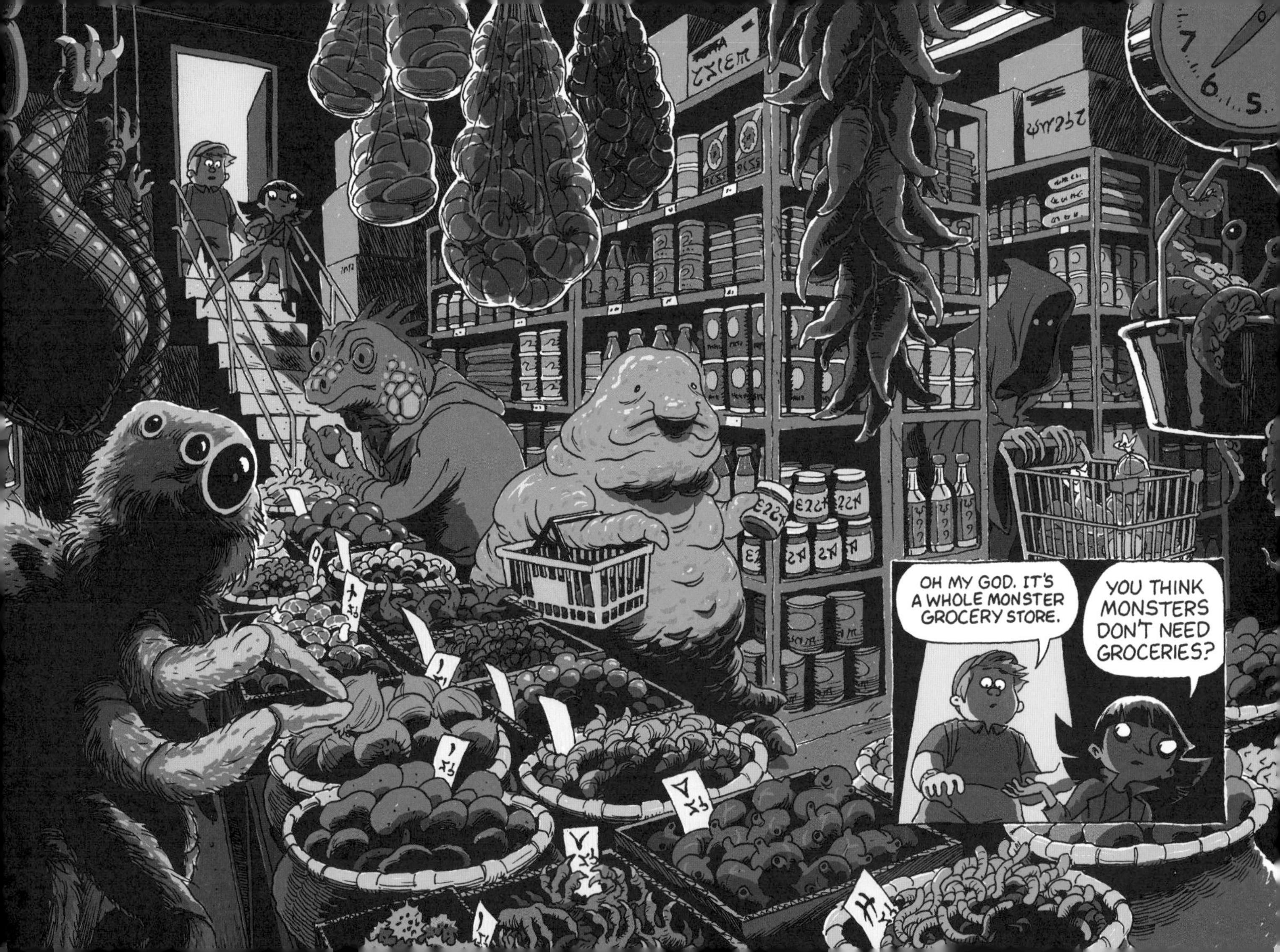
OH MY GOD. IT'S A WHOLE MONSTER GROCERY STORE.
YOU THINK MONSTERS DON'T NEED GROCERIES?

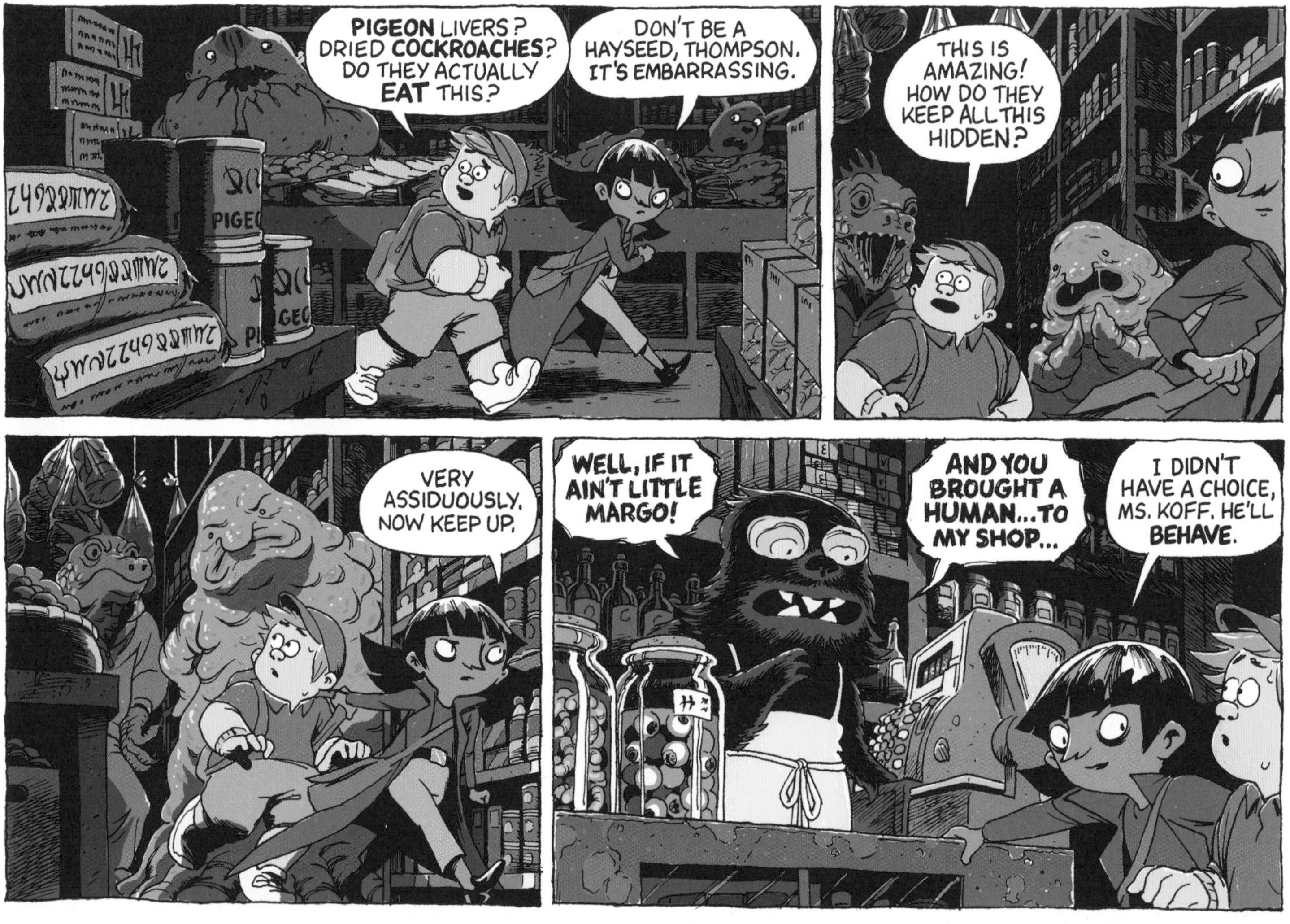
PIGEON LIVERS? DRIED COCKROACHES? DO THEY ACTUALLY EAT THIS?
DON'T BE A HAYSEED, THOMPSON. IT'S EMBARRASSING.
THIS IS AMAZING! HOW DO THEY KEEP ALL THIS HIDDEN?
VERY ASSIDUOUSLY. NOW KEEP UP.
WELL, IF IT AIN'T LITTLE MARGO!
AND YOU BROUGHT A HUMAN... TO MY SHOP...
I DIDN'T HAVE A CHOICE, MS. KOFF. HE'LL BEHAVE.

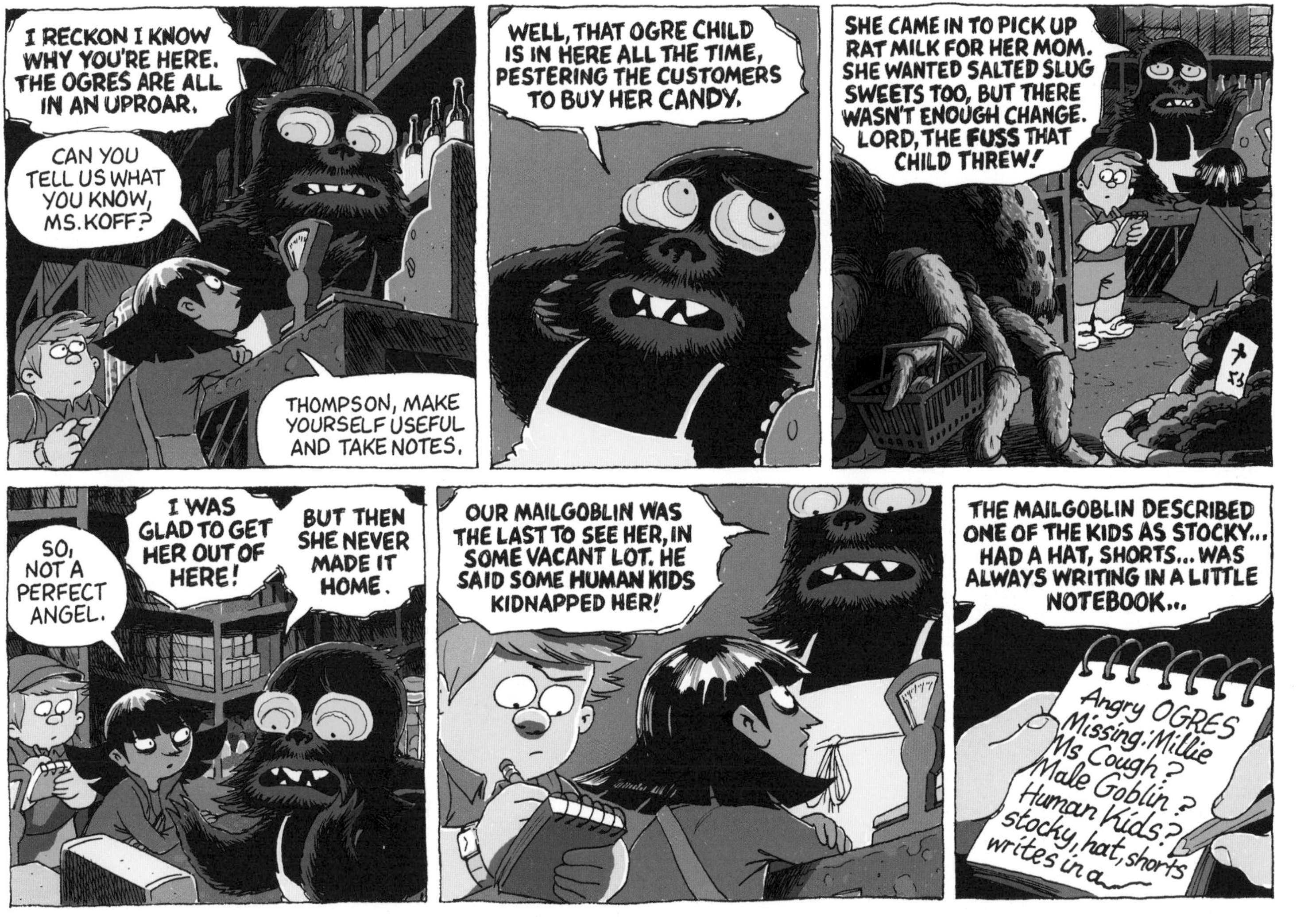
I RECKON I KNOW WHY YOU'RE HERE. THE OGRES ARE ALL IN AN UPROAR.
CAN YOU TELL US WHAT YOU KNOW, MS. KOFF?
THOMPSON, MAKE YOURSELF USEFUL AND TAKE NOTES.
WELL, THAT OGRE CHILD IS IN HERE ALL THE TIME, PESTERING THE CUSTOMERS TO BUY HER CANDY.
SHE CAME IN TO PICK UP RAT MILK FOR HER MOM. SHE WANTED SALTED SLUG SWEETS TOO, BUT THERE WASN'T ENOUGH CHANGE. LORD, THE FUSS THAT CHILD THREW!
SO, NOT A PERFECT ANGEL.
I WAS GLAD TO GET HER OUT OF HERE!
BUT THEN SHE NEVER MADE IT HOME.
OUR MAILGOBLIN WAS THE LAST TO SEE HER, IN SOME VACANT LOT. HE SAID SOME HUMAN KIDS KIDNAPPED HER!
THE MAILGOBLIN DESCRIBED ONE OF THE KIDS AS STOCKY... HAD A HAT, SHORTS... WAS ALWAYS WRITING IN A LITTLE NOTEBOOK...
Angry OGRES
Missing: Millie
Ms Cough?
Male Goblin?
Human Kids?
stocky, hat, shorts
writes in a

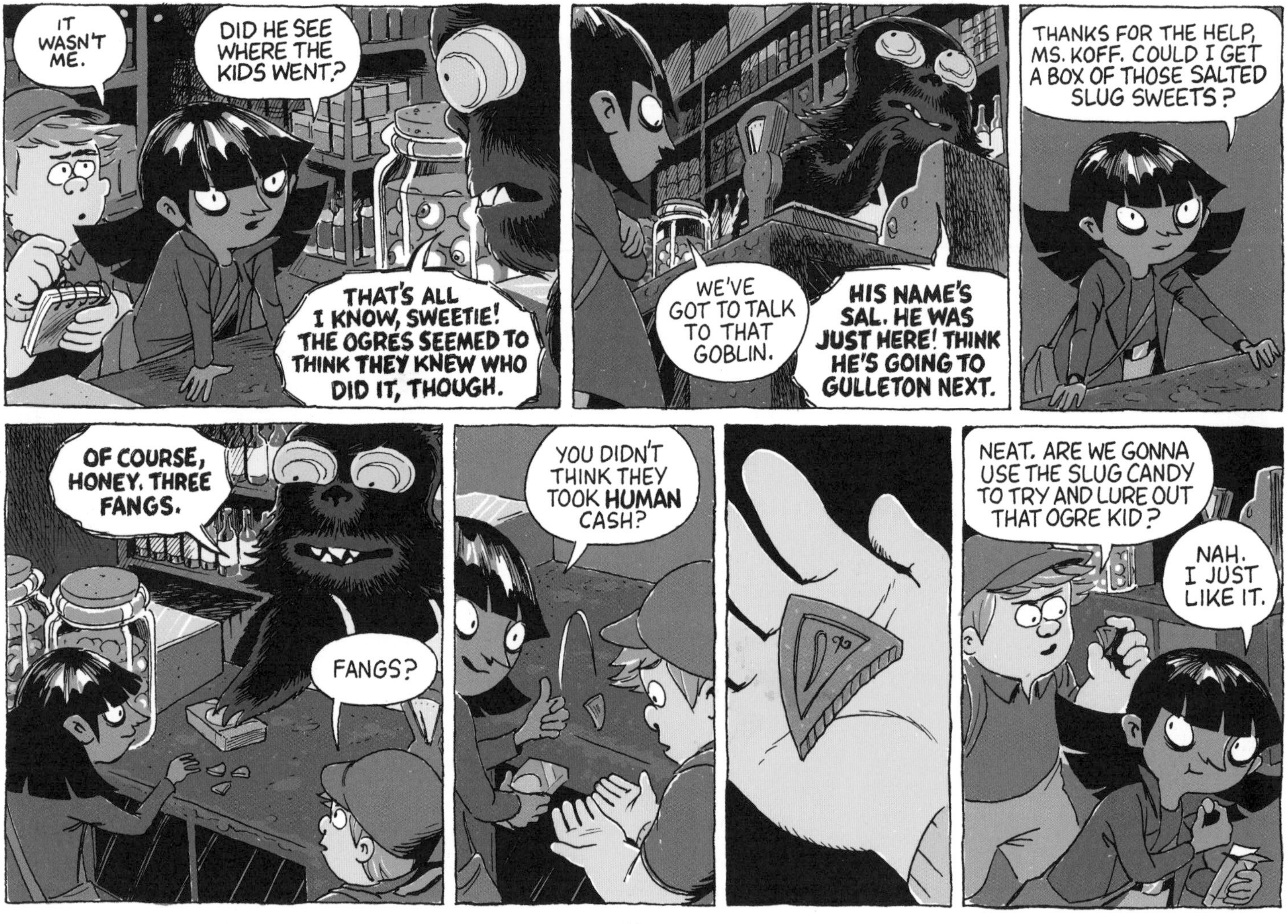
IT WASN'T ME.
DID HE SEE WHERE THE KIDS WENT?
THAT'S ALL I KNOW, SWEETIE! THE OGRES SEEMED TO THINK THEY KNEW WHO DID IT, THOUGH.
WE'VE GOT TO TALK TO THAT GOBLIN.
HIS NAME'S SAL. HE WAS JUST HERE! THINK HE'S GOING TO GULLETON NEXT.
THANKS FOR THE HELP, MS. KOFF. COULD I GET A BOX OF THOSE SALTED SLUG SWEETS?
OF COURSE, HONEY. THREE FANGS.
FANGS?
YOU DIDN'T THINK THEY TOOK HUMAN CASH?
NEAT. ARE WE GONNA USE THE SLUG CANDY TO TRY AND LURE OUT THAT OGRE KID?
NAH. I JUST LIKE IT.

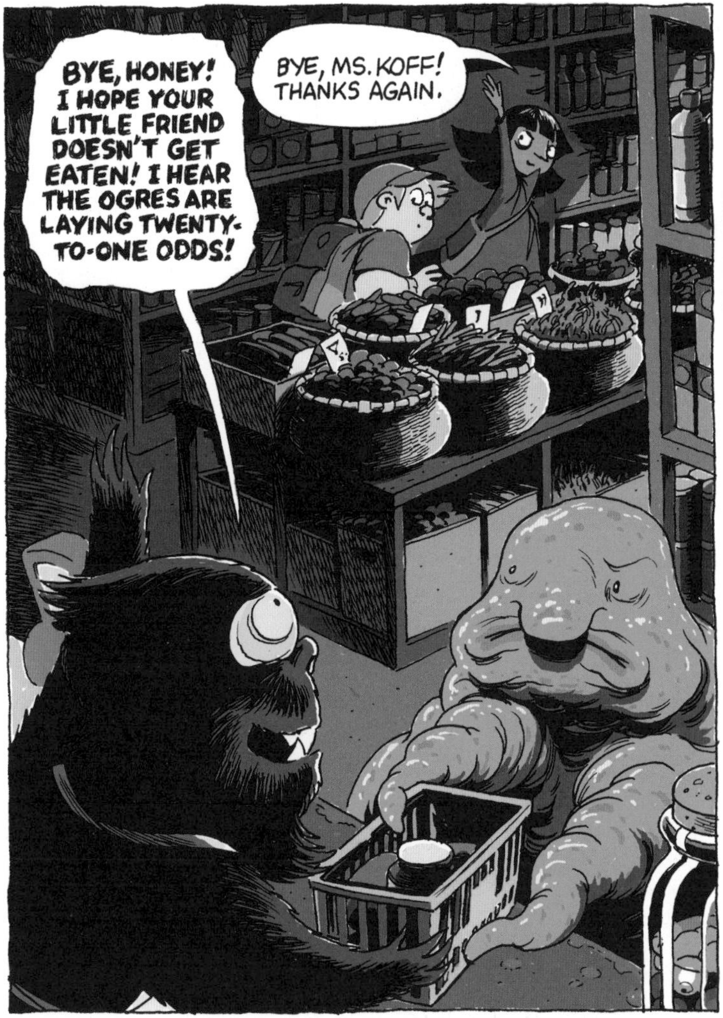
BYE, HONEY! I HOPE YOUR LITTLE FRIEND DOESN'T GET EATEN! I HEAR THE OGRES ARE LAYING TWENTY-TO-ONE ODDS!
BYE, MS. KOFF! THANKS AGAIN.

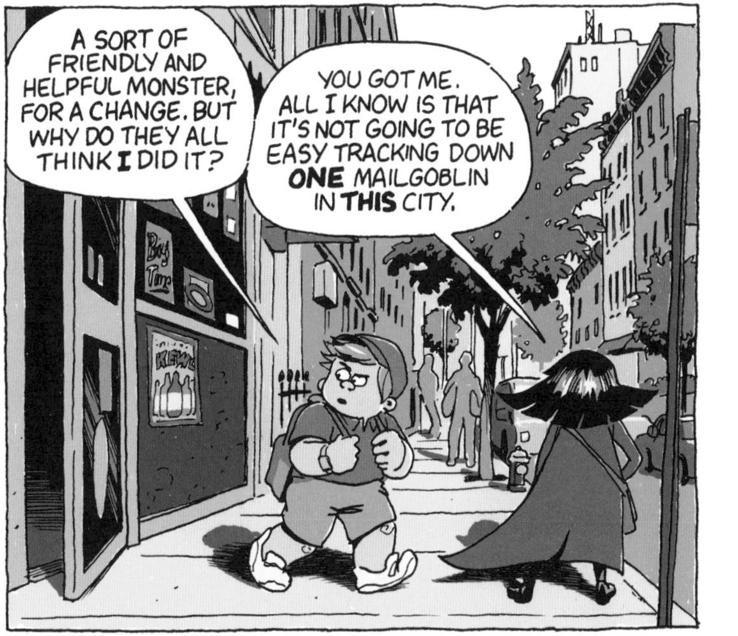
A SORT OF FRIENDLY AND HELPFUL MONSTER, FOR A CHANGE. BUT WHY DO THEY ALL THINK I DID IT?
YOU GOT ME. ALL I KNOW IS THAT IT'S NOT GOING TO BE EASY TRACKING DOWN ONE MAILGOBLIN IN THIS CITY.

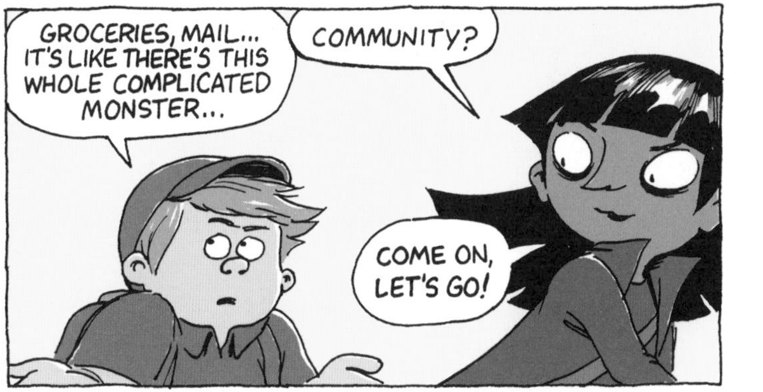
GROCERIES, MAIL... IT'S LIKE THERE'S THIS WHOLE COMPLICATED MONSTER...
COMMUNITY?
COME ON, LET'S GO!

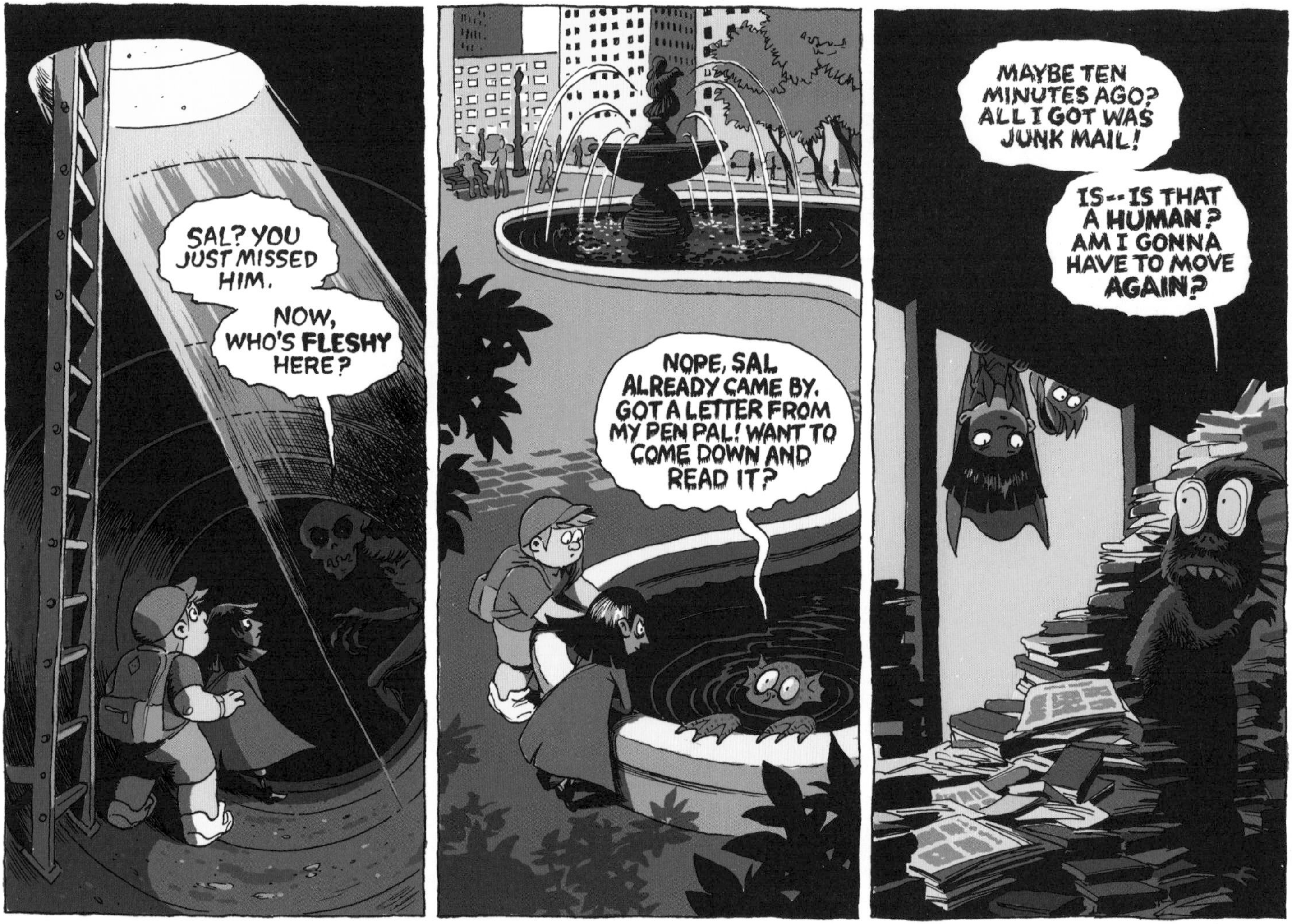
SAL? YOU JUST MISSED HIM.
NOW, WHO'S FLESHY HERE?
NOPE, SAL ALREADY CAME BY. GOT A LETTER FROM MY PEN PAL! WANT TO COME DOWN AND READ IT?
MAYBE TEN MINUTES AGO? ALL I GOT WAS JUNK MAIL!
IS--IS THAT A HUMAN? AM I GONNA HAVE TO MOVE AGAIN?

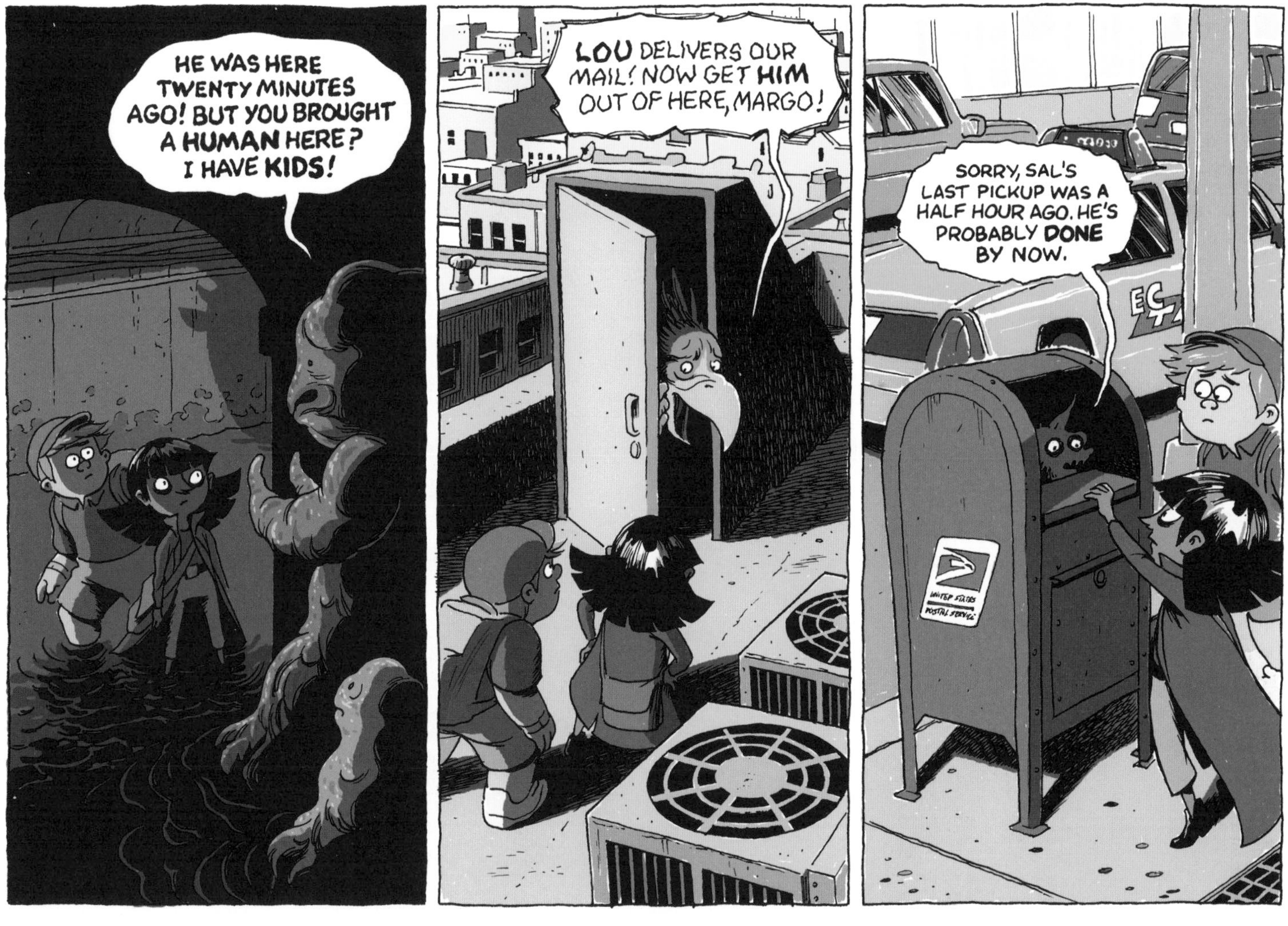
HE WAS HERE TWENTY MINUTES AGO! BUT YOU BROUGHT A HUMAN HERE? I HAVE KIDS!
LOU DELIVERS OUR MAIL! NOW GET HIM OUT OF HERE, MARGO!
SORRY, SAL'S LAST PICKUP WAS A HALF HOUR AGO. HE'S PROBABLY DONE BY NOW.
UNITED STATES POSTAL SERVICE

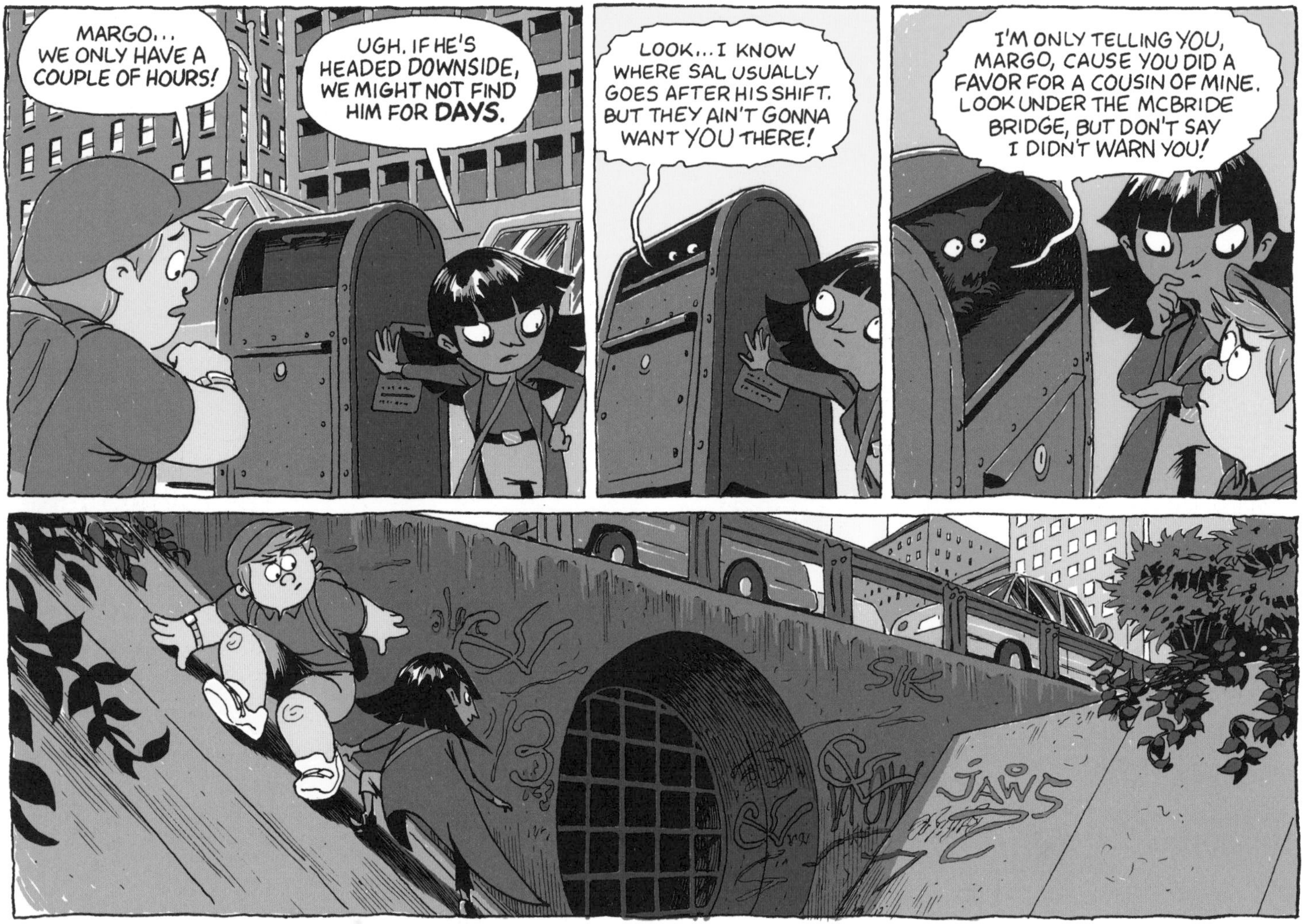
MARGO... WE ONLY HAVE A COUPLE OF HOURS!
UGH. IF HE'S HEADED DOWNSIDE, WE MIGHT NOT FIND HIM FOR DAYS.
LOOK... I KNOW WHERE SAL USUALLY GOES AFTER HIS SHIFT. BUT THEY AIN'T GONNA WANT YOU THERE!
I'M ONLY TELLING YOU, MARGO, CAUSE YOU DID A FAVOR FOR A COUSIN OF MINE. LOOK UNDER THE MCBRIDE BRIDGE, BUT DON'T SAY I DIDN'T WARN YOU!
SIK
JAWS

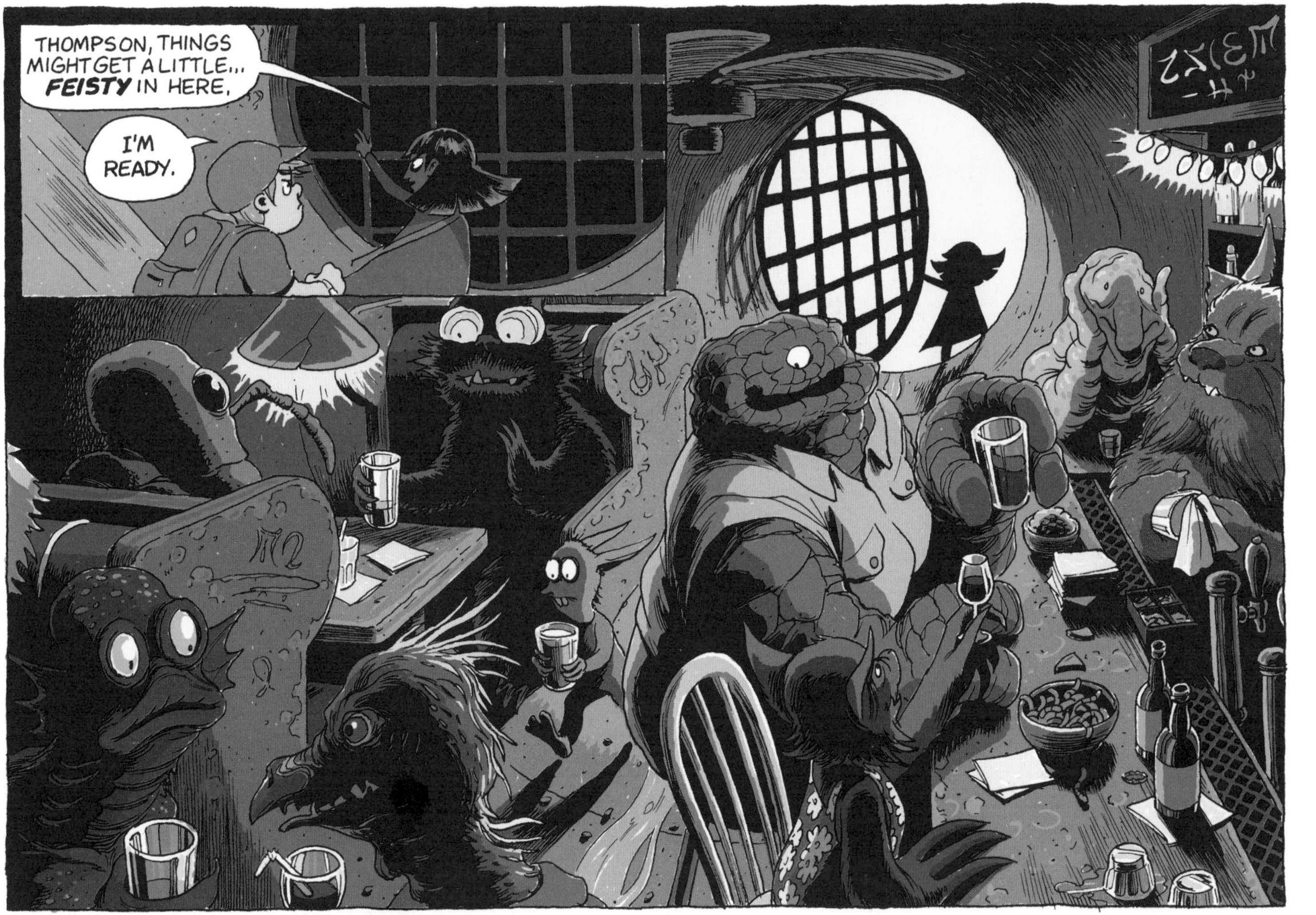
THOMPSON, THINGS MIGHT GET A LITTLE... **FEISTY** IN HERE.
I'M READY.

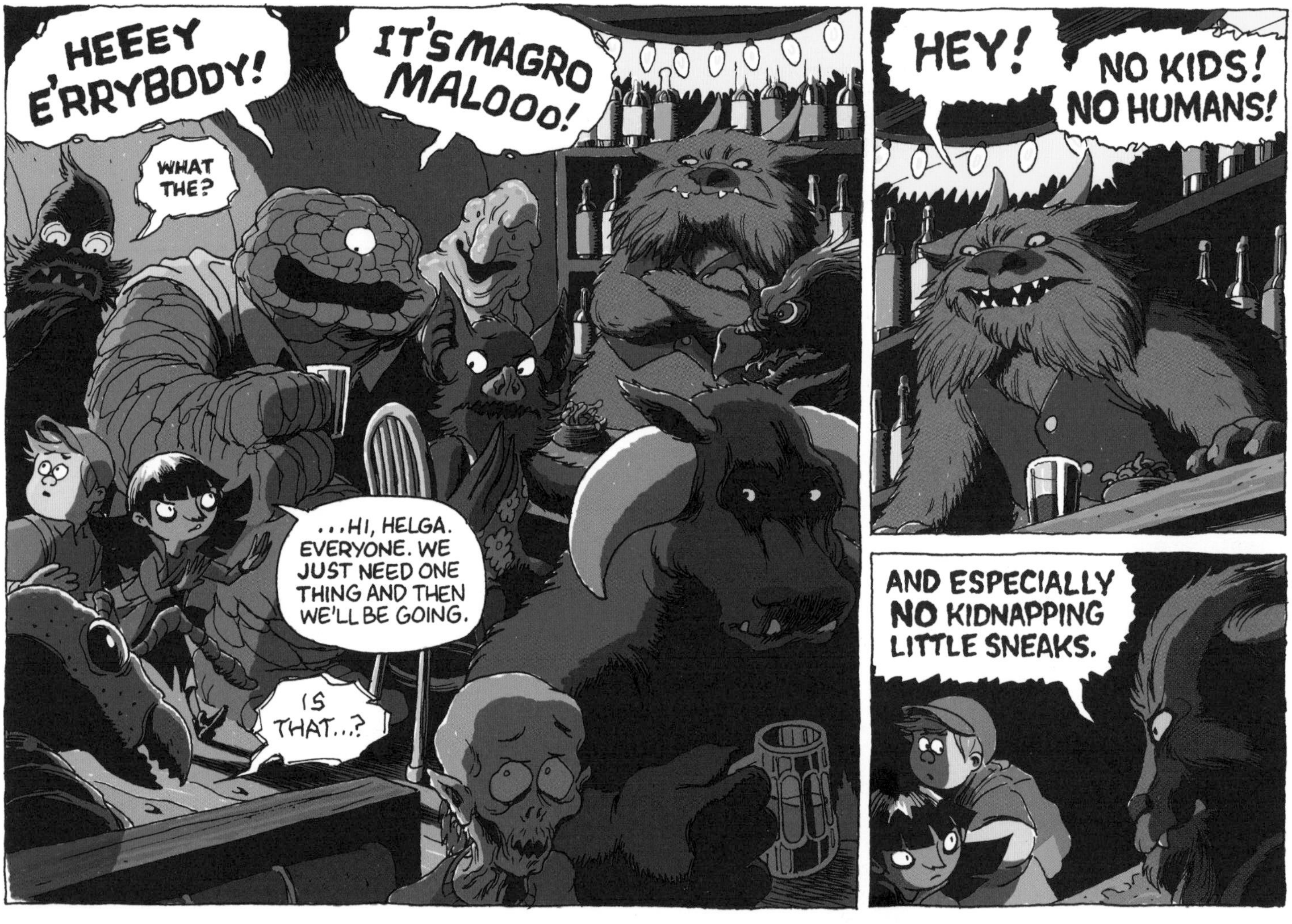
HEEEY E'RRYBODY!
IT'S MAGRO MALOOO!
WHAT THE?
...HI, HELGA. EVERYONE. WE JUST NEED ONE THING AND THEN WE'LL BE GOING.
IS THAT...?
HEY!
NO KIDS! NO HUMANS!
AND ESPECIALLY NO KIDNAPPING LITTLE SNEAKS.

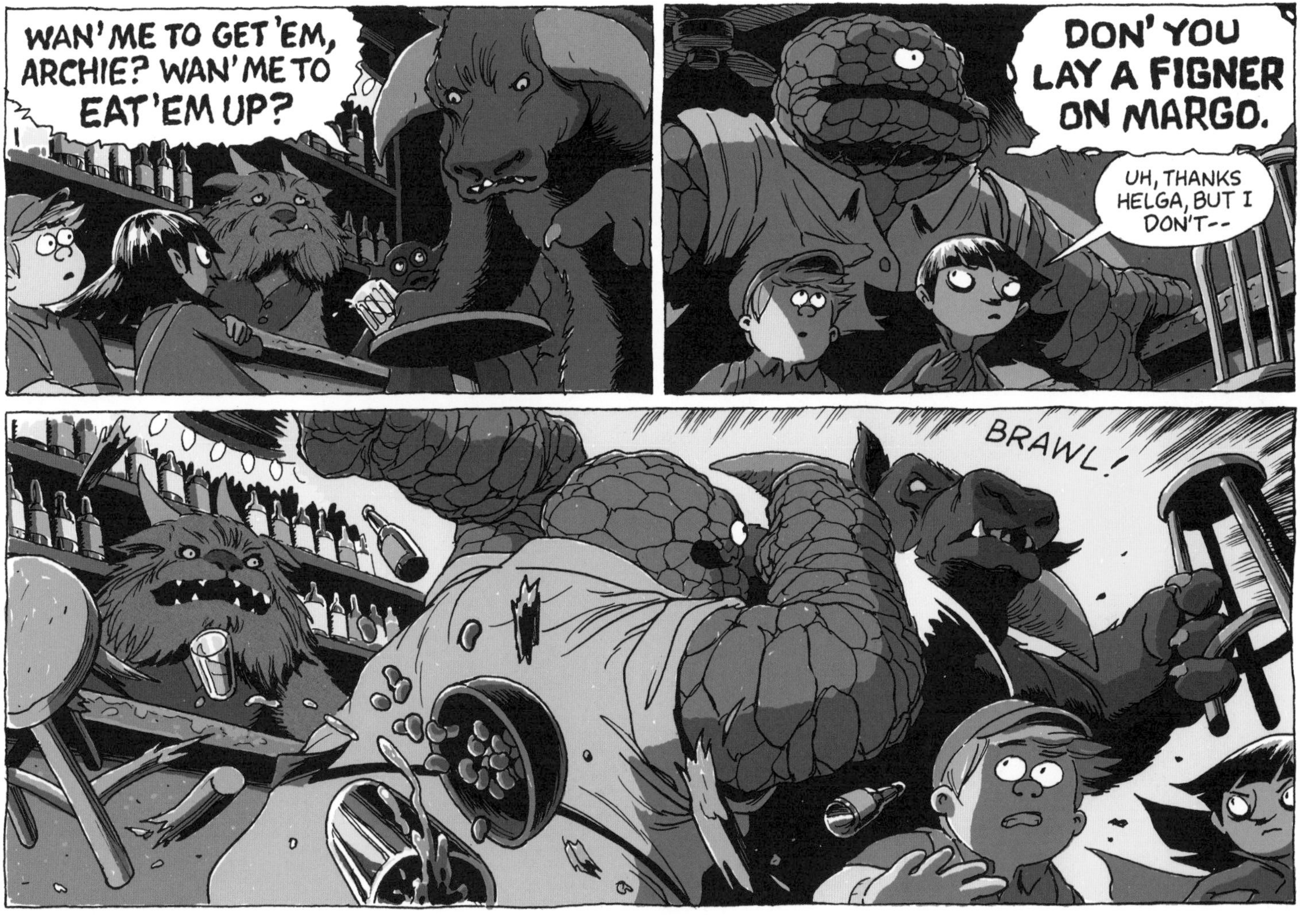
WAN' ME TO GET 'EM, ARCHIE? WAN' ME TO EAT 'EM UP?
DON' YOU LAY A FIGNER ON MARGO.
UH, THANKS HELGA, BUT I DON'T--
BRAWL!

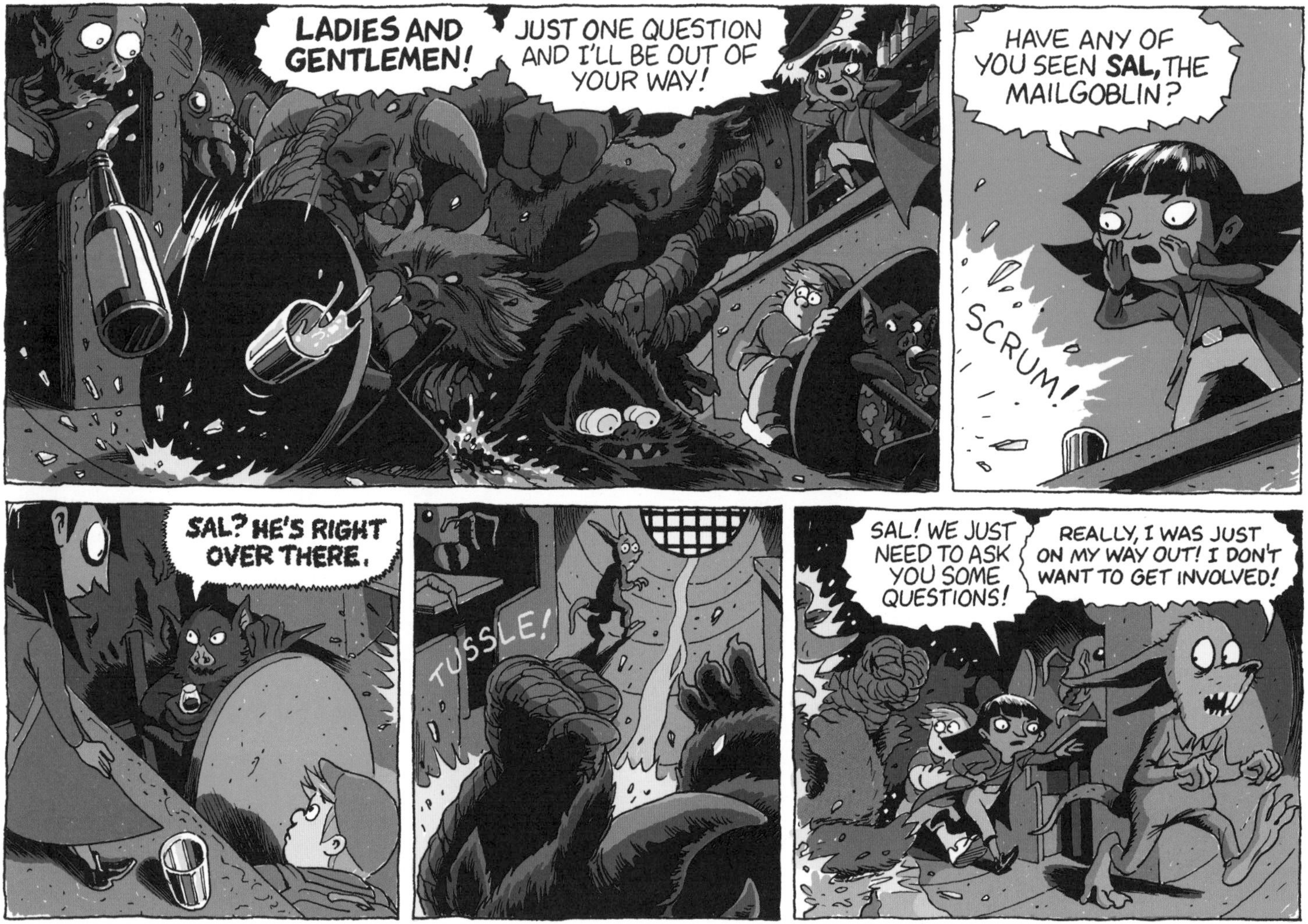
LADIES AND GENTLEMEN!
JUST ONE QUESTION AND I'LL BE OUT OF YOUR WAY!
HAVE ANY OF YOU SEEN SAL, THE MAILGOBLIN?
SCRUM!
SAL? HE'S RIGHT OVER THERE.
TUSSLE!
SAL! WE JUST NEED TO ASK YOU SOME QUESTIONS!
REALLY, I WAS JUST ON MY WAY OUT! I DON'T WANT TO GET INVOLVED!

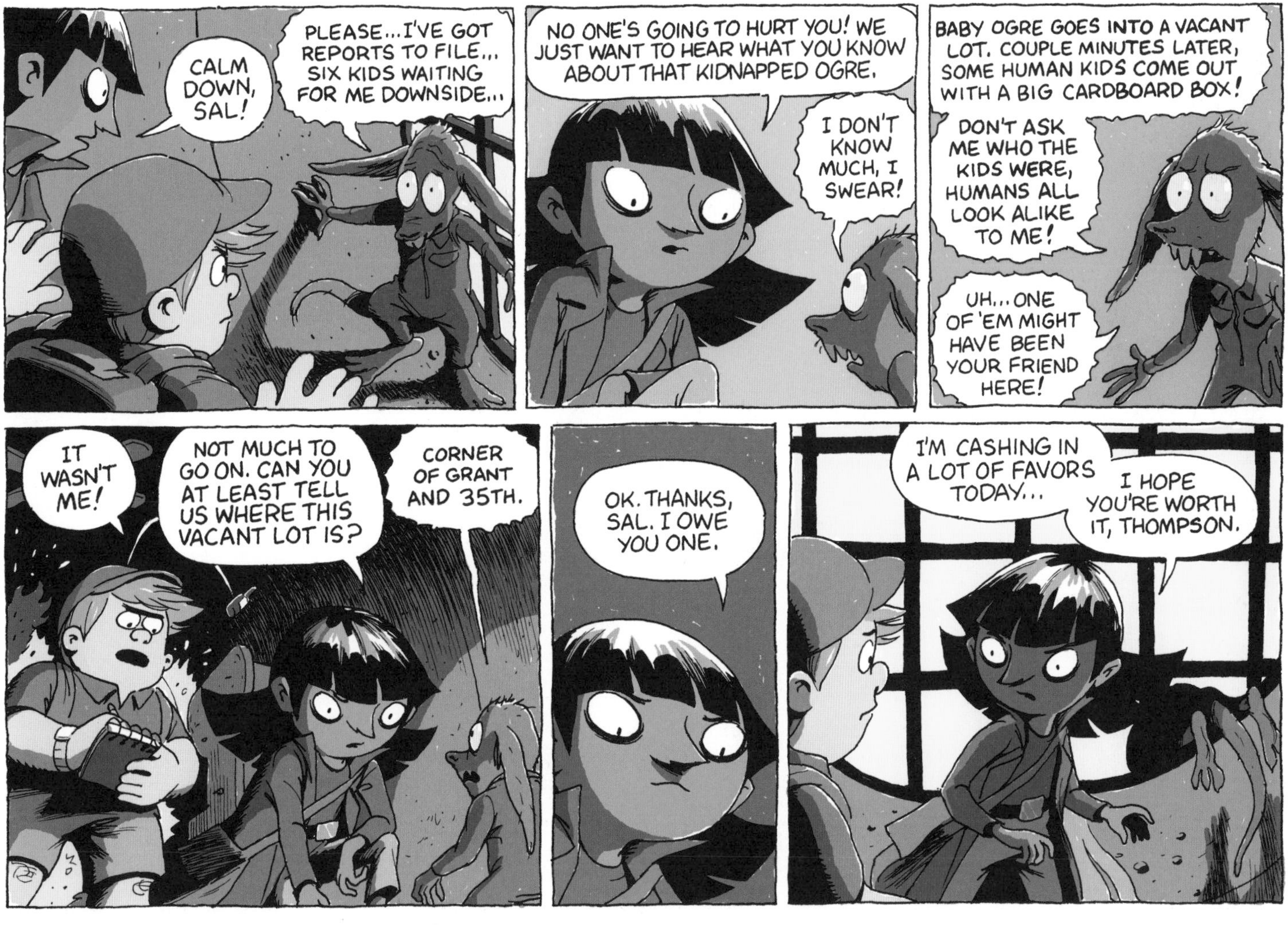

CALM DOWN, SAL!
PLEASE... I'VE GOT REPORTS TO FILE... SIX KIDS WAITING FOR ME DOWNSIDE...
NO ONE'S GOING TO HURT YOU! WE JUST WANT TO HEAR WHAT YOU KNOW ABOUT THAT KIDNAPPED OGRE.
I DON'T KNOW MUCH, I SWEAR!
BABY OGRE GOES INTO A VACANT LOT. COUPLE MINUTES LATER, SOME HUMAN KIDS COME OUT WITH A BIG CARDBOARD BOX!
DON'T ASK ME WHO THE KIDS WERE, HUMANS ALL LOOK ALIKE TO ME!
UH... ONE OF 'EM MIGHT HAVE BEEN YOUR FRIEND HERE!
IT WASN'T ME!
NOT MUCH TO GO ON. CAN YOU AT LEAST TELL US WHERE THIS VACANT LOT IS?
CORNER OF GRANT AND 35TH.
OK. THANKS, SAL. I OWE YOU ONE.
I'M CASHING IN A LOT OF FAVORS TODAY...
I HOPE YOU'RE WORTH IT, THOMPSON.

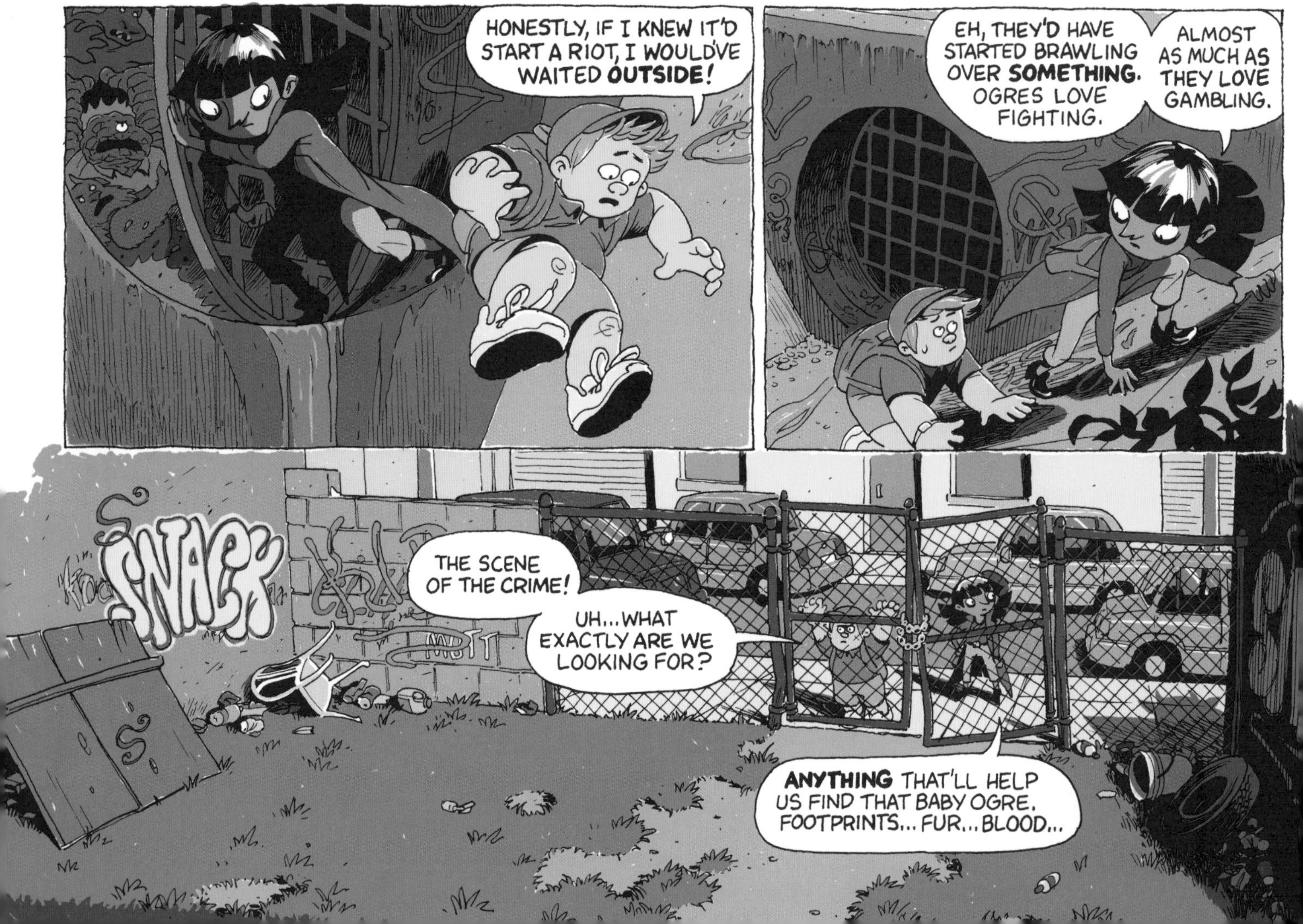
HONESTLY, IF I KNEW IT'D START A RIOT, I WOULD'VE WAITED **OUTSIDE**!
EH, THEY'D HAVE STARTED BRAWLING OVER **SOMETHING**. OGRES LOVE FIGHTING.
ALMOST AS MUCH AS THEY LOVE GAMBLING.
THE SCENE OF THE CRIME!
UH... WHAT EXACTLY ARE WE LOOKING FOR?
ANYTHING THAT'LL HELP US FIND THAT BABY OGRE. FOOTPRINTS... FUR... BLOOD...

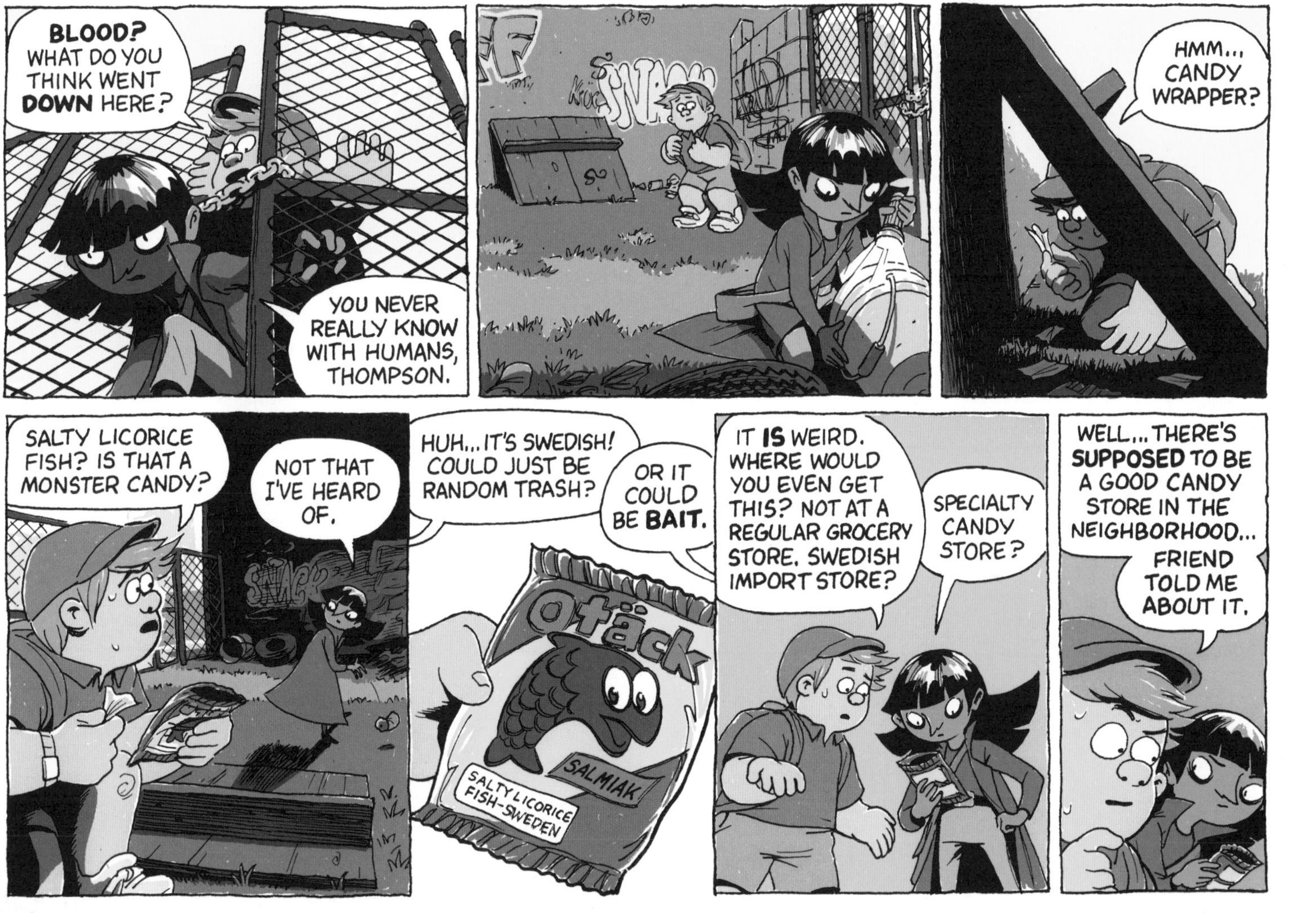

BLOOD? WHAT DO YOU THINK WENT **DOWN** HERE?
YOU NEVER REALLY KNOW WITH HUMANS, THOMPSON.
HMM... CANDY WRAPPER?
SALTY LICORICE FISH? IS THAT A MONSTER CANDY?
NOT THAT I'VE HEARD OF.
HUH... IT'S SWEDISH! COULD JUST BE RANDOM TRASH?
OR IT COULD BE **BAIT.**
Otäck
SALMIAK
SALTY LICORICE FISH-SWEDEN
IT **IS** WEIRD. WHERE WOULD YOU EVEN GET THIS? NOT AT A REGULAR GROCERY STORE. SWEDISH IMPORT STORE?
SPECIALTY CANDY STORE?
WELL... THERE'S **SUPPOSED** TO BE A GOOD CANDY STORE IN THE NEIGHBORHOOD...
FRIEND TOLD ME ABOUT IT.

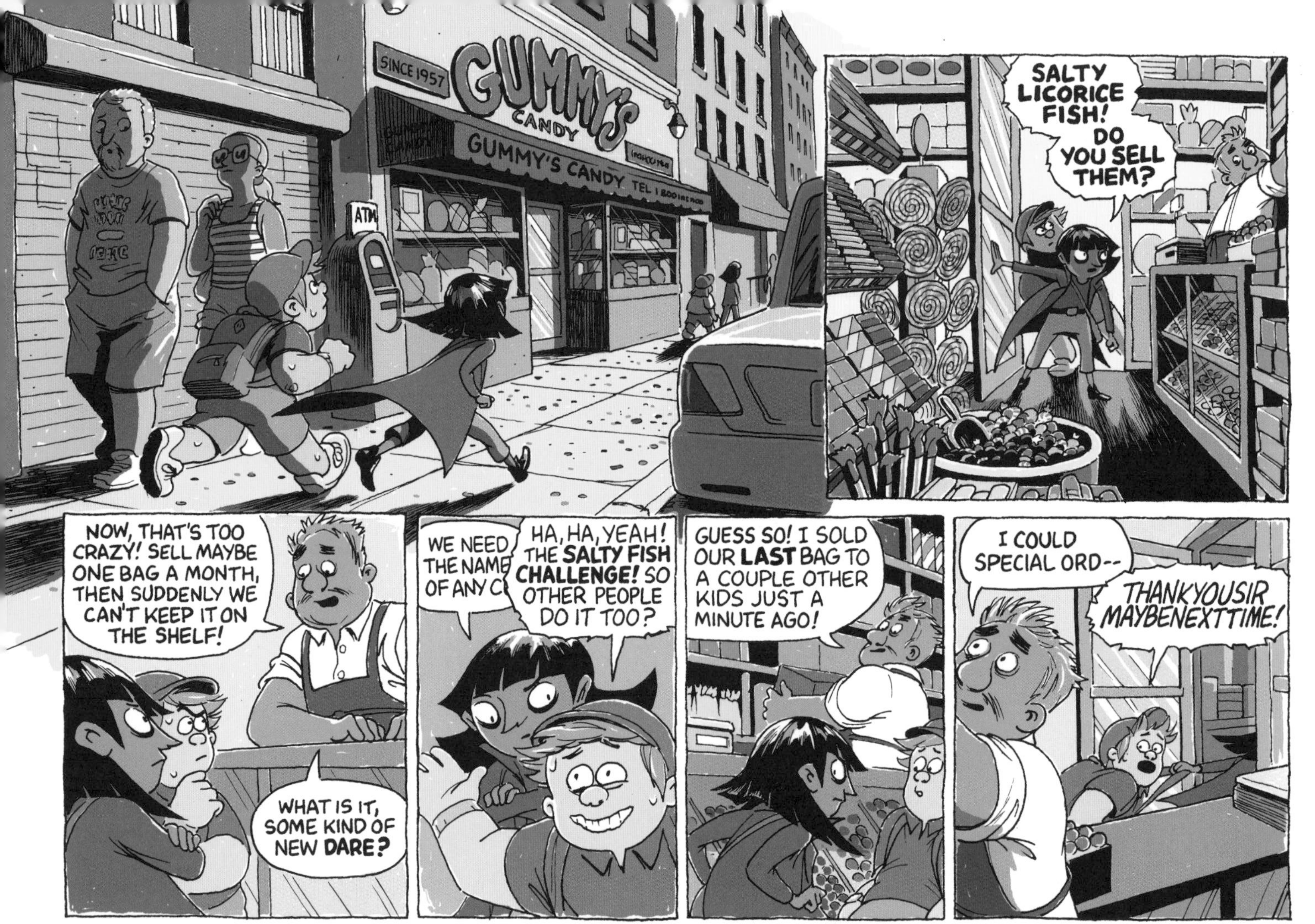
SINCE 1957
GUMMY'S CANDY
GUMMY'S CANDY TEL
ATM
SALTY LICORICE FISH! DO YOU SELL THEM?
NOW, THAT'S TOO CRAZY! SELL MAYBE ONE BAG A MONTH, THEN SUDDENLY WE CAN'T KEEP IT ON THE SHELF!
WHAT IS IT, SOME KIND OF NEW DARE?
WE NEED THE NAME OF ANY C
HA, HA, YEAH! THE SALTY FISH CHALLENGE! SO OTHER PEOPLE DO IT TOO?
GUESS SO! I SOLD OUR LAST BAG TO A COUPLE OTHER KIDS JUST A MINUTE AGO!
I COULD SPECIAL ORD--
THANKYOUSIR MAYBENEXTTIME!

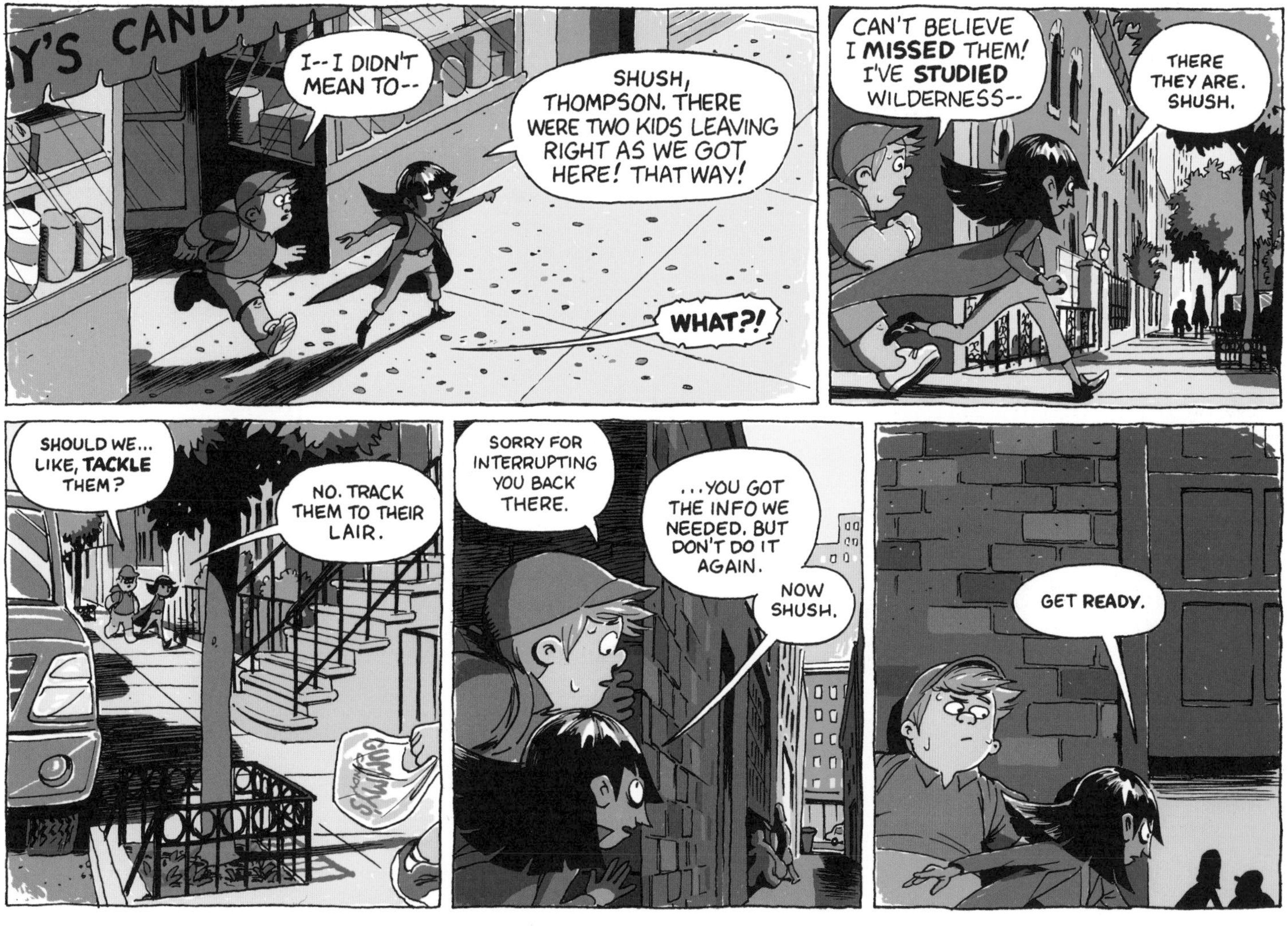

Y'S CAND
I-- I DIDN'T MEAN TO--
SHUSH, THOMPSON. THERE WERE TWO KIDS LEAVING RIGHT AS WE GOT HERE! THAT WAY!
WHAT?!
CAN'T BELIEVE I **MISSED** THEM! I'VE **STUDIED** WILDERNESS--
THERE THEY ARE. SHUSH.
SHOULD WE... LIKE, **TACKLE** THEM?
NO. TRACK THEM TO THEIR LAIR.
SORRY FOR INTERRUPTING YOU BACK THERE.
...YOU GOT THE INFO WE NEEDED. BUT DON'T DO IT AGAIN.
NOW SHUSH.
GET **READY**.

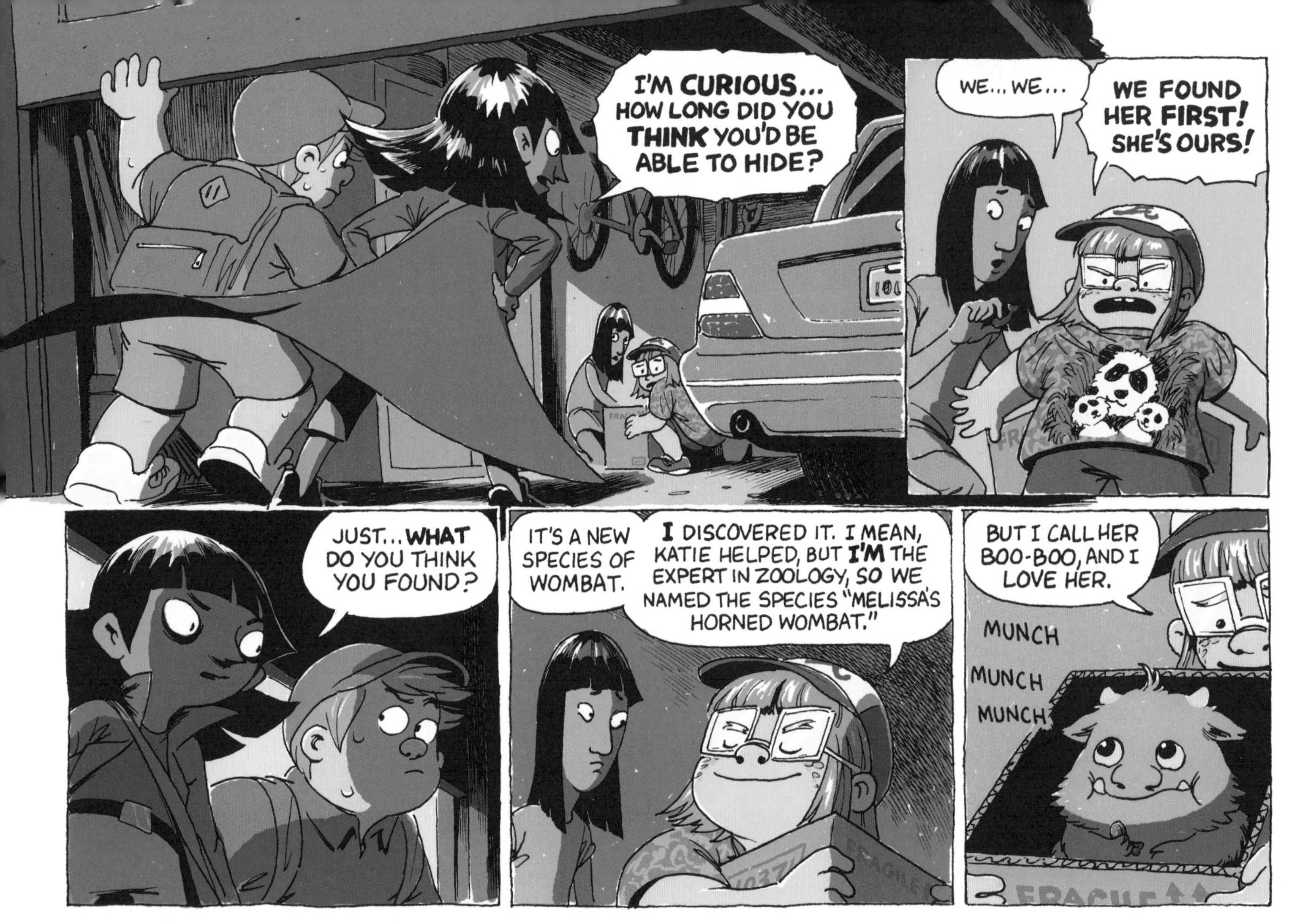
I'M CURIOUS... HOW LONG DID YOU THINK YOU'D BE ABLE TO HIDE?
WE... WE...
WE FOUND HER FIRST! SHE'S OURS!
JUST... WHAT DO YOU THINK YOU FOUND?
IT'S A NEW SPECIES OF WOMBAT.
I DISCOVERED IT. I MEAN, KATIE HELPED, BUT I'M THE EXPERT IN ZOOLOGY, SO WE NAMED THE SPECIES "MELISSA'S HORNED WOMBAT."
BUT I CALL HER BOO-BOO, AND I LOVE HER.
MUNCH
MUNCH
MUNCH

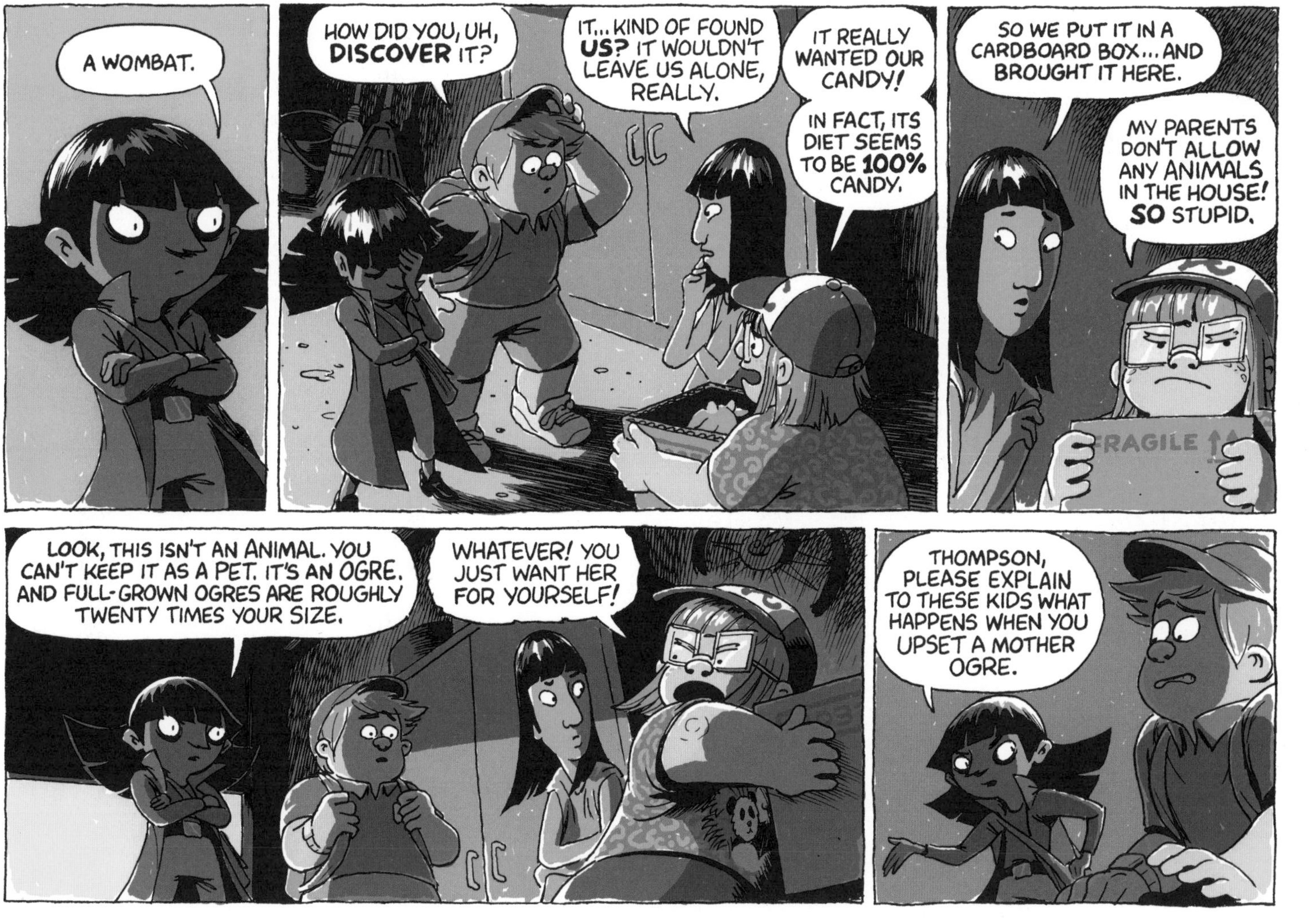
A WOMBAT.
HOW DID YOU, UH, DISCOVER IT?
IT... KIND OF FOUND US? IT WOULDN'T LEAVE US ALONE, REALLY.
IT REALLY WANTED OUR CANDY!
IN FACT, ITS DIET SEEMS TO BE 100% CANDY.
SO WE PUT IT IN A CARDBOARD BOX... AND BROUGHT IT HERE.
MY PARENTS DON'T ALLOW ANY ANIMALS IN THE HOUSE! SO STUPID.
FRAGILE
LOOK, THIS ISN'T AN ANIMAL. YOU CAN'T KEEP IT AS A PET. IT'S AN OGRE. AND FULL-GROWN OGRES ARE ROUGHLY TWENTY TIMES YOUR SIZE.
WHATEVER! YOU JUST WANT HER FOR YOURSELF!
THOMPSON, PLEASE EXPLAIN TO THESE KIDS WHAT HAPPENS WHEN YOU UPSET A MOTHER OGRE.

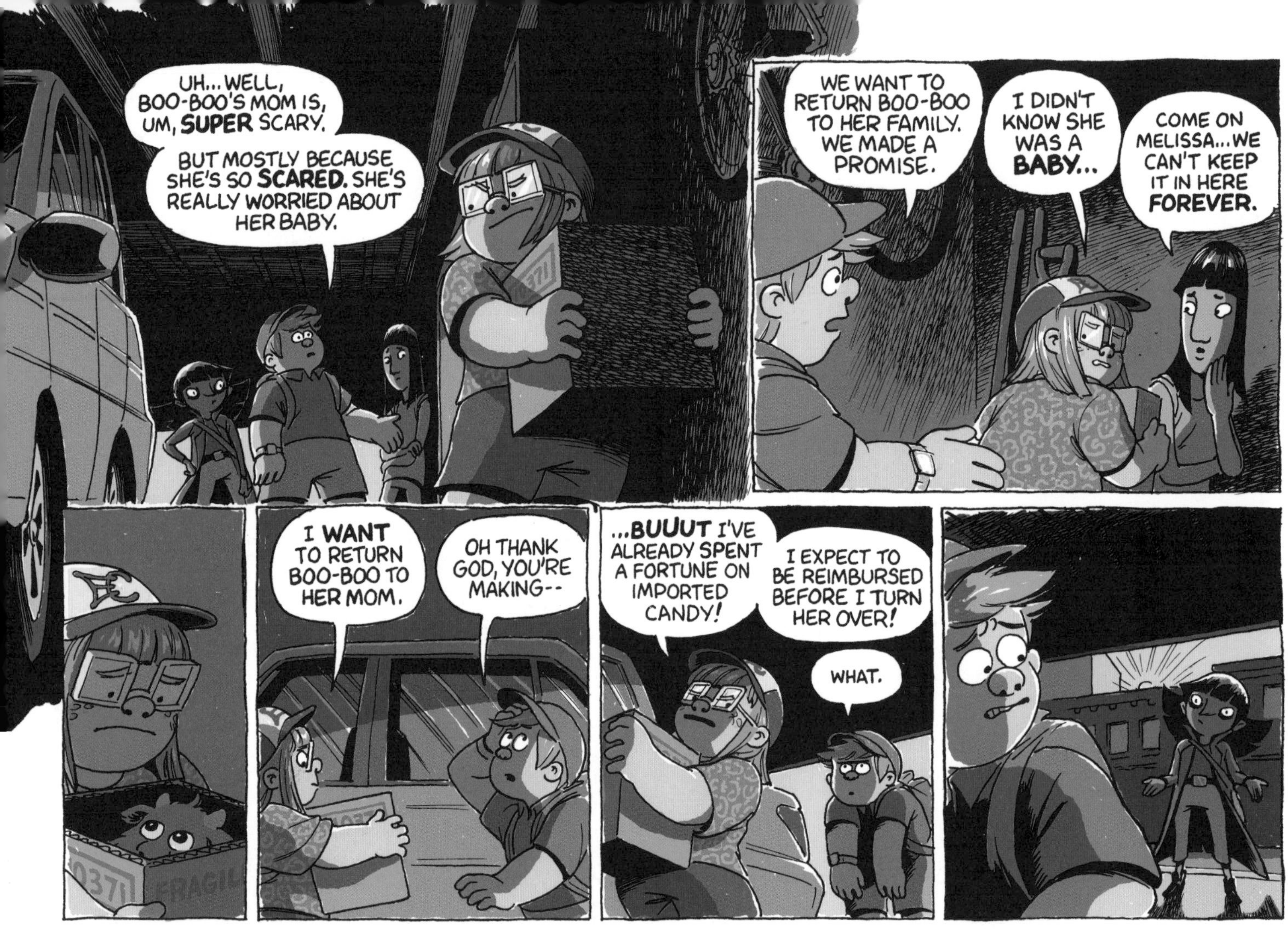
UH... WELL, BOO-BOO'S MOM IS, UM, **SUPER** SCARY.
BUT MOSTLY BECAUSE SHE'S SO **SCARED.** SHE'S REALLY WORRIED ABOUT HER BABY.
WE WANT TO RETURN BOO-BOO TO HER FAMILY. WE MADE A PROMISE.
I DIDN'T KNOW SHE WAS A **BABY...**
COME ON MELISSA... WE CAN'T KEEP IT IN HERE **FOREVER.**
0371
FRAGILE
I **WANT** TO RETURN BOO-BOO TO HER MOM.
OH THANK GOD, YOU'RE MAKING--
...**BUUUT** I'VE ALREADY SPENT A FORTUNE ON IMPORTED CANDY!
I EXPECT TO BE REIMBURSED BEFORE I TURN HER OVER!
WHAT.

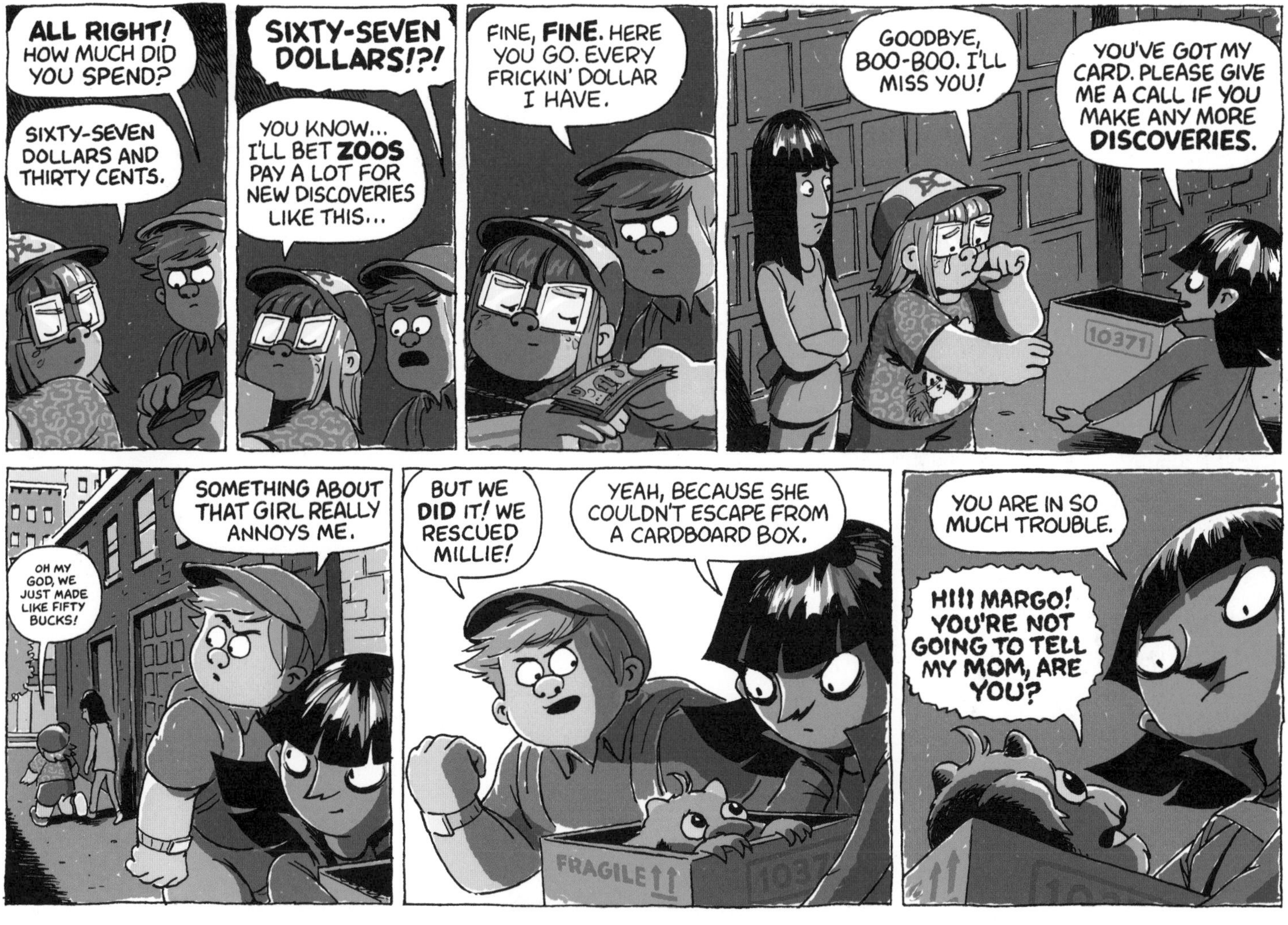
ALL RIGHT! HOW MUCH DID YOU SPEND?
SIXTY-SEVEN DOLLARS AND THIRTY CENTS.
SIXTY-SEVEN DOLLARS!?!
YOU KNOW... I'LL BET ZOOS PAY A LOT FOR NEW DISCOVERIES LIKE THIS...
FINE, FINE. HERE YOU GO. EVERY FRICKIN' DOLLAR I HAVE.
GOODBYE, BOO-BOO. I'LL MISS YOU!
YOU'VE GOT MY CARD. PLEASE GIVE ME A CALL IF YOU MAKE ANY MORE DISCOVERIES.
10371
SOMETHING ABOUT THAT GIRL REALLY ANNOYS ME.
OH MY GOD, WE JUST MADE LIKE FIFTY BUCKS!
BUT WE DID IT! WE RESCUED MILLIE!
YEAH, BECAUSE SHE COULDN'T ESCAPE FROM A CARDBOARD BOX.
FRAGILE
YOU ARE IN SO MUCH TROUBLE.
HIII MARGO! YOU'RE NOT GOING TO TELL MY MOM, ARE YOU?

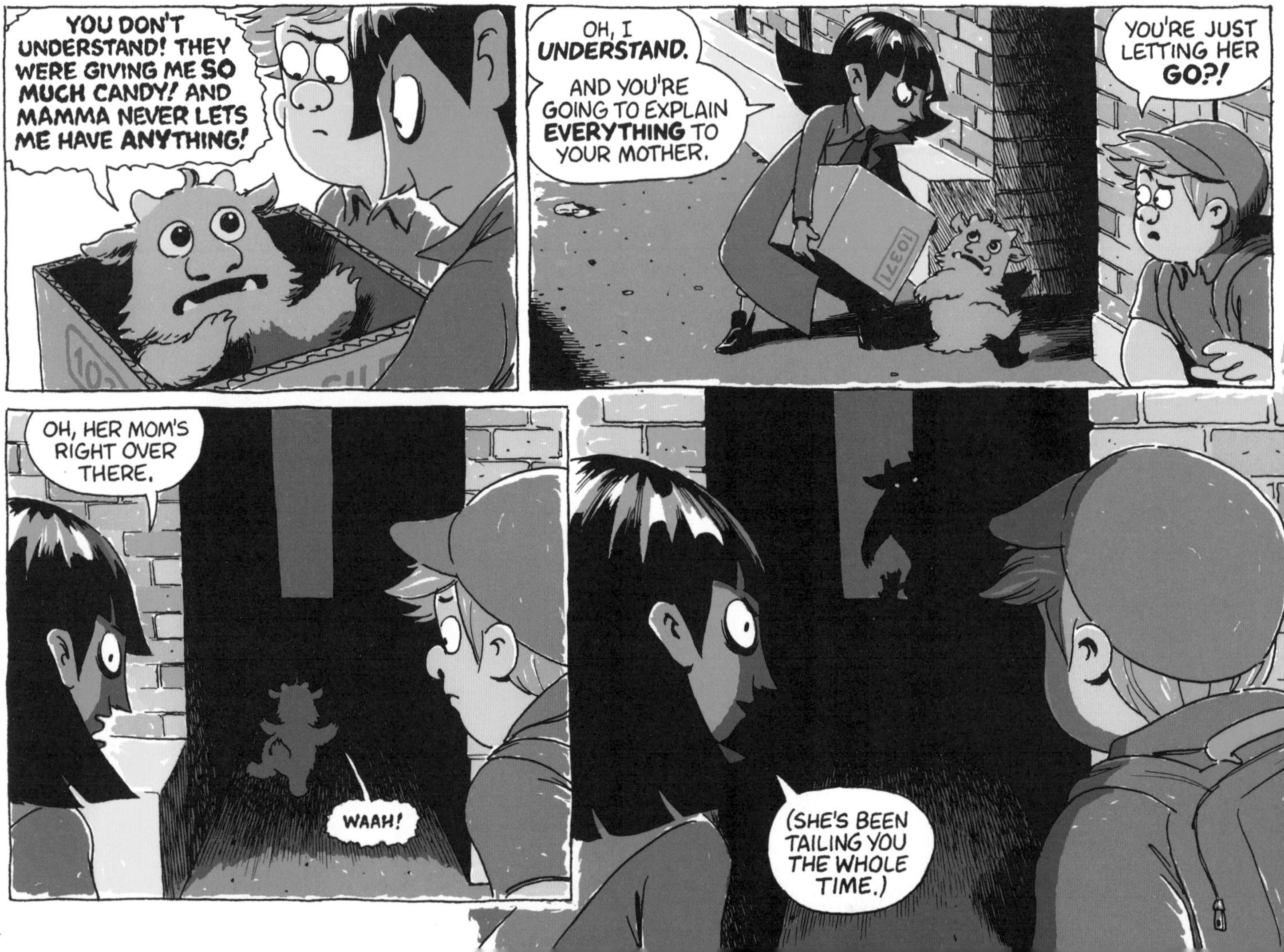
YOU DON'T UNDERSTAND! THEY WERE GIVING ME SO MUCH CANDY! AND MAMMA NEVER LETS ME HAVE ANYTHING!
OH, I UNDERSTAND.
AND YOU'RE GOING TO EXPLAIN EVERYTHING TO YOUR MOTHER.
YOU'RE JUST LETTING HER GO?!
OH, HER MOM'S RIGHT OVER THERE.
WAAH!
(SHE'S BEEN TAILING YOU THE WHOLE TIME.)

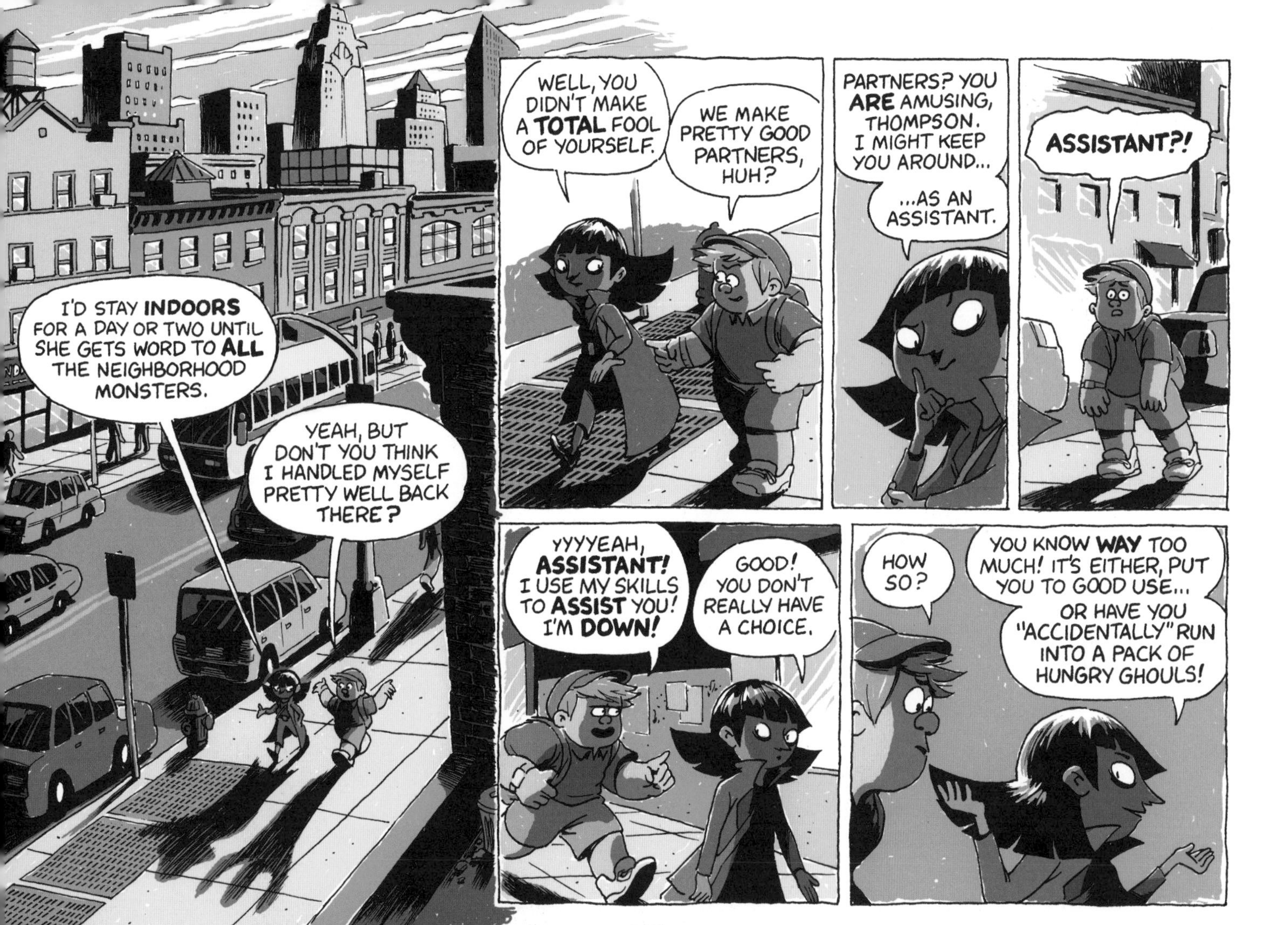

I'D STAY **INDOORS** FOR A DAY OR TWO UNTIL SHE GETS WORD TO **ALL** THE NEIGHBORHOOD MONSTERS.
YEAH, BUT DON'T YOU THINK I HANDLED MYSELF PRETTY WELL BACK THERE?
WELL, YOU DIDN'T MAKE A **TOTAL** FOOL OF YOURSELF.
WE MAKE PRETTY GOOD PARTNERS, HUH?
PARTNERS? YOU **ARE** AMUSING, THOMPSON. I MIGHT KEEP YOU AROUND...
...AS AN ASSISTANT.
ASSISTANT?!
YYYYEAH, **ASSISTANT!** I USE MY SKILLS TO **ASSIST** YOU! I'M **DOWN!**
GOOD! YOU DON'T REALLY HAVE A CHOICE.
HOW SO?
YOU KNOW **WAY** TOO MUCH! IT'S EITHER, PUT YOU TO GOOD USE...
OR HAVE YOU "ACCIDENTALLY" RUN INTO A PACK OF HUNGRY GHOULS!

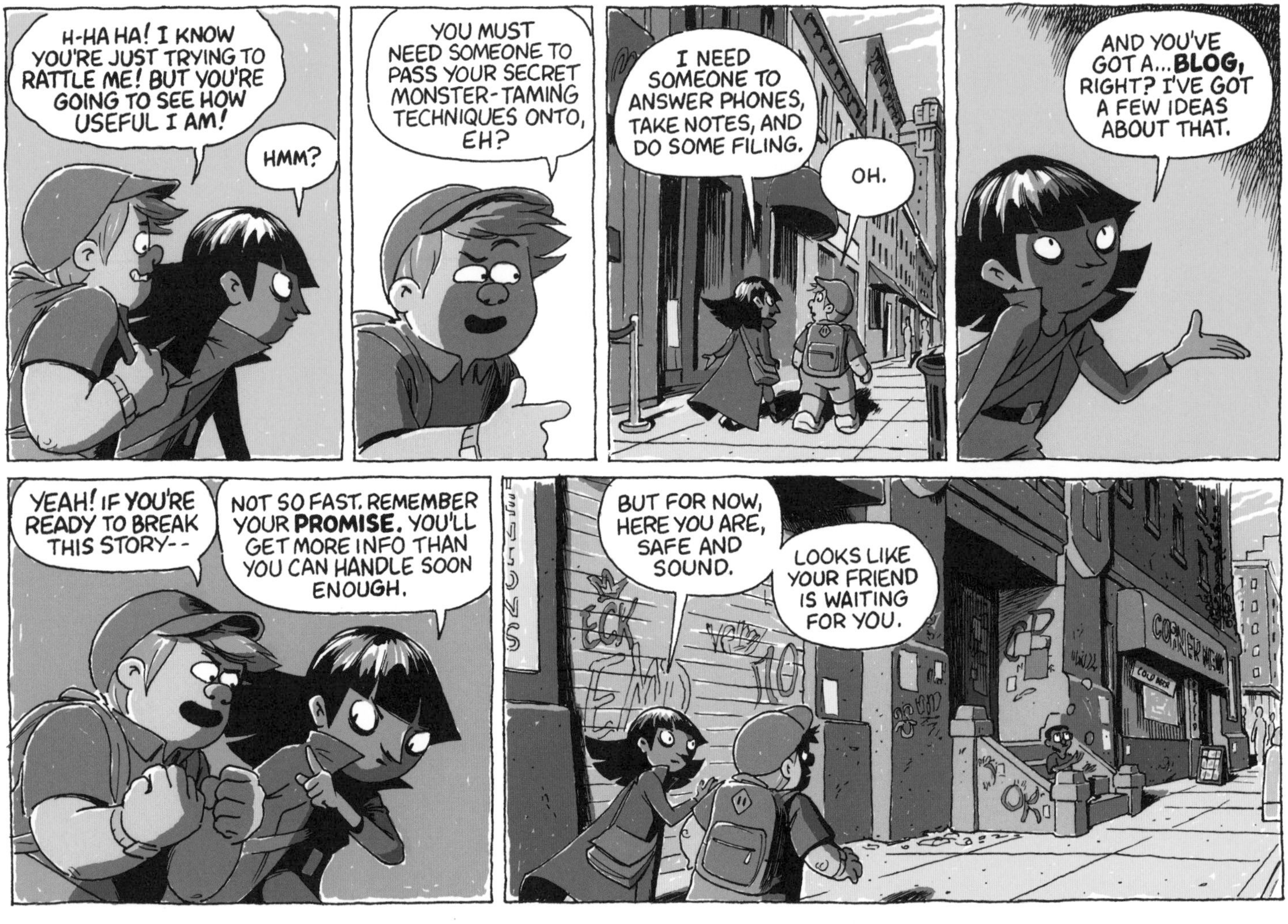
H-HA HA! I KNOW YOU'RE JUST TRYING TO RATTLE ME! BUT YOU'RE GOING TO SEE HOW USEFUL I AM!
HMM?
YOU MUST NEED SOMEONE TO PASS YOUR SECRET MONSTER-TAMING TECHNIQUES ONTO, EH?
I NEED SOMEONE TO ANSWER PHONES, TAKE NOTES, AND DO SOME FILING.
OH.
AND YOU'VE GOT A...**BLOG,** RIGHT? I'VE GOT A FEW IDEAS ABOUT THAT.
YEAH! IF **YOU'RE** READY TO BREAK THIS STORY--
NOT SO FAST. REMEMBER YOUR **PROMISE.** YOU'LL GET MORE INFO THAN YOU CAN HANDLE SOON ENOUGH.
BUT FOR NOW, HERE YOU ARE, SAFE AND SOUND.
LOOKS LIKE YOUR FRIEND IS WAITING FOR YOU.
COLD BEER

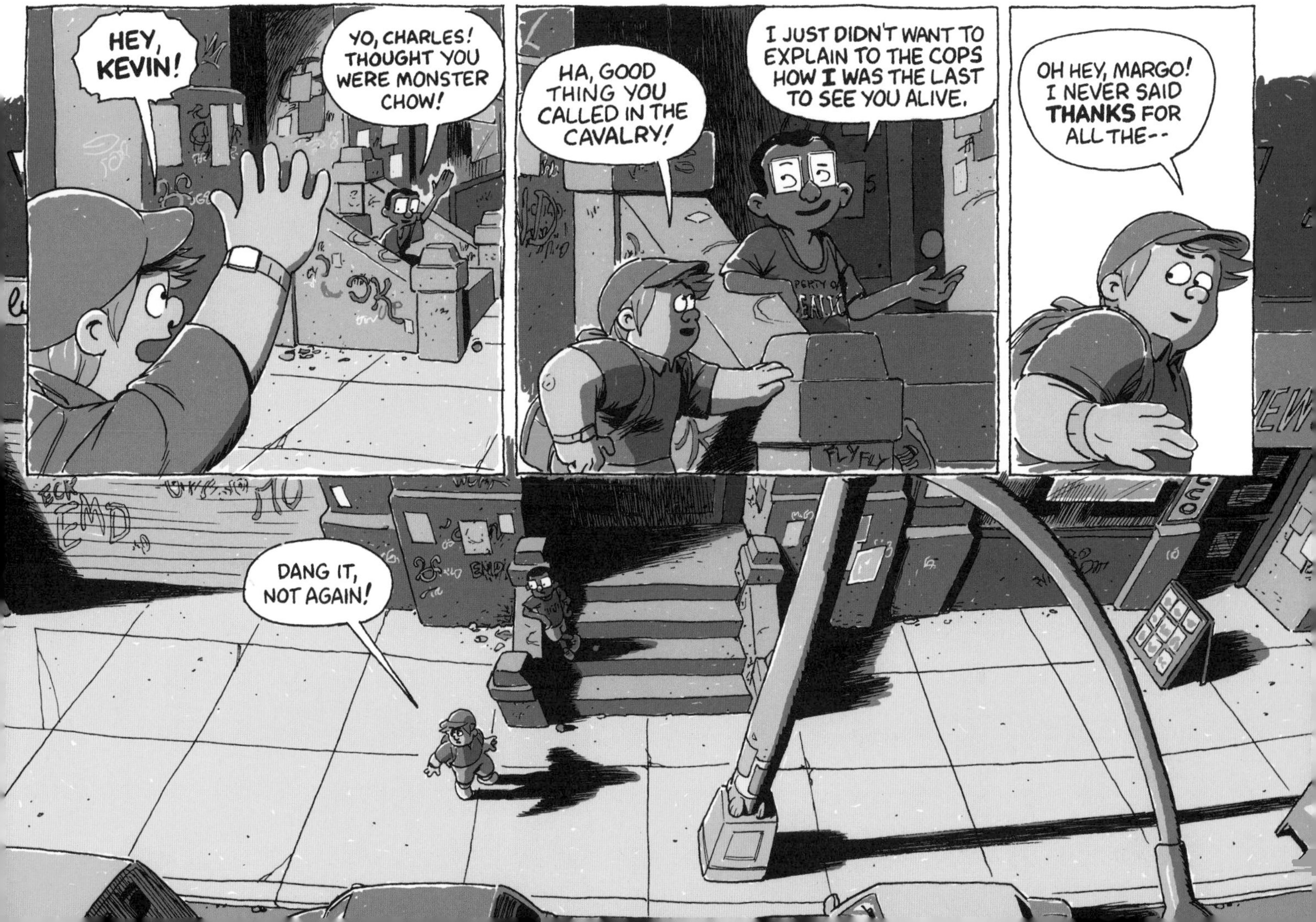
HEY, KEVIN!
YO, CHARLES! THOUGHT YOU WERE MONSTER CHOW!
HA, GOOD THING YOU CALLED IN THE CAVALRY!
I JUST DIDN'T WANT TO EXPLAIN TO THE COPS HOW I WAS THE LAST TO SEE YOU ALIVE.
OH HEY, MARGO! I NEVER SAID THANKS FOR ALL THE--
DANG IT, NOT AGAIN!

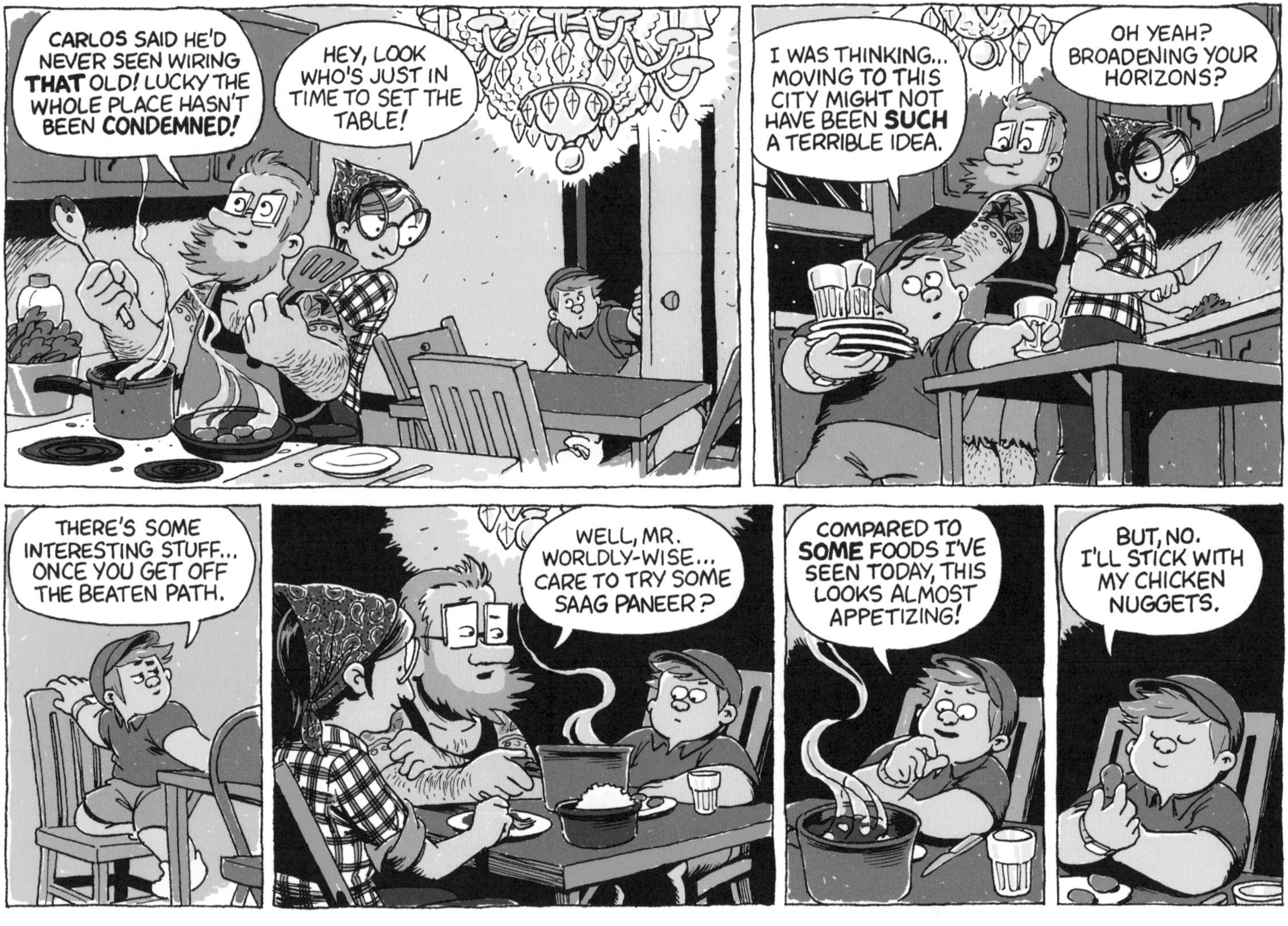
CARLOS SAID HE'D NEVER SEEN WIRING THAT OLD! LUCKY THE WHOLE PLACE HASN'T BEEN CONDEMNED!
HEY, LOOK WHO'S JUST IN TIME TO SET THE TABLE!
I WAS THINKING... MOVING TO THIS CITY MIGHT NOT HAVE BEEN SUCH A TERRIBLE IDEA.
OH YEAH? BROADENING YOUR HORIZONS?
THERE'S SOME INTERESTING STUFF... ONCE YOU GET OFF THE BEATEN PATH.
WELL, MR. WORLDLY-WISE... CARE TO TRY SOME SAAG PANEER?
COMPARED TO SOME FOODS I'VE SEEN TODAY, THIS LOOKS ALMOST APPETIZING!
BUT, NO. I'LL STICK WITH MY CHICKEN NUGGETS.

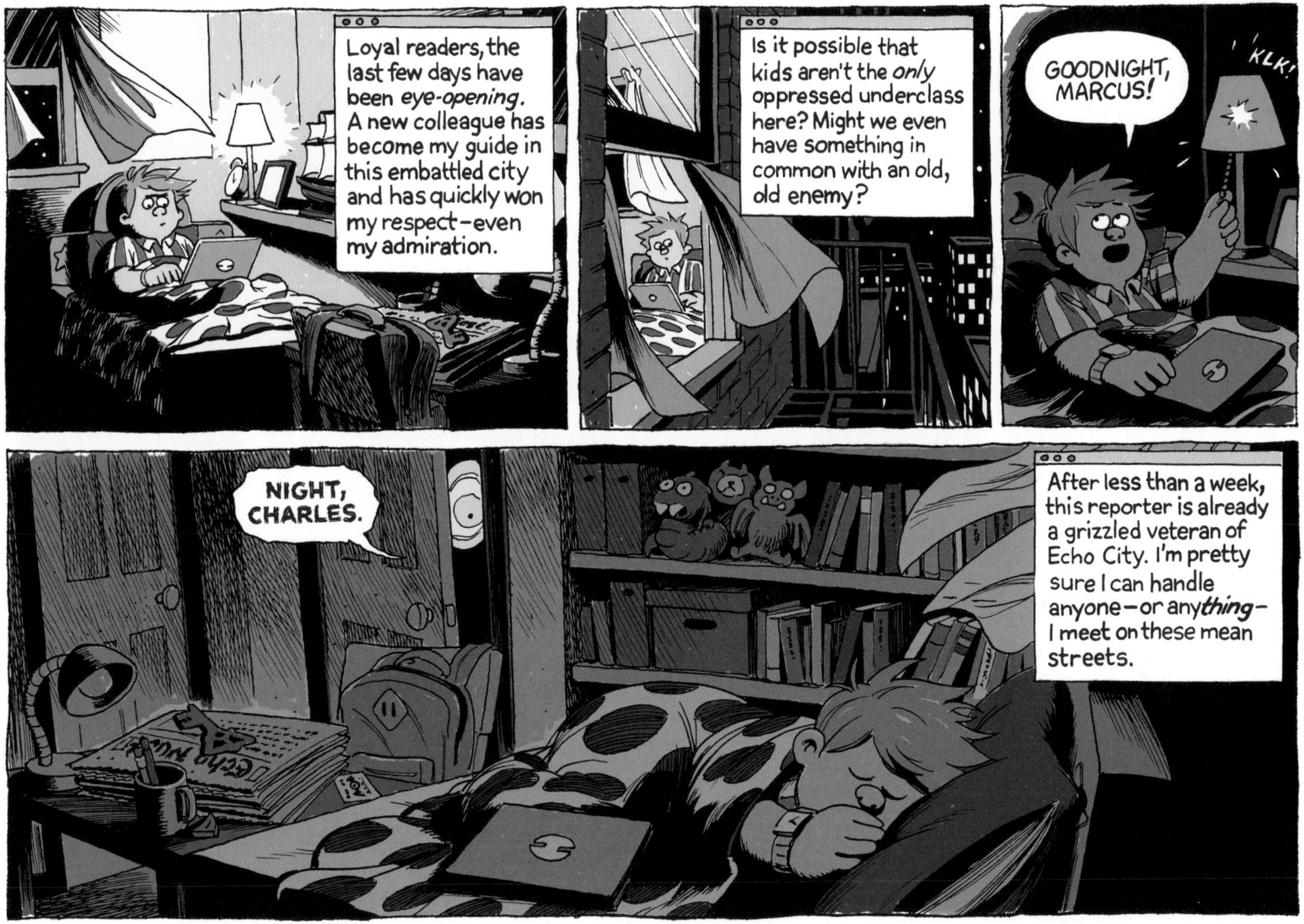
Loyal readers, the last few days have been *eye-opening*. A new colleague has become my guide in this embattled city and has quickly won my respect—even my admiration.
Is it possible that kids aren't the *only* oppressed underclass here? Might we even have something in common with an old, old enemy?
GOODNIGHT, MARCUS!
KLK!
NIGHT, CHARLES.
After less than a week, this reporter is already a grizzled veteran of Echo City. I'm pretty sure I can handle anyone—or any*thing*—I meet on these mean streets.

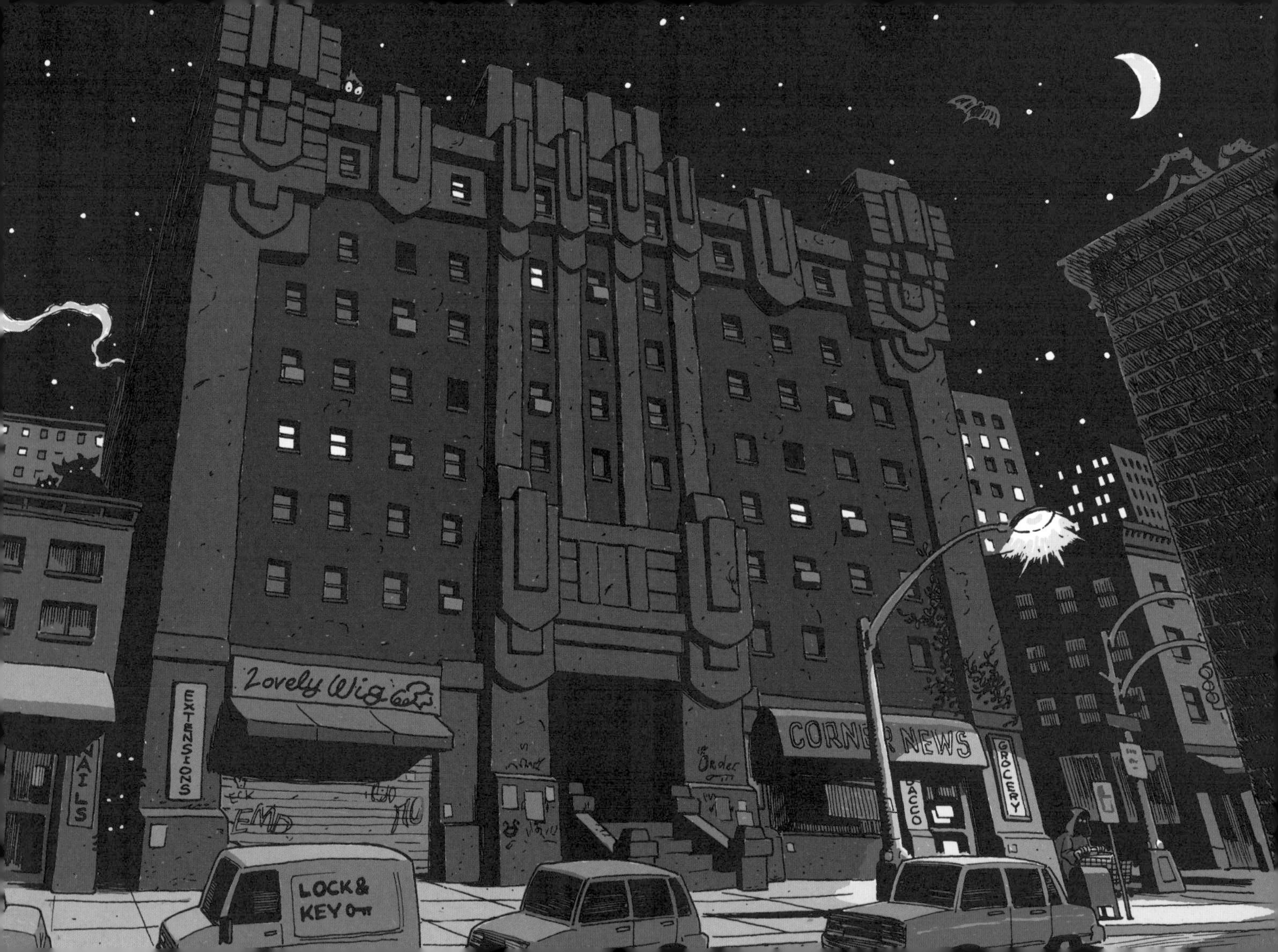
Lovely Wig
EXTENSIONS
NAILS
CORNER NEWS
GROCERY
LOCK &
KEY

Infinite, boundless, unspeakable, *unthinkable* amounts of love and gratitude to my wife Eleanor Davis—who co-created Margo in the first place, and then helped make this thing happen at every step along the way. Thanks to all the patrons who helped support me as I made this book, and to my friends for sticking around in the meanwhile. Oh, and thanks to my family, who for some reason thought it was actually a good idea for me go to comic book school so many years ago. Finally, thanks to Danielle, Robyn, Calista, Gina, and Mark at First Second for their infinite patience for my persnicketiness.

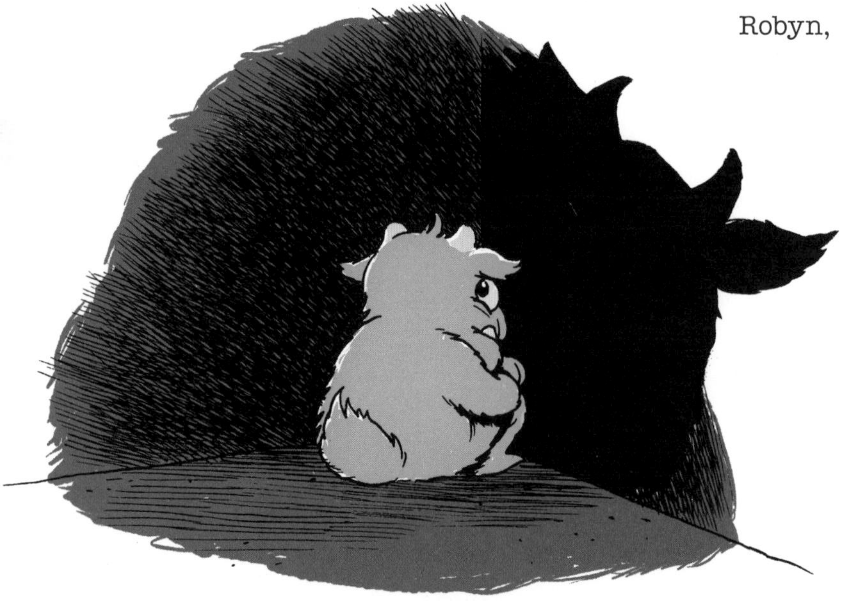

Ghosts

Ghosts (Lemures phasmatis) are a fairly rare, vaporous, nearly intangible species of monster, often mistaken as a spirit of the restless dead.

Appearance: Ghosts are cloudy, with a pillowy body and a long tendril-like tail, but their exact appearance and size is always shifting. They often emit a soft glow. Little is known about the specifics of ghost biology, but they seem to be composed of gas and are extremely cold to the touch. Ghosts are so vaporous that they can easily slip through the tiny cracks in most walls.

Behaviour: Ghosts are extremely solitary, and don't seem to have any sort of societal structure. Ghosts tend to become attached to specific places, and can become quite protective, attempting to scare off all intruders. Little can touch them or harm them. The limits of a ghost's lifespan are unknown, and many have been around for centuries.

Diet: They seem to utilise some sort of photosynthesis. They need very little sunlight to survive, and may actually find too much sunlight ~~xxxxxxxx~~ harmful, as they tend to habituate dark places.

Danger Level: **Guarded**
Ghosts are quite terrifying in appearance and their touch is unpleasantly cold, but it's yet to be determined whether ghosts pose any physical threat. Hmm...

A human encountering a ghost is more at risk of injuring themself trying to escape, than from the ghost!

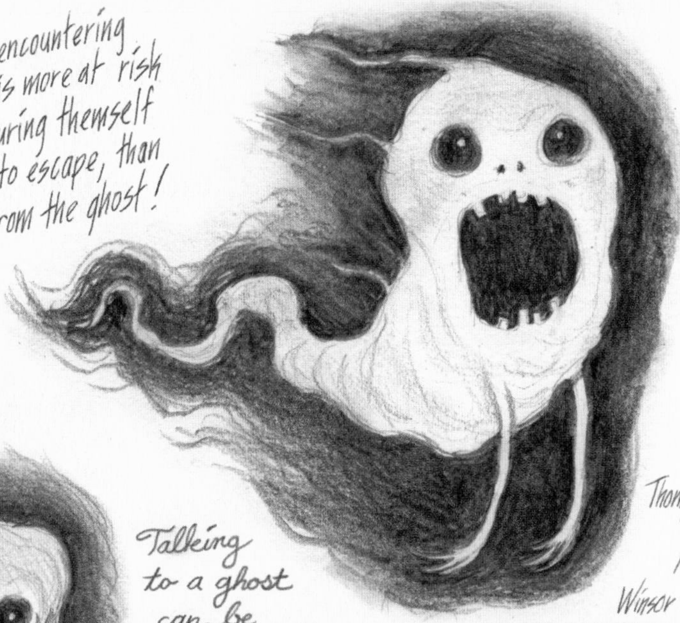

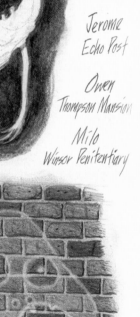

Jerome
Echo Post

Owen
Thompson Mansion

Milo
Winsor Penitentiary

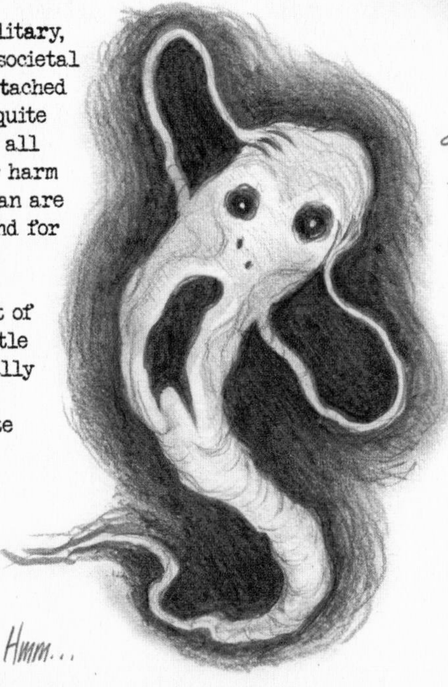

Talking to a ghost can be frustrating
Especially the old ones!

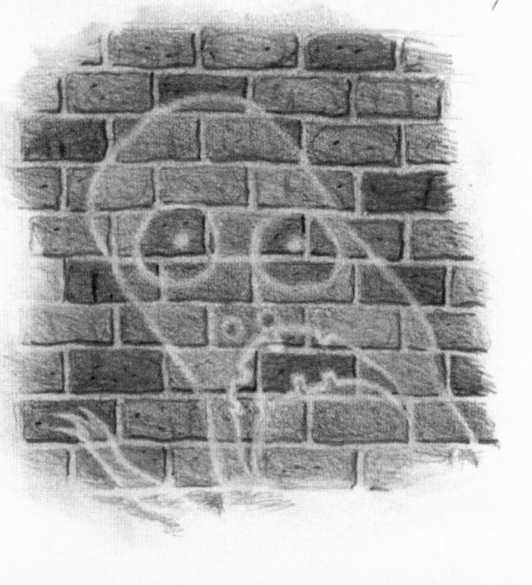

When they choose, ghosts can fade to invisibility
Almost!

Goblins 2/7

Goblins (Gobelinus Murine) are small, ratty, nervous monsters that are one of the most likely to be encountered in Echo City.

Appearance: Goblins typically have pointed noses, large crooked teeth, long prehensile tails, and are covered with sparse hair. They range in colour from a drab greyish blue to greyish brown. They tend to wear xxxxx dungarees, boiler suits, or other work uniforms. Adult goblins are usually only 1.5 to 2 feet tall, and weigh 10 - 20 lbs.

Behaviour: Goblins are very bureaucracy-minded, and goblin society is a convoluted network of communal warrens. It seems nearly all goblins are members of multiple unions, and sit on several committees. Goblins seem to fill many of the menial jobs of monster society - delivering letters, repairing electricity and plumbing. The goblin leader (job title: Chief Administrator) is elected by a complicated system of nominating committees.

Taken for granted by other monsters!

Diet: Goblins are omnivorous, and especially love insect-based foods.

Danger Level: Low
Goblins seek to avoid humans at all costs, though they can deliver a nasty bite if cornered.

Who woudn't?

3:30pm
12th & Reynolds

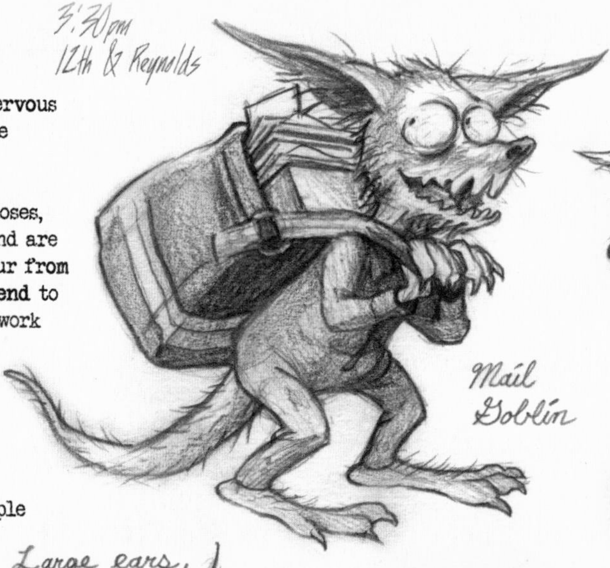
Mail Goblin

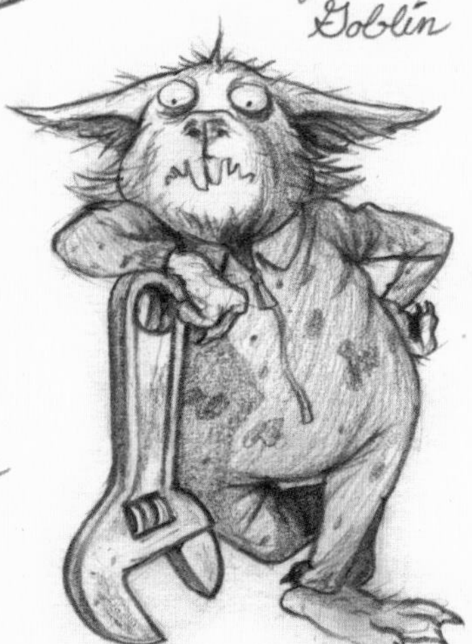
Repair Goblin

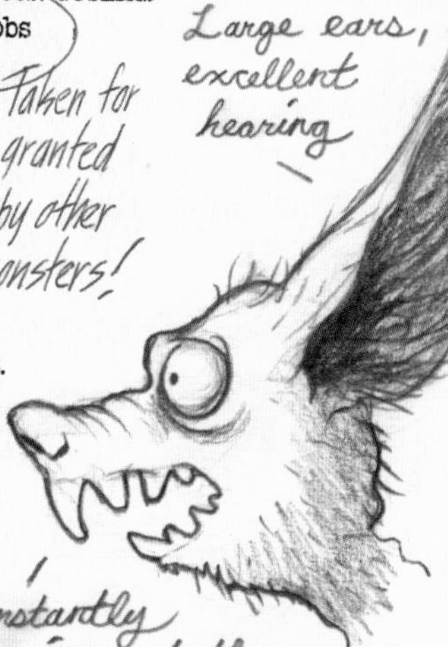
Large ears, excellent hearing
Constantly growing teeth

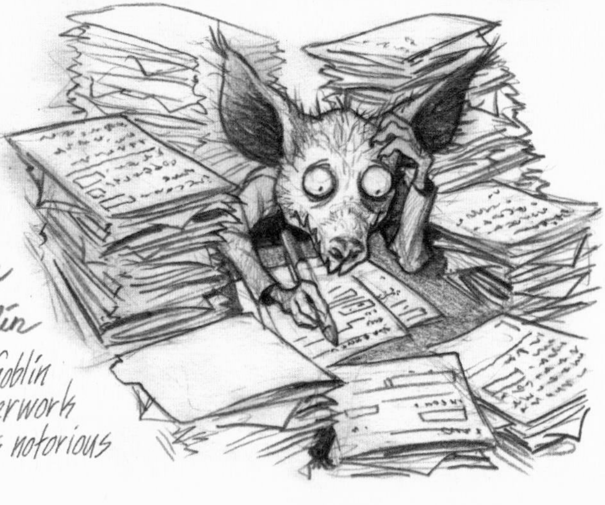
Office Goblin
Goblin paperwork is notorious

Ogres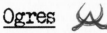

Ogres (Orcus Magnum) are a large species of monster, known for having a good-natured if somewhat aggressive demeanour, but not too well known for intelligence. *Depends on the ogre!*

Earl owes me: 76¢
Gertrude owes me: 102¢

Ogres come in many shapes & sizes

Appearance: Ogres are furry, with powerful arms, undersized legs, and horned animal-like heads with beady, orange eyes. Ogres' fur comes in many bright colours. Full-grown ogres tend to be **6 - 12** feet tall, and weigh from **400 - 900** lbs. Females are usually even larger than males.

Behaviour: Ogres live in dens of 10 - 20 adults and young. Ogres are very athletic and physical, and even adults engage in wrestling and **roughhousing**. They love games and feats of strength, and placing bets on the outcomes. Ogre society seems to be largely tied together through a complex system of **gambling debts**. *Pit Boss*

Diet: Ogres are omnivorous, and generally have large appetites. They especially love sweets, and an easy way to win favour with an ogre is to give them candy.

Danger Level: High
Even in a good mood, an ogre can underestimate their strength, to unfortunate ends. But an angry ogre is **terribly dangerous**. They are especially protective of their young.

Of course! Never get between an ogre and their baby!

Eyes blaze bright orange when angry or afraid!

The larger the horns, the older the ogre

Trolls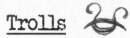

Trolls (Congero lucubro) are a nocturnal, mostly subterranean species of monster, known for their hoards.

Appearance: Trolls are large and shaggy, with fur colour ranging from dark blue to dark green. Their size varies from 4-9 feet tall, 400 - 1500 lbs. Their huge luminous eyes allow them to see in the dark, and they are deceptively limber and stretchy for their size, able to squeeze through quite narrow cracks and crevices.

Behaviour: Trolls are solitary creatures who prefer large, hidden spaces where they can tend to their hoard. A large hoard is a status symbol, and the most dominant trolls usually have the largest. Trolls trade between themselves and with other monster species for coveted items, and deals can be struck if the troll is in a good mood and not too hungry.

Diet: Trolls are omnivorous, but love meat and have a taste for human food. *esp. fast food!*

Danger Level: Elevated
Trolls generally avoid human attention, but beware if you encounter a troll in its lair - they will protect it at all costs.

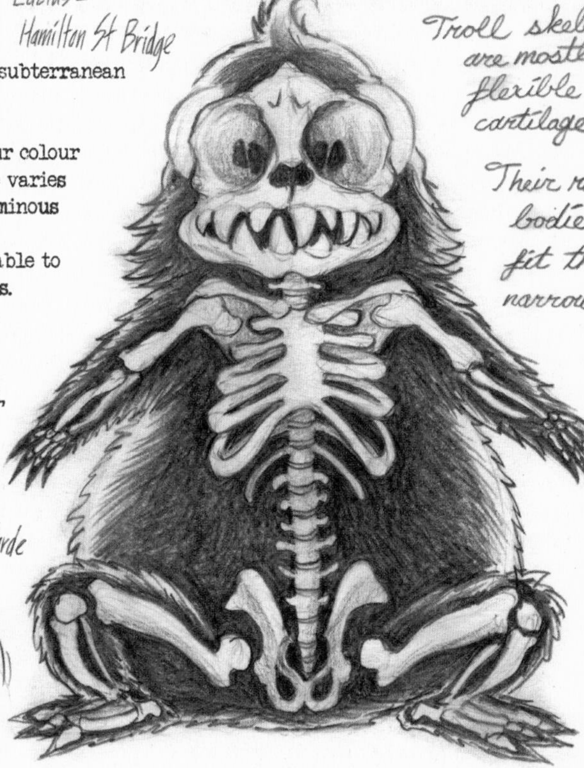

Trolls have distinctive ringed yellow-green eyes

Lucius - Hamilton St Bridge

The Lord of the Horde

Troll skeletons are mostly flexible cartilage

Their rubbery bodies can fit through narrow gaps

Troll society is organized into five main clans. Each clan has items they traditionally value in hoards:
- *Stashmasters - Tools, implements of destruction*
- *Trovestows - Gadgets, lights, modern technology*
- *Garnerkeeps - Jewelry, furniture, luxury items*
- *Pilehighs - Books, newspapers, the written word*
- *Cachegathers - Clothing, shoes, adornment*

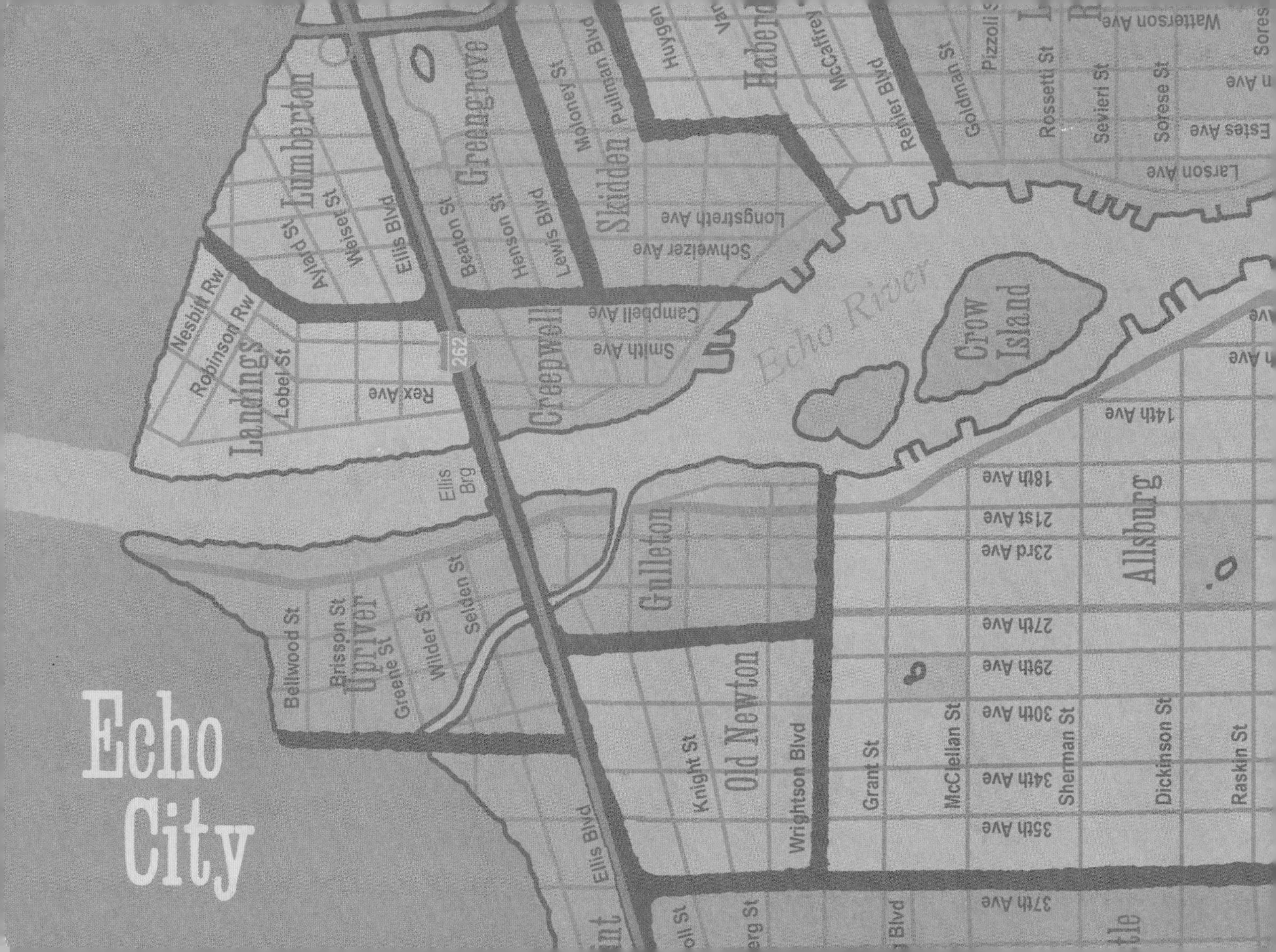

Echo City
Echo River
Crow Island
Lumberton
Greengrove
Skidden
Habere
Landings
Creepwell
Gulleton
Upriver
Old Newton
Allsburg
262
Nesbitt Rw
Robinson Rw
Lobel St
Aylard St
Weiser St
Ellis Blvd
Beaton St
Henson St
Lewis Blvd
Moloney St
Pullman Blvd
Huygen
McCaffrey
Renier Blvd
Goldman St
Pizzoli
Rossetti St
Sevieri St
Sorese St
Watterson Ave
Estes Ave
Larson Ave
Longstreth Ave
Schweizer Ave
Campbell Ave
Smith Ave
Rex Ave
Ellis Brg
14th Ave
18th Ave
21st Ave
23rd Ave
27th Ave
29th Ave
30th Ave
34th Ave
35th Ave
37th Ave
Bellwood St
Brisson St
Greene St
Wilder St
Selden St
Knight St
Wrightson Blvd
Grant St
McClellan St
Sherman St
Dickinson St
Raskin St